First Paperback Edition, March 2021

Cover Design:

Map design: www.startwithadoodle.co.uk

Paperback ISBN: 9798709359574

Hardback ISBN: 9798758941201

About the Author

Jacqueline Florence is originally from the East End of London. She achieved her dream of joining the Woman's Royal Naval Service before eventually gaining an MA(Hons) in Psychology at the University of Aberdeen and a Postgraduate MSc in Urban and Regional Planning at Herriot Watt, Edinburgh. She has two grown up children who, over time, have made various attempts to leave home, but so far, only one has been ousted successfully. She now lives in Aberdeenshire with her husband and various other animals.

Also by Jacqueline Florence

The Kelan Sagas

Blue Star Rising
Sapphire Tree

For Emily, for believing that
however unlikely the outcome,
anything is possible.

Acknowledgements

First of all, I want to thank my daughter Emily; for believing in me and gave me the courage to start telling my stories. Also, many thanks must go to my best friend, Carolyn Forrest, for many much needed hugs, pep talks and the occasion medicinal glass of wine — or two! To Jemma Body, Barbara Forbes and Keith Hill for your invaluable input and critique; to Patrick and Juliet Serrell of the Kilted Frog, Inverurie, for keeping me topped up with tea, and no doubt too much cake, while I spent many hours battering away at my laptop; to GetCovers Design, for their fabulous work and patience; and to Gail Armstrong of Startwithadoodle for bringing Kelan to life with her amazing map. Finally, but definitely not least, my husband Bill, who has not only read my stories countless times, but who has listened to all my plot lines without calling for the men in white coats. He has picked me up so often when I have been down, and he's never doubted me, even when I did, I appreciate it more than you know.

Prologue

pplying the age-old principle, that if you hit the button hard enough and often enough, it will undoubtedly open faster, Jean battered frantically at the door release button. She needed to get away, and fast.

'Open, open, open. Oh come on, just sodding well open will you?!' She scowled at the offending panel as if it was being deliberately obstructive.

The sound of heavy booted feet approaching caused her to falter — shaking fingers hovered as her heart missed a beat. It wouldn't be long before a whole company of very pissed off Breen would appear around the corner.

Finally, after what seemed like forever, the door relented to the constant hammering and opened. Jean Carter ran inside the room, hitting the close button with the same vigour as its counterpart outside.

'Close, close, close. Oh come on, now you're just taking the piss.'

The door slid closed with a hiss.

Outside, in the corridor, the boots slowed down, they knew she had to be somewhere around here. Clutching at her aching ribcage Jean felt along the bulkheads, making her way further into the room. All around were whirring consoles with blinking lamps as the only source of light; she'd found the comms room and thankfully, it was empty.

Determined to put as much distance between her and the door, Jean stepped further into the room. She rested beside a large humming cabinet, intent on staying upright while she caught her breath. Wiping the blood that still trickled down the left-hand side of her face, Jean noted, with relief, that the wound was already starting to heal. However, the accompanying headache throbbing in her temples, was threatening to be a real bundle of laughs later.

Exhausted and hungry, Jean had been unprepared for the counterattack when it came. She had made the rookie mistake of forgetting that, if it looked too good to be true, then it probably was. A job that was supposed to be a simple extraction, had turned very quickly into a vicious fight, one that she was in no fit state to take part in. The Breen had taken her completely by surprise, and the whole operation almost become a deadly mistake.

Almost, but not quite. Well, not yet.

The sudden impact of a right hook to the left-hand side of her forehead, had left her dazed and with blurred vision. It was

3

when she had been winded by a side kick to her ribcage, that convinced her she needed to get out fast. To top it all, it had cost her the damned crystal.

Now Jean faced the prospect of having to go through it all again, but this time with bruised ribs and a real doozy of a headache on its way. Trying to gather herself together, she needed time to recover, but time wasn't on her side. Moving further into the darkness of the shadows, she heard the door behind her open.

Shit!

The Breen entered the room and started their search, Jean felt the tell-tale signs of their life force pervading her senses; anticipation and fear, fear, yep that was always a good one. Then there was the adrenalin, with its unmistakeable signs of raised heartbeats, shallow breathing and heightened senses. All served with a generous dose of adrenalin, in fact, far too much for her liking.

Shit, shit and more shit!

Now she had a couple of huge, highly trained killers on her trail, who were hell bent it seemed, on killing her in particular. And to top it all, they were on some performance enhancing, super soldier drug.

Well, could this day get any better?

There was one saving grace though, one of them had the crystal; Jean could feel the familiar gentle tug. It was just a case of finding out which one of them still had it. How simple it sounded? She would have laughed if she didn't feel so bloody crap.

Feeling the darkness closing in, Jean only had the light from the terminals, attached to machinery and bulkheads, to see with;

4

her peripheral vision was still shaky and unreliable. That, alongside the pain, hunger and exhaustion too, meant all she wanted was to get out of there, have something to eat and finally get some much needed sleep.

The far off sound of the engines hummed, while the reek of an unwashed body hit her nostrils; apparently one of her pursuers was averse to using soap.

He approached and Jean wrinkled her nose while her empty stomach clenched, threatening to make an already aching gut throw up. Shaking her head, she tried to focus, determined to keep her exhausted brain alert while she concentrated on her two pursuers.

If the smelly one was just around the corner, then where the hell was the other one? Probably still smarting from the broken nose she'd manage to get in after gaining her own mind-numbing crack around the head. She was still annoyed that the crystal had been allowed to fall back into the Breen's hands; it was a waste of valuable time.

Movement to her right brought the bulk of the smelly one into view.

Dear gods, he has to be seven-foot-tall and built like a bloody ox, what the hell do they feed these people?

His strong, high tech, flexible body armour had already made using her daggers awkward. Jean would need to be close enough to get to his weak spots, but that would leave her vulnerable too. Fortunately, the unclean sweaty one removed his helmet, leaving his head and neck exposed, she hoped it was enough.

Slipping her daggers silently from the small of her back, Jean sighed. Life was so much easier in the days of dull thugs depending on ineffective firearms for defence, the look of surprise when their weapons didn't work, soon changing to horror when they realised the danger, was priceless. But now it was all intensive training in close combat with knives and swords; whilst body armour was the height of modern warfare technology. Suddenly, your average, run of the mill gangster, was now a bloody ninja.

Oh, for the good old days.

He didn't see the blow coming as she kicked out and caught his hip, the force sending him into the side of the bulkhead with a crunch; he only recovered in time to receive a jarring elbow to the head.

With his own practiced training, and the inability to feel pain due to the drugs they were given, he sent a hefty punch to Jean's face in retaliation. The force knocked her against one of the electronic cabinets, and she ducked instinctively as he followed through with another punch, smashing into a computer panel and sending sparks everywhere. Exposed and mangled electrical wires, along with circuit boards, were ripped out by her now enraged adversary. His lack of concentration while he flailed at the blinking lights, almost cost him his life, as Jean aimed a dagger to his exposed throat. Only his mate with the broken nose managed save him from a fatal stab wound, grabbing Jean from behind and pinning her arms to her sides.

Where the fuck did he come from?

Jean kicked out as she was lifted off the floor, dealing several cracking blows to his legs, but the adrenalin coursing through his body made the impact of her flailing body ineffective. She doubted if he'd have felt any pain even if she had

6

disembowelled him, which she considered more appealing by the second.

The first assailant, taking full advantage of her predicament, had recovered enough to lay a smashing punch to her solar plexus; the air was forced from her lungs and her body loosened as it struggled to take in air. She fell to the floor as the second guy let her go, but only so he could give a bone jarring kick to her ribs and stomach instead. By now she was struggling for breath. Trying not throw up as she felt everything around her begin to spin.

Curling herself into a ball, Jean made a futile attempt to protect her vital organs and head, while the vicious blows found their mark. She knew she had to bring the fight onto a more even keel; if she didn't, she would die here, and that was not an option. Despite the consequences, she had to get the crystal and leave this shit hole of a ship behind.

In the brief time before the next deadly blow, Jean unlocked the doors in her mind, that dark place that held the chaos of the emotional world at bay. Mentally bracing herself, she felt the full force of the effects of the drug fuelled adrenaline that spilled from her attackers. Allowing the turmoil of their own rage to flood into her mind, stimulating her brain to respond to their attack.

Her heartbeat soared, while her own breathing slowed, the world around her becoming instantly crystal clear.

Barely perceiving what should have been the excruciating pain from her ribs, her lungs forced air back into her body. The constant waves of nausea began to subside, the world stopped spinning and her focus cleared.

Jean stood and faced her attackers and, for a moment they faltered.

Noting the sudden change, they realised too late that this woman had become very dangerous.

The second guy succumbed to her daggers almost immediately, his blood arching from his exposed throat as he staggered forward to fall dead on the floor. The stinking bulk of his friend now threw caution to the wind. Lunging towards his fallen comrade, he rushed past Jean and rummaged through his pockets in a desperate attempt to take the crystal from his lifeless body.

Excellent, that saves me the bother of searching the dead one later.

Bolstered by his new acquisition and its possible power, the last one fought on, his training and drug induced brain not allowing for the possibility of defeat. But even the giant he was had to concede that this was no normal warrior he now encountered. Her strength seemed to grow as his ebbed. Relentlessly she forced her attack with blow after blow, until eventually, the Breen found himself backed against the ship's hull.

He had heard stories about this woman, of a wild female warrior who had struck terror into the hearts of her adversaries across the passage of time; he'd even trained for the possibility of meeting her in combat. But never did he think that he would actually come up against her, the woman who had become more legend than reality.

In a final attempt to save himself, he wrenched out the crystal and smashed it against Jean's head, his eyes blazing with the possibility of victory.

He would be the one to finally defeat the un-defeatable.

There were tales of these crystals causing horrendous burns to victims when used in combat, even stories of people so overcome by the stone's power that they disappeared. But this time there was nothing, the bloody woman had nothing more than a mark where he had struck, certainly no scorched skin or mortal injuries. She hadn't even flinched.

He stared in horror. In that moment, he finally knew he was lost; nevertheless, he was damned if he'd go down quietly. Lunging forward, he made ready to deliver as many punches as he possibly could to this mythical opponent. But then suddenly, the huge man found himself shooting backwards, his arms and legs flailing. His lungs burned as they tried to suck in air, but they were unable to work; while an impossible cold engulfed his body.

Why it was so bloody cold?

His arms whirled slowly in front of him, and it took a moment for him to understand that where his hand should have been, there was now only a bloodied stump. Eyes opening wide, his jaw dropping, he stared, stunned at his damaged arm in complete confusion. His vision was beginning to fail due to lack of oxygen and cold. In the distance, past the ruin of his arm, he saw a ship moving away, leaving him behind. Anger and disbelief finally overwhelmed him; the bitch had shoved him out of a fucking airlock.

Prising the crystal from the disembodied hand, Jean Carter forced the doors, to the emotional world around her, closed and pushed them into the deep recesses of her mind. Breathing deeply, slowly and calmly, she brought down the huge adrenalin

9

rush; struggling against the need to seek out and tear something apart.

Finally, leaning her battered body against the bulkhead, she fought back her own emotions that threatened to engulf her; anger, fear and disgust. The pain of her injuries flooded in and she doubled over, retching in agony as her empty stomach could discharge nothing but bile.

The urgency of her situation meant she needed to get out of there while she still had the crystal, and before more Breen came looking. Seeking the peace and sanctuary of her own ship, Jean projected her thoughts outward, the familiar feelings of a moment's weightless suspension surrounded her. Travelling through time and space in less than a heartbeat was now as natural to Jean as breathing, and soon her pain racked broken body was once more on her spaceship, the home she affectionately knew as NiCI.

Part one

Kelan

1

Guardian

aving no idea how long she had slept, if at all, Jean woke to the familiar internal alarm that persisted and refused to be ignored. It was like a bad case of tinnitus in her head until she was fully wide awake; the remnants of the alarm still rattling about her brain as she tried to focus. Endeavouring to sit up, she swore loudly as her ribcage reminded her of the beating she had received previously. Glancing at the clock that sat beside her bed, she noted that she had at least gained a few hours' sleep. Though to be fair, she felt as if she had been hit by a very large truck and she could quite easily crawl back under the covers.

She had arrived onboard her spacecraft knowing, that with her injuries, what she needed more than anything else was rest and food to mend. However, her kitchen cupboards were almost bare, and with all the chaos of the past few days, shopping had taken a bit of a back seat. But rest she could do, and her bed had beckoned her to a glorious, if all but brief, oblivion.

Making her way to her quarters, Jean had thrown the hard won crystal into a bowl full of other identical crystals. She frowned as she noted that the bowl was looking considerably inadequate to the task now, its contents already threatening to spill over the brim onto the table surface.

Note to self, add another larger bowl to the shopping list.

Barely giving a second glance to the overflowing dish, Jean still wondered what it was about these crystals that pulled her to them. But she was no nearer to finding the answers now than when she was at the beginning, only that the brilliant, diamond like stones, were capable of causing chaos in the wrong hands.

Having seen the devastation these crystals could do, she had made it her own personal mission to retrieve them when she felt their presence; which wasn't often fortunately. But it was still a pain in the arse.

What was curious though, and Jean was still none the wiser as to why, was that they had no negative impact on her — as the smelly Breen had found to his cost. In fact, they were nothing more than a gaudy stone that kept her busy when she needed something to do.

Having given final instructions to NiCI, (Neurological, Cognitive Interface) her onboard computer, to direct the ship to their hidden dock — an asteroid that orbited an unnamed moon on the far side of the universe — she then directed herself towards some desperately needed sleep. Right now, she could feel every one of the centuries she had existed for, and she breathed a sad, exhausted sigh. Regretting it immediately, she winced painfully as her ribs gave a stabbing reminder that breathing was to be taken very carefully.

In her quarters, Jean had taken off her overcoat and stripped off her own lightly armoured suit, before attempting to sit down on her bed. Gingerly she tried to lie down, but it took a while for her body to stop objecting to her efforts. Eventually though, she was horizontal, under the bedsheet, with her aching head on the pillow. Sleep had begun to envelop her as the pain slowly started to dissipate, eventually succumbing to the draw of, hopefully, dreamless bliss.

Now, as the alarm in her head continued, she was making another attempt to sit up, but this time with a little more care. Once upright, Jean tried to tune into the irritation whirring within her still sore brain. It was tough to explain exactly what she felt when these warnings came. After the initial audible alarm, they were more like that nagging feeling you had when you forgot something, and you couldn't remember why. But she had understood long ago, that these warnings were a prelude to an imminent relocation and to ignore them was not only pointless, but had the potential to be very embarrassing. Once, she had been enjoying a long hot bath, when she ended up in the backwater of nowhere, stark naked; it was a valuable lesson to make sure she was ready for her future missions in plenty of time.

Where these missions took her to however, were in the hands of the gods, literally. It was the gods who had been instrumental in creating her, and it was they who sent her on her assignments.

This was one of the few things Jean could remember from that time, when she had accepted her fate as Guardian. The gods said it was her calling, Jean said it was a very big bag of horse shit.

How she had actually honed her craft as a warrior though, was a complete memory blank. She knew that she had been taught her skills, but for some reason she could not remember any of it; she had no idea who had been her teacher, or where it had taken place. Learning to fight and stay alive wasn't something she knew instinctively. It had taken time and a lot of work to perfect what she did, but how she did it was beyond her. Only that short time before, when Jean learned who she was, and the time after, when she had made her vows and received her weapons — there was nothing in-between.

What she did know however, was that despite the belief of so many differing faiths that she had met throughout the universe, the gods played no actual part in the lives of those who lived within the cosmos. They were not omnipotent beings that decided the fate of mortals, they had no direct contact with them at all, in fact, there were times when Jean seriously questioned why her own intervention was required. But that was another thing she had learnt not to ask, it was what it was, and she had to get on with it.

As always, life rarely runs smoothly, while the gods accepted that the natural course of life within the universe usually involved it's countless creatures trying to annihilate each other. There were circumstances when forces were involved that had the potential to upset the normal progress of the existence of life; anomalies that threatened to unravel the very fabric of time and space. When these times arose, it was Jean's responsibility to go in and sort it all out, so that the everyone could go back to the everyday business of killing each other again.

But the job was taking its toll.

Jean groaned as the headache that had threatened earlier, was now beating a tattoo on the inside of her skull.

Was this really happening now?

Doubting she could barely walk, let alone fight at the moment, Jean was concerned at her ability to keep herself, or anyone else safe. But she knew it was pointless in moaning, no one was listening and the mission would happen anyway.

Making her way to the bathroom, she looked into the mirror and winced at her reflection, she regretted it immediately.

No beauty contests for you yet Jean my girl.

The sore and puffy face that looked back, was already showing the yellow tinge of bruises on the wane. It was a saving grace that her body mended so much faster than normal humans, but the downside was the process hurt a hell of a lot more too.

Sighing, Jean gingerly peeled off the undergarments she had slept in, then stepped into the sonic shower. Gods, what she wouldn't do for a soak in a good old fashioned deluge of hot water.

Her weakened and sore body was pounded by the throbbing ultrasound, while the blood and dirt was scoured away under its unforgiving pulses. She hated feeling like this, vulnerable to her own pain and self doubt, having to accept the reality of her life now and who she had become. The pain tore at her heart. NiCI, her spacecraft, had become a parody of her life; a ship floating in the vastness of space, nowhere to go to be welcomed home. The only world she had ever belonged to, that she

16

considered home, was lost to her. No matter how hard she searched, she could never find her beloved Earth.

Leaning against the cubicle wall, the internal emotions that had threatened before began to break through; she was exhausted, hungry and alone. Jean knew she was losing herself to the misery of a life she struggled to see a way out of. Her soul cried out to just curl up and go to sleep; to never wake up and welcome the sweet call of oblivion. Tears escaped and ran down her sallow cheeks and her knees buckled under the weight of her sorrow. Self-pity and loneliness had eventually overwhelmed her own tired, rational brain. Curling her battered body up on the floor, she sobbed.

Eventually, Jean gathered herself together, knowing that time was short. She really didn't need another naked humiliation, so reluctantly, she got dressed, ready for the unknown task ahead. Pulling on clean underwear before stepping into her own, newly cleaned body armour, that had also just undergone a sonic wash, she shut down her internal emotions, pushing them behind well-built walls in her mind. Time was moving on, and knowing she would soon be somewhere far away from her ship, she had to be ready.

By the time Jean left her quarters she was in control, ready to face whatever came her way, albeit with a bit of caution for her ribcage. She pulled on her blue overcoat, with many useful pockets, and grabbing her rucksack, she checked her provisions. Jean noted, not for the first time, the lack of food, remembering that technically she had only herself to blame. When she had procured her ship, it had a perfectly good replicator that provided plenty of food; but she hated the results and refused to let go of old habits. So, disconnecting the replicators, she had

17

reclaimed one of the other sleeping quarters, converting it into a fully working galley kitchen. However, as water in space was a prized commodity, she had to accept that sonic showers were the price to pay for real food on her table.

At last, the alarm that had indicated a new mission such a short time ago, now alerted her that transit was imminent. Checking her left-hand coat pocket, her fingers touched the familiar data pack that resided there. Then bracing herself for the unexpected, her empty stomach grumbled, and Jean was taken from her ship into the unknown; a different world, in another distant part of the universe.

2

A Cheese and

Pickle

Sandwich

*S*hit!
Whatever part of the universe Jean had arrived at, she found the world had unexpectedly turned upside down; surrounded in darkness she had suddenly gone from upright, to horizontal very quickly. Her already sore body,

protested painfully as she slammed into a hard, uneven surface. Laying still for a few moments, her brain tried to comprehend what had happened and where she was.

The wind had been knocked out of her as she landed and she hurt everywhere. Trying to draw in air, Jean smelt the sickly scent of mouldy hay and straw, causing her empty stomach to churn again. Wincing in pain at the effort, she began to carefully lift herself up; aware that anything or anyone could be watching her. Though to be honest, she wasn't sure she would be in any fit state to do anything about it right now anyway. Normally she could sense the presence of life around her, but as experience had sadly shown over the years, immediately after one of these uncontrolled relocations, her senses were completely knocked out of kilter.

Is that why I can't see now?

Her stomach clenched in fear at the thought of being blind; no matter how temporary.

Shit.

If that was the case, she was screwed big time.

A chink of light appeared from somewhere above and she squinted to try and focus. Relief washed over her, realising she hadn't gone blind after all; it was just a simple case of her eyes adjusting to the gloom of wherever she was. Looking up, Jean saw that the chink of light, was in fact, filtering through a shingle in a far from watertight roof. Letting out a small moan, she uncurled her stiff limbs and attempted to force herself to stand up.

Dear gods, I'm too old for this lark.

Once upright, Jean reached out and slowly moved forward until her hands came in contact with a cold stone wall, which became wooden slats at about head height. Assuming she must be in some kind of outbuilding which was partially subterranean, she continued around the wall looking for a way out, eventually coming to a flight of wooden steps.

Her eyes were better adjusted to the poor light now and she soon discovered the reason for her fall. Half of the room was taken up by a mezzanine level, its rotten wood partially collapsing when it had to take the unexpected force of her weight. Obviously not a well-maintained building. Jean made a mental note to be careful when climbing the stairs, which led up to a small door set into the wooden slatted wall. Cautiously, checking each footing as she went, she made her way up to the door, giving a quick thanks to any deity that may be listening when the door opened without any problem other than a gentle squeak of its rusting hinges.

Nathan leaned his back against the wooden bench, allowing himself to be hidden within the shadows cast by the flames of the large open-fire that burned beside them. His companions sat with him around a table, set near to the fireplace that provided enough heat to the rest of the taproom of the tavern. It was to be their lodgings for the night, an establishment they had used many times before, which also meant they knew the landlord well. He had ensured they had a private table, set apart from the main hubbub of the rest of the room, and most importantly, where they wouldn't be disturbed.

Breathing in slowly, Nathan closed his eyes, thinking of how ridiculous it was, having to drag along an entourage as useless as Kleinstock and his cronies. Fortunately, the landlord had set them at a table on the opposite side of the taproom, so at least

Nathan and his three companions didn't have to put up with them this evening. He felt his frustration rise when he thought about how well that bloody woman had caught him in her web, and how hopeless he was to deal with it. Here they were, on a simple journey, a courtesy call on an old loyal friend who was dying — Nathan considered it inconceivable not to make a final visit to see him. His wife however, thought he was mad to go out of his way for someone she considered a nobody. But to be fair, he couldn't care less what she thought, he just had to put up with Kleinstock and his rabble instead.

A serving girl had come over to their table and laid out their food, along with a jug of ale and four tankards. His three companions had ordered themselves bowls of meat stew served with large chunks of bread. But he had no appetite for heavy food tonight. Instead he had ordered himself a cheese and pickle sandwich, a favourite of his, and he was feeling particularly indulgent. As the others tucked into their stew, his sandwich remained uneaten on the table in front of him. *Perhaps*, he thought, *he would tackle it later.*

The taproom was busy that night as it had been market day, and by now most of its patrons were well and truly drunk. Two large men had attempted to give a rendition of some fairly bawdy drinking songs, but unfortunately, despite their enthusiasm, they weren't very good at it.

'What is that bloody awful noise?'

Nathan glanced across the table at Stephen. A tall blonde man, voicing his objections while scowling into his tankard of ale. But it was Daniel, sitting next to him, who slapped him on the back and laughed. Stephen's scowl deepened as ale slopped down the front of his shirt. Daniel just grinned.

22

'They are happy, leave them alone. The gods only know they need some joy, don't be so grumpy.'

'We could all do with some of that.'

The three of them turned to the man who sat next to Nathan, his name was Damien and he looked up from the map he had been studying. Stephen had skewered one of the last pieces of meat that remained in his bowl with his fork, bringing it to his mouth but not eating it straight away, instead he turned his scowl onto Damien.

'Hmmmm, well they might be feeling joyful, but it sounds like a bloody racket to me.'

He popped the meat into his mouth and chewed, dropping his fork into the bowl. Sitting back in his chair he crossed his arms, his gaze settling on Nathan, still nestled within the shadows.

'Is there any way out of this do you think?'

Nathan raised an eyebrow.

'It's only a few drunken songs, they'll be off to their beds soon enough. Besides, I've heard you sing this same song before and you don't sound any better.'

Damien and Daniel sniggered; Stephen didn't seem impressed.

'I'm not talking about the singing, though I object to your lack of appreciation for my vocal talents.'

Nathan joined in with the other two in their laughter, Stephen lurched forward and thrust his face toward Nathan. The laughter stopped immediately.

'I'm being serious Nathan. How much longer do we have to put up with this for?'

Nathan leaned forward and placed his arms on the table, holding Stephen's gaze. It was Stephen who looked away first, sitting back in his chair again, eyes fixed on the table in front of him. Damien and Daniel shared a glance before Nathan spoke.

'I don't know how long we have to put up with this for, but throwing our weight around and upsetting hard working folk, who just want to have some fun, is not going to help matters.'

Stephen looked back at Nathan and nodded his head in agreement.

'Yes I know, of course I know, but it is so bloody frustrating.'

Nathan held Stephen's gaze a little longer, he didn't say anything, he knew he didn't need to. He then leant back against the bench, satisfied the moment had passed.

Daniel looked behind him, before also leaning onto the table conspiratorially, gaining their attention.

'What we need, is us.'

The others stared at him, then at each other, then back at Daniel. Damien put his map down.

'Nope, you're going to have to explain that one.'

Daniel sighed as if they had missed his obvious point.

'I mean, this is the sort of thing we do, isn't it? Only we can't do anything now ourselves, so we need us. Or someone like us, to sort things out.'

Damien leaned forward and slapped him on the shoulder.

'Damn good idea, anyone in mind?'

Daniel gave him a withering look.

'Very funny, but you know what I mean.'

'Of course we do, but there is little chance of that happening is there?'

Daniel humphed and sat back in his chair. He looked as if someone had stolen the punchline of his favourite joke.

Nathan felt for his friends, they were as fed up with the whole situation as he was, he didn't blame them for wanting a way out, he just wished he could provide them with one. Looking down at the map that Damien was studying, he nudged his friend.

'What the hell have you got that map for? Surely you should know where you are going by now?'

Damien grinned. 'I swiped it off of Kleinstock earlier, he didn't seem to have much need of it, so I acquired it.'

'How do you know he didn't need it? Perhaps he just wanted to know where we are.'

'Maybe he does, but it was unlikely to happen.'

The others looked at him, confused. Damien began to chuckle.

'The idiot was reading it upside down.'

There was a moment of silence, then suddenly the four of them burst into laughter. Nathan picked up his tankard and drank deeply, he was just about ready for his sandwich now.

Finding herself in a dark alley, the only light from an open door further down the track, Jean took note of her new surroundings. Large puddles had formed amongst the broken cobbles, indicating a recent downpour of rain. The air smelt damp and fetid, and the shadows felt oppressive, she didn't need to be empathic to know that there were eyes watching her from hidden windows and doorways.

Despite still feeling very confused with the expected disorientation from her shift in location, and the uncomfortable feelings of hunger, Jean had sensed there was something else in the air. She noticed it as she left the fetid atmosphere of the subterranean barn. It was weird, as if she was in an odd bubble, but strangely it wasn't an unpleasant feeling. She put it down to the effects of concussion, making a point of mentally closing off the outside world for a while, so as to stop her picking up false readings.

Looking up and down the alley, it disappeared into darkness to her left. To her right, there was the light she saw earlier, coming from an open doorway. Further on, there was a junction that showed the glow of lamps from another street beyond it. She decided to head towards the light and the open doorway, taking a speculative look in whilst still being careful not to be seen.

Careful to avoid the puddles she made her way cautiously down the alley. Flattening herself against the building wall she peered around the open door jamb. Inside was all the makings of a bar taproom. Jean had seen enough in her time in all their glorious forms, and if she was honest, thrown out of enough of them too. However, this bar room scene was odd somehow, she couldn't quite put her finger on why though. The room itself was full of men and women having a good time; nothing unusual there. People in well-worn work clothes, that marked them as labourers, took up most of the space in the room. Half-eaten food and spilt drink littered tables, whilst the customers were enjoying the entertainment of two robust men, who had obviously spent most of the day imbibing; singing very loudly, and very much off key. Jean's stomach growled at the thought of all that wasted food, then winced at the onslaught to her already aching head from the appalling noise.

To her left, near what seemed like the main door, was a group of well-dressed men and women; the gaudy cloth and the vulgar but expensive trinkets of the nouveau riche didn't go unnoticed. They looked and sounded like peacocks, guffawing and raising their voices; sneering at their fellow drinkers and nibbling at their food as if it would choke them. Yet at the same time they swilled their drink as readily as the workers, who now deemed it necessary, to join in with the painful singing.

At the opposite side of the room by the fire, hidden in the shadows of high-backed benches, was a very different group of four men. Dressed in dark clothing they sat around their table, heads close in conversation, seeming indifferent to the raucousness of their fellow drinkers. Before them they had tankards of ale and mostly empty plates, but one dish remained, with what looked like a cheese sandwich. Jean's mouth watered at the thought. Then her eyes widened with delight.

Bingo.

At last, something positive; spread out on their table was a map. Sending another silent prayer of thanks, Jean hoped that if the gods would just keep the good luck going a bit longer, it would be a map of the local area and she could find out where the hell she was.

There were few choices available to her at this point; she could go straight up to the men at the table and ask for the map of course, but this had its own risks. She was completely new to this world, she had no idea of its social structure, and more importantly, who the good and bad guys were. As her senses were completely up the wall at the moment, she would be effectively going in blind into a potentially dangerous situation. If things didn't go well, Jean doubted she would be in a fit state to do anything about it. She took another look at the four men sitting at the table. They were fit, strong, and by the look of it, well fed.

Another possibility was to cause a diversion. Clearing the bar would make acquiring the map much easier and a lot less of a risk, the problem was of course, how to create a suitable distraction. Bearing all this in mind, Jean turned away from the taproom, making her way further down the alley. She arrived at a junction which opened onto a wide street. To her left, the road led off into the distance and to her right, were the front buildings of the inn and the rest of the street disappearing around a bend in the road. Checking the way was clear, she turned right into the street, passed the closed front door of the tavern, then ducked under the inn windows so as not to be seen. She eventually came across the entrance that she assumed was the inn's main livery yard, a few stable lads were still busy putting the horses to bed for the night.

Looking around, a couple of drunks slumbered in a darkened, shop doorway across the road. Lights within rooms above the shops were partially shuttered, but there was little movement around. Apart from the awful noise that the carollers were still making inside the tavern, the whole area looked and felt abandoned. It gave her the creeps.

About to explore the street further, Jean heard the sound of a number of feet heading in her direction. Melting into the shadows of the yard entrance, she waited to see who was about to arrive.

They appeared to be a group of five men and women, although admittedly not a particularly ordered one, but they were armed with thick wooden cudgels and, Jean was impressed to see, quite sober.

At first she assumed they were just going to carry on down the street, so she waited for them to pass out of sight. But as they approached the drunks, who snored contentedly in their doorway, the group stopped. Jean was shocked when suddenly, one of the men kicked out at the drunks. Yelps of pain announced they had woken one of the slumberers, and by the sound of it, they had found a particular sore spot too. Jean winced in sympathy and contemplated stepping in to help.

However, it would appear that the drunks were not as inebriated as the thugs with cudgels first thought. Unhappy at such a rude awakening, the first victim had woken his friend and now, sobering quickly, the drunks fought back with a vengeance. Within moments, both sides were punching and kicking, causing a hell of a racket; upper windows were flung open and people began pouring out of the inn to see what was happening. The two carollers were amongst the growing crowd from the inn, and on seeing the uneven fight, set about joining in with the melee. Soon fights broke out amongst the crowd and the whole area was now in mayhem. Jean grinned; she had inadvertently found her diversion.

Not daring to question her luck, she quickly made her way past the crowd and retreated back up the alley towards the open side door. Making sure her hood was up, she made ready to rush in and grab her map and victuals; clearing off sharpish before anyone noticed she was there.

However.

Shit, double shit and bollocks.

While the rest of the inn had vacated to see the show in the street, the four men had remained at their table, apparently oblivious to the commotion outside. Her luck had run out.

Sod it.

It wasn't ideal, but she had no choice, she was hungry and in pain. Brazening it out, she stepped forward and hoped these were the good guys.

Making her way across the taproom floor, the four men were curious as they watched her enter and approach their table. Assessing the stranger, they didn't move, their faces gave nothing away other than an impassive intelligence. But Jean knew soldiers when she saw them, and was under no illusion that they were ready to react if provoked. However, she needed that map; and hell, that sandwich looked good. On reaching their table she laid her hand on the map and attempted to give a disarming smile, the bruises on her face objected however, and she found herself wincing instead.

'I'm sorry gentlemen but I need to take this map, I'm sure you wouldn't begrudge a lady this one request.'

They didn't move, but continued to stare at her, she also noticed the slight twitch of a smile form on their faces; but still they didn't speak. Making no movement to stop her taking the map, Jean felt a little confused at their lack of reaction. She tried to clarify what she wanted.

'Please, I don't want to hurt anyone, I just need to take the map'

This raised a few eyebrows, apparently the thought that she could possibly hurt any one of them seemed to be amusing.

Well, looks can be deceiving gentlemen, so don't push it.

Seeming to come to a decision, one of the men closest to her leant forward as Jean made to take the map. She thought he was going snatch it back, but instead, he gave a quick glance to the man sitting in the shadows beside him. Then taking a pen out of his jacket pocket, he made a mark on the paper. As he looked up, his dark eyes met hers and her heart seemed to do a flip. The barriers she had spent so long building to protect herself shifted, for a brief moment she felt very vulnerable and had to fight the urge to run. However, before she could react, he pointed to the mark he had made on the map, and in a clear, calm, deep voice he told her, 'We are here'.

Then he thrust the treasured map toward her.

Both amazed and emboldened by her apparent good fortune, and knowing she was probably chancing her luck, Jean decided that if she was going to be brazen, she needed to go the whole hog, she made a bid for the sandwich.

She reached out her hand and the delicious morsel was very nearly in her grasp, but then another hand was suddenly clutching hers. Jean gasped.

The man furthest away, who was partially hidden in shadow, moved forward and two strikingly blue eyes caught her gaze. A stunning shock of, what seemed to be, recognition passed between them, and inexplicably, in that moment she felt as if she could not bear the thought of him letting her hand go. Then, saying nothing, he loosened his grip and pushed the proffered cheese and pickle delight towards her.

Suddenly, very confused, she felt bereft and relief all at once. Still trying to make sense of what had happened, a jug of ale was then thrust into her other hand by the blonde man sitting opposite. Mr Dark Eyes stood up, and as she was still trying to figure out what the hell had happened, he took hold of her arm and almost forced her through the open side door.

The fight outside was being broken up by more of the thugs armed with cudgels, and howls of pain could be heard, as those not fast enough to head back into the bar were dragged away. No doubt the cudgels and a few well aimed kicks were used in the process. The man who still held Jean's arm leaned in, with his face close to her ear, his voice became urgent,

'Stay out of sight until dawn, when the town gates will be opened. You can leave with the rest of the labourers as they head for their days work in the fields. Head west to Parva'.

He looked down into her face for a moment, before she was unceremoniously shoved into the alley.

Jean was barely aware of the door closing behind her, before she was once again shrouded in darkness. Stunned by what had just happened, she began making her way back up the lane away from the ruckus in the street beyond. Bypassing the shed she had arrived in, she found a barn where fresh, clean hay was stored and slipped inside.

Aching and exhausted, she made her way out of sight of anyone who may need to come in during the rest of the night. Climbing up a ladder that led to where she could hide amongst the straw, she settled down with the map open in front of her. Then with the light from the torch she kept in her pack, she studied it while hungrily tucking into the sandwich and ale.

Eventually though, despite all attempts to stay awake longer, Jean finally succumbed to desperately needed sleep; drifting off into dreams of armed men beating people up, while singing raucous songs, badly. Watched silently by bright blue eyes.

She was even oblivious to the fate of her torch that had fallen from her hand as she slept, its inner workings dissolving and evaporating into the ether.

3

A Curious

Horse

Niall scowled down at the young man trying to burrow further into his blankets.

'Come on, get that lazy carcass out of bed, the morning is almost gone, and we have to be on the road if we're to be home before dark.'

Layne made a valiant attempt at opening his eyelids, but they seemed to have gained enormous weight overnight. Sharp blades of sunlight, thrust through to the back of his brain, compounding the thumping head he daren't lift off the pillow. It took all his concentration to hold back the waves of nausea threatening to wash over him.

'Gerroff. It's too early and my head hurts.'

Burrowing deeper amongst the bed clothes, Layne hoped that Niall would give up and let him be. Sadly, however, it appeared Niall had other ideas.

'If you're not out of that bed right now, I'm going to haul that lazy arse of yours down the stairs feet first.'

Niall whipped the bedclothes off to emphasise his point.

Layne curled himself into a ball to to protect his aching head from the light and Niall's, increasingly louder, voice. He tried to shout his anger at being disturbed, but the pain in his head soon reduced it to a desperate croak.

'Alright, alright, I'm up.'

'Good, you get the horse and cart sorted and I'll settle up with the landlord.'

Protesting audibly, but only as loud as his aching head allowed, Layne uncurled himself, squinting his eyes against the sun's glare, and got himself dressed before leaving their shared room, scowling. Gingerly he made his way down to the stables.

Niall looked around the room and thought it wise to open a window; two men on the ale last night, as well as sharing a confined sleeping space, didn't provide a particularly pleasant atmosphere. Dana would have kicked them both out to the barn overnight, making sure they had a dunk in the pond before they were even considered back in the house the following day. Touching his own delicate head, he regretted having raised his voice so loud to get Layne moving. Whatever evil creature resided in his brain at the moment, it was taking great delight in wielding a very large hammer around his skull. He really should make an effort to remember he couldn't drink like he used to.

A final look around the room and Niall was satisfied they had everything packed up, he then took his wounded pride down to the main bar, meeting the landlady waiting for him and his money.

'Morning Niall, that was a fair skinful you and your lad had last night. Not like you to get so drunk.'

Niall had the grace to look bashful and slowly nodded his head, too much movement seemed to set the hammer wielding demon in his head off again.

'Aye Jess, that wasn't how I expected the day to end. But with all the troubles going on and a tough day at the market, drowning my sorrows seemed a good idea at the time.'

Jess cautiously looked around her and drew nearer to her friend.

'Shhh Niall, you know it is best not to talk about what's going on. The inn by the West gate, The Three Maids, they're all but bankrupt now, ever since *that* group had their lively discussion about the Emperor's wife.'

Niall scoffed at this. 'Surely that can't be the reason why.'

'I'm telling you Niall, be careful, these are different times now, nowhere is safe anymore.' Jess lowered her voice further. '*They* have spies everywhere.'

'Don't be daft woman.' And Niall laughed at her paranoia, though even he felt it was hollow, there were too many changes happening to ignore the signs. Clearing his throat, he hoped he could at least leave on a happy note as he bid farewell.

'Well Jess, that's Layne and I away. Tell that husband of yours I was asking for him.'

Handing the landlady his dues for the previous evening, he then turned towards the door that led to the livery yard. Waving his goodbyes, he strode out into the sun, taking care to pull his cap over his suffering eyes; there was a slight limp to his right leg.

Jess watched his back, and as she always did, admired the man who had once brought her husband back home safely. Both of them had served the Empire together, but Niall had saved her Piele's life, bringing him home to recover when he was invalided out of the Order. Now Niall himself had paid a hefty price for his service, but neither he nor Piele would regret any of it. Jess sighed and set to work about the inn, soon her customers would be arriving, and she didn't have time to reminisce about old times.

Picking up her broom, she continued about her usual chores, Niall and Layne already a fast fading memory.

The morning following her abrupt arrival to this new world, Jean woke to sunlight breaking through the chinks in the wooden slats of the barn. Shielding her eyes, she moved away from the glare, her head still throbbing from yesterday's battering.

Was that really only just yesterday?

Looking out of a small window facing east, she realised the sun had already risen well above the town walls; she had slept much longer into the morning than she had intended. Cursing herself for her tardiness, Jean at least acknowledged that the extra rest had helped her heal. Her ribs were still sore but that was because they were bone, but the bruising had reduced dramatically to a few dark splodges around her face and ribcage.

Needing to work out the aches in her body Jean stood and stretched, feeling her muscles unfold, relishing the sweet pain of movement, as she eased them into the yoga positions she had learnt so many years ago.

Feeling better, she began tidying up the remnants of the ale and sandwich from last night and gathering up her meagre possessions. She felt a slight panic when she couldn't find the torch, she was sure she used last night. Searching through the straw she finally found the remnants of the device, but as she picked it up, it fell to pieces in her hand. Staring at the broken pieces, all she could think that had happened, was that she had kicked it during the night while she slept — but she wasn't convinced. However, there was nothing else she could do about it now, she had to leave.

Placing the broken bits in her pack, she decided she would mull over the problem when she had more time. At least she had found the pieces, the thought of anyone finding an electronic torch in a world without any obvious signs of electricity, was something she would rather didn't happen.

Newly energised, though decidedly peckish, Jean ventured out of the barn. With one more important task to do, the prospect didn't appeal to her but it had to be done; she needed to pee, and she didn't imagine indoor plumbing had much of a role to play in this world by the look of it. Her plan was to leave the town as quickly as possible and find the nearest secluded bush. Checking up and down the alley, making sure the way was clear, she ventured back towards the main road.

The side door to the inn was open again, though this morning the bar was empty, but for a woman and man swabbing down the floors, preparing for the day's trade ahead. Leaving them to it she carried on to the main road, Jean was relieved to see it was bustling with life now. Observing the people as they passed, carrying out their daily chores, she felt the same unease as she did last night. Something didn't feel right. There was tension in the air, heads were bowed, and no-one stood long enough to talk to their neighbours. Fear and sadness rose up to greet her.

The energy she felt seemed at odds with the town itself, the streets and buildings were well maintained and clean. There were no closed or broken shutters, and everywhere looked lived in; all of which spoke of a prosperous market town. But these people went about their business like suspicious and desperate people of poorer, depressed regions Jean had encountered over the years.

A shudder travelled up her spine, she needed to get away from here, the negativity was making her feel sick and she longed for the fresh and open air promised outside the town gates; besides, the need to pee was getting desperate. Working her way through the crowds as quickly as she could without drawing attention, she headed westward to the edge of the town and the gate that would join the road there. She remembered the words of the dark eyed man from the previous evening telling her to leave early, but she'd missed the exodus of labourers heading to their day's work hours ago. There were still a fair few people milling around the town's walls though, so she tagged onto a small group passing out of the West gate, until finally she was leaving the sad little town behind.

To her relief, the town was surrounded by plenty of trees away from the main road and prying eyes!

Making her way west along the road, Jean reflected on her decision to take the advice of the dark eyed man. In some ways it could be considered foolhardy to proceed on his suggestion, but she took his proposal purely on the basis that she had no reason not to. Normally she could tell the intentions of those around her, no matter how hard they tried to hide it; but the men from last night were a different matter altogether. She didn't know why, but they were able to mask their feelings, and that in itself should have raised alarm bells.

But it didn't.

What was it about the man with the blue eyes?

She brushed her right hand subconsciously as she remembered the curious, but not unwelcome, feeling as it had touched his; a brief frisson ran through her body. Shaking her head, Jean concluded that she was probably still suffering from the previous day's injuries, and anything else was just fanciful thought. At the end of the day, the simple fact was, Jean had decided to see where his friend's advice led her. So, heading west, she set her goal on the largest city on the map, Parva.

Breathing in the fresh air and relishing the peace and quiet after all the troubled urban air and noise, Jean eased into a steady pace; taking in the landscape surrounding her. After a while, the traffic on the road thinned as people went about their own business amongst the farms and villages scattered around the countryside. It was good to be out of the confines of a spacecraft and walking on solid ground again.

To the north, was a continuous line of mountains, their peaks still covered in snow, while lower down the slopes, heather and pine trees clung to the poor soil; the green and brown, contrasting sharply with the white snow and beautiful blue sky.

To the south, a river ran towards the west, its waters were high, probably due to snow melt from the mountains and the recent rain. Here the soil was much richer, and trees grew thicker; forests of oak, elm and elder were already showing the first buds of spring. Sheep and cattle grazed the land, with fields tilled ready for planting.

Memories of a previous life when things were so much simpler came into her mind. Sighing, she felt the pangs of homesickness tug at her heart, and though she tried to suppress the feelings of regret and nostalgia — it was pointless dwelling on the past and things she could not control — memories of a life long ago flowed through her mind.

A clatter of hooves and cartwheels brought her back from her reverie. She spun around just in time to see a pair of big brown eyes staring at her, along with a soft nose nuzzling her pockets in the hope of a snack. Looking up from the hopeful horse, Jean saw a barrel-chested man in labourer's clothing; his skin had the colour and lines of someone who worked outside in all weathers. A wide brimmed hat protected his face from the day's sun; Jean suspected he was probably nursing a hangover judging by the unhealthy pink of his eyes. But despite this, his open friendly face wore an amused grin as he leant forward, resting his elbows on his knees, the reins loose in his hands. When he spoke, it was with a clear deep baritone.

'Are you deliberately trying to get yourself run down? Because if that's the case, I'll have to back up and take a run at it. This old boy doesn't do speed anymore, but we'll give it a go if you want.'

It took a moment to realise what he had said, then with a grin, which evolved into an amused giggle, she returned his laughter. The sudden noise roused the horse's curiosity again, resulting with more snuffling and snack searching. It seemed a long time since she had laughed and the feeling was amplified by its pleasure. Aware that her mind had been elsewhere and negligent of her immediate surroundings, Jean deserved the ribbing, appreciating the man's humour. But she did make a mental note to be more careful, she was a complete stranger in this world, and she needed to keep her wits about her, not daydreaming and having to dodge traffic on the road.

It was something she had begun to notice more and more since she had come to this world; she was becoming far too relaxed. Now was not the time to drop her guard. However, she couldn't ignore the fact that having left the unhappy atmosphere of the town behind, Jean noticed how much the air still felt different, that not unpleasant feeling she had when she first left the confines of the subterranean shed. Or was it something else? Whatever it was, she seemed to have become far too comfortable and was becoming oblivious to the possible dangers around her. Fortunately though, this time, the only danger seemed to be losing half the contents of her pockets to an over curious horse.

Laughing at the horse's persistence, she rubbed at his soft nose and begged the man's forgiveness.

'I'm so sorry, I should be more aware and spend less time daydreaming.'

She moved off the road to allow the cart to carry on past, but the farmer didn't urge his horse on. Instead he studied her and seemed to come to a decision.

'Are you wanting a lift? I'm heading on this road for a few miles yet and would be happy for the company. Layne here doesn't have the most interesting of conversations, and we exhausted those a long time ago.'

Pointing his thumb towards the rear of the cart, Jean saw a surly young man, who was dozing amongst the cargo. He barely opened one eye to acknowledge she was there and Jean began to appreciate the older man's words.

'If it's not too much trouble, I would certainly appreciate the lift, as well as the company.'

She scrambled up beside her new friend and held out her hand introducing herself.

'My name's Jean by the way.'

'Niall, and pleased to meet you too.'

Taking his hand, she noted the hardness and callouses of a person used to work, in particular a swordsman. He was a soldier or at least had been trained as one. The glance he gave he hand as he clutched it suggested he had come to the same conclusions about her. He had given the slightest pause, but Jean had noticed it, this man was no fool and she had to be careful not to lose his trust. Friends on the road were a rare commodity and not ones to be lost lightly. Hoping she was giving him her most open smile possible, she beamed at him while he gave a barely perceptive nod of his head. Settling back, Niall gave a flick of the reins and sent the horse forward at a slow and steady pace.

While Jean was thankful for Niall's suggestion of a lift, it wasn't entirely surprising to her that he offered her a seat on his cart. As an empath, and a particularly intuitive one, she was not only able to sense the emotions within others, but in her definitive efforts to control her own thoughts and emotions she seemed to emit an aura of trust. This had become very useful over the years, proving valuable in reducing time wasted while gaining people's trust. Of course, the calm she tried to maintain within had to make way for stronger, hostile thoughts eventually, she wasn't in the business of peace and serenity. But she would deal with that when the time came, as it always inevitably did.

The cart trundled on and Jean watched the backside of the horse sway lazily from side to side, his tail swishing at unseen flies. She was unsure of how to explain her presence on the road and it was an inevitable question that Niall was going to ask. She was alone, and apparently unarmed, which was unusual in the very least. To not know where she was and why she was there, would surely be pushing her credibility to the limits.

She had to say something eventually.

Niall, on the other hand, was a jovial man and was more than happy to fill in the silence for a while. It seemed he was returning from the market that had taken place the day before in the town they had just left. She had discovered last night, from the mark the man had placed on the map still in her pocket, this town was called Rassen. A small but busy community that ministered to the local farmsteads and villages. Niall and Layne, whom she discovered was his stepson, had enjoyed the hospitality of one of the taverns, where they had hired a room to stay rather than face the prospect of dealing with the Patrols. It would appear that the group of thugs, she had seen attacking the sleeping drunks the previous evening, were members of these Patrols.

Two raging hangovers later, had meant they had left the town long after they should have done; they were now very tardy in returning home and didn't relish the reception they were likely to receive when they got there. Jean smiled at Niall and his obvious wariness of facing a very unhappy wife at home.

He told her that their farm was predominantly cattle with a few sheep, though they grew their own food crops. Any produce left over went to the local council for distribution to the poor and infirm. She gave Niall a surprised look, this form of community altruism intrigued Jean.

'You actually give your produce away? But it's your food, why not sell it for profit? You did all the hard work after all.'

Niall looked at her askance, it was a few minutes before he replied, his answer measured.

'You're obviously not used to life within the Empire Jean, so are unaccustomed to our community values. Those who are in need, are just as valuable as those who have plenty.'

Again, he paused before continuing, Jean's uncomfortable silence suggested he had hit a sore mark and he watched her carefully. She became acutely aware of the scrutiny.

'Admittedly you have an excellent grasp of the Kelan language, but you still have the accent of someone from Earth. I'm not sure why a member of the Patrols should be out on the road, alone and unarmed, but you seem woefully unprepared to survive for very long.'

Jean was temporarily speechless. Apart from the fact that this man, whom she had mistaken as a country bumpkin, more concerned with his cows than politics, was very much on point with his knowledge and facts. It was that he knew she was from Earth originally that completely poleaxed her; though the fact that he should associate her as a member of the Patrols did make her feel uncomfortable. She hadn't heard anything of her home planet for so long, despite many fruitless attempts to find Earth and get back there. Yet here was a man, countless lightyears away from a world that, to her knowledge had still barely reached the boundaries of its own solar system, was speaking as if it was the village next door. Jean felt as if she had been turned on her head and spun round very fast.

She was beginning to feel vulnerable.

Niall explained that the Patrols were recruited mainly from Earth. Apparently, as the people who lived within this Empire were still considered too loyal to their Emperor, people from Earth, according to Niall, were enlisted from less scrupulous, criminal members of society to the Patrol's ranks. Grasping the possibility of a workable story Jean formulated her reply carefully, though she didn't much like the idea of the association.

'Since I've been here, I've seen that the Patrols are nothing more than thugs.'

A nod from Niall encouraged her.

'I was recruited myself as a member of the Patrols. But they are lawless in themselves and have little, if no honour at all. I don't like the way they carry on and unfortunately, I voiced my opinions too loudly. I was subsequently beaten for my insolence and I left as soon as I could, in fear for my own life.'

He looked sideways at her. 'I didn't take you as a criminal, what have you done to pique the interest of Ephea's thugs?'

Jean shrugged. 'I think I was in the wrong place at the right time, a case of mistaken identity.'

46

Niall didn't look convinced and Jean didn't blame him, but he didn't question her further on the matter and changed the subject.

'So, you haven't been on Kelan long?'

She shook her head. 'No, I've barely been here and know practically nothing about Kelan at all.'

This last statement was so true, that when Niall paused and assessed her reply, he seemed to accept it without question.

'I doubt if the Patrols take kindly to deserters, and normally I would be sickened to have one anywhere near me. However, the Patrols have no honour and are despised in Kelan, they have no place in my world. So, anyone who is happy to speak out against them and is willing to suffer the consequences for it, has a place at my hearth.'

Jean understood, the Patrol that she saw last night was obviously part of a much bigger network. They had run roughshod over the lives of these people, who gladly gave away their food to the poor in order to serve their society and strengthen community ties. The citizens of Kelan were beginning to intrigue her, they were people she wanted to know more about. Urging Niall on, she encouraged him to tell her more about this world, and why its idyllic life was so suddenly being torn down.

Behind them snores began to emit from Layne as he finally succumbed to his own hangover.

4

Ti'akai

The hours past pleasantly as they travelled on the road leading westwards. For the next few miles, Niall and Jean discussed how the local people around Rassen were dealing with the relatively recent arrival of the Patrols. Apparently, they were still only openly present in small towns like Rassen, among the hamlets and villages, dotted around the countryside.

However, due to the presence of Garrisons manned by highly trained and well-armed soldiers, that Niall referred to as knights of the Order, the Patrols were more of a menacing presence rather than an all-out threat, unwilling to provoke the military arm of the Empire. Niall himself had apparently been one of these knights, and he spoke proudly of his days at Pernia, where all knights of the Order trained. His warm baritone was comforting as he spoke and Jean felt at ease, urging him to continue his stories.

His time within his beloved Order had come to an end when he was badly wounded. Niall was reluctant to speak of what happened at first and Jean didn't push him, she'd seen soldiers badly injured and then forced to leave their friends behind; for many it was the only family they had ever had and the trauma of leaving that life behind could be devastating.

After his injury though, he had been offered the opportunity to remain in the Order as a knight, but the damage to his body meant he would be stuck behind a desk for the rest of his career. To Niall this was his idea of hell, so he had taken an early pension and reluctantly left the Order, making a new life as a civilian. After revealing such personal information, he was quiet for a while and Jean could sense his feeling of loss and left him to his own thoughts.

Eventually, she asked what had happened since he left the Order, he took a few moments before grinning.

'Surely I have bored you too much about my life? There must be better subjects to talk about.'

But Jean was reluctant to discuss her own history, it wasn't your average person's story and she wasn't ready for that much disclosure just yet. Besides, she was fascinated with Niall's own tales and wanted to learn more about this world she found herself in; as well as this amiable man.

'Absolutely not, keep going, I want to know more.'

Allowing himself a smile, Niall urged the slowing horse forward and carried on talking. It would seem that Layne, who was dozing behind them, was actually his stepson and Niall had adopted him as his own when he had married his mother Dana; a widow whose husband had died after a long, drawn out illness. Niall was apparently a distant cousin and they both met during a family get together. They soon found they had a lot in common. The farm was hers, but it had been hard to work on her own with a young son to look after as well. She didn't have the means to pay someone to help her at the time, but Niall had offered to help as long as he had a place to stay. The arrangement had worked out well and it didn't take long before they realised they were going to be more than just friends. The farm began to be profitable and eventually they were married, with twin girls born soon after. Niall had a wistful look on his face as he talked about his wife and family, he seemed contented.

The couple were happy, and the farm had given them everything they needed. Even the recent arrival of the Patrols in the towns hadn't really affected them, as they lived so far away from the difficulties. But Niall wasn't a fool. He could feel the tension rising, and there were recent rumours that there were those within the Order that had been tempted to turn a blind eye for the odd incentive. Even now, when they went into Rassen for market days, there was more chance of trouble starting and reluctantly, people were beginning to stay away. So now everyone was beginning to feel the burden of shrinking profits.

Jean pondered his words and asked why the Emperor hadn't done anything about it if he was so powerful? Niall looked away for a moment, seeming to gather his thoughts. When he turned back, Jean noticed his eyes were moist. Feeling uncomfortable at such a sudden show of emotion, she was surprised that someone like an Emperor, so distant from the life of a farmer, could instil such a strong reaction.

She turned her attention onto the rolling countryside instead and was again in awe of its open untouched beauty. They were passing through a valley, where the mountains in the north were now closer and their sides much steeper. A spectacular waterfall fell down a sheer cliff face, rainbows arced in the sunshine as thousands of gallons of water plummeted downwards into a basin before rushing to join the main river Par; which had wound round a copse of trees on the farthest bank. Its flowing waters were now churning among the rocks as it met with the influx of water from the cascade.

Niall drove the wagon across a bridge that spanned the smaller, tributary river and Jean breathed in the air. She enjoyed the scent of spring flowers pushing up along the riverbanks and feeling the spray of the water as they passed over. All around, birds were busy in their preparations for nesting and she sensed that the other animals around were also waking to the natural call of spring.

The noise and spectacle had given a brief moment for Niall to gather himself. When he was ready, he talked as a teacher would to a child, imparting important information that should not be forgotten and so the child must concentrate. Jean was intrigued by the change in tone, but its significance soon became apparent.

'As it seems you really have no idea about Kelan, the Empire or the Order, I'll try to give a brief outline of it's history. I won't go into the details of the universe and I certainly won't try to explain the reasoning of the gods; I know there are forces that have moulded our history that I could not possibly comprehend, let alone try to relate to a stranger.'

He paused again and Jean was holding her breath. If nothing else Niall knew how to throw together a good yarn and keep his audience listening.

Niall continued. 'Around ten thousand years ago, the gods created a group of men who would work together to unite the seven Primary Worlds; these would eventually become known as the Empire. However, this Empire was not about dominance and subservience, but created to ensure the security of the universe by uniting the Seven Sectors.'

Niall was about to get into the flow of his story, when Jean put her hand on his arm.

'What Seven Sectors? What Primary Worlds?'

'Of the universe, there are seven parts to it.'

Seeing her still blank look, he closed his eyes and sighed, projecting an air of someone trying to remain calm and patient, while speaking to a child that is refusing to understand a simple statement.

'You are surely aware that when the universe was created there were seven Sectors. The Seventh Sector, the one that Earth is the Primary World of, had to be severed from the rest of the universe because it couldn't cope with the Ti'akai.'

Jean was by now completely confused and her face obviously showed it.

'They really haven't told you anything before you came to Kalen have they?'

Jean just shook her head slowly, *you have no idea.*

'The universe is made up of many things, I'm not a physicist, so I'm not going to mention all of them but predominantly, the Ti'akai is the substance that keeps it all together. It is the power and life force that we all rely on. However, millions of years ago in the Seventh Sector, there was a problem, it seems the Ti'akai was actually attacking the very fabric of that part of the universe. So the gods decided the best thing to do, was to sever it from the rest of the universe and the other six sectors; removing the Ti'akai altogether and leaving it to survive alone.'

Jean was speechless and could only just sit in silence, totally bewildered by what she had just heard. Niall, oblivious, carried on.

'No-one really knows what happened to the worlds that existed there, but it seems that at least some survived, including Earth. But because of the absence of the Ti'akai, it took longer for life to evolve, and on Earth at least, they have only just begun to catch up with the other Six Sectors; though they have had to rely heavily on such inefficient power sources as electricity. Of course, with the huge populations that now exist there, life has become a bit of a nightmare. Mind you, despite all their problems and inadequacies, the people of Earth are dealing with their issues. After all, they aren't extinct, yet.'

Trying not to splutter, Jean finally found her voice.

'What do you mean Earth is only just beginning to catch up? Inadequacies? We have advanced considerably with modern technology.'

Admittedly she hadn't been there for a very long time, and she didn't have a clue as to the actual date now, but the home she remembered seemed pretty ahead of the game with its technology.

Niall watched her indignation with a smile.

53

'Advanced eh? How is the necessity to fly planes, drive cars, produce toxic waste to provide power, advanced? How is the divide between the rich and poor going? And have all the diseases been eradicated since I was last there? Besides, I can guarantee most of those advances in technology you talk of were because the Empire helped to produce it.'

Jean made a deliberate effort to keep her voice calm, but it was becoming difficult.

'Planes? Cars? You ask that while we sit in a cart being pulled by a horse? That power you talk of provides aid to hospitals that help the sick and poor.'

Jean wanted to defend her own world further, but even she thought her arguments sounded hollow, remembering the wars and suffering that no doubt still occurred since she was last there.

'We don't have thugs on the street attacking the defenceless.'

She broke off, unable to carry on, even she didn't believe that. Of course Earth did, for most cities it was a fact of life. Living on the streets was dangerous and made people easy targets for abuse and much worse.

Niall didn't seem to notice her consternation but continued to answer her questions.

'Why should we need planes? We use the Portal Gates if we need to travel far, and that includes travel between the rest of the worlds in the Empire. Except of course Earth, that one is restricted. But cars? Why use cars? There is no need to move at a speed that requires such vehicles; and if haste is required, we have the Gates.'

Niall paused and sighed for a moment.

54

'Regarding the thugs that haunt our towns, yes, I concede that is not good; but that is only a recent occurrence. Normally the Order would have eradicated that problem as soon as it started, but they have left them unchecked. I don't know why; I can't imagine what would make the Emperor leave his people to the mercy of the Patrols the way he has.'

Niall suddenly looked so sad and unhappy; Jean felt her annoyance subside.

'How do you know what Earth is like? Unless you've been there you surely can't comment on it.' Jean asked.

'Oh, I've been to Earth, and I am very much aware of the troubles that exist there. How do you think I got this injury?'

He lifted his trouser leg above his boots and Jean saw now that the lower part was a prosthetic, not wooden as she would expect from a medieval society, but one made of metal and other materials she wasn't sure of. It looked like something they would recognise on Earth in a specialised hospital unit. Aware that Niall had returned to the subject he mentioned earlier, but was reluctant to expand on, Jean gently encouraged him to tell her more.

'What happened?'

Niall sighed again. Jean found Niall did a lot of sighing when he was impatient.

'I was an engineer, in charge of adapting the existing and unreliable machinery that provided clean water for remote areas. There were two of us, but some of the local rebels didn't take kindly to our being there; apparently helping those in need was not good for their business.'

He rolled his eyes and shook his head in disgust.

'They tried to frighten us off, which included death threats. Armed men would attack at all times of the day and night, but they couldn't understand why their guns and explosives didn't work around us. Unfortunately, they eventually resorted to other tactics.'

He sighed again and Jean found herself biting her tongue. He went on.

'We had become arrogant and lax in our security, and we'd become complacent in believing we were untouchable. It was a fatal mistake.'

He pursed his lips, reliving past grievances.

'If nothing else, the people of Earth are resourceful, the rebels had forced the local civilians to secretly undermine the building we were working in, causing it to eventually collapse. We were trapped under the rubble.'

He looked away and seemed to take longer this time to compose himself. He tapped his leg.

'My friend was killed, and my leg was badly crushed, I had to lose it below the knee, but it was the damage to my spine that did for me. I was rushed to Aria, here in Kelan, and Lord Steven himself worked on me. He managed to sort the damage on my spine, but he couldn't save my leg too.'

Jean saw tears form in Niall's eyes and she looked away, studying the flowing river again. When she turned back, he had wiped the offending wetness away.

'I'm so sorry Niall, that's a horrible thing to happen, I don't know what to say.'

'Ah lass it's not your fault, I have my life now and a good wife and family. I just have to see it as a different adventure.'

He gave her such a broad happy smile on his weather-beaten face, she couldn't do anything else but return it.

'Just spend some time in Kelan Jean, you'll grow to understand. Even the air feels different away from the Seventh Sector.'

It was then that Jean realised this was the weird feeling she was getting here. It was the Ti'akai. She looked around her, viewing this new world through different eyes, maybe she shouldn't be so quick to judge what she was seeing. Niall was right, she'll give it time and if nothing else, she had no desire to return to where she came from that was for sure. But most of all, for the first time she may have found a way to get back home; to her broken and battered Earth.

She closed her eyes and let her mind drift back to memories she had tried so hard to suppress, finding it was her turn to shed a tear.

5

Raging Bull

While Niall and Jean talked, the countryside passed by slowly, with the mid-afternoon sun shining down to warm their skin. Jean could feel herself becoming drowsy while Niall's words played around her head, trying to come to terms with the extraordinary and unexpected information regarding this Empire that he was so proud of. However, something was tugging at her thoughts, something Niall had said in passing, but she knew was important.

Shit.

Her eyes shot open and she spun round in her seat to face Niall.

'Niall, what do you mean, none of their guns and explosives worked?'

Niall gave a start and looked up surprised, he seemed to have completely forgotten she was there for a moment. Rapidly blinking away his confusion, he tried to focus. Jean apologised and tried not to laugh.

'I'm sorry Niall, I didn't mean to startle you, but when you spoke of the people who killed your friend, you said that guns and explosives didn't work. What did you mean?'

Having composed himself, Niall returned his attention to keeping the old horse moving. Relaxing his elbows onto his knees he answered.

'Ah, well it's part of the Ti'akai; guns, explosives, electricity and probably more, can't work within the Six Sectors; they can't be used against anyone who originates from there either. So, when someone from Earth tries to use guns on us, they jam, eventually falling apart. Quite funny seeing the shock on their faces when it happens.'

Niall gave a wicked grin and Jean grinned back; she'd seen that startled look many a time on her own adversaries.

'Interesting.'

Niall took this at face value and chuckled, but Jean found the scenario more than just a bit interesting. As far as she had been concerned, she was the only person this phenomenon had happened to. But now she was learning that there is apparently a huge chunk of the universe, that this has always been an accepted norm.

Very, very interesting.

Jean mulled this new information over as they trundled further along the road, passing under a glorious blue sky and

59

warm spring sun. But if only people from the other Six Sectors were affected this way, why did it also happen to her? She was after all, from Earth originally.

Niall sat up and stretched. Layne, in the back, was still fast asleep judging by the snores coming from his direction.

'Look, we're about an hour away from the farm and it's already getting late, we have a space above the barn that is used by any extra help we have over the summer and harvest. There is one farmhand, George, who helps Layne and I, he lives in the house with us. But if you are looking for somewhere to keep your head down for a while, you are more than welcome to use the barn. All we ask is for help on the farm. Besides, I think Dana would be glad of some female company that isn't a couple of rowdy five-year-old twin girls.'

Niall smiled wistfully as he talked of his family and again, Jean found herself warming to this man. The idea of having somewhere safe to stay while her injuries healed was a godsend. It would also, hopefully, help her to gather more information about this world called Kelan, that was beginning to be more of a puzzle and far from the backwater it had at first appeared to be.

'I would certainly appreciate the offer Niall, and I am more than happy to help out on your farm. It would be good to get some fresh air into my lungs, and some solid hard graft to work out this battered old body.'

Niall snorted. 'You're nothing but a spring lamb, you wait until you're my age before you start talking old bodies.'

She smiled. *Oh Niall, if only you knew.*

Some time later they were travelling up a long winding lane, reaching the farm as the sun was beginning to dip below the mountains far off to the west; Layne had finally woken up but still looked a little worse for wear. By now all three of the weary travellers were looking forward to getting off the cart and enjoying a good meal and a tankard of ale. However, as they approached the little huddle of farm buildings, that Niall and Layne called home, the shouting, barking and squawking that ensued suggested that dinner may be sometime away.

Once they had reached the yard, the noise had become deafening, the scene was one of complete chaos. A young man was running around the yard, attempting to herd, what appeared to be, a very pissed off and terrified bull, whilst trying to keep away from its lethal horns as the beast swung its head from side to side in panic.

A dog ran in and out at the bull's legs, barking its head off, apparently having the time of its life. Ducks, geese and chickens also joined in the mayhem; squawking and screeching for all they were worth, scattering in all directions. Though Jean was pretty sure they were actually having a rare old time too, probably taking great delight in winding the chaos up further.

In the doorway of a small two storey farmhouse, a woman stood with a couple of little girls peeking from behind her legs; their eyes wide while watching the fiasco.

The woman looked furious as the commotion unfolded.

'George, stop winding the beast up and get him back in the field.'

Poor George hearing his mistress, turned around and indicated that he was indeed trying to steer the beast into his field. The bull, however, had other ideas, and George was very nearly impaled on its horns, only dodging the danger by a hair's breadth. By the time Niall had pulled up into the yard, the carthorse had also figured out that life had just become far more interesting, stamping his feet and tossing his head, eager to be out of his harness and in amongst the melee.

Jumping down from the cart, Layne, now wide awake, immediately ran to help George, who had just narrowly missed being disembowelled by the flailing horns again. Niall was already shouting orders to his wife to 'get the girls inside' before he had even alighted from the cart, demanding they bolt the door behind them.

At the sound of his master's voice, the dog seemed to take great delight in increasing the decibels of its barking. Weaving around Niall's legs, as well as the panicked bull, running back and forth, scattering the ducks and chickens in its wake. The air was full of noise, feathers and shouting.

Trying not to laugh at the fiasco taking place, Jean stood up and decided that she really needed to sort this out, preferably before someone got seriously hurt.

Ok girl, now's the time to get to work.

She began by turning her senses inwards and gathering her thoughts. Then slowly, Jean opened the metaphorical doors in her mind and allowed the emotional chaos to enter. A gentle vibration worked through her body, down her arms to her fingertips; sensitive to the world as it came flooding in. Jumping down from the cart, now on the verge of being dragged back out of the yard by the excited horse, she touched the beast's flanks as she passed, sending out her own soothing peace. Almost immediately the horse began to calm, until eventually he stood quietly, unconcerned with the noise.

There you go boy, stand still and wait.

As if he read her mind, the horse let the mayhem pass over him, remaining unconcerned by the commotion that continued around the yard. Jean then pushed her own calmness further outward, and the atmosphere in the yard began to change. Sensing something new, the barking dog faltered, he looked confused and stopped running around; his barks turning to whimpers of submission. He seemed to now be aware of the possible danger he was in and began to back away from the still terrified bull, seeking out the safety of his master and running to Niall's side.

Jean looked over at the flapping birds and rolled her eyes; birds were always a bloody nightmare. However, the lack of barking appeared to have lessened their resolve, and as the bull threatened to trample their own safe roosts around the yard, they scattered for cover, only indignant squawks belaying their whereabouts.

Niall, Layne and George looked around in confusion at this inexplicable change in their animals; Niall's eyes eventually resting on Jean.

The stranger was walking steadily across the yard towards the bull, his head, with the vicious horns, moving from side to side as he tried to understand the change in the atmosphere himself. The beast's whole body was shaking, his eyes rolling in terror as he turned around to confront any new onslaught that came near. His focus finally rested on the figure approaching him. Instinct told him he had to get away from danger, to protect himself, but somehow, he no longer felt he was in danger. He looked around, sure there must have been some reason to be afraid, or maybe there wasn't. His familiar surroundings seemed a comfort now, why had he been so anxious before?

Eventually, the quivering animal began to calm, his clambering heart reduced to a more sedate speed and his breathing slowed. Still confused, he tried to make sense of what was happening, shaking his head, still unsure. The familiar men that stood around him were there, but at a distance, shouting, but their voices seemed so far away.

All the bull could focus on was the strange human walking towards him, soothing his thoughts. He felt a calmness wash over him, until finally, he bowed his head; exhausted and in shock. The new stranger was now so near, she held out her hand and he felt her touch his head. The words, were they words? Reassuring and calming.

Peace my friend, no one will hurt you now.

He could feel the familiar halter pass over his head, and he allowed himself to be led back to the safety and security of his field. Grateful for the feel of grass under his cloven feet, breathing in the smell of grass and soil while beginning to slowly munch on the sweetness of his evening meal; the blinding terror of a few moments before, now forgotten.

Jean concentrated her mind on gently closing the doors to the emotions of the chaos, sensing a fragile harmony easing throughout the yard while man and beast came to terms with the strange events. From behind, within the yard, she was aware of a very different reception, this time from a thoroughly perplexed farmer, his family and the lad, George.

But the expected onslaught of questions and finger pointing didn't come. Instead, as Layne and George were about to open their mouths, Niall silenced them, giving orders to clear the yard and sort the horse and cart, before giving instructions to see to the rest of the farm. He turned to his wife, who was again standing in the farmhouse doorway, two very curious little girls with grubby faces still peering out from behind her.

'Dana, take the girls inside please, we'll be in shortly. Is dinner ready as I am starving and I'm sure our guest is as hungry as I am?'

Dana's head turned to Jean and her eyes narrowed slightly. There was a moment of silence, but then she nodded.

'Aye, by the time you've washed up, it'll be on the table.'

A brief nod from Niall, and Dana turned, ushering her children inside. At last he returned his focus on Jean, who was a full head taller than he was now they stood together.

'I think that's enough drama for one day, there'll be time enough tomorrow to explain that little party trick.'

Looking deep into her eyes Niall studied Jean, it took nearly everything she had not to turn away. He put his hands on his hips and before she could say anything he spoke again, his voice calm but full of authority. Jean could imagine he had been a formidable soldier.

'I don't know who you are Jean Carter, but I know damn fine you have never been part of any Patrols on Kelan, or anywhere else for that matter. However, I do know that bull trusted you when it was terrified and panic stricken.'

He breathed in slowly, with a determined look that suggested he was making some effort to remain calm, and steadied his gaze on her.

'I've been around beasts for long enough to know that they are pretty good judges of character. So, if that bull trusts you so will I.'

He stepped forward and lowered his voice while keeping her gaze.

'But the gods help you if you betray that trust.'

Sighing silently with relief, Jean inclined her head.

'I understand Niall, and yes you are right. I have nothing to do with the Patrols here, but I ask that you keep that to yourself, at least for the moment. I promise I have no desire to hurt you or your family, and I am truly grateful for your belief in me. I just hope I am able to repay your trust.'

Reaching up Niall placed a hand on her shoulder and gave her one of his most disarming smiles.

'A few weeks labour and believe me, you'll be a welcome addition to our little family. No rest for the wicked around here I'm afraid.'

And with that he led her to the yard trough, a few tugs on the pump handle and fresh water flowed. They both washed the grime of the road from their hands and faces, then slaked their thirst, before walking side by side into the farmhouse, where Layne and George were also heading. The smell of freshly cooked food filled their nostrils and Jean's mouth watered as she stepped inside.

After dinner, the dishes had been cleared and the children were finally asleep in their beds. Nothing like a bit of chaos and a fascinating stranger to keep sleep at bay for curious little ones. Layne and George had gone outside to make sure all the animals were finally settled for the night.

Niall, Dana and Jean sat by the fire, relaxed in each other's company and talked for a while. The conversation mainly stuck to general gossip around the neighbours, Dana's growing up on the farm, and how Niall had literally been her knight in shining armour when he came to help after her first husband's death. It was all perfectly amiable and could be any night-time farmhouse scene.

True to his word, Niall mentioned nothing of what had happened earlier, and the evening passed pleasantly enough. Jean knew that tomorrow was going to include a lot of questions she wasn't entirely sure how to answer, but for tonight, she was determined to put that aside. She hadn't felt so relaxed and at peace in a fair while, a feeling that was long overdue, she soon felt her eyes begin to glaze and her head start to nod.

By now everyone was feeling tired. Fortunately for Niall, Dana put his fatigue down to the events of the day, but he knew it probably had more to do with the previous night's shenanigans. Not wishing to push his luck, he suggested an early night for everyone, and he beckoned Jean to follow him out to the barn.

He showed her the steps, to the rear of the large outbuilding, that led to a door on the first floor. As they entered, Niall opened a small box that sat on a shelf just inside the door, it contained a bright shining orb that lit up the room. Jean looked at it curiously, it looked like insects were flying around within, she turned to ask Niall what it was. He picked up the sphere and held it in his hands.

'These are simply known as Light Orbs. On the world of Juno, there are little insects that exist in pockets within the rock, that are totally devoid of oxygen. They live in the darkness with only the glow from their own bodies to see with, preferring to live in small, confined spaces.'

'But what about food?'

'Well, that's the weird thing about these creatures; they eat their own dead.'

She grimaced. 'Lovely.'

'Well, as revolting as that may be, they are able to survive within these orbs for a considerable length of time. Each generation feeding off of the previous ones before breeding.'

Jean took the orb from him and looked within its centre again, but the light hurt her eyes and she put it back in its box. Niall then turned and left the room saying he would be back shortly.

Looking around her surroundings, she saw was in a small room that contained a couple of beds, a table with two chairs and a small dresser. A window looked out over the back of the farm and Jean could hear the babble of water of an unseen stream somewhere in the darkness. On further inspection, she discovered a small closet that held, to her complete surprise, a toilet and a sink with running water.

Once Niall had returned with some bedding, he checked that Jean had everything and made to leave. When he saw the look of surprise on her face he asked what was the matter?

'You have internal plumbing in your barn. There's a toilet!'

'Of course there's a toilet. What do you expect, a dash to the nearest bush every time you need a piss?'

Jean had a flashback of that very morning and her own dash behind a few convenient trees.

'Surely you must have seen the public lavatories in Rassen?'

Feeling herself redden, she tried to brazen out her awkwardness.

'Of course, I just didn't expect to see one in a barn that's all.'

Feeling mortified that she had bared her own backside amongst a pile of dead leaves, when she had probably passed a perfectly good public convenience, she bid Niall good night.

He gave her a questioning look before saying his own farewells and leaving her alone. She raised her palm to her forehead.

'Good grief Jean, you're and idiot. That will teach you to make assumptions.'

Once he was gone, Jean made up one of the beds, then undressed before thankfully crawling between the sheets. Another box on the bedside cabinet revealed a smaller orb containing the cannibalistic insects.

The comforting smell of the horse stabled below, mingled with that of the hay loft tugging furiously at her brain, sleep could not be ignored any longer. Even as her head touched the soft, clean pillow, she wrapped herself in the warmth of her blankets and Jean was soon drifting away into a dreamless, peaceful sleep.

6

Squashed Tomato

F allon Kleinstock stood in the bright hall, waiting at the bottom of a flight of sweeping stone stairs, contemplating his life so far. The spring sunshine was pouring through the tall windows, causing sunlight to shimmer off the mirrors and highly polished furniture around the room. Unfortunately, the fenestration remained firmly shut, as the smell of fresh air and bird song seemed to annoy the lady of the house. As such, the fragrances of the various displays of flowers that adorned every table, had become mixed with the perfumes and body sweat of all those standing around the room. The air became cloying and hot. Even the blooms had started to wilt in the stifling heat.

He closed his eyes, his mind wandering back to what seemed a lifetime ago. To the boy he was then, and how he had come to be here, the man he was today.

His father had told him he was vain.

Fallon liked to think that he just had more refined tastes, compared to the sort of people who often frequented his parents' company anyway. After his father had left the Order, his family had made a good living within their little town of Bratten. As merchants of fine cloth, they had made sure that their children enjoyed all the advantages that young men and women could desire at their ages.

Being the oldest of his siblings, Fallon had taken full advantage when his parents were so willing to pick up the bills. But life had become so boring; he had had to find other, more exotic, ways to keep himself amused. It wasn't his fault his mind needed more stimulation than his siblings.

Unfortunately, the sort of stimulation Fallon preferred to indulge in cost a lot of money, and his parents had decided that they wouldn't pay for him anymore.

How could they desert him like that?

He had debts that needed to be cleared, and the shame of not being able to pay his bills was awful. Even his friends understood his humiliation, leaving him alone in order to save face before they contacted him again; well he assumed that must be the reason, because he hadn't heard from them for a while.

What was even worse, his father had made Fallon stand before him one evening, his mother looking on; only the redness of her eyes belying the tears it cost her to fight her son's case. But her husband didn't want to hear any more. He had heard enough about Fallon being young; how he had to get out and see the world, have some fun before he settled down and take his place within the family business.

However, Fallon didn't want to take over the family business, hating the boring repetitiveness of meeting clients and suppliers, the monotony of bookkeeping. He also had a nasty feeling his father had begun to figure this out, and now was refusing to invest in his son's social life anymore. Especially if Fallon had no desire to put the effort in to make the business work.

Fallon had felt humiliated as his father listed the outstanding creditors that would now have to go unpaid. Unless, of course, Fallon decided to work off his debts, with his father, in his office. Believing at first, that his father was just firing his usual shots about having to grow up and take responsibility, he'd made the fatal mistake of sighing and then rolling his eyes. His father on the other hand, had come to the end of his patience with his wayward son, startling him with a slap to his face. Looking back at the memory of the pain and shock made the young man wince. Remembering the stinging of his cheek, his hand moving to his face unbidden, rubbing the sore spot while looking at his mother for help. But she just stood there and watched, while his father humiliated him. He hated them both.

His father had sneered in disgust and disappointment, sending Fallon away, hoping this was the way to force him to be responsible for his own actions.

So, an arrangement had been made that he be sent to an Aunt in Parva. She accepted her nephew into her household, on the clear understanding of course, that he was to work for his keep. This didn't go down well for Fallon and he was soon looking for ways to avoid the labours he was being forced to do. His saving grace however, was during a rare afternoon free, when he found himself in a shady bar away from the usual haunts of his aunt's household. It was there he met the people who said they would be willing to give him back the life he deserved; *if* he was willing to serve the new wife of the Emperor.

Apparently, she needed her own court as her husband's inner circle was stifling; far too stiff and colourless for such an outgoing and bubbly personality as the Duchess Ephea. When he had queried why she was still referred to as Duchess and hadn't been crowned Empress yet, the looks they gave him made him think of his father before he received his slap. He had backed down then, lowering his eyes. He had learnt he could do humility if it meant no pain.

Now, bringing his mind back to the present, he stood within the beautiful white walled hall of his mistress. Having served her diligently for the past three years, he had been rewarded handsomely for his efforts. He had his own associates now, who looked to him for honour and profit; there were even those among them he would be happy to mark as his friends. He could feel their presence now, standing behind him, their backs pressed against the pristine walls. Though it made him sick to admit it, he wasn't sure if they were there for support, or morbid curiosity.

He gave an uncontrollable gulp and noted his throat was dry with nerves.

All alone, Fallon stood in the centre of the room, his shoulders slumped, trembling despite the heat. He barely kept himself upright with his nerves, his gaze fixed firmly on the floor. Above him, he heard a door open and he felt himself gulp again, whilst he gripped his hands behind his back to stop them from shaking.

Still unwilling to raise his eyes completely, he only saw the expensive billowing red skirts of the short, fleshy woman in his peripheral vision. This was unfortunate, as the only image he seemed to be able to make out was that of a badly squashed tomato. He felt sick.

The clack, clack, clack of her shoes on the marble stairs, reminded him only too well of the reality he was about to face.

Behind him he felt, rather than heard, his fellow associates. Or maybe they *were* friends? They had, after all, come with him when he was summoned. Fallon could feel tears well in his eyes and his throat constrict, self-pity began to overwhelm him.

The awful billowing, red apparition had reached the bottom of the stairs and begun to shimmy slowly across the floor, closing in on him.

Clack, clack, clack.

Eventually, the hem of the appalling dress covered a particularly interesting tile that he was determined to focus on. Time had run out and he was forced to acknowledge his fate.

With all the will he could muster, Fallon raised his own eyes to meet her dark, beady ones, his tall frame towering over her own stout form. She had to stand with her head back, her chin thrust out, in order to ensure she was able to take the stance of looking down her nose at him. It was a position she had adopted years before and had become her natural posture — it did nothing to enhance her already ridiculous image.

Trying not to gulp again, Fallon stood alone and waited. His stomach churning when her childish voice broke the silence.

'Tell me Fallon, how is it in your *letter...?*'

The last word was sneered as she pulled out a piece of paper from within the folds of her skirts. 'You speak of a stranger talking to *them.*'

This time she spoke the word 'them' as if it caught in her throat, as if to utter *their* names would choke her.

'But you don't have any information to help identify who this stranger is? Surely, as you shared an entire evening with *them*, no-one should have escaped *your* notice.'

She shook the piece of paper in his face as if to prove a point.

Mustering all the strength he had left, Fallon finally found his voice. Even he had to admit to how weak it sounded in this vast cavern of a room.

'My lady, this person had a hood and their face was obscured in the dim light.'

His dry throat cracked at the effort of talking.

Slap!

A bejewelled back hand caught his face, a deep cut began to bleed down his expensively barbered chin. Visions of his father swam before his eyes and he hated himself when, again, his hand betrayed him, reaching up and brushing his burning cheek.

'What were they? Man? Woman? What did they do? What did they say?'

Fallon's eyes watered and he tried to block back the tears.

'I…I couldn't hear them, they were too far away. They were tall, but I don't know what sex they were.'

His voice had become petulant, the pout on his lip disappearing as she dealt him another vicious blow. This time much harder.

Slap!

Another red gash appeared, and blood began to mix with the tears that now flowed unchecked.

'Why not?'

Her voice began rising to a shrill pitch, spittle hitting his expensive shirt and waistcoat. The heat in the room was becoming unbearable and his throat burned as he swallowed the bile that had risen from his empty stomach.

'You were there all evening, you should have been watching. Why weren't you near enough to hear?'

In his panicked state, the whimpering man tried to save himself.

'There was a commotion outside. We all went to check to make sure it was safe for *them*.'

'Safe? You wanted to keep *them* safe?'

She began what could possibly have been a laugh, but instead it seemed to border on hysteria.

'Did they move? Did they leave to see if it was *safe*?'

His eyes fell to the floor, realising any hope of a reprieve had been lost.

'No, My Lady.'

This time the slap became more of a punch and Fallon recoiled against the force.

'Then you shouldn't have left either.'

By now she was screaming, her arms flailing with anger, his jacket was pitted with her spit.

'Instead you all spent the evening eating and drinking yourselves senseless.'

She flung her arms out to those standing around. They flinched, trying to push themselves further against the walls in a desperate attempt not be seen.

'You then looked for sport, watching idiots kicking the hell out of each other.'

She had to stop for breath and stood back, her heaving breast sucking in the stinking air.

'In the meantime *they* are having a clandestine meeting with someone, and *you* missed it.'

Her rage had reached its pinnacle. Raising her taloned hands, she rushed at the pathetic man that now disgusted her so much. Throwing punches at his head and chest, not stopping until he was a cowering, sobbing mess on the floor. Not content to end her retribution there, she began to kick and stamp, her high, spiked heels finding soft flesh; soon the floor was running with his blood.

In her rage a heel snapped from one of her shoes. Furious, she gave a final enraged kick, before turning and practically running back up the stairs. Her blood-soaked skirts leaving a scarlet trail across the monochrome flagstones.

Ephea's bloated face was now an unhealthy florid colour due to the labours of her violence, her broken shoes once more reverberating on the stairs.

Clack, thump, clack, thump.

Behind Fallon, the unwilling spectators peeled themselves from the walls, nervously approaching the bloodied heap on the floor. Together they helped their fallen comrade out of the heat and stench, his fate of no concern to the departing figure.

Closing the door to her private apartments, Ephea breathed deeply and tried to gather herself. She had let herself become emotional again — not something an Empress should ever allow. She silently hoped the useless lump that made her so angry died slowly and painfully. Her voice calmer, but still breathless, she turned and addressed the figure that stood at the window.

'Captain, find out what you can about this elusive stranger, I want to know who this person is and why they are here. But bring whoever they are back, alive.'

She seemed to consider something else and continued.

'That is, as long as they can speak, I'm not too concerned about the rest of their body.'

Captain Karen Johnson nodded before taking her leave, quietly closing the door behind her.

Alone in her rooms at last, Ephea looked around her sumptuous surroundings. Her expensive jewels lay sprawled across the dressing table from earlier; she hadn't been able to decide on which sparkling gems she would display today. Eventually she had settled on the rubies to go with her beautiful new dress. She scowled when she remembered that it was nearly ruined by the stupid maid helping her to get ready. Ephea was pretty sure the nasty little wretch had deliberately pinched the cloth so it wouldn't fit properly. Then smirked when she thought about the swift kick to the maid's shins, followed by a good tug on her hair before throwing her to the floor. Silly girl used the excuse of playing with the stays of her mistress's corset; but Ephea knew better, the only reason she wore the damn corset was to help enhance her curves, and that boney bitch wasn't going to imply anything else.

She smiled in satisfaction that the maid was now on her way out to a farm, far away from Parva, so her vicious gossip couldn't spread amongst the rest of servants — she expected loyalty from her staff.

Raising her eyes in disgust, she considered servants; why couldn't that bloody stupid husband of hers accept that they were just there to make life simpler? They were there to serve her, so they were servants. He could get as pissed off as he liked about how she treated them, but she knew best and he was just a stupid old fool.

Stripping off the red silks, she began the arduous task of undoing her laces. Of course, if her maid was still here, she would have done it, but thanks to her uselessness, Ephea now had to do it herself.

She sighed, it would take time to find someone else to trust enough though, so it was one of those burdens she would have to bear in the meantime. As the last lace was loosened, her *curves* were released from the corset's restrictions and they succumbed to the inevitability of gravity.

Ephea idly scratched under her left breast and made her way to the room that was her inner sanctum. No-one was allowed to enter here, only her.

Unlocking the door with a key she kept on a long chain that nestled between her ample breasts, Ephea stepped inside and closed the door behind her. The stresses of the morning slipped away and she knew, that at least here, she was completely alone and safe.

Opening a small box on the shelf to her right, an orb shone bright and lit the small room in which, lining one side, were rows of very expensive wigs. Moving around the room, she opened another two orb boxes and further light bounced off a mirrored table that ran along another wall. Pots of makeup and creams were arranged neatly on its surface. Taking down a dressing gown that hung beside the door, she covered her naked body, then sat at the table and stared into the mirror.

As always, Ephea took a deep breath before she reached up and removed the auburn curls from her almost bald head. The wisps of hair, that clung desperately to her scalp, were now grey and sparse. She knew she should just cut them off, but it was all she had left of the beautiful head of hair she once had. Her mother would sit with her at night and brush her curls, whispering how beautiful she was. Regaling stories of fairytales where handsome princes would whisk maidens away on their noble mounts. But it was all a lie, there were no handsome princes, only foolish men with too much power and not enough balls to wield it. A silent tear dared to spill onto her cheek, she angrily grabbed a handful of cream and began to rub off the thick mask she painted on every day.

She scrubbed at her skin and the stark reality was revealed underneath, a grey face, aged before her time; lines around her sullen eyes and cheeks creased her ravaged face. She had to fight down the bitterness that threatened to overwhelm her, this was the price she had to pay for the riches and power she now happily held. But there were times at night, when she shed tears of self-pity for the woman she once was, but could never be again. Who could possibly understand what sacrifices she had made? Her sisters? No, they didn't care and why should they? They had their own problems to deal with.

Why did the bastards have to make life so difficult?

Once Ephea had finished removing the last of her makeup, she made her way to the bathroom and ran hot water into the large tub, pouring in copious amounts of bath oils and bubbles. What she needed was a good soak, along with a bottle of wine — or two. The bath filled while she went in search of a glass and bottle from the cabinet kept for such occasions.

Johnson stood on the landing, noting the devastation below, before descending the magnificent, sweeping staircase. She had to admit that the ugly, mad, old bat may not have much in the way of charm, but hell, Ephea wasn't afraid to get her hands dirty. Barging past servants scurrying to clean the mess that had spread over the tiled floor, the Captain made her way down a corridor that led towards the back of the house. No-one spoke or acknowledged her as she passed through the back door and crossed to the stables, meeting up with two men standing with their horses waiting for her.

'Road trip to Rassen it is then boys.'

The two men nodded and the three of them mounted, leaving the yard through big iron gates and riding out into the warm, busy streets of Parva.

A huddle of people was carrying a bundle into a carriage further along the road, but the riders ignored them. Instead they urged their horses into a trot, forcing passers-by to hurry out of their way, earning themselves a barrage of curses in the process. The riders' passive faces barely even acknowledged the chaos, carrying on regardless, heading for the East gate and the portal that would eventually take them to their quarry at Rassen.

7

Empath

It had been five days since Captain Johnson and her fellow riders had left Parva, and she was in a bad mood, having had to travel all the way from the city of Vernia — a small city south of the river Par. They had been forced to travel from there as it was the nearest public portal to Rassen. Any portal that was closer, was within a garrison of the Order, or in public buildings manned by the Order. Ideally Fallport, a large Imperial garrison, was less than half a day's ride from their destination; but no Patrolman willingly puts themselves within reach of the Order's curiosity. Especially out here in the country, where if the odd Patrol member were to go missing, it would be unlikely that many tears would be shed, let alone a public outcry raised to search for them.

Of course, there was the added pressure that the Captain would rather not have to answer any awkward questions as to why she, and her men, were there in the first place.

Once the riders had travelled the five extra days needed to get to their destination, they were in a far from congenial mood. Johnson thought at least this encouraged the people they met on their journey to keep out of their way.

It was late in the evening by the time Johnson and her men had ridden into the centre of Rassen, she had decided to stay in the same inn as Fallon and his companions had done the week before. The Dog and Bucket was the largest tavern in the town, with ample rooms to accommodate a fairly large party of travellers. Even so, Fallon and his party would still have had to share rooms for everyone to have a bed that night.

Johnson's men made sure their horses were stabled, with suitable threats given, ensuring the high standard they expected for the welfare of their mounts. Satisfied their accommodation was sufficient, the party of three then made their way into the large taproom. As it wasn't market day, along with the local Patrols making sure that people didn't venture out after dark unless it was an absolute necessity, the bar was virtually empty. All except for a couple of old locals sat huddled by the fire, that was until Johnson turfed them out of the way. Mumbling their disgust quietly at such rudeness, the old men settled in the farthest corner, their eyes averted and voices low.

Once settled and eating their evening meal, the Patrolmen made a brief but thorough interrogation of the landlord and his staff. Their efforts revealed little more than they already knew.

'Yes, of course they remembered the evening well.'

Such clientele is rare, even before such austere times.

'Yes, the fight outside in the street was quite a spectacle.'

Apparently, one of the men involved in the scrap was still nursing a nasty head injury in the hospital at Aria. It wasn't mentioned directly, but there was a hint it wasn't his sparring partner that caused the damage to his head, but a rather over enthusiastic member of the Patrol wielding his wooden cudgel.

Not wishing to get caught up in grievances about local enforcement, be it lawful or otherwise, and bored already with the gossip, Johnson and her men had retired to their beds. They rose early the next morning, making sure they were in time to be at the town gates as they opened for the morning traffic. They had better luck here, when their enquires gleaned that a tall woman, that the Watch hadn't seen before, had passed through the gates sometime during the day. Apparently, just over a week ago.

It had taken some effort on her part, but Johnson had bitten her tongue and after, what she would consider some gentle prompting, the lad on the gate confirmed that it must have been the day after market day.

'The woman had left around midday.'

The young man finally thought of this when he remembered that a cart, carrying a farmer and his son who lived out in the next valley, left soon after her.

'They must have caught up with the woman not much further down the road.' He suggested, 'Though their horse preferred a more sedate pace.'

A few more questions had gathered that the farm was a good four hours ride along the Imperial Highway. Unfortunately, it also passed very close to the Fallport Garrison. Johnson had to play things carefully, this stranger had already shown she had friends in very high places, friends who also had the full support of the Imperial Order. Satisfied they'd learned all they could from this godforsaken town, the riders secured directions for Niall's farm and set off on the road west.

Later that day, the heat had slowly burnt off the low-lying fog that had formed after the previous night's rain. Jean and George had been out early with Niall, seeing to the cows and their calves; the bovines had been happily munching the new spring grass up on the gentle slopes of the hills that skirted around the farm. After ascertaining that Niall was indeed the most highly esteemed manager of bovine happiness, they made their way back to the farm for a well-earned breakfast.

Passing the pond and stream that ran past the back of her barn, Jean told George and Niall that she would meet them back at the house later. She felt a quick dip was exactly what she needed in this heat, to wash away the filth from the mornings work. They left her to it, with George stating a dunk of his head in the farmyard trough was all that he needed.

Jean stood and watched them return to the house, before contemplating the inviting pool.

George you couldn't possibly understand, unless you've been battered to the point of destruction by relentless sonic waves, just to feel remotely clean.

It also occurred to her, that this was another region where Niall had a point in the civilisation rankings; the sheer pleasure of water. There was a bath and shower in the house that Jean could use whenever she wanted to, but the clear, cooling waters of the pond looked too inviting to miss. Enjoying the cold water envelop her body, she reflected on the conversation that she and Niall had had the morning following her first night at the farm.

She really had no idea then how much, or how little she should let this man, who had shown so much trust in her around his home and his family, know of her true identity. But, in the end Jean had decided that being a bit circumspect was probably wise. If nothing else, the last thing she needed was to possibly put the family in danger just because they knew too much.

Niall had cornered her while Layne and George were in the back field fixing fences. He and Jean had been assessing the damage from the previous day's animal antics; there were a number of boards on the barn that had been battered by the unhappy bull, which definitely needed replacing. Niall took hold of a board and absently started to wiggle it while seemingly lost in thought.

'Well, now seems as good a time as any to put your cards on the table Jean, suppose you tell me who you really are and why you are here.'

Jean had been waiting for this but was still reluctant to be completely open about who she was, although to be honest, it was probably better to go with what Niall had obviously figured for himself. Leaning against the warming wall of the barn and feeling the heat of the morning sun on her face, she began.

'Well, no doubt you have realised I have some empathy with animals.'

Niall shrugged his shoulders in acknowledgment, she was going to have to give a lot more for this man to be happy.

'I am empathic, not telepathic before you ask, I can't read minds, but I can empathise with the emotional states of others. It is much easier however with animals, as they naturally communicate without all the complications of speech and the desire to conceal their true feelings as people do.'

Niall contemplated this. 'So, you can speak to animals?'

'No.' Jean sighed, always the same assumption she was Dr bloody Doolittle. 'No, I can't talk to animals, but we can communicate through the perception of emotion. Humans are so much more complicated as I said, just purely because they are barely honest with themselves let alone to anyone else.'

Stabbing the ground with her booted toe she carried on.

'The daft thing with people is, the more they try to hide their feelings, the easier it is to see the real ones inside.' She pursed her lips and frowned. 'My biggest problem though, is keeping the emotional state of the general populous at bay; otherwise there is this huge emotional overload that completely overwhelms me. However, now I can control the effects and can open myself to read those I want and when I need to, but then close it down again afterwards; to protect my own sanity if nothing else. I call it building walls; different walls for different needs.'

Niall nodded his head; this obviously wasn't a huge surprise to him, and he seemed to accept this quite naturally. She got the feeling that very little would surprise this man.

'So, you've already made an assessment of me and my family then?'

He looked at her with his head to one side, it seemed a casual question, but the answer would mean a lot to him and how their relationship would continue. She chose her words carefully.

'When you offered a lift to me, I admit yes, I did gauge whether it was safe for me to accept, but even if I weren't empathic, I know a good man when I meet him.

87

'People actually have good instincts of their own, the only problem is, some still choose to ignore them, even when the signs are blatantly obvious against them.' She paused for a moment. 'You are a good example of someone who is good at trusting his instincts.'

'Me?'

'Yes Niall, you! You offered to give me a lift on your cart, making an assessment there and then that I wasn't an immediate threat, and later inviting me to stay and work with you for a while. You considered your instincts and made a decision; I hope I have the opportunity to demonstrate that you haven't made a bad one.'

Jean felt a little guilty, while what she said was true, she didn't mention that she had a knack of ensuring people's trust anyway.

Niall looked into her face and her green eyes gazed steadily back. Grinning, he jovially slapped her on her shoulders.

'Aye lass, I'm happy with my decision, but you still haven't told me where you have come from and why you are here. Because you sure as hell don't come from Kelan.'

Laughing back, Jean inclined her head.

'True, I don't come from Kelan. I was born and brought up on Earth, London to be precise. But I haven't been there for a very long time.'

Jean looked away, aware that despite her best efforts the homesickness was creeping back again. Niall said nothing, he just watched her face as the emotion fleeted across it. Closing her eyes, she steadied her thoughts and continued.

'I've spent the last few years in the Seventh Sector, traveling around, trying to stay out of trouble — failing miserably most of the time.'

It felt strange referring to a universe that she had spent her life assuming was a whole, was actually only one-seventh of it; the vast expanse of space she knew, had suddenly got a hell of a lot bigger.

'You could say I'm in the security business; sorting out problems that are often too big to be dealt with normally.'

'And *you* are the one to sort the problem out?' Niall raised a sceptical eyebrow.

'Funnily enough, yes. I do have certain attributes that help.'

'The fact that you're empathic?' More scepticism.

Come on Niall I need you to stay with me here.

'Yes, that plays a part, but not everything.'

She was getting to the point where she really didn't want to tell him anymore than she already had. 'You really don't need to know all of that, but I can assure you, it has no bearing on you or your family. As to why I am here, I haven't figured that one out yet; I've rarely, if ever, been given instructions beforehand, but it will no doubt become apparent over time.'

Niall returned to the loose board of the barn and started to wiggle it again. Eventually he gave up and turned back to Jean, who had been watching him in silence.

'Fair enough, I'm going to take a leap of faith and accept that you are not going to harm my family or my home.'

Jean smiled and nodded, she made to move away with Niall in order that they could carry on with the work they had started, but then she felt his hand catch her elbow and she turned back to him, puzzled. His face had gone dark and Jean felt the tension within him.

'But if you cause me to regret that decision Jean Carter, you will learn what it is to piss me off.'

Jean understood completely, she covered his hand with hers.

'I swear Niall, your family's safety is paramount to me.'

He kept her gaze for a while longer, then turning, he headed towards the chicken coop beckoning her to following him.

'Let's get these bloody chickens sorted before they cause anymore havoc around the yard.'

Jean smiled and once again felt an enormous affection for this man, gladly following him to sort out the *bloody chickens*.

Having enjoyed her daydreaming and the dip in the pond, which probably took a lot longer than it should have done, Jean dried herself and dressed, ready to join the rest of the family for breakfast and farmyard chores. She was climbing the grassy slope up to the bottom of the stairs that led to her room, when she became aware of people approaching the farm. She couldn't see them, and they couldn't see her behind the barn, but she felt hostility and arrogance approaching. It was as she ascended the steps, she heard the sound of horses entering the yard. Riders, not wagons. Experience over the years had taught her that discretion is often far better, so quietly, she entered her room and crossed the floor to where a ventilation hatch had been cut into the wall and listened.

Within the yard, Niall took one look at the visitors and immediately was put on his guard; there were three riders, one woman and two men, but they had the bearing and uniform of the Patrols. Beside him, the dog growled and his hackles rose along his back; Niall touched his head with his fingers.

'Steady boy, we don't need trouble.'

He shot a glance at his wife.

'Dana, take the dog and get inside and keep the girls safe. Lock the doors.'

Dana stayed where she was and looked at Niall with a mutinous glint in her eye. Niall returned her gaze and briefly, Dana glanced towards the barn; fear gripped at him.

Surely, she wouldn't?

'Now, Dana.'

This time his voice brooked no argument. Dana gave a last fleeting glare to her husband, then ushering her daughters, they went inside the house; the door slamming shut behind her.

Years of training had made the old soldiering in Niall cautious, stepping forward, he met his visitors with a straight back, arms relaxed at his side, but his mind alert for danger. George and Layne stood either side of him but a pace back. Silently he prayed Jean stayed out of the way.

Johnson had sensed the atmosphere as soon as she had entered the farmyard, she also noted the defensive stance of the older man before her. The other two younger men that stood just behind him seemed to be happy to let him be in charge. Dana's unhappy retreat hadn't gone unnoticed either; this farmer understood trouble when he saw it. This could be interesting.

The riders came to a stop and Niall stepped forward.

'Can I help you?'

Niall's rumbling voice was loud, commanding and clear, carrying across the yard leaving Johnson in no doubt that this was a man with at least some military training. A slight nod of her head and her two henchmen urged their horses so they were more spread out. She wanted this man to concentrate on her and be less aware of what her men were doing. Somehow, she couldn't see this farmer's boys having the same mettle as him.

The silence lengthened, while Niall and Johnson continued to eye each other up; The man painfully aware of the other riders at the edge of his peripheral vision.

Finally, Johnson broke the silence.

'You were in Rassen a week ago.'

It was a statement, not a question. She spoke in English knowing that if this man was an ex-member of the Order, as she suspected, then he would understand; English was taught as standard at Pernia apparently.

She spoke with a strong Australian twang and waited for his response. It was pointless in denying his whereabouts on that day, he no doubt knew she would ask around.

'I was. It was market day.'

The man wasn't going to give information away easily, and Johnson bit her tongue to keep her frustration in check.

'You waited until the next day to come back to your farm. Wouldn't they have missed you here?'

'My son and I had a few too many ales after the market, we decided it would be better if we stayed and left for home the next day. I am confident in my family to keep the farm working while I'm away.'

The Captain watched him for a while, he was hiding something but she didn't know what it was. For all she knew he could be selling illegal liquor on the side, if so, she couldn't give a shit if the Emperor lost a few coins in tax revenue. She tried again, her patience wearing thin.

'On your way home did you meet anyone? Give them a lift on your wagon perhaps?'

Niall narrowed his eyes.

'Aye, I met a woman going our way on foot, at least part of the way that is. She wanted to get to the Garrison at Fallport, apparently wanting to travel onwards via the portal gate there.

Johnson stiffened.

Shit, if she'd got to the portal, she could be anywhere in the Empire by now; on top of that they didn't even know if this was the same stranger as the one they were interested in.

She tried another tack.

'What did you talk about on your way home? It must have been a good couple of hours before you gained the crossroads leading to Fallport.'

Niall shrugged as if unconcerned.

'To be honest I was nursing a horrendous hangover and she was more the silent type. We barely talked. I'm not even sure we got her name properly.'

Turning to Layne he cocked his head questioningly and deliberately reverted to Kelan.

'Greta? Gaynor? Did you manage to catch it?'

Layne was more than happy to play along if it got these strangers as far away from their farm as possible.

'Aye something like that, to be honest I wasn't really interested, my head was killing me.'

Johnson's frustration was growing. Speaking in English, she turned her focus on the young lad.

'So, you didn't hear anything at all other than her name, which you can't remember?'

Layne looked uncomfortable with the sudden attention from this horrible woman, he seemed to suddenly lose his power of speech and stood opening and closing his mouth like a landed fish.

Niall stepped forward between her horse and his stepson.

'He doesn't speak English.'

Johnson's patience was hanging by a thread, she tried again, but this time in Kelan. Niall winced as she butchered his native tongue.

'You went to the market with your father?'

Layne nodded slowly.

Johnson gritted her teeth.

Jesus, the boy is an idiot.

'Did you speak to the woman your father offered a lift to on the road home?'

Niall grimaced, she spoke slowly as if talking to a fool, making her sound even more ludicrous.

This time Layne shook his head and Johnson was getting more and more angry, something her men had noted, they didn't want her taking it out on them later.

'You had better not be lying to me boy, I won't be taken for a fool'

The Captain gave a barely perceptible nod to the rider closest to the lad, and with a speed that caught Layne completely by surprise, he kicked him full in the face. The boy fell back to the ground, clutching at his face, blood flowing from his now broken nose. Niall's face was a picture of fury he lunged at the rider, but the horse spun around, knocking him off balance.

Had he had both legs intact, Niall may have kept himself upright. But while he prided himself on his ability to get around without barely any impediment, this time his prosthetic limb failed him, he fell hard.

George ran to his aid but was pushed away in frustration by his master.

Niall vented his fury and humiliation.

'Get off my land, get out.'

Johnson had remained impassive throughout the incident, but she had noted the old man's disability. Sneering at what she considered as a broken man and two useless boys, she turned her horse and beckoned her riders to follow.

She was about to urge her horse into a trot when she stopped and rode back to Niall. He was still lying prone on the ground. Moving her horse so close it was almost standing on him, she leaned down and stared deep into his eyes. Niall met her gaze without flinching. Johnson's voice was low and menacing.

'If I find that you have lied to me old man, I will come back, and I will have your pathetic farm torched and your animals slaughtered.'

She kept his gaze a little longer to emphasise her point, then spinning her horse round, she cantered back down the lane, her riders in pursuit.

As they disappeared out of sight, Dana ran out of the house, panicking at the sight of her bloodied son and prone husband. Niall had succumbed and allowed George to help him to his feet, though he still seemed shaken. Dana made sure her husband was not harmed and then turned her attention to her son, helping him up and walking him into the house.

From the barn, Jean approached the scene; sick to the stomach that she should be the cause of so much pain. George saw her first and tensed, causing Niall to turn and see Jean walking towards them, her face was drawn and unsure. Gently pushing the concerned attentions of George away, Niall stood to face the woman who had become more than just an enigma to him and his family. She tried to say something as she approached, but the words seemed pathetic and shallow.

'Niall, I don't know what to say, I'm so sorry, I have no idea who that woman is.'

Niall held up his hands to calm her.

'Come in lass, we can do better discussing this inside.'

With that, Niall turned and entered the house considering the matter settled. George followed close behind, while Jean tried to settle her stomach, briefly hesitating before following and closing the door behind her.

Niall had settled, gingerly, at the kitchen table that was set for breakfast. He was pushing a protective George away again, this time with a little more force, telling him to put the kettle on, stating a cup of tea would do them all the world of good right now.

By the sink, Dana was mopping at Layne's face. It seemed the blood had finally stopped flowing, though it looked as if he was going to have a spectacular set of black eyes later.

When Dana noticed Jean standing by the door, she gave vent with every bit of motherly love she had. It was only Niall, risking another stint on the floor by grabbing her waist and pulling her to him, that stopped her actually physically attacking Jean. It didn't however stop her voice.

'Who the hell do you think you are? Get out of my house. Take your things and go. I never want to see you again.'

Her face was red with fury, tears had begun to flow with her anger and frustration.

96

'Dana, she's not going anywhere.' Niall's voice was calm and gentle.

Jean looked at Niall confused, surely, he didn't expect her to stay here, not after what had happened.

It seemed Dana agreed with her, and with increasing decibels; she spun round to face her husband.

'Have you seen Layne's face? Look at him, he's only a boy. And you, you're hardly in a fit state to take on armed horsemen. You could have been killed. And what use would George have been?'

The look on the men's faces echoed the irony of Jean's thoughts. In one bold swoop, Dana had managed to irritate the very people she cared for and loved so much, by implying their ineffectiveness and lack of masculinity.

It didn't go down well.

At the cooker, George slammed the kettle down, causing water to spill everywhere. Layne had removed the cloth his mother had been using to mop his face, then stood up, planting his feet, in what he hoped, was a manly manner. Niall let go of his wife and set her firmly away from him, turning to Jean and speaking as calmly as he could manage. Had the circumstances been less emotional she would have laughed, instead her face remained passive.

'Do you have any idea who those people were and why they are looking for you?'

Jean slowly shook her head.

'No, I swear I have never seen them before, I don't even know why they are looking for me. When we met on the road I had barely spoken to anyone; I had spent the previous night in a shed. All I can assume is that they know something I don't.'

She paused for a second and looked into his face, then at those of the rest of the room.

'I can't be responsible for hurting your family, Niall, I have to leave.'

'And go where?'

His voice was calm and gentle, as if talking to a child.

'Parva, if there are answers, that would be as good a place as any to start looking.'

Niall nodded. 'True, that would be the natural place to start, which is what they...' He pointed out of the window, '... expect you to do. As soon as you are on the road, either they, or others, will find you.'

He sighed and looked at his wife, who stared back with incredulity; her hands on her hips as she made her defence.

'You can't be serious Niall, the woman will bring every Patrol member here; our farm, our home, will be destroyed.'

Niall assumed the voice of someone talking to a child again.

'No, if Jean is found on the road near here, then it will be obvious that we lied, then they will come to destroy the farm. But if Jean stays and lies low, they will eventually take their hunting elsewhere.' He paused to consider something and turned back to Jean.

'Though it would probably be better if you spent the night up in the mountain woodlands, I have a feeling we may have another more illicit visit tonight.'

Jean understood and nodded in agreement. His words made sense, but she wasn't sure his family would be so reassured.

Dana certainly wasn't convinced. 'But...'

Niall seemed to have come to the end of his patience, he stood to his full height and again Jean saw the younger man, the proud soldier, in him.

'No, I have made my decision, Jean will stay here, and we will welcome her. Whoever she is, those we consider our enemies are looking for her and we have a duty to protect her.'

He walked over to the door and faced Jean and spoke in the same commanding voice.

'As such, I expect you to not do anything that may give cause for the Patrols to return to our home. Do we understand each other?'

Jean again nodded her understanding.

'Of course, I will do whatever I can to ensure your protection. I will also make sure that what has happened here today is not forgotten, that bitch will pay one way or another.'

Niall studied her face and seemed satisfied.

'Fair enough. George.'

The farm hand looked startled at his name and exchanged a glance with Layne in panic.

'Yes?'

Niall turned back to the table and gestured for Jean to sit, while also settling himself down, he then turned his head to the confused lad.

'Has that bloody kettle boiled or are you heating it by hand?'

Relief passed over the young man's face and he busied with the kettle and tea pot. Dana went to resume her ministrations of her son, but he pushed her away, obviously still smarting about her earlier remarks suggesting he was still a boy. He sat down in his chair next to his father, and Dana, who was now looking hurt and mutinous, sat at the table as far from the rest of the group as possible.

Two little girls moved away from the shadows in the corner where they had been hiding, watching everything that had happened. Coming across the kitchen to be with their mother, they kept wary eyes on the others in the room. Gathering them to her, Dana held them close, knowing that whatever happened, she would protect her family. So, while she may not like it, for now they would abide by Niall's decision. But if he, or that damned woman, put her children in danger again, she wouldn't hesitate to let them know where her priorities were; and to hell with the consequences.

Until such time as it may become necessary however, she would put up with it, but right now a cup of tea seemed like a very good idea.

8

Denfield

nathan stared through the French windows and out over the balcony to the walled garden beyond. Trees and flowers grew in abundance, which made an exquisite place to walk amongst when the sun shone. On a clear day, you could see over the far wall and right out across the tree filled valleys beyond, to the edges of the beautiful, exposed wilderness of Dartmoor.

But not today. Today there had been a constant drizzle that obliterated the view, leaving a dreary veil over the rest of the estate. It made the garden look dark and forbidding.

The French windows ran the length of the kitchen wall, leading out onto a raised balcony that also served as a patio, with sweeping stairs either side that led down to the walled garden. Sighing to himself, Nathan placed his forehead against the cool, clear glass. He remembered the happy summers they had all enjoyed out there on the patio, along with the new discovery of Earth's passion for barbecues. It was a novelty, which had been quickly been adopted by anyone from the Empire who managed to get themselves invited to one. The whole idea had become so popular, that Simon, an engineer by trade, had even set his hand to building one in the gardens of the Retreat at Parva. Nathan smiled as he remembered, that despite his expertise in astrophysics and quantum mechanics, the sheer pleasure on his friend's face when he'd finished his handiwork, and subsequently burnt his first steak, was one of pure elation.

But alas, it had been at least four years, — or was it nearer five now? — since a summer gathering at the Retreat. Their home, their one place for privacy within the Empire; where they could just be men, be who they really were, without fear of anyone else intruding. No-one to see the daft antics they got up to, especially when Daniel and Damien decided to pull one of their pranks. It was a fact of life, that to the outside worlds the Knights were serious and without humour, figures surrounded in mystery and treated with awe. At the Retreat however, or if they were off on some assignment elsewhere within the universe, their dynamics were complex, humorous and on occasion, volatile.

Now the Retreat was secured and impenetrable. Nathan himself had created the barrier, that he alone, could unlock around their precious house and gardens. It had to be protected for the future. A beacon of hope, that one day this nightmare would end, and they could return to how it used to be. Until then, its place in their lives was too precious to fall within the hands of Ephea and her sisters. It made them all feel sick to consider the possibility, so until the threat was ended, they accepted their home at Parva was out of bounds.

One saving grace though, was the fact that their recent work on Earth, had meant that they had set up their own separate homes here. Nathan had felt an affinity with the contrasting worlds of moor and forested valley of Devon, in the South West of England. He had invested in land and created a house that, for the first time, belonged only to him. His home was an old, two storey house that had fallen to nothing more than a pile of granite stones when he acquired it, but with a huge imagination and a hell of a lot of money, (he still remembered the cold sweat and wince on Damien's face when he saw the bill) he had created a space he lovingly could call his own home, Denfield.

Over time, he had come to consider this little part of Devon as precious as that of the Retreat, creating invisible barriers of energy to protect its borders. Even now, despite having their own homes scattered around the country, the other Knights often migrated to Denfield to meet, refusing to let old habits die out.

Behind him, Nathan could feel his cousin, his second in command, Damien, resting his gaze on his back. Watching, while the others sat in silence, probably also letting their thoughts wander to other, happier times. They had been helping themselves to Nathan's Balarian Brandy, a luxury that he prized highly. He also noted how liberally it was being shared around the table.

They had all gathered in Denfield's kitchen, a huge room warmed by a large range cooker at the business end, and a wood burning stove surrounded by large sofas at the other. It used to be the perfect place to come back to, to sit and relax after a day's Imperial work. However, now it was used more and more as a place to meet and discuss the very business he used this space to escape from. The large circular kitchen table that covered the floor between the kitchen counters and sofas, had been commandeered as a boardroom. Since early that morning, until half an hour ago, in-depth discussions had been ongoing, with problems considered and decisions made. Despite the continuing turmoil within the Empire, they were all determined to ensure that the everyday bureaucracy of government continued to function, without too many distractions from the unfortunate events currently taking place elsewhere in the Empire.

Nathan had to admit, it was becoming increasingly more difficult to maintain the status quo. For many years they had worked hard to achieve a stable economy; a security for those living within the Empire. Never did they think it would be threatened like this. Of course, there were those who tried their hand at taking power, but they were soon dealt with and such inconveniences were few and far between. If he was completely honest, Nathan had never really considered any of them very seriously. Unfortunately, to his constant chagrin, he had failed to see that this time, it was different. Constantly going over the horrendous events, he had tried to work out how he would have done things differently; but he knew he wouldn't have. Nathan was beginning to feel impotent at the possibility of failure, a concept almost alien to him, haunting his thoughts day and night.

He closed his eyes against the grey dreary view before him.

But what if? Was there a possibility of hope?

They had finished their meeting; the minutes had been covered and relevant tasks delegated. Now they were left to contemplate 'All other business' that was unlikely to be recorded in any minutes read outside these walls. In particular, their thoughts regarding the strange encounter in Rassen. It had definitely been unexpected, though whether it held any actual significance was difficult to ascertain.

Unfortunately, it wasn't as easy as it once was to investigate such incidences. The likelihood of raising suspicions from unwanted quarters was all too possible now. People were already disappearing, not many, but enough to make those remaining, wary of involving others. Luckily, some information was still able to slowly filter through, and recent intelligence had brought the subject of Rassen back to the fore.

Nathan turned his back on the grim weather outside and faced the six men sitting around his kitchen table.

'And you're sure it's Johnson who's been sent to find out about this 'mysterious' stranger?'

The day's business tidied away and the detritus from their lunch, which had been eaten without a break from their work, was now moved away to the kitchen counter. Only the brandy and their glasses, that Nathan noted had been refilled, remained on the table. He didn't begrudge them their indulgence, it had been one of those days, and only a Balerian brandy seemed the best solution to, if not lift, at least, ease their spirits. Though he considered that at this rate, his drinks cabinet and wine cellar, were going to require restocking soon.

Damien had been playing with his own glass, swilling his brandy around, before relishing the amber liquid. Putting down his glass, he gave his cousin, and friend, his full attention as he replied.

'It's definitely her. She was seen leaving Brooklake and heading on the road north to Rassen about three weeks ago. The landlord at the Dog and Bucket has confirmed it. Later when the lad on the West gate was asked if he saw anything, he described Johnson perfectly. Though apparently, he also turned an odd shade of green at the memory, I don't think he is going to forget the encounter anytime soon unfortunately.'

He picked up his glass again and he drew his brows together as anger flashed across his face.

'There have also been several reports of people being assaulted in Johnson's quest to find out information.'

Nathan completely understood Damien's anger, as the Duke of Lorimar he would take it as a personal affront that his own people were being harassed this way. Nathan knew it would only take a single gesture and his cousin would travel to the Garrison at Fallport and drive out every member of the Patrols in the area. But he couldn't, he daren't.

The others around the table listened in silence and Nathan joined them and sat down. Paul leaned forward, his elbows on the table, while cupping his own glass in his hands.

'The question is, is this the same woman who you saw that night?'

Damien nodded.

'Yes, I think we can safely assume this is the same person that has piqued Ephea's interest, but whether such investigations are warranted I don't know. Well, not yet anyway.'

'Oh I think they are definitely warranted.'

Everyone turned to Nathan as he relished another warming mouthful of brandy. He met their gaze and continued.

'Whoever she is, she is definitely not from Kelan.'

They all looked at him in silence, curious as to how he had come to this conclusion. He put down his glass and gestured with his palms upwards.

'Why would she want the map if she was from Kelan? It doesn't matter where you come from in the Empire, you'd know where Parva was, also, that you were in Lorimar. The fact she didn't, is curious enough.'

'Unless of course you're from Earth.'

'True.' Nathan nodded; Daniel was as pragmatic as always.

'But when she spoke, her Kelan was perfect.' Damien reminded him.

Nathan nodded. 'Yes, exactly, too perfect. Unusual don't you think?'

His hands mirrored his enthusiasm for his own argument. He turned to Damien who sat to on his left.

'And she was almost grateful when you pointed out exactly where we were, where *she* was, on the map.'

Daniel nodded slowly, understanding where Nathan was going with this.

'As if she had no idea where she was at all.'

'Exactly.' Turning back to Daniel he smiled with encouragement, seeing his comprehension.

'What are you getting at Nathan?'

Stephen, sitting next to Daniel looked enquiringly at Nathan, aware that an idea was forming in his mind. It had been a long time since he'd had such a spark of positivity and Stephen was intrigued. He wasn't disappointed.

'Someone arrives in a place that they are totally unfamiliar with, yet they have an ability to speak the local language. Albeit without all the nuances, usually picked up by a lifetime's use. Doesn't that sound familiar to you?'

Nathan looked around the table, the faces of his closest friends stared back stunned. Simon broke the silence from his seat opposite.

'Of course it's familiar, it happens to us all too often.'

He looked around the table and then back to Nathan, who returned his gaze with a smile.

'Go on.'

Simon was incredulous. 'Are you suggesting this stranger, this woman, is like us?'

Nathan held his gaze a moment longer, then shrugged his shoulders, before sitting back in his chair.

'No idea; but it's not something I'm going to dismiss just because it seems unlikely. We know all too well of the possibility of the unlikely becoming entirely probable.'

Nodding heads and mutters of ascent around the table confirmed his statement.

Daniel cocked his head to one side.

'So, you believe that my remark about needing someone like us to come to our aid, has actually come to fruition?' He looked at Damien. 'That is why you gave her the map?'

'Well it wasn't as if we needed it, and at the time it seemed like a good idea.'

Damien turned to Nathan, as intrigued now as everyone else.

'Fair enough, so how do you want to handle this theory of yours?'

Nathan picked up his glass again.

'At the moment, nothing.'

'WHAT?' They all sat forward, not sure if they had heard properly; but it was Simon that voiced their concerns.

'What do you mean nothing? Surely if someone is here, who is possibly the answer to this god awful mess we're in, we should be doing something to help them.'

This was followed by much nodding from the rest of those at the table. Nathan raised his hands in order to ease the tension that had arisen.

'I am not abandoning anyone, or anything, that may help our situation. My concern is that by interfering and stomping all over the place, we may put our visitor in more danger. I am merely suggesting that for now, we just keep our eyes and ears open, gleaning whatever information we can before taking any action.'

There was a collective sigh around the table in understanding, though it was difficult to consider sitting doing nothing, when there was a possible means to the end of the chaos. Nathan took up the brandy bottle that still sat in the middle of the table, emptying its contents into their glasses. Raising his own he made a toast.

'To the possibility of the unlikely.'

All around his words were echoed, and silently he prayed it wasn't a false hope.

Later that evening, Damien and Nathan sat alone by the fire in his sitting room, another bottle of brandy opened. Damien had been pondering in silence, considering Nathan's revelation earlier, now he looked over to his friend.

'There's something else isn't there?'

The look of innocence he received in return didn't fool him one bit.

'There is another reason you believe this woman is not just a normal traveller, landing herself in an unfortunate quagmire of trouble.'

Nathan chuckled. 'There is no chance of fooling you is there? But you're right, there is something else that has been prickling the back of my mind.'

Nathan put down his glass and looked serious.

'Do you remember she took a liking to my sandwich?'

Damien laughed at the unexpected question.

'Yes, and I seem to recall you were not overly impressed as you had been looking forward to it too.'

'Quite, I was starving. But that aside, as she leaned forward to take and I grabbed her hand, there was something, I don't know what, but it was…. something.'

Nathan paused, trying to recall the moment, when those green eyes looked back into the blue of his own.

'It was as if I had known her before, but more than that; it was as if I was looking back into my own soul.'

Damien just stared at him, unsure how to respond. He knew Nathan to be capable of many things, but being fanciful was, absolutely, not one of them. He drew his eyebrows together and Nathan tried to explain.

'I know how strange this sounds, that is why I didn't mention it earlier in front of the others. But it was real Damien, I can't explain it, but it happened.'

Damien nodded his head slowly and smiled back.

'Very well, I am the last person to doubt it. However, we really don't need you to go all weird on us. Not now.'

110

Nathan grinned. 'Thanks, I'll bear that in mind and keep all weirdness to a minimum shall I?'

They laughed amiably, continuing to enjoy their brandy in silence, staring into the fire for a while as both contemplated this new information. Damien spoke first.

'Well, whoever she is, it is certainly going to be interesting to finally meet this young lady again one day. Let's hope she survives Johnson's little hunting trip long enough for that to happen.'

Nathan felt a pang of annoyance.

'I stand by my decision to do nothing, not until we know what is going on.'

'I know, but what if our only chance is lost, because Ephea's nasty little Antipodean dog becomes overzealous?'

'We have to have a little faith; we've been in enough tight scrapes ourselves, but we've always come through in the end.'

Damien looked sharply at Nathan.

'That isn't exactly a ringing endorsement, do you remember Ixeer?'

Nathan found himself unable to stop the shudder that ran down his spine at the memory, conceding that Damien had a point. He nodded, but still stood his ground.

'True, but I still think we can end up doing more harm than good if we interfere.'

'Yes, alright, I agree. But I hope you're not going off your head and that you know what you are doing.'

Nathan looked up sharply and Damien chuckled.

'Bastard, you nearly had me there.'

'If I thought for one moment you were losing your marbles, do you really think I'd let you carry on?'

111

'No. Of course you wouldn't.'

'Exactly, but it is bloody difficult sitting around doing absolutely nothing at all. Let's hope this woman knows what she has to do and manages to keep her head.'

'Maybe a little bit of healthy madness will help along the way. It's not done us any harm.'

They both looked at each other and laughed out loud. This time it was Damien who raised his glass in a toast.

'May the gods look kindly on our avenging angel, and may she be blessed with a sprinkling of healthy madness.'

Nathan grinned. 'I'll gladly drink to that. To faith and madness.'

Later that evening, they had both retired to their own rooms and Nathan undressed and got ready for bed. He knew he had probably had too much to drink but was beyond the point of caring. Now as he stripped naked, he caught himself in the full-length mirror that stood in the corner of his room. Tall and strong, he had the physique of a warrior, hard muscles wrapped around a solid frame, built and honed to fight.

The tell-tale white lines of the scars he had gained over time, criss-crossing his body, barely registered in his thoughts. Unlike the scars that remained red and prominent across his back, weals reminding him of a nightmare that refused to leave him. No matter what Stephen had tried, he could not remove, or even lessen, the damage that scarred his body. It wasn't even the remembered pain of receiving them that hurt so much, though that was bad enough, it was the fact that the other Knights, his friends and comrades in arms, had had to endure the same agonising fate as well — and he had been helpless to stop it.

Ixeer.

A hell full of monsters, where in order to escape it, he had been forced to become a monster himself. What frightened him most was that it was dark side of him that had surfaced so easily; a part of him that he would rather remained buried, but was now lurking beneath the surface, waiting for the time it could rise again — when he wouldn't be able to stop it.

As he looked back at his reflection, he saw that he had been clenching his fists. Glancing down at his hands, he realised his nails had dug deep into his palms, in places, drawing blood; a sheen of sweat covered his body and he felt a chill against his skin. In an attempt to warm himself up he made his way to the bathroom, standing under a hot shower and feeling the hot water scour his body, forcing himself to deal with the pain he felt he deserved.

It was some time before he turned off the deluge and dried himself, finally slipping between the sheets of his bed, knowing it would be a while before he would get any sleep.

He looked out into the darkness of his bedroom, considering his conversation with Damien earlier. Why was he so convinced this woman was there to help them? No matter how many ways he tried to consider the rationality of it, the answer always came back to the simple fact that he just knew it. Just as he knew the sun would rise tomorrow.

But still his tired brain refused to shut off, thoughts of Ephea and her family, the awful things they had done. His own inability to do anything about the fate of his people at the hands of the Patrols, and the frustration of the Order, forced to remain confined to barracks.

Somewhere he had missed a point, a simple detail that would bring everything into focus, but no matter how he tried he could not see it.

He balled the bedsheets in his hands, frustration gripped at his heart, and he forced the bedding away from him. Getting out of bed, he began to prowl around the floor of his bedroom feeling his anger rise within. Eventually he stopped at the window and looked out over the same vista he had seen earlier, downstairs in the kitchen. But this time the sky was clear, and a new moon shone down onto the gardens below.

Nathan breathed deeply and slowly, knowing that his anger would serve no-one, he drew the familiar veneer of calm serenity around himself, forcing the darkness within to stay silent.

He was unsure how long he had stood there, staring out into the garden and the valley beyond. But by the time he finally crawled into bed and fell into an exhausted sleep, the first rays of dawn were creeping over the horizon.

9

Running Out
of Time

niall had been getting it in the neck for the past two weeks, Dana was not happy with Jean's continued presence on the farm and now, as they were settling down to bed after another busy day, she showed no signs of relenting her onslaught.

Even as she was closing the bedroom door behind her, Dana rounded on her husband.

'When I picked up the twins from school today, there was more talk about those riders roaming the countryside looking for a female stranger. Word is they are getting more and more violent, just because they can't find her, they're getting desperate Niall.'

She walked up to him with her hands on her hips, her face close to his; he knew he was in trouble now.

'And we have her here, in our barn! What if they come back and find her?'

Dana's eyes were dark and dangerous. Niall had to fight the urge to step back as her chin thrust further forward.

'If you, Layne or George get hurt because of her, the gods help me, I will kill her with my own bare hands.'

While Niall doubted that Jean would actually allow herself to be seen off by his wife, he didn't, for one moment, think any less of her promise. Dana could be pretty quick with a frying pan and if you didn't duck fast enough, she was more than capable of laying you out flat. He also understood his wife's concerns; he himself, had spent many a sleepless night recently with the stories he'd heard from around the other farms, there was a lot to be concerned about. It was reputed a couple of farm lads, across the valley, had ended up in the hospital at Aria due to Johnson's anger. It was also an indication that the Captain's lack of success was causing her to be indiscreet and take more risks.

However, Niall still believed the last thing Johnson needed, was to pique the curiosity of the Order. Even with her reputation, she wasn't going to give them cause to ask unwanted questions. Though this in itself was a cause for concern, he couldn't imagine why the Order still wouldn't do anything about three members of the Patrols causing so much trouble amongst the populace. He felt angry that the Order was doing nothing to help the people they vowed to serve, but even worse, the Order had always been incorruptible, a beacon that shone, lighting the way to safety and peace. Now it seemed to him, they were as lost as everyone else.

He sighed and looked back into his wife's big beautiful brown eyes, he lowered his forehead to gently touch hers.

'Sweetheart, I understand, really I do, and I *will* speak with her tomorrow. Please try not to worry, we will get through this.'

The words sounded hollow even as he spoke them, he received an equally sceptical look from Dana as he wrapped his arms around her waist, pulling her closer to him.

'Look on the bright side, one of the good things about Jean being here, is we've managed to be so far ahead with the workload, that I'm sure we can afford some time away from the farm.'

He felt her relax slightly, taking this as a hopeful sign, he thought he may get a reprieve yet.

'What if we take a picnic up to the gully by the falls tomorrow? The girls will love it, and it would be good to spend some family time together. What do you say?'

Dana looked back up into his face, her features softening and he felt her love wrap around him. To get away from the farm, if only for a short while, would be a welcome blessing. Giving him a watery smile, she nodded her agreement.

Relief rushed over him, and Niall felt his heart swell with love. He would do anything to protect this wonderful, beautiful woman. She had come into his life when he desperately thought it was over, and now, he couldn't imagine a life without her, or their treasured family. Brushing her damp teary cheek with his finger he drew her chin up to him and kissed her. She responded to his tenderness and Niall drew her enticingly towards the bed.

Their visitor would have to take care of herself from now on. There was nothing else he could do, and his family were far too important to lose.

Jean had also been thinking about having to leave the farm soon. She had been brought to this world for a reason and was pretty sure it wasn't to keep Niall's cows happy in the fields. Relaxing in her room above the barn, working out a few knots in her muscles, she enjoyed the satisfaction of tiredness from hard manual labour; especially within the expanse of the countryside and with fresh air filling her lungs. She felt fitter and healthier than she had done in a very long time.

She found that she was feeling a lot of things she hadn't felt in a long time; the pleasure of other people's company, to feel part of a family, to be fed regular meals — now that was always a bonus. Constantly wondering where the next meal was coming from, was a stress she normally had to deal with on a daily basis. But here, with food, shelter and good company, Jean knew she was becoming too accustomed to a life she was going to have to end soon.

Of course, she had understood Niall's concerns about leaving immediately after the visit from Johnson and her riders. Then it was a bad idea, but she couldn't stay indefinitely. From what she had gleaned from Niall, Layne and George, this Captain Johnson was renowned to have a vicious reputation and was certainly no fool. Eventually the riders would be back, and this time they would do more than just rough up Niall and the boys.

During her time on the farm, the days had grown progressively longer and warmer, the seasons were changing, and summer was definitely on its way. Jean finally made the decision that tomorrow, or the day after at the very latest, would be a good time to go. So, even if it was with a heavy heart, she would make a point of speaking to Niall tomorrow, though somehow, she didn't think that Dana would be too heartbroken about the news.

Johnson was looking morosely out of the window of an inn in Fallport Village, she and her two riders were to stay there that night, despite being dangerously close to the garrison. She was getting desperate, forcing her to start taking more risks. The sun was dipping behind the mountains after another glorious spring day, but she wasn't impressed. For nearly three weeks now, they had been trudging around the countryside, looking for an elusive stranger they didn't even know was still in the area. She was beginning to feel her blood boil again at the frustration, picking absentmindedly at a spot that had started to grow on her chin. Information she had received from Parva, suggested that the bloody woman hadn't turned up anywhere else within the Empire, but that could just mean she was simply lying low somewhere, out of sight of the Patrols.

Her mood had darkened over the past few days, any suggestion, in correspondence she had made, of returning back to the city, had been immediately dismissed. It had been made clear that she was not to return, not until she found her quarry.

Slamming her fist down onto the table, she tried to vent her fury on the furniture. She was going around in circles, no-one knew anything about the *fucking woman* or where she had gone.

Even after threats of a spell in the Prison at Belan didn't glean any more information, Johnson was running out of ideas. Now in a very bad mood, everyone around her kept well out of the way. Dornov and Hanz, her riders, were doing their utmost to steer clear of her when they could — they were both currently seeing to the horses. She rolled her eyes, as apparently it now took two of them to complete the task.

If nothing else, this wild goose chase had made her consider what she wanted to do with her future. Despite all the advantages she had gained while on Kelan, Johnson was beginning to feel it was time to leave. She needed pollution in her lungs, and a vehicle with a lot more horsepower than just one.

She needed to go home.

Having been thinking more about her past life lately, she considered the road that had brought her to where she was today. Her career in the Australian Army had been fairly short due to, what she regarded, as an admin error. The admin in question was the snitch in the General's office who had ratted on her after she had been caught selling drugs; bastard! The end result being dishonourably discharged, then kicked out onto the streets of Melbourne.

She was alone with no money and no future, but by then it was too late.

The armed forces had taught her many things, including how to use some pretty impressive firepower. And while she had never been one to mix with the crowd, she missed being part of the machine, having a purpose that counted.

Not one to like leaving loose ends, she had eventually found the bastard who had snitched on her. She had cornered him in a bar one night and broken his nose, and possibly his arm too, but she didn't stick around to make sure. It helped to teach him his mistake and she would have dearly loved to have done more, but his friends rallied and protected him, forcing her to leave a job half done in her mind.

As far as her real family were concerned, she was a lost cause. They had made it clear they didn't want anything to do with her, and she found she really didn't care about that half as much as she did being kicked out of the army; good riddance to them as far as she cared.

But she needed to find a way of making money and Johnson had soon discovered a new lucrative career in drug trafficking on the city streets. The Army had even been good enough to teach her sufficient skills to make sure she survived working in such a dangerous world. Especially as guns and blades were par for the course in this line of work. She was particularly proud of her ability to excel in sword craft, having obtained a Katana, a prize a rather odorous competitor had left behind — he didn't need it after all since his demise. She soon found that with a fair bit of practice, she was pretty adept with it herself.

Eventually she had gained a fair reputation among other gang members, a few had lost a limb or two, some their lives, it all went to boosting her rise among the lower depths of gangland society, and her ego. While such notoriety amongst the gangs may be useful, it did also mark her out with the local police force. After one particularly messy incident, she was in need of somewhere to lie low, and fast.

Such an opportunity arose, when Johnson was approached by a man in a sleazy bar at the proverbial wrong end of town. He told her of a world that she could hide in, and that she could have real power with her talents. He was obviously drunk and talking utter bollocks, but he was a determined bastard.

His proposition had annoyed her. She hated nut jobs and now was not the time to piss her off. However, a timely raid by the police, after an anonymous tip off, meant she had to make herself scarce yet again, so she, and the nutter, were soon fleeing through a back door of the bar.

It should have led to a pile of stinking bins but had somehow turned into the top of a cliff overlooking a huge city by the sea. While it had been nearly midnight when she was drinking in the bar, the sun here was high in a bright blue sky.

Completely disoriented and confused, she had intended to take out her annoyance on the drunk, but an unforeseen attack found her flat on her back, with the man holding a knife to her throat. Apparently, he wasn't the mad drunk she thought he was, in fact he seemed remarkably sober as well as armed to the teeth with knives. She also later suspected he was the anonymous tip off that had forced them to flee the bar in the first place.

The world in which she had landed was literally, completely alien to her. She learnt that apparently her skills on Earth had been observed for some time, it was therefore suggested that she could do well in this world they called Kelan. They were right. It hadn't taken long for her to rise up through the ranks of the disreputable newly formed Patrols. Before long, she had worked her way to within the inner circle; entrusted with tasks that needed a certain kind of talent, and discretion. Once more she was notorious with a dangerous reputation, but now no-one dared touch her.

While she had been musing over her past, her hand had strayed to her pocket and the small crystal that resided there, hidden since she stole it from Ephea's rooms. Her emergency exit when she decided it was time to finally leave Kelan behind, start a new venture elsewhere. That time was approaching faster than she expected, and she was surprised at how much she was looking forward to the prospect.

Dornov, hurrying through the door in an excited state, forced her back to her present reality and she shot him a dangerous look that brought him up sharp.

'What?' She barked.

'Ma'am, I've just heard some news from the garrison.'

Johnson narrowed her eyes as she studied him. 'Go on.'

'One of the traders has returned from there, he was bemoaning that they still haven't got the portal up and working properly yet. Apparently, they have had problems for a few weeks now.'

Johnson would have prayed thanks to the gods if she had believed in them; instead she leapt to her feet and slapped Dornov on the back, making the man flinch.

'At last, a break. If the gate hasn't been working this whole time, that means this woman has been here and had to travel over land. She couldn't have left the area; our spies would have told us had she been on any of the roads.'

She allowed a spiteful grin to creep across her face.

'I think it's about time we made another visit to our one-legged farmer. We'll see if he's more talkative when we have hold of his boy and threaten to cut bits off him. We leave at first light tomorrow.'

The look on Johnson's face as Dornov left was joyous, maybe she would put off leaving for a while yet.

A grin spread across the face of Dornov as he made his way back to the stables, at last she was in a good mood, and the chance of meting out some decent leverage was always a bonus.

10

The Picnic

B y the time the sun had risen over the farm, the day's work was already underway, and by mid-morning, Niall and his family were finally ready for their day out and some much-needed time together. The twins had been excited since they learned of the day's events at breakfast, spending most of the morning running around and squealing at the top of their voices. Niall and Dana were hoping that the walk to their picnic spot would help work off their offsprings' excess energy.

Layne was to join them with the food later, while Jean and George were to stay behind to keep an eye on the farm.

When at last all the chores were completed, Niall finally considered it was safe for him to leave the farm for a short while.

Dana had given him enough looks of warning that the girls were driving her mad, but when she seemed to be taking a particular interest in the frying pan, he decided they had better be leaving soon — if only for the sake of self-preservation.

Eventually, the family found themselves on the trail to the gully and falls, looking forward to relaxing in the sun and enjoying the spectacular views. The farm was slowly disappearing from view when Dana, unable to contain herself any longer, turned to Niall.

'So, have you spoken to her?'

Niall winced, they had barely started the journey, bracing himself he tried to brazen it out.

'Not yet.'

Dana came to an abrupt halt; anger flashed dangerously in her eyes.

'What do you mean, not yet?'

Seeing the imminent danger, Niall raised his hands in appeasement.

'I have it in hand. I'm going to speak to her this evening, when the girls are in bed and the farm is quiet. I said I will sort it and I meant it.'

'Until another excuse comes up, I suppose. I'm warning you Niall, if you don't say something I will.'

The twins, who had been happily skipping ahead of their parents, stopped and turned at their mother's raised voice. Niall scowled, this is not how he planned to have a nice relaxing day with his family, he waved his hand at the children.

'Move along you two, I'm sure there is plenty of mischief you could be getting into.'

The girls cautiously walked up the path again, they weren't used to hearing their parents argue in front of them and Niall felt guilty for frightening them.

'It's alright, we're right behind you.'

There was a moment's hesitation, then the desire for adventure finally took over and the girls turned and ran up the path. Satisfied he only had his wife's attention, Niall turned to her.

'Look Dana, I know you don't particularly like Jean and I'm not convinced it's just because of this Johnson business, but whether you like it or not, she has been a big help around the farm. She's also been true to her word, keeping her head low. I told you I will speak to her, but it will be when I am ready and at the right moment.'

Dana pursed her lips, and looked as if she was about to argue some more. But to Niall's relief, she decided to relent this once; he had a reprieve, at least until this evening. Putting on an apologetic face she smiled.

'I'm sorry Niall, I know you'll do things right, let's just enjoy today with the twins.'

Then putting her arm in his, she urged them forward. Niall wasn't fooled though; he knew that if he didn't speak to Jean tonight he was going to be in the doghouse for the foreseeable future. Vowing to make sure he got Jean alone tonight, he allowed himself to be led up the path, the sun beating down on their happy family.

It was a few hours later that Jean and George enjoyed their own lunch in the hazy sunshine. Backs against the newly fixed wooden barn wall, they listened to the insects buzzing lazily around, soaking up the warmth of the sun. Layne had left about an hour after his parents and sisters to join them on their picnic, so it was George and Jean who had finished the daily chores. It was while they dozed in the heat, that they heard the bull bellowing in his field. George sighed, making to get up to see what had set the beast off.

'What's the matter with the old fella now?'

Jean laid a hand on his arm and told him to relax.

'I'll have a look, you stay here and clear away this.' Indicating the debris of their lunch.

George nodded and let Jean go, the dog bounding along beside her as she made her way across the fields. She'd already impressed him with the way she seemed to communicate with the animals, no doubt she could deal with the bull better than he could. As she made her way to the fields, his gaze followed her tall figure and watched how she moved so easily. He felt himself blush, to his horror his manhood was stood to attention and he looked around frantically making sure there was no-one to see.

Fuck sake George, get a grip, she's never going to be interested in you.

He spent the next few moments trying to readjust himself, hoping to the gods that Jean didn't turn around and see him fiddling around with his nether regions. But still, just before she disappeared from view, he stole another longing look, then shaking his head and another a final readjustment, he hurried back to the kitchen.

While he cleared and tidied away all of their food, George became aware of the sound of horses approaching the yard. Feeling relaxed and in a good mood with the day so far, he was off his guard when he went outside to investigate.

'Hello, how can I......?'

He trailed off, unable to finish his sentence. His mouth dried up when he saw who their visitors were.

Johnson looked down at him from her horse, leaning forward with her forearms relaxed on the pommel of her saddle.

'Well hello to you too.'

Her words were charming and oily, but her eyes were hard.

Seemingly bored already with the conversation she continued in a cooler tone.

'Where's the old man? I want to speak to him, now.'

Her gaze didn't leave the young man's face and George felt himself wince, he backed off towards the house, but the two male riders soon cut off that means of escape. He tried to speak, but only succeeded in opening and shutting his mouth like a landed fish. George felt himself colour at his lack of control.

Johnson gave an exasperated groan.

'This is ridiculous. The boy is an imbecile.'

George blanched at the insult, but still couldn't find the words to reply. The Captain moved her horse so that George was in line with her saddle and she leant down and grabbed him by the front of his shirt, forcing him to stand on his tip toes.

Raising her voice, she repeated her demand.

'Where is he?'

Gathering all the bravery and strength he could muster, George stared back, his chin raised in defiance. He knew he would gain a beating for it, but he refused to betray the family he now called his own. Johnson cuffed him hard around the head with other hand, whilst still holding onto his the front shirt, George felt his ears ring.

'Where?'

Despite all his efforts he couldn't stop his eyes straying towards the trail, hoping that no-one would appear on the path after enjoying their day out.

Johnson saw it.

Letting him go, he fell backwards but just managed to stop himself from landing on his backside. Sitting up on her horse Johnson looked in the direction of George's gaze, seeing the path leading up behind the farm and through the trees. Narrowing her eyes, she grinned in triumph.

'I think it's about time you had a good walk, don't you?'

Pushing George in front of her horse, forcing him to lead the way, he felt the tears forming in his eyes, he felt disgusted with himself for his treachery.

Jean was crossing the paddock where the farm horse was grazing lazily; he munched on, unconcerned with what was happening in the yard, enjoying the sun on his back. The house had come into view on her return from dealing with the bull, just as she saw George leading three riders up the path behind the farm; two men and a woman. Her stomach clenched as she thought of the danger Niall and his family were suddenly in.

It wasn't a difficult leap to assume these riders were the same ones who had visited the farm a few weeks ago, despite not having seen them herself at the time. However, if she was going to deal with them, she would prefer it be away from the farm, rather than allow an unfortunate visitor to stumble across any unexplainable incidences. So, until she knew exactly what

Johnson intended to do, Jean decided to follow the small group at a distance.

Keeping the dog at heel as she approached the farmyard, she walked him up to the house and shut him in. He wasn't impressed with the situation, but she didn't want a dog jumping around while she tried to stay out of sight; he gave an indignant bark and a filthy look before slouching off to his bed beside the stove in the kitchen.

Opening her mind to the surrounding area, Jean managed to ascertain that these three were still alone and not relying on reinforcements. That was a blessing at least. Also, whilst mentally exploring the area she considered the strangers. It wasn't a comfort to George's plight, when she felt the distinct emotions of disgust, contempt and anger, but it was the existence of elation that concerned her most. It seemed Johnson believed she was finally on the right trail and her quarry was at last in sight.

As George and his captures approached nearer to the site of the gully and falls, Johnson began to push George harder and faster. Several times he stumbled, causing the Captain's impatience demand that Dornov dismount and sort the boy out. Her henchman was not happy about being made to walk, especially as his fellow rider, remained quite comfortable on his own horse. When George had fallen for a third time, Dornov lashed out and kicked at the prone figure, venting his own anger, before grabbing his hair and finally hauling him to his feet.

By now the lad was black and blue with bruises, covered in the dirt from the trail, and after his last fall, a cut over his eye which had begun to bleed down the side of his face.

Niall heard the horses before he saw George and his unwanted escort arrive. Immediately put on his guard, his old training kicked in and he told Dana to gather the girls. Already sleepy from the day's excitement and the copious amounts of food they had eaten, they whined at the sudden change in their parent's mood. Layne hurried to his mother, helping to lead his sisters into a copse of woods nearby, determined to keep them safe, no matter what.

When Johnson did come into view, with George looking considerably worse for wear, Niall's heart sank.

Where the hell was Jean?

Johnson pulled up her horse and dismounted, with Hanz following suit, he took all the horses to a tree, where he tied them while they grazed.

Johnson approached the forlorn figure of George and she grabbed him by the scruff of the neck, bodily dragging him along with her. His eyes watered with the pain and Niall saw the terror reflected in them. The twins were crying somewhere behind him in the trees; they loved George and to see him so hurt would distress them deeply.

'Keep the brats quiet.' Johnson barked.

From behind Layne, Dana desperately tried to comfort her children, seeing them so upset he put himself firmly between his mother and sisters, not wanting them to see the people who had caused so much pain to him and Niall not so long ago. His own heart went out to George, but he felt impotent to his plight. Like his father, he was beginning to wonder where Jean was.

Once the girls were quietened to a whimper, the Captain chose to ignore them.

'Where is she old man?'

Niall made a vain attempt in bluffing it out, but even he knew it was pointless.

'Who?'

'You know the fuck who. I told you what would happen if I found you had lied to me.'

Her voice was low, clear and angry. Niall looked on in horror as she put a knife to George's throat, pressing hard until blood began to trickle where the sharp blade pricked his skin.

'Please no.' Niall was imploring now. 'I really don't know where she is. If she wasn't at the farm, then she must have gone.'

'Don't play games with me, if you don't tell me now, you'll be minus one scrawny farm hand.'

To emphasise the point, she pressed the blade harder and George's blood began to flow more freely.

'I swear I don't know why you didn't see her there. Perhaps she saw you approaching and ran off.'

Niall tried not to believe the woman he had become to consider a close friend, someone he trusted, was a coward. But why wasn't she there for George? Had she really fled at the first sign of trouble? What did he really know about the strange woman he had met on the road only a few weeks ago?

A hard lump began to form in the pit of his stomach, the thought of the betrayal and the awful consequences to his family gnawing at his heart. Fear and anger began to swell within him, the look of George's terrified face, along with the continued whimpering of his daughters, stoking his rage. He clenched his fists in frustration when he heard a familiar voice.

'What do you want Johnson? It is Johnson isn't it?'

From somewhere along the trail a figure stepped into view.

There seemed a momentary suspension in time as everyone in the clearing was alerted to the newcomer. Niall found himself both relieved and ashamed. How could he have believed that Jean would desert them like that?

'You've been scouring the countryside looking for me, well here I am.'

Johnson and her men spun round, seeing a tall woman blocking the entrance to the path back to the farm. When she had moved, the captain's knife had dug deeper into George's throat and nicked the artery, his blood had now begun to flow in the rhythmic pulse of his rapidly beating, and panicked, heart. Jean pursed her lips, she needed to sort this out sooner rather than later, George wasn't going to last long at this rate.

'You wanted to see me and now I'm here, let the lad go, these people are no threat to you.'

Though tempted to keep her captive just for the fun of it, Johnson decided to let him go and forced him away from her. Blood was beginning to soak into her clothing anyway, it was always a nightmare to remove.

George fell, clutching at his throat and Niall, throwing all caution to the wind, rushed forward and dragged him away to safety. Jean watched with relief, as Niall placed his own hands over the wound, staring into his young friend's eyes, willing him to hang on.

'Stay with me lad, you'll be fine.'

He glanced up and his eyes briefly met Jean's.

Johnson ignored him and George, she had what she wanted, and Jean was happy for her to believe it would remain that way, for now.

'Well, well, you are quite the elusive quarry. I've been all over this shit hole looking for you.'

Jean saw the other woman assess the potential threat that stood before her. She would see a tall woman that was apparently unarmed, but if she was wise, she would look out for potentially hidden knives. Either way, Johnson was looking confident and that suited Jean down to the ground.

Dornov and Hanz had also noticed Jean's lack of weapons and they moved around, ready to cut off any chance of her running away.

Jean would have enjoyed teaching them the error of their ways at her own leisure, but she could see George lying prone with Niall desperately trying to stem the flow of blood. Assessing that she didn't have long, there certainly wasn't going to be any time for prisoners. Opening her mind, Jean sensed the effects of adrenalin that was by now flowing freely around the small glade. She allowed the emotions it created to heighten her own; heart beating fast, breathing shallow, senses heightened. Over the years she had honed this skill so that she was ready to act when needed, without the shock of a sudden adrenalin hit; however, the sudden change within her body was still something she had to brace herself for.

Focusing on George and the danger he faced, along with the need to protect Niall and his family, Jean set about teaching this bitch and her pet thugs a brief lesson in mistaken presumptions.

It was Hanz who fell first, feigning a swerve to her right she made a jab to her left, a fist slammed into the man's throat and

135

it went a fair way to crushing his larynx, forcing him to bend double. He hadn't expected so much strength behind such a blow and the man struggled to take in a breath, his face contorted with the pain surging through his windpipe. But he refused to go down.

Aware that the other man to her right wanted to get in on the action, Jean ducked his punches and put the struggling man between her and her new opponent. A swift kick to the balls and Hanz, already short of breath, buckled to his knees.

Dornov wasn't put off by his friend's plight and lunged at the woman, determined to get a fist in that smug face of hers. Unfortunately for him, Jean had other ideas and he fell sideways as Jean kicked out just above his knee and knocked him off balance. Before he could regain his feet, she made contact hard between his legs too. He lunged forward in agony, Jean following through with a stabbing punch to his solar plexus.

Falling forward, Dornov broke his nose on her knee as she brought it up, forcing his head down with a hard thrust of her hands behind his head. Finally, she finished the job with a strong hard twist to his neck, a sickening crack followed by his limp body falling to the ground.

Shocked, though silently impressed, Johnson made to deal with this bloody woman herself. However, to her annoyance, Hanz had considered himself sufficiently recovered to have another go and was trying to stand up. Unwilling to allow anyone to get in her way now, she had drawn her sword and with a savage thrust, she ran her own rider through.

Barely even acknowledging the look of shock on his face, she furiously kicked his lifeless body from her blade, his wide-open eyes reflecting his shock at her treachery.

Indifferent to the fate of her cohorts, the Captain now turned back to face Jean; one woman armed with a bloodied sword, rage surging through her body, the other remaining relaxed but ready, her thoughts and emotions focused on getting the job done as soon as possible.

George didn't look a good colour at all.

Jean felt the rise in anger from Johnson, but she ignored it as a pointless emotion that was of no use to her. It just meant the Captain was more likely to make even more mistakes.

'Who the fuck are you?' Johnson was snarling now.

'Trust me, you don't really need to know, and to be fair, you won't be around long enough to appreciate the knowledge anyway.'

'You have to try to kill me first.' Johnson jeered, standing ready, light footed and bred for combat. Unfortunately for her, it was on the Melbourne city streets, and they were a long way from Australia.

Niall groaned inwardly. While Jean's skills were surprisingly impressive, to face an experienced swordsman, with this woman's notoriety; and to be unarmed as well, was practically suicidal.

However, his groan soon turned to surprise, as for the second time that day, Jean proved his scepticism wrong.

From out of nowhere Jean Carter drew her own sword.

Surely not; how is it possible? But only they….

Johnson halted for just a moment, confused at where the other woman had drawn her sword from. Then she realised she didn't care, she wanted blood and that was all that mattered. Lunging forward she made a charge.

Blow by blow Johnson moved forward, buoyed on by her continuing advance, pushing her opponent ever backwards, forcing Jean to defend every thrust.

But Jean was relaxed, she was trained in sword craft to a level Johnson could only dream of. Every step back she took was balanced and surefooted. Each blow from Johnson was parried away.

Eventually though, Jean stopped moving backwards.

Johnson, who was still on her advance, found herself suddenly, very up close and personal to her opponent.

Swords crossed, they faced each other, eye to eye.

A smile caught at the corners of Jean's lips and Johnson faltered: something was wrong.

With a force that caught Johnson completely off guard, Jean thrust her opponent away. Barely able to gather herself, Johnson now found that *she* was the one being forced backwards; but unlike Jean, she struggled to cope with the uneven ground, barely fending off the blows now raining down on her fast and hard.

Johnson's arms and hands ached with the force of Jean's blows. Confused and exhausted she stumbled and fell back onto the grass, Jean knocking her precious Samurai blade out of her hands, out of reach.

Terror spread across Karen Johnson's face and Jean stepped forward, allowing the Captain time enough to realise the horror of her fate.

'You really shouldn't have pissed me off Johnson.'

Then raising her sword, Jean thrust it hard into Johnson's chest. Blood flowed from the wound and her body jerked as

Jean twisted the blade to free it from the Captain's body. Her eyes, like Hanz, wide open with shock.

Barely even acknowledging the prone body that now lay strewn over the grass, Jean was cleaning her own sword on a rag ripped from Hanz's clothing, whilst hurrying to Niall's side. The increasingly pale features of George stared up at her.

Niall briefly noted the markings that ran the length of blade that Jean now sheathed. He involuntarily gulped.

Dear gods, it's a miracle.

Either that or he was definitely losing his wits.

He was brought back to the present as his wife tried to stop the twins rushing forward, wanting to satisfy their curiosity now the fighting had ceased. Instead their mother and Layne were corralling them back into the trees and they were voicing their disgust loudly. Mother and son exchanged looks of concern and confusion, they were farming folk not soldiers, they just wanted their quiet life back.

'How is he?'

Jean's green eyes were now wide with concern as they searched Niall's for answers.

'He's lucky the blade only nicked the artery, or he'd most certainly be dead by now. He can't be moved though, in case the wound completely ruptures, the whole vessel would rip open.'

Niall was still trying to stem the flow of blood as he looked imploringly at Jean.

'You need to run back to the farm. In the kitchen there is a box on the top shelf of the dresser, in there is a crystal we can use to get George to Aria.'

'What are you talking about? What crystal? And what does it do?'

Niall sighed impatiently.

'All knights get them in case of emergencies. And this is a bloody big emergency. I need you to hurry Jean, George doesn't have long.'

George began to whimper at Niall's panicked voice, his blood was beginning to flow faster.

'Jean, please.'

Shaking her head, she laid her hand on his arm.

'You obviously know where this Aria is.'

She looked up and took in the scene of Dana and Layne, still struggling with the girls. Her voice became urgent.

'Think of Aria Niall, and trust me.'

Niall didn't understand, but even as he thought of Jean's instruction, the image of the Prime Imperial Hospital, within the lands of Aria, sprang into his mind. Suddenly the gorge, the falls and trees, all disappeared and they were all within a compound of many stone buildings.

The picnic area was now silent, even the birds that had sung throughout the day seemed to want to avoid the place. Only the horses that grazed by the tree where they were tethered moved, the stench of blood and death rose around them and their nerves made them twitchy. They sensed movement nearby, they couldn't see what it was at first, but they strained at their ties, stamping their feet in fear.

Karen Johnson, Captain of the Patrols, loyal to Ephea, the wife of the Emperor, was dying. Pain was shooting through her chest and her breathing was so shallow as to be barely there. But it was the lack of pain in her legs that frightened her the most, she couldn't feel anything below her waist. Panic began to take over, she could feel herself shaking as adrenalin from her fear pulsed through her body, her heart forcing her lifeblood out onto the grass surrounding her.

From somewhere within her terrified brain a voice told her to stay calm, to stop panicking, she just needed to find help.

How the fuck could she find help? She couldn't feel her fucking legs!

Then she remembered. The crystal, her emergency exit. This wasn't the emergency she envisaged but it was all she had. Thankful she could still move her arms she reached into her pocket and felt her trembling hands enfold the crystal that rested there. It was warm to the touch and she felt relief wash over her. Tears came unbidden and she found she didn't care, she needed to be safe and that meant getting home no matter what. For the first time in years, she pictured the face of her mother and gripped the crystal hard. Then, just as quickly, as Jean and the others had disappeared, so did Karen Johnson; the clearing still and silent, the horses once more grazing in peace.

The first thing Jean noted was how much hotter it was here, then there was the sound of Dana and her children hurrying to their sides — she seemed agitated.

'I didn't know you had the crystal on you. Why did you bring it? Did you know there was going to be trouble?'

Dana paused briefly, considering something and her brows furrowed.

'How did you bring Layne and I here, along with the twins too? Surely we weren't near enough for you?'

Her questions were rushed and slightly garbled, but all Niall could do was shake his head and look at Jean. Finally, he found his voice.

'It wasn't me; the crystal is still at home.'

At his words Dana and Layne also looked at Jean, waiting, it seemed, for an explanation.

Aware of the scrutiny, Jean looked away and gave her attention to George. He was now being attended to by a group of people who had run out of one of the buildings surrounding them. His body was being placed on a gurney and they were already setting about him to stem the flow of blood; even as they were attempting to wheel him back towards the hospital.

George caught at her hand, forcing them to stop, a tear spilled down his cut and bruised face, he looked at her imploringly. Squeezing his hand back, she leant forward and kissed his cheek.

'Get well soon my friend, I'll come and see you. I don't know when, but I promise I will.'

He managed a brief smile before the impatient hospital staff whisked him away. Dana scurried behind with the twins, refusing to look at Jean any longer, anger and worry etched into her face. Layne made to follow but then hesitated, he looked back to Jean and nodded, then following his mother, he also disappeared inside.

Alone now with Jean, Niall was unsure of what to say regarding everything he had just witnessed, or whether he really did see it at all. But it was Jean who broke the silence first.

'Niall I'm so sorry for the pain I have caused your family. I swear I'll set this right; but right now, I have to get rid of a lot of evidence back at the picnic site.'

142

She looked away, unable to face him as she spoke. 'Then I'm just going to leave. I still don't know why I'm on Kelan yet to be honest, or how I can help, but nothing is going to be done here while I stay with you and your family. So, I am going to continue the journey I started to Parva.'

Turning back, she reached out and held his hands in hers.

'You and Dana have allowed me into your home and offered me your trust when most would have gladly turned me away, I will never forget that.'

Niall looked sad, but Jean didn't miss the slight look of relief too, she didn't blame him at all.

'You are an amazing man Niall, and I am honoured to call you my friend. As such, I have probably far outstayed my welcome.'

Niall began to protest, but Jean wasn't having any of it.

'No Niall, we both know I have, but I've got to go. I promised George that I would return, and I will. But until then my friend, stay safe.'

Niall allowed the tears to run down his face, only now did he realise how much of a friend Jean had become, and how much he would miss her. Jean held out her hand out for him to shake, but instead he shook his head and grasped her hand with both of his, pulling her to him in a huge bear hug. Momentarily stunned, she returned it gratefully. When he pulled away, his voice was the same strong baritone as always and his cheeks were once more dry.

'Go back via the farm and take whatever you need for your journey.' He squeezed her hands. 'Try to stay out of trouble Jean Carter, though I have a feeling you flout safety as a way of life. My prayers go with you and I hold you to your promise to

143

return, else George will make my life a bloody misery otherwise.'

They both laughed, then regretfully, she let go of him and gave a final smile before raising a hand in farewell. Then she was gone, one moment she was there and the next, Niall was looking at an empty space where she had been. Sighing and offering a silent prayer to the Gods, he then turned, following his family and George into the hospital.

Arriving back at the gully, Jean wiped her own tears from her face and set about clearing the food and scattered remains of the happier part of the day. The first thing she saw was the empty space where Johnson had fallen. Blood covered the grass, but nothing else to suggest where the Captain had gone. There were no marks where she could have moved herself, or evidence that others had arrived, Jean felt uneasy and angry. She should have made sure Johnson was dead, but she was so concerned for George and getting him to safety she hadn't checked.

Staring at the blood stained grass, she had a horrible feeling she may regret that one day.

Having to accept that there was nothing she could do about the missing body of Johnson, she set about clearing up the rest of the area. Once evidence of the family was packed away, she went over to the horses still tied up. Removing their saddles and bridles, she put her hands to them and made the connection that would urge them to get as far away from this place as possible; preferably at a distance from humans. With any luck it would be a long time before anyone found them. Taking the tack, she then investigated the gully, flinging it into the deepest part of the ravine. Once satisfied it wouldn't be seen, she returned to the two remaining bodies.

144

Now for the easy bit.

Standing before them, Jean held out her hand, and within her mind muttered an incantation. Slowly, blue flames began to rise within the dead forms of Johnson's men. It wasn't long before they were engulfed in a fire that, though seemed unnaturally cool, soon reduced the bodies to dust. Eventually, after a short time the flames began to recede, when all that remained were piles of dark ash. With a flick of her hand the ash rose into the air, momentarily suspended, before dispersing into the winds.

After a final survey of the site, Jean picked up the picnic remains and retraced her steps back down the trail to the farm. By the time she had dropped off the picnic and gathered her own meagre belongings, the sky was beginning to turn pink with the setting sun. Aware that it was unlikely Niall would be back until late, Jean set about putting the food away, then made sure the beasts were secured in their paddocks.

She took enough food for a few days, and an oilskin cloak Niall had given her when she had been soaked in a deluge while out in the fields. Jean settled her pack over her shoulders and without a further glance back, set off down the track to the main road that would take her west to the City of Parva.

Part Two

Parva

11

Fog

It was still a long walk to Parva, but fortunately, it was that time of year when farmers were hiring itinerant labourers to help in the fields. Jean had fallen in with a gang of such workers, who had a schedule to work at a number of farms heading west. They were always ready to accept extra help, and over the next few weeks she found plenty to keep her fit and well fed. She was also pleased to receive a wage for her endeavours.

There was much gossip and speculation about the Patrols and their continuing presence. Even now they seemed to be getting bolder; not only gaining strength in the small towns and villages, they were also venturing out into the open countryside. It seemed their fear of the ever-present eye of the Order was diminishing, as on more than one occasion, a group of two or more mounted riders were seen on the horizon as Jean and her colleagues worked. But they didn't come any closer, they just sat and watched, before riding away into the distance.

Jean was more aware now of how much people were beginning to feel unnerved, they felt abandoned and insecure, angry the Emperor and the Knights as well as the Order, weren't doing anything to help. Eventually, on the odd occasion there was grumbling amongst her fellow workers, dissent had begun to set in, and more than one drunken fight had to be broken up. What concerned her more, was that with the rise in mistrust and anger, she had to accept that her own perception and emotional state was changing. No longer was she laid back and willing to go with the general flow of her surroundings, she was becoming more assertive.

It was a trend that she had learned to recognise over time, it was part of who she was. No matter how much Jean tried to suppress the effects, the emotions and steel core that lay within her would eventually rise to the surface. It was an inevitable response to the situations she so often found herself in, and it was the only way she survived. But she hated it.

Over the years she had turned to various ways of controlling her anger, her desire to crush the wrongs that existed within the universe. The quiet unassuming result was often a misconception by the people she met; that she was a poor defenceless woman travelling alone. It was a mistake many only made once.

Becoming more assertive and stronger, meant those travelling with her found they often looked to Jean should a problem need dealing with. But it was people who were themselves more aggressive, that fed into her trust now; those of a more peaceful nature either avoided her, or more often than not, had nothing to do with the escalating troubles she found herself in. And so, it was happening here, while the life she enjoyed on Niall's farm was quiet, she felt at peace and calm. But when amongst the farm workers and their boisterous outlook and tough life, she felt the flame of retribution rekindle. It was subtle, but to Jean she understood that while she slowly changed, life was definitely going to start to become more interesting.

By the end of a long eight weeks of hard work and good company, it was time for Jean to say goodbye to the farmhands and finish her journey. She knew from her procured map, that the city of Parva was set along the coast. She had heard that it had a large seaport, where goods were brought in and transferred to inland craft, that sailed up and down the river Par. It was on one of these craft that Jean had gained passage, and now she was settled on the deck as the captain, Geof, and his small crew of Lisse and Marco, kept their boat on course. It was mid-morning on a bright early summer's day that they followed the river west, passing through a large area of woodland that grew either side of the river banks.

When they finally broke through the tree line into the bright sunshine, they were once more among the familiar fields of crops and livestock. They slowly glided under one of two bridges that traversed the waters connected by a small island in the middle of the now wide slow moving river. In the distance there was a huge circular rise, a fortified wall with towers running around the entire ridge line. The river ran alongside the main highway, which was broad and carried plenty of traffic

149

in both directions; to and from the fortification. A ravine cut through the ridge to the north, with large gate towers crossing both freeways.

At last she had finally reached Parva.

Approaching the city Jean realised that the ridge line was in fact the remains of a long extinct volcano caldera. The sea level had long since risen and several millennia of erosion meant that now all that remained was a huge crater, with the ever-winding river running through the city centre, before disappearing out to sea.

Jean had, on more than one occasion offered to help out on the boat, but Geof was precious about his craft, it was his livelihood and home. He knew how to handle her, and she could be a bit temperamental apparently. Jean smiled at Geof's obvious affection for his boat, which she noticed was mirrored by his crew; who were also his children and heirs to their father's lucrative business.

So, taking a rare opportunity to travel without having to do anything, Jean appreciated the moments of peace, enjoying the time to sit and reflect on what possibly lay ahead.

Looking at the information she had gathered so far about this world called Kelan, Jean had concluded that it was an autonomous society with an Emperor at its head. Councils were elected by the populace, with a High Council over seeing all. But these factions answered ultimately to the Emperor. Jean still wasn't entirely sure how this worked precisely, but apparently, up until about five years ago, it had been, and to a large extent still was, a highly efficient, well respected form of government. Providing a secure society, with a solid social and economic regime.

So, what had gone wrong?

The only thing everyone could agree on, was that problems began when the Emperor married the Duchess Ephea. This in itself was evidently quite a surprise for the rest of the Empire, as rumour had it that he was a confirmed bachelor, and despite many attempts in the past, no-one had secured his affections enough to warrant the sound of wedding bells.

The subsequent marriages of Ephea's two sisters to the Lords Damien and Daniel, were even more of a surprise. Since then, many rumours had run rife as to what these women had over such powerful men; because it was generally agreed, none of these marriages had anything to do with romance. There was also talk that Ephea, the Emperor Nathan's wife, was particularly furious at her husband's refusal to give her the title of Empress. It seemed that under normal Imperial law, both partners took on the most senior rank of the two, they would then retain the responsibility of that rank, which would then also hold them accountable to the people within their authority.

However, the only rank this didn't include was that of the Emperor himself, he alone could allow his wife his rank, but only if he wished it so. If he didn't, then she would only hold his other rank and title of Duke of Pernia. Ephea was apparently so upset with her husband's refusal to give her what she wanted, that she wouldn't even allow others to refer to her as Duchess, as she considered this as confirmation of a lower rank than she was entitled to. It was an interesting situation, and one that Jean felt was a key factor to the whole mystery of the Patrols and the disharmony occurring around the Empire.

While she pondered, Jean felt a slight breeze from the river caress her face. She could smell the scents of riverside flowers and felt the hot sun on her skin. She had long since become used to the difference in the air from the Ti'akai and had learnt much more about its role on her travels. This force within the universe that Niall had told her about on their first encounter, was more than just a feeling in the air. Apparently, it could be harnessed by a metal called brattine, that was only found within the six sectors. Its ore was mined on the world of Lode, a planet that was one of the seven worlds that made up the Empire. Lode was so abundant with this metal, that it was kept strictly under the control of the Emperor and the other six Knights. When Jean had expressed her concern that this was unfair and surely should be questioned, she was met with dark looks and hostility. No matter how much she pressed, no-one was willing to discuss the matter with her further; clearly, she had burnt her bridges with that subject.

However, it did fascinate her how the Ti'akai and brattine worked together. It would appear that anything made from this metal, required only a very small catalyst before it was able to enhance the energy to provide power. Either through heat, or even the turning of a water wheel, the metal was able to power whatever it had been cast into. The main equipment Jean had seen that utilised this was the humble, household cooker; with a small fire set inside to get it going, the appliance retained the heat for a long time, even once the flames were out. Again, Jean considered the fact that this substance should not be held by a small group of men to the exclusivity of others, but no-one was willing to discuss it, so she had to remain in ignorance for now.

On reflection, Jean realised that despite the obvious unease that was happening around her, and regardless of the fact that she had a mission to fulfil — whatever that was — she hadn't felt more at home anywhere than she did here on the world of Kelan. She felt a pang of fear at the thought that one day, possibly very soon, she would have to leave this place and return alone to NiCI. The thought made her heart sink and she felt slightly sick.

Trying to bring her mind back to the present work in hand, Jean returned her gaze to the approaching city. It was only now that she realised just how large it was. The crater itself was a solid granite wall that was virtually impenetrable, except through a natural fault line with a ravine allowing the river and road to pass though. The fortified walls, built on top of the ridge line, had towers spaced throughout their length. In order to create a continuous access to both sides of the ravine, a bridge had been built traversing the expanse over the river and road. Over each tower flew a large black flag with a large silver tree; the symbol of the Empire.

Soon they passed through the gates and under the bridge high above. At last they were arriving at the city of Parva, Capital of the Kelan world and centre of the Empire. Passing the towers that housed the gates, Jean got her first glimpse of the famed knights of the Order that she had heard so much about. Bearing the same title as the Knights who ran the Empire, a proud legacy they inherited on leaving their training at Pernia. They stood guarding the highways, seeming relaxed but alert, watching as the traffic of the road and river passed to and from the city. Their black uniforms stood out from the colourful clothes of the populace, the silver trees on their collars denoting the Empire they had sworn to protect. Other insignia were also worn on their uniform sleeves and lapels, Jean assumed these indicated rank and possibly regiments, but she had no idea. It was something she would have to investigate further.

These were the men and women who stood for the Emperor and all he symbolised. Yet, for some reason, they had been obstructed in dealing with the Patrols and their obvious infringements of the law, leaving the populace to their uncomfortable fate. Jean could only imagine how frustrated the Order must feel, understanding how dangerous such suppressed bitterness and resentment could be if left unchecked.

They followed the river towards the far side of the city and the seafaring ships that were berthed there, passing under bridges that connected the North and South Banks, as they were known. Large houses and gardens crowded on either side, private jetties with boats of varying types and sizes tied alongside — for the exclusive use of their owners of course. Some were working craft; some were for more leisurely use. At times Jean could see lock gates along the South Bank leading into private quays that allowed larger ships to remain moored, even when during low tide.

Geof pointed to the North Bank and told Jean that they were the lodgings of the University staff and students. His tone suggested that they were overindulged, and he didn't hold much truck with the likes of the highly educated. He indicated the South Bank and here he seemed even less enthusiastic; these were the houses of merchants, owners of the quays and wharfs further downstream. Jean noted how much smaller the area to the north was, with the majority of the city lying to the south of the river.

Passing under two further bridges, Geof and his crew tied up alongside a large quay already bustling with the day's activity.

154

He refused to accept any payment for her passage, he stated it was just good to have the company. Jean couldn't recall the captain being particularly talkative during their trip, but thanked him anyway and at last she stepped ashore onto dry land.

Her stomach told her it must be about lunch time, so following advice from Geof, in one of his rare, more articulated moments, she made her way from the South Bank into the city itself in search of lodgings.

Geof had suggested a small townhouse owned by a relative of his sister's husband. He did give Jean a brief idea of what his actual connection to the landlady of this particular establishment was, but she had to admit, it might as well have been through a relative of her cat's adopted aunt for all the sense he made.

When she finally found the establishment, Jean just mentioned that Geof had recommended it and left it at that. Fortunately, the landlady, who went by the name of Mrs Moore, was more than happy to make up for Geof's lack of communication, and Jean was pleased to find the room available was clean and warm. A month's rent up front secured the deal, which was pleasantly celebrated with a large pot of strong tea with a plate of sandwiches, followed by homemade cake and a generous dose of city gossip.

'You've come at a tough time to visit our beautiful city I must say Jean. I don't know what has become of our Emperor, but it's not a happy time.'

Mrs Moore dabbed at her eyes with a lace handkerchief, but Jean was hard put to see any tears.

'Are there any of the Patrols within the city? I've heard that they try to stay away from the Order.'

'Well, there you have the crux of it dear. Up until a few weeks ago you wouldn't have seen any of those *foreigners*, but now, they are quite brazen as they walk around. Can barely speak their own language let alone try and learn Kelan.'

Jean was bristling under the *foreigner* attack, as she herself was effectively a foreigner here; an alien even. However, she didn't need to set her landlady against her now, but she would be careful what she said in front of Mrs Moore. Jean got the impression she wasn't too worried about which ears she whispered her gossip into. She was about to settle into listening to the general local gossip of Mrs Moore's neighbours, when the older woman leant her head forward and lowered her voice to a more hushed, conspiratorial tone.

'Then of course there's the *murders*.'

She mouthed rather than spoke the last word, as if uttering the word 'murder' would cause the harbinger of death to come calling at her door. Jean couldn't be done with such superstition and had no intention of holding a whole conversation in furtive whispers.

'Murders? What murders?'

Mrs Moore seemed to consider Jean for a moment, assessing whether she should confide such important details to someone so bold and brazen. But apparently, the opportunity to be the first to tell all the juicy details to a captive stranger was too good to miss. Leaning a forearm on the kitchen table and turning her head to give one last sweep of the kitchen; you can never be too sure who is hiding behind the tea towels, she began.

'Oh, it's been awful, absolutely awful. It must have been about two weeks ago…'

Mrs Moore held her hanky to her lips as she considered the details.

'No, it must be nearly three weeks now. A young baker's boy was found dead. Cold as the grave.' More dry tears and much dramatic waving of her hanky hand indicated this was apparently how Mrs Moore liked to punctuate her speech. Jean breathed silently inwards and tried to concentrate on the woman's words and encouraged her to continue, Mrs Moore seemed delighted to oblige.

'Throat cut from ear to ear. Blood everywhere.'

Jean caught the teacup that nearly went flying, as arms were thrown in order to exaggerate, just how much blood there really was. She obviously didn't want Jean to think this was just a needless death of meagre proportions.

'Do they know why he was murdered?'

'Oh no, that's the thing, no-one knows why any of them were done in. They reckon the boy was on his way home late the previous evening, but he didn't make it. His mother alerted the police when he failed to come home and they found him some hours later, down a dark, lonely alleyway. His poor mother was beside herself; you could hear her wailing streets away. Quite a racket she made.'

Jean tried not to sputter her tea at the callous indictment of the tragically grieving mother. Mrs Moore, completely unaware of Jean's shock, carried on her tale.

'It was two nights later that a woman was attacked, they reckon she put up a bit of a fight because she not only had her throat cut but was stabbed too. Quite a mess from what I heard.'

'I'm sure it was. Do they know why *she* was killed?'

'No dear, as I said, none of them seemed to be dead for any reason other than a madman on the loose.'

Jean wasn't so sure, but she encouraged Mrs Moore to carry on.

'Well, then it started to get really bad, four nights in a row, a body a night. No reason for it, it didn't matter if you were man, woman or child. Dead. Throats cut, and stabbed. The streets of Parva awash with the blood of the innocent and the police are getting nowhere.'

'I am sure they are doing everything they can, but if there is no apparent motive and the victims appear random, I can imagine their task is huge.'

Mrs Moore looked indignant.

'Well, there has been another three murders, two on the same night. That's ten people dead. How many more have to die before we can rest safe in our beds?'

Mrs Moore leaned further across the kitchen table.

'It's those bloody *foreigners* I tell you. Those Patrols are behind this. Mean characters the lot of them. But will the police do anything? Of course not. Too scared if you ask me. And all the time more people are dying.'

Mrs Moore threw herself against the back of her chair and crossed her arms as if to emphasise her point. Daring Jean to argue with her.

On the contrary however, Jean wasn't prepared to either agree or disagree with her new landlady's arguments; but she would rather base any conclusions she made on facts and not prejudice and local gossip.

It was a further twenty minutes before Mrs Moore considered that Jean had caught up on all the other gossip from around the city. Rising from her seat, she declared that Jean shouldn't keep her talking for so long, as she had far too much work to do. Then, piling up the dishes and uneaten food, she bustled away and left Jean under no doubt that she was expected to get out of her way.

Leaving her landlady to deal with her *work*, Jean set to exploring the city and assessing for herself the extent to which the Patrols had made their presence known, along with anymore information about the spate of gruesome murders that had besieged the city.

The sun was high in the sky and the streets were busy with people going about their business, if the city was living in fear of unprovoked attacks it wasn't apparent in the brightness of the day. Jean passed shops and market stalls, selling everything from all regions of the Empire, full of fruit and vegetables both familiar and exotic, alongside stalls with spices and herbs that made her mouth water. Precious stones and metals were sold by jewellers and goldsmiths within their own quarter of the city, tailors and drapers selling cloth of every fabric and colour imaginable, occupied another. Jean studied her own now battered clothing and considered a change in wardrobe may be an idea. Besides, if and when she needed the protection of the subtly armoured gear she wore, it would need repairing in quite a few places. She had acquired a few extra bits of clothing over the weeks from her fellow farmhands, old trousers and shirts to wear while working the fields. Ideal for labouring in the fields, but not walking around the streets of the city.

By the time she returned to her lodgings, Mrs Moore was out in the garden chattering to one of her neighbours; a stout woman standing over the fence, highly engrossed in the information her neighbour was imparting. Jean hurried to her room before being spied and then, no doubt, would have to undergo the scrutiny of Mrs Moore's neighbour.

In her small but scrupulously clean room, Jean took her shopping from their packaging. Trying on her new clothes; trousers, two shirts and a lightweight long jacket with plenty of pockets — her current thick coat was too warm for the summer heat — she was impressed by the quality, they were well made and comfortable. She kept her own boots on, but knew they were going to have to be replaced soon, otherwise she was happy with her purchases.

She had even found a shop that dealt entirely in underwear, Jean nearly cried when she left with her new acquisitions. While she had always been meticulous in her own personal hygiene making sure she kept clean underwear on every day when she could, even she had to admit that her knickers had more resemblance to old string now.

Now, newly kitted out, Jean was ready to find somewhere for a decent evening meal. Closing the front door behind her and entering the street, Jean noted a change in the air. A mist had started to roll in from the sea, and as evening approached the brightness of the day's sun was slowly consumed by the swirling grey of fog. Somewhere towards the west, a loud foghorn blasted out to sea; an ominous warning of imminent danger. An irony that wasn't lost on Jean as she ventured into the evening.

Despite the fear that had apparently spread regarding the recent murders, the streets were full of people; either finishing their day's business and hurrying home before the fog got any thicker, or heading out to meet up with friends. No doubt there were also those who had assignations that they would rather not be noticed by the rest of the world.

As the fog thickened the crowds became less distinct, with people looming out of the shadows as they rushed past, their footsteps muffled by the thick, damp air. Jean could feel the caution, even fear, coming from those around her, it mingled with a deeper underlying feeling of discontent and anger. Fear and despair seemed to ooze out of the walls and up from the ground, the pervading fog doing nothing to dispel these feelings. Jean considered that Parva may be renowned as a beautiful and prosperous city, but there was an ugly side that was pushing its way through to the surface.

Feeling herself caught up with the encroaching darkness, Jean made a point of getting off the streets and into the light, looking for somewhere to eat as soon as possible.

Her salvation came from the buzz of laughter somewhere near to her right. Making her way in the direction of the sound, aware that the fog can play tricks on a person's senses, she found a small bistro type of affair. On entering she was welcomed by the sight and sounds of people enjoying an evening out. The smells coming from the kitchen were promising, and when a short, round man wearing a long, white apron approached, she gladly followed him to a small table to the side of the busy room. The fog outside may be having a negative effect on the streets of the city, but the people themselves were still determined to keep their spirits up. Jean spent a quiet couple of hours of the evening enjoying a small dinner, and relishing the hot strong tea that the people of Parva enjoyed so much.

Eventually, deciding that it was time she ventured back out into the foggy night, she attempting to find her way back to her lodgings. As she stepped outside, the evening had already turned to night, and the fog also seemed to have thickened. The orbs of the streetlights had been uncovered, giving off their eerie glow at intervals down the lanes and main roads. Little orbs of light seeming to float within the fog like willow the wisps; giving hope in all the gloom, but still the feeling of danger hung in the air. Hoping her sense of direction wasn't going to let her down, Jean turned into a lane that would lead to, what she hoped was, her lodgings. To her left, the foghorn still continued its steady, booming blasts, obliterating all other sound. With her sight and hearing badly impaired by the fog and horn, she relied heavily on her empathic ability; sensing for any approaching danger.

The streets were virtually empty now, as people preferred to keep to the light and safety of indoors. Occasionally, large groups of people loomed out of the fog, gathering in numbers for safety.

Walking swiftly, Jean suddenly found herself against a stone wall, she had nearly walked headlong into it, but for a cat screeching and running in front of her, stopping her in her tracks. As she looked up and reached out her hand, she felt the cold stone of the wall and confusion set in. She had obviously missed a turning somewhere, and now she was in a small lane with no idea where she was. Swearing to herself, she turned to retrace her steps, hoping to get back to the main street, and from there, be able to find her bearings. She froze as she heard a scuffling noise to her right, a muffled cry came from an area that seemed to be a dark alleyway. Opening her mind, Jean tried to sense anything that may be lurking in the darkness, instantly feeling terror and pain, along with malice and contempt. There were two people there, and one was being attacked by the other.

Suddenly there was an ear-piercing scream, followed by the sound of a hand slapping flesh.

'Bitch.' An angry man's voice.

By the time Jean had found the entrance to the alley in the near pitch darkness, a figure was charging out at her. He was about the same height as Jean, and he held a small light orb in his hand that he had just retrieved from within his jacket. The glow lit up his face from below, he features were contorted into a mask of fury, his eyes wide. Jean was pleased to see that whoever else was down that alley, they had made sure they had left their own mark on their attacker. Sucking at his left hand where blood was flowing, the man barely acknowledged Jean as he rushed past and she considered going after him; but the feeling of terror and pain was still emitting from within the alley somewhere. She had to see if whoever was there was alright.

Reluctantly letting the fleeing man go, she entered the passageway. Feeling her way along the alley wall, she called out to whoever was there.

'Hello. Can you hear me? Are you alright?'

There were little whimpering sounds coming from a short distance ahead, and by the time Jean had got to the body of the young girl slumped against the wall, the whimpering had turned to painful sobs.

'It's alright, I'm here, are you hurt?'

The girl grabbed at Jean, squeezing her arm hard, crying out in pain as she tried to sit up. Behind them, back at the alley entrance a woman's voice called out.

'Police. Who's there? Where are you?'

Jean looked towards two bobbing lights heading in her direction.

'Here. There's a woman who's been attacked, I think she needs a hospital.'

Two figures came into view, and all she could think of was the pictures of Bobbies that worked the beat of a fog shrouded, Victorian London, the only thing missing was the big round helmets. It was so surreal Jean had to stop herself from laughing at the irony.

The two figures hurried to the girl lying on the ground, then looked to Jean enquiringly.

'Who are you? Do you know this girl?'

Jean was brought back to the seriousness of the situation by the woman who was now attending to the young girl. In the light provided by the orbs, she could see the blood that was flowing from below the girl's skirts.

'Lyal, get help, this girl needs a hospital.'

The other *Bobby* turned and headed back up the alley at speed. The woman was trying to stem the girl's blood.

'You still haven't answered my questions, who are you and what's happened here?'

'My name is Jean Carter, and I have no idea who this poor girl is, I was heading back to my lodgings and got completely lost in the fog. I heard a scuffle and a scream, then a man ran out of this alley. I came to investigate and the next thing, you are here.'

'How do you know it was a man who ran out of here?'

'He held an orb in his hand, I saw his face as clearly as I see you now. He also had blood on his hand, I think this poor girl managed to bite and draw blood before he ran off.'

The woman nodded her head in understanding, more people joined them, and soon the girl was being seen to by a group of people that she assumed were medics. Swiftly taking away their patient, the medics made their way back up the passageway, closely followed by the female '*Bobby*'.

'Wait, where are you taking her?'

The woman looked frustrated as she turned back to Jean.

'To the hospital, where do you think?'

The woman then nodded to her comrade.

'Give your details to Lyal here, and someone will take a statement from you tomorrow.'

Jean stepped forward; she wasn't being fobbed off just like that.

'What? No. I'm coming with you. I saw the man that did this, he might still be nearby, watching what happens.'

The woman stopped and gave her a look that seemed almost pitying. Jean felt her hackles rising.

'Have you seen the weather? This man you saw could be standing less than ten feet away and we wouldn't see him. Go home and we'll speak to you tomorrow, it isn't safe to be about in the city alone at night.'

She came very close to telling this haughty, arrogant policewoman that she didn't need to see this bastard, she would know him anywhere. The rage and arrogance that emanated from him had left a distinct mark on her memory; she could

165

point him out in a crowd easily. However, for now, she bit her tongue and tried a new tack.

'That would be very difficult because I don't actually have a clue where my lodging is. As I told you before, I am completely lost, unless of course you fancy trawling the streets, trying to find out where I should be?'

The policewoman closed her eyes, obviously trying to stay calm, whilst at the same time aware that the young girl was probably already in the hospital being seen to. She held up her hand in exasperation.

'Fine, you can come to the hospital, but stay out of the way. Lyal will keep an eye on you.'

Glancing at the young man hovering beside her, he barely seemed to be at an age to be shaving.

What is it they say about getting old and policemen getting younger?

She held up her hands. 'I'll follow you, shall I?'

The PC made a noise, that Jean was sure was a growl, in the back of her throat, before striding off after the medics. Jean and Lyal hurried on after her. By the time they arrived at the hospital the young girl was being examined by a doctor. Jean and both *Bobbies* found themselves in the waiting room until further news of her condition was available. Jean felt it was probably best if she tried to build a few bridges, especially in light of all the troubles that had besieged the city so far, it was better if she kept the police on side, rather than provoking them.

'Look, we haven't started off on a good footing, have we? As I said before, my name is Jean Carter.' She indicated the young lad. 'I'm assuming this is Lyal, so you are…?'

The PC took a while before answering, Jean began to wonder if she was actually going to have to keep considering

166

her as the *female Bobby*. Eventually, however, the woman seemed to relent and stood up.

'Police Constable Croft.'

She held out her hand and Jean shook it, obviously PC Croft still wanted to keep everything on an official level. Before Jean could say anymore, the door opened, and two elderly people were ushered in by a nurse. When they saw PC Croft and the familiar sight of her uniform, they rushed forward, demanding to know what had happened.

'What is going on? What has happened to Morna?'

The couple held on to one another and their faces showed the fear for their daughter. PC Croft tried to corral them over to some chairs set against the wall. At first, they were reluctant to move, but Jean placed her arm around Morna's father and leading him forward, his wife followed with PC Croft. Lyal stood looking uncomfortable and PC Croft sent him off in search of some tea.

A doctor came in soon after the couple were given a hot beverage, their faces were drawn and grey with worry and Jean had to close down part of her senses as their pain washed over her. Putting the drinks down they stood and rushed to hear his news, the tea was forgotten; She wondered if it would be really rude if she acquired one instead.

The doctor was obviously used to dealing with distraught family members, and he managed to sit the couple down as he explained what had happened to their daughter.

'First of all, Morna is going to be fine, there is no permanent damage and we have managed to stop the bleeding. She's resting at the moment, but I will take you through to see her soon.'

The couple nodded their thanks and to Jean's regret, they picked up their tea. PC Croft took the doctor aside and Jean moved to make sure she was just within earshot.

'So, what happened doctor? Was she sexually attacked?'

The doctor flinched and seemed reluctant to pass on such personal information to the police.

'This is important doctor, if there is a predator out there, we need to know. If this is our murderer and he's started to sexually attack before killing, with this fog there are plenty of opportunities for him to strike again.'

The doctor looked over to the couple huddled together, then turned back to PC Croft. He gave a barely perceptible nod, then made for the door before he was asked anymore awkward questions.

Shocked, she exchanged a look with the PC before lowering her own voice to a whisper.

'What is the matter with him? Surely, he understands the brutality of rape? And to assume that she will be perfectly fine after dealing with that?'

'I know, but it is still one of those things that many don't want to talk about in certain circles.'

Jean looked at her blankly.

'It wouldn't do, it's not the done thing to have a rape victim in the family.'

She inclined her head to the couple. Jean could feel the rage at the injustice and arrogance of his attitude growing inside her, it took a lot of effort to push the emotions back down. It was then the door to the waiting room burst open and three people entered. They were an older couple, who unlike Morna's parents, stood upright and slightly apart; the man had a haughty expression that suggested he expected to have his way without question. The woman also wore an arrogant expression, but hers was more like a mask, hiding the reality underneath. Jean however, barely glanced at them, as they were followed by a young man who had changed his clothes since Jean had last seen him. She noted his hand was also neatly bandaged, but she would know him anywhere. Motioning to the two police officers, she suggested they go outside into the corridor to give the family some space. Croft was about to protest that she should stay in the room, but the look on Jean's face made her follow anyway. As the door was shut behind them, Jean walked a little further down the hall before turning and pointing back to the room.

'It's him. He's the man who attacked Morna.'

'What? Are you sure?'

'Oh, I am absolutely positive, that young man in there is a rapist.'

12

Denial

Police Constable Croft looked horrified and stared at Jean in disbelief, stunned that she should even consider such a ridiculous accusation.

'What do you mean that's him? How can it be him?'

'I'm telling you, that's him. He even has a bandage on his hand where Morna must have bitten him.'

Croft was shaking her head.

'Do you have any idea who his father is? He is a General in the Order, he is a man of respectability, and he commands a lot of power in Parva.'

'I don't give a rat's arse who his bloody father is, I saw that man's face as clear as day, and I have excellent facial recognition recall. No matter what your fancy General thinks of himself, the fact remains, he has a rapist for a son.'

Croft stared at Jean, momentarily speechless, then looked over to Lyal, who appeared as horrified as she did. Finally shaking her head, she moved over to a row of seats against a wall and sat down heavily.

'You can't be right in this Jean; do you have any idea what this would mean?'

Jean joined her and sat down too, trying to control her temper and frustration.

'All I know is, there is a girl who has gone through a horrendous nightmare at the hands of that man, she deserves justice. Someone needs to make sure he can't hurt anyone else.'

Croft sat silently for a short while, just staring at the floor. Jean was beginning to wonder if she was alright, when suddenly, the PC looked up and gave instructions to Lyal.

'Have all of Morna's clothes been bagged for analysis?'

Lyal nodded. 'Yes, and a member of the forensics team was with the doctor as they took samples from under her nails and, erm, other places.'

'Good, I want you to make sure that they are all safely secured, I don't want anything happening to them. In fact, find out where they are and don't let them out of your sight until you have the results.'

The young policeman made to leave when Croft called him back.

'And Lyal, make sure you bring the results directly to me as soon as you get them.'

He then hurried off, thankful for something to do. Jean stared at Croft slightly taken aback.

'You have a forensic team?'

'Of course, we have a forensic team. We have to make sure that we glean as much evidence as we can if we are going to build a case against this bastard, we have to make sure it's watertight.'

'You believe me then?'

Croft turned in her seat to face Jean and for the first time seemed to soften.

'Yes, I believe you.'

'Why? Why now?'

'You obviously have no idea who our important General is?'

Croft couldn't keep the sneer out of her voice, there was clearly no love lost there.

'He is General Victor Bales. Five years ago, he was just another officer in the Order. He wasn't anything particular, in fact it was doubtful he was ever going to be a candidate for any promotion let alone fast tracked to the lofty position of a General. Yet, here he is, a General, with much power and influence. There are rumours that Ephea has been particularly interested in his career.'

Jean nodded understanding.

'But how do you know so much about him?'

Croft sighed. 'My mother is a Major in the Order. She was picked out for excelling within the ranks and expected to rise quickly. But since the Emperor married Ephea, my mother, and others like her, have been carefully shunted out of the way, leaving the road clear for the likes of Bales.'

Croft sounded bitter and Jean could well appreciate how her family would feel towards this General.

'It sounds as if the whole family are rotten, if you think he's been gaining undue influence from high places. I can imagine, however, that the last thing that family would want, is to have their son convicted of such a heinous crime as rape.'

Croft nodded and for the first time smiled. 'Ella.'

'I beg your pardon.'

'My name is Ella, Ella Croft.'

Jean smiled back. 'Pleased to meet you Ella.' She felt more confident about the possibility of justice at last. 'I think we have a bastard to hang out to dry.'

'Huh, I don't know if that will actually happen.'

She felt the confidence ebb away. 'Why? If you can get all the evidence, then surely it should stand up in court.'

'Jean, I doubt if this will even get past a brief, but intense, conversation in the police station. To have the stigma of a rapist in the family would be unacceptable. They will do whatever they can to keep the family name clean.'

'But he needs to be brought to justice. I don't care about whether his family like it or not.'

'It's not how it works I'm afraid. Even Morna's family will want to keep this quiet, they won't want to have their daughter tainted with the label of rape victim.'

'So, you are not going to do anything?' Jean was shocked.

'Of course we're going to do something, we're going to do everything we need to get this to court and gain a conviction. I just think you need to know, that there is every likelihood it will be stopped before we have chance to get anywhere. That's why I've sent Lyal to secure the forensic evidence; I don't want anything unfortunate to happen to it.'

Suddenly there was an almighty crash from the family waiting room.

'What the hell…?'

Jean and Ella were on their feet and running back up the corridor. Raised voices were heard as they burst into the room where they saw Morna's father pinning General Victor Bales against the wall; with both of their wives desperately trying to pull him off. The younger man stood back against the farthest wall in silence, watching with interest.

Taking Morna's father by the shoulders and, with a strength that took the man by surprise, Jean heaved him out of the way. Both men were now yelling at each other across the room, while Jean and Ella tried to gain some peace.

'SHE SHOULDN'T HAVE BEEN LEFT ALONE, WHAT WAS THAT USELESS LUMP DOING WHILE SHE WAS BEING ATTACKED? OFF IN SOME BAR OR GAMBLING DEN NO DOUBT.'

'HOW DARE YOU? MY SON WOULD NEVER LEAVE MORNA UNPROTECTED, THE SILLY GIRL PROBABLY WANDERED OFF. SHE'S NOT THE BRIGHTEST OF THINGS IS SHE?'

Morna's father lunged forward, further enraged by the slur on his daughter. Jean pushed him back against the wall, and Ella finally managed to make herself heard.

'That is enough both of you. Now calm down.'

'It's his fault my daughter is here, ask him where he was.'

Morna's father had thrust his finger towards the silent man in the corner. When he realised everyone was now looking at him, the smirk on his face disappeared, adopting a more solemn

174

expression. Jean felt sick to the stomach and had to push down the urge to grab him by the front of his shirt and punch his face.

You bastard, I know your secret, just give me a reason to wipe that smile right off that arrogant little face of yours.

His mother, seeing the attention her son was now gaining, ran forward and placed herself protectively in front of him.

'How dare you? My son has done nothing wrong and doesn't need to answer to you or anyone.'

Ella wasn't having any of it.

'Actually, I would be very interested to hear what your son was doing while Morna was being attacked. I would also like to know what she was doing out on a night like this on her own, especially when there is a killer on the loose.'

It was his mother who spoke for him, her chin raised in defiance.

'Aleix is Morna's fiancé. She was having dinner with us when she started moaning that she didn't feel well, she wanted to go home.'

Rolling her eyes as if this was typical behaviour, she continued.

'We tried to dissuade her obviously as the weather is awful, and that she should just stay with us and retire early. I even offered to bring her something to help her sleep, but she would have none of it. So, Aleix, being the gentleman he is, said he would walk her home.'

His mother stood there, arms crossed over her chest as if this was a perfectly good explanation and no further comment was needed from her son.

'It doesn't explain where he was when Morna was attacked though does it?'

Before his mother could reply, Ella added.

'And I would like to hear the explanation from Aleix himself.'

Aleix scowled at Ella, then looked up towards his father, as if expecting him to step in and do something about the interfering PC. His father however, just looked away realising there wasn't much he could do about it — at the moment anyway. It was the first time the young man had spoken, and to Jean, his voice sounded weak and petulant. She had to stop herself from gagging and punching him.

'I started to walk her home, but she was still complaining that she felt unwell. She started to wander off into the fog and when I tried to call out to find her, there was no response; she had disappeared, I couldn't see her anywhere.'

He looked down at his bandaged hand and seemed to have a moment of inspiration.

'I even cut my hand on a broken wall as I went looking for her.'

He held his hand up as if to prove the point.

'You should get that looked at then, perhaps we should call a doctor in to look at it. Why don't you take the bandage off and let him see?'

Croft looked at him with an air of concern, but Aleix snatched his hand to his chest protectively.

'No, it's fine, I don't want a fuss.'

His mother smirked as if this proved how brave he was. Croft had other ideas and wasn't going to let it lie that easily.

'So, you were nowhere near Morna when she was attacked?'

'Of course not. I went home to see if I could get help in finding her. I hated the idea she was so alone and lost in the fog;

and with the killer around, anything could have happened to her.'

Jean heard Morna's father growl quietly beside her. What possessed Morna to want to marry such a weak, pathetic man was beyond her. Ella took a step towards Aleix, she was so close his mother had to move aside, the affronted look on her face suggested what she thought of the PC and her apparent rudeness.

'It's strange that you say you weren't anywhere near the place where Morna was attacked. I don't believe I actually mentioned where it was, so how could you know if you were nearby?'

She enjoyed the smug look on his face slip as he realised his mistake, she carried on.

'Also, I have an eyewitness who saw you leave the scene immediately after the attack. Your hand was bleeding at the time.'

This was too much for his parents to accept and they both lunged forward at the PC, demanding she apologise for such a grievous slur on their son's name. They made so much noise, that two members of the hospital stuff rushed in to see what was happening. By now, after the initial shock of hearing that his future son in-law was probably responsible for his daughter's attack, Morna's father had gathered himself and lunged at Aleix, pushing passed Jean and Ella, before laying a pretty impressive punch on the young man's nose.

Chaos once more ensued, as both fathers were now yelling at each other again. Ella and Jean tried to calm things down, and with the help of the two hospital staff, that they took to be nurses, they managed to pull them both apart. The men stood opposite each other, pinned against the walls by Jean and the two male nurses; Ella stood over Aleix while he blubbered through his fingers, trying to stem the stream of blood from his nose. His bandage, wrapped around his hand, soon soaked red with the flow. It had been poorly applied, and Ella took full advantage, pulling the lad up and rather adeptly managing to loosen the gauze. Underneath, the wound was quite obviously a bite mark. Aleix snatched his hand back, trying to get as far from the PC as possible, backing further into the corner.

By the door, only Morna's mother had remained silent throughout the whole scenario, tears rolling unchecked down her cheeks. Despite all the emotion that was hurtling around the room, it was the pain of a mother's heart breaking, that caught Jean most earnestly.

Then, beside the girl's mother, the door opened again, and Jean saw a short man enter. His uniform was similar to Ella's but, Jean noted, there was a lot more braid and he carried himself like a man comfortable with his authority. Ella looked at him and then at Jean before sighing.

'Hello Sir.'

'What the hell is going on here PC Croft?'

The voice of the man belied his limited stature, even Jean found herself standing taller. Ella gulped and Jean felt the young woman's nervousness as she spoke.

'Well Sir, a young woman was attacked tonight, and it has just been established that her fiancé…' She indicated the cowering lump in the corner, '…has been lying as to his whereabouts at the time.'

'What has that got to do with anything other than he is a bad liar?'

The newcomer couldn't stop the sneer of distaste in his voice as his eyes fell on Aleix's crumpled form. Jean liked him.

'We also have an eyewitness who saw him fleeing the scene.'

'Really? And where is this witness now?'

Ella glanced at Jean, and realising this was her cue, she stepped forward. Everyone looked in her direction.

'Yes, I saw this man.' She pointed squarely at Aleix. 'Leaving an alley immediately after I heard a scuffle and a scream. I managed to get down the alleyway, despite the fog, to see that Morna was in some distress. PC Croft and her fellow PC, arrived shortly after.'

The small man stepped closer to Jean and looked her in the eye.

'And how, exactly, did you manage to see anyone in this weather?'

She was ready for this.

'He pulled an orb out from under his jacket, it lit his face up perfectly. I have absolutely no doubt that this man was the one I saw running from the scene.'

Before she could be questioned any further, General Bales pushed past the male nurses and confronted Jean.

'But you didn't actually see him attacking the girl.'

Jean noticed that father and son were reluctant to use Morna's name.

'No I didn't.' She conceded. 'But he has already lied about his whereabouts at the time, and forensic evidence has been taken. A sample from the lad should prove or disprove his involvement.'

179

'My son will not be giving anything. I expect to see a warrant and have a solicitor present before anything further is said about this matter.'

The General thrust his weak jaw at the senior policeman, daring him to say otherwise.

'How will forensics help prove he attacked my Morna? Surely, as he spent the evening with her, his DNA will be present on her clothes.'

A small voice from the door broke through the awkward silence and Jean was once again caught on the back foot.

They can check and compare DNA here?

Then she realised, of course, the families didn't know that Morna had been raped; they thought she had just been badly assaulted. Jean's heart sank, the truth was going to devastate her parents.

Ella was the one who stepped forward, and she broke the news as gently as she could, Jean admired her courage.

'I am so sorry, but the attack on Morna was of a sexual nature.'

Croft held her hand out as Morna's mother seemed to crumple, giving a heartbreaking cry and falling into Ella's arms, sobbing onto her shoulder. Finally seeming to realise his wife's distress, her husband rushed forward and rescued Ella. Taking his wife into his own arms, tears were coursing down his face by now too.

It was also clear that Aleix's parents were unaware as to the severity of the attack on their future daughter-in-law, they too were looking at each other, shocked. They seemed reluctant to look at their son, still cowering in the corner.

'PC Croft, can I see you outside? And you too?'

The small officer beckoned to Jean to also follow. The two nurses stayed in case there was another outbreak of violence. The three of them walked back down the corridor, towards the seats that Ella and Jean had occupied earlier. The family room opened behind them and the Bales' family swept down the hall, refusing to acknowledge anyone as they passed. Aleix followed in his parents wake, his nose no longer bleeding but his eyes threatened to be an impressive sight in the morning.

Jean looked at Ella. 'Are you just going to let him go?'

'We can't do anything without further evidence. If we just went into court with your testimony alone, we'd be laughed out of court.'

The senior policeman nodded his agreement.

'We have to wait until forensics get back to us and we have permission, or a warrant, to gain a sample off the lad.'

Jean was frustrated but understood. Personally, she thought of all the ways she could deal with the bastard herself, but she kept her own counsel around current company.

'Well Croft, are you going to tell me who this apparent eyewitness is?'

Ella seemed to jump to attention again.

'Of course Sir, my apologies. This is Jean Carter. Jean, this is Inspector Graves.'

Jean and the Inspector shook hands.

'I hope to the gods you know what you two are doing? General Bales is not a good man to upset, and you know he has the ear of *that bloody woman.*'

Ella looked aghast at his obvious disregard of the Emperor's wife, he had bit of a chuckle to himself. 'Tell it like it is Graves.'

Jean definitely liked this man.

Once again, the door to the family room opened and Morna's parents were escorted out by the two male nurses. They glanced briefly in the direction of the two police officers, before hurrying in another direction, presumably to see Morna. Jean returned her attention back to the Inspector.

'Somebody needs to be on guard outside Morna's room. What if Aleix comes back to keep her quiet?'

A look of irritation passed across the Inspector's face.

'I can assure you the young lady's safety is well in hand Miss Carter, you needn't worry yourself. Croft, make sure our witness here gives her statement and is escorted home safely.'

Realising she had obviously stood on his toes, she had the grace to look apologetic, but before she could say anything, the Inspector had bid them good evening and was striding towards the door.

'Don't worry, he's just worried how this could affect not only our station, but Parva's police force in general. On top of all these killings he's getting a bit stressed out.'

Jean had the feeling, *a bit stressed out,* would be an understatement in Graves' opinion. Making their way to the seating area, the two women sat down while Ella formally took Jean's statement, recalling her version of the evening's attack on Morna, and Croft wrote them down word for word. Once the formalities were finished, they were soon back out into the darkness and gloom of the fog.

Ella was obviously at home among the streets of the city, but Jean, even with a good sense of direction, had to admit the twisting and turning roads and alleyways, had completely turned her brain around. They were finally nearing Jean's lodgings when she suddenly froze, sensing there were other people around, but with an underlying menace about them she didn't like. Ella, aware that Jean had stopped walking, looked back quizzically. Jean pressed a finger to her own lips to indicate she should be quiet.

As the strangers approached, she took Ella's elbow and ushered her into a nearby lane, just as a group of five men and women came into view. They were dressed as members of the Patrols, but now, instead of cudgels, they carried knives. Ella caught her breath as she too saw the lethal weapons in their hands. Jean pressed her further into the alley. One of the Patrol members began to speak in a loud whisper, in English, and if Jean's memory was anything to go by, it was a pretty thick Scouse accent.

'Where the hell did they go? I know I saw them go this way.'

A fellow Liverpudlian answered. 'I don't know how the fuck we're supposed to see anything in this shit. I reckon we should just go back and tell them we lost them in the fog.'

Several voices agreed with this sentiment, but the first Scouser wasn't so sure.

'We were given clear instructions; we were to make sure the woman didn't live to see the morning.'

'But if we can't find her how the hell can we kill her? Do you know where she's staying.'

Apparently, there was much shaking of heads, before it was finally agreed to abandon the search and the unhappy group carried on. A few seconds later there was a crash from further up the road.

'SHIT.'

Followed by suppressed sniggering.

'Trust you to fall over something.'

'It's not fucking funny, it hurt.'

'Well it's your own bloody fault, you should look where you are going.'

'How can I fucking see where I'm going in this fucking weather? I hate this fucking fog, I hate this fucking city, I hate this fucking world!'

'Calm down mate, and stop shouting, you'll wake the whole sodding street.'

'I don't give a fucking rat's arse about the sodding street. I'm fucking pissed off and I want to go fucking home.'

'That's enough.'

All humour was lost now among the group. Whoever had just fallen, was making far too much noise and there were a number of lights going on in windows around them. There were a couple more grunts, then it seemed the Patrol had finally moved on.

Jean and Ella waited a while, until Jean felt it was safe to leave their hiding place. Making their way back to Mrs Moore's, Jean kept her senses on alert, but the rest of the journey was Patrol free. Once inside and sitting at the kitchen table, both women resolved to meet tomorrow and discuss this new turn in events. It took a while for Jean to convince Ella that she should still be involved with the investigation, but when Jean reminded her of the Patrol that was looking for her, she gave in. It seemed that Jean had piqued the interest of someone, and Ella's inquisitive nose wanted to know why. But for now, Ella had to return to the station and see if Lyal had managed to gain anything from the forensic team. If there was anything useful though, she knew it would be a while before any real evidence would be available.

'Are you sure you are ok travelling out there with those Patrols on the loose? And there is still a killer at large somewhere.'

Jean didn't like the idea of the young PC alone on the streets, but Ella just laughed.

'I know these streets better than anyone, I'll be careful. But don't worry, I will be back at the station before you know it.'

They bid each other farewell, and as the PC disappeared into the fog, Jean considered following her to make sure she stayed safe. But having thought about it, she realised there was more chance of her probably get completely lost again, so decided against the idea; she had to trust Ella and her instincts. With this thought, she wound her way up to her own room and a welcome bed, making the most of the rest of her first night in the city of Parva.

13

Wives

I n his office within the Palace at Parva, Nathan sat at his
desk, his head in his hands. Before him an array of the
morning's newspapers was spread out, all leading with
variations of the same headline. Last night the son of a
General of the Order was accused of raping a young girl. Who
was held responsible for such a heinous crime depended on
which paper you read? They ranged from his parents, society as
a whole, the young girl herself or even the Emperor.

Scattered throughout the tabloids, the same questions were
repeated in some form or other.

**Where was the Emperor when you needed him? He
should have prevented this awful thing from
happening.**

Inevitably, they referred back to the vicious murders that had plagued the city over the past weeks, and the lack of any progress available in bringing the culprit to justice.

Was the same person responsible?

Nathan shifted in his chair, whether he liked it or not, he couldn't help but agree with the sentiments written. It was all a horrible, bloody mess. However, at some point all the tabloids mentioned the *new Duchess,* how this sort of thing never happened before *she* was around. Then of course it became the Emperor's fault again, he married her in the first place.

Nathan felt sick.

This whole sorry mess was down to him, who else could accept responsibility? He felt more desperate and alone than he had ever done in his life, and was struggling to find a way out of the situation. The stranger that had offered so much hope weeks ago seemed to have vanished, along with the hope for his people with her.

He was roused from his despondency, by the sound of raised voices from outside his closed office door. His secretary was in full, indignant flow; someone was getting it in the neck, and unfortunately, he had a strong idea who that person was.

'You cannot go in there, the Emperor does not accept visitors without a prior appointment, and you Madam, are not on the list.'

Nathan chuckled to himself.

You tell her Val.

'I don't need an appointment to see my husband.'

He groaned when he recognised the voice.

You don't always have to be right Nathan.

187

'I can assure you, that *you* definitely do have to have an appointment.'

'I am not having this, get out of my way.'

There was a thump against the door.

'What are you doing you stupid woman, get out of my way.'

Nathan had to admit, even he was now intrigued, and bracing himself, stood up and went to open the door that led to the main office.

Valèria Cornice, his long time and currently, long suffering secretary, practically fell into his arms as he opened the door. Evidently, she had thrown herself against the door in order to bar Ephea from entering. Val had been his secretary for over thirty years and Nathan was touched by her loyalty and devotion, even if it had come to include the physical defence of her boss. Ensuring Val was standing firmly on her feet, he gave her a small smile of gratitude. He saw a slight tear form in her grey eyes as she nodded back, before straightening the jacket of her business-like suit.

He inclined his head and said. 'Thank you Val, I'll deal with this.'

Val squared her shoulders and set her chin.

'Very well my Lord.' Giving Ephea a steely stare, Val became the consummate professional. 'Would you like me to bring tea?'

It took everything for her not to spit out the words, but instead she remained calm. Nathan, however, didn't feel so generous today, so with barely disguised venom, replied with a simple but firm.

'No.'

Val, satisfied that she was no longer required, swept passed Ephea and returned to her desk. Ephea, having given up expecting any respect due to a wife from her husband, bustled past Nathan and into his office. She was already in a bad mood, now she was furious.

Nathan took a slow, deep breath as he closed the door to the outer office with a gentle click. He could smell her cloying perfume begin to ooze into the room and made his way to the windows and opened them. It was mid-morning, but the sun was obscured by the swirling fog outside; the foghorn was still booming it's forlorn low cry.

Ephea watched him through lidded eyes, and shuddered.

Why was he always opening windows? Surely, he must realise how bloody freezing it was out there.

She watched him warily as he moved around his office. He was a tall, strong man, a long-seasoned soldier with the air of authority that left no doubt of who was in charge. At well over six-foot-tall, he towered over her; she was barely five foot in her stockinged feet. As such, Ephea preferred that in the few times they had to bear each other's company, they remained standing apart. Her corsets had little give, making it impossible to look up when so close to someone without getting a crick in her neck. She was relieved when he went to sit behind his desk, though she also noticed he didn't ask her to sit down too.

It was purely down to the years of diplomacy and the need for civility and patience, that stopped Nathan from showing the deep contempt and dislike he had for this woman. Instead he just gazed steadily at her before speaking — but she could stand while doing it.

'What are you doing here Ephea? Apart from upsetting my secretary.'

Ephea sniffed with distaste, diplomacy was never one of her own fortés.

'The damned woman should know her place. You should talk to her about manners.'

Nathan raised a surprised eyebrow.

'I can assure you that Valèria has manners of the highest standard. You, on the other hand could learn a lot from her.'

Ephea slammed her hands down on Nathan's big heavy desk; the solid oak didn't budge, and the expression on her face showed she regretted it instantly as the pain shot up her arms. Nathan just sat back in his chair and watched, saying nothing. Turning around and walking towards the cold fireplace, Ephea rubbed her sore hands, so he couldn't see how much her outburst hurt. When she turned back, he was still sitting there, silent, waiting. Her neck and face reddened as the anger rose within her.

'Where is she? What have you done with her?'

'Who?' Nathan stiffened slightly in panic, was she talking about the stranger?

'Johnson of course? What have your knights done with her?'

Relaxing with relief, he said.

'I have no idea what you are talking about. Why should I want to have anything to do, with any of the criminals, you seem to feel necessary to surround yourself with?'

Ephea began to bristle and Nathan couldn't help getting further under her skin.

'The last I heard, your pet bully was roaming around Northern Lorimar, irritating the hell out of the locals. Perhaps she just got bored, annoyed with running around on a wild goose chase, and finally decided to go home.'

Ephea's eyes were wild with indignation.

'It was no wild goose chase; she was after one of your spies; and she would never abandon me. My staff are loyal.'

Nathan raised an eyebrow, Ephea was more delusional than he thought, if she believed they put up with her through loyalty and not the amount of money in her purse. Though he clenched his teeth, when he remembered that her purse was predominately filled from the coffers of his own.

'I have no idea what harebrained schemes you have, that you believe I would need spies keeping an eye on your barely educated thugs. However, I can assure you that the loss of your *loyal* Johnson, has absolutely nothing to do with me, or those of the Order. I suggest you send a search party to the Australian Outback.'

Standing with her hands on her hips Ephea gave a small smile.

'For someone who denies any knowledge of her whereabouts, you seem to know a lot about her.'

'It's hardly a secret is it?'

Nathan had had enough; he wanted the foul smell that permeated from this awful woman out of his office.

'Everybody knows who she is and where she is from, her criminal and army records are pretty impressive reading.'

He looked to a pile of files on his desk and Ephea blanched.

'You've investigated Johnson?'

Nathan gave a small mirthless chuckle.

'Ephea, I make sure I know all about the people who I consider most dangerous to the Empire.'

He watched her gulp and the colour slowly drained from her face before continuing.

'Now, if there is nothing else, I have plenty of work to do, you can let yourself out.'

Ephea again made to slam her fists down onto the desk, but this time stopping just short of the surface, placing them carefully onto the highly polished wood.

'Be careful Nathan, be very careful. Your ego and pride can get a lot of people killed remember.'

Nathan rose from his seat, slowly put his own hands down on his desk, leaning forward until his whole frame towered over hers. His deep voice, low and menacing.

'Now would be a good time for you to leave *Ephea*.'

His eyes never left hers until she looked away. She knew then she had stepped too far. No matter how much power her family believed they had over this man, there was always a point of caution you didn't cross, and she had come close. Turning on her heel, Ephea made for the door, aware all the time he was watching, his fury only barely hidden behind the steel blue of his eyes.

It wasn't until she was on the other side of the door, that Ephea realised that she had been holding her breath. Gulping in air, she put her hand to her ample breasts, before noticing that his secretary was watching her. She sneered at Val as she strode past.

What are you looking at bitch?

Val just shook her head and continued with her work. Ephea hurried out into the main office, past the three secretaries that worked for Nathan, Damien and Daniel, into the open space, where clerical staff worked on the business of the Empire. She was flushed and almost stumbled in her haste to get away, catching herself on a desk to stop herself from falling. Its occupant barely hid their contempt as Ephea swore under her breath.

Her exit from Nathan's office did not go unnoticed by those working in the rest of the outer office. Here clerks busied themselves with the work generated by the Emperor; Nathan, the Chancellor; Damien and the Lord Justice; Daniel. No matter what the High Council debated and considered regarding the government of the Empire it was within these offices alone that the ultimate seat of power existed. Those who worked within these walls were fiercely loyal, and as such, there were no friends of Ephea and her cause here. They watched her silently, as she stumbled awkwardly through the forest of desks and filing cabinets. Feeling the eyes of mistrust and dislike as she passed, only breathing again, once she gained the stairs that led down to relative safety.

There was a window open at the end the lower corridor and she rushed to it, gulping in air. The fog was as thick as it ever was, and the blast from the foghorn made her jump. She braced herself against the window ledge for a few moments, gaining her composure before she began her descent to the lower levels of the Palace.

A sudden prickling up her spine warned her that she was no longer alone.

Spinning round, she saw the eyes of someone she felt she should recognise, but for the life of her she couldn't think where from. The look on the scarred and drawn face was one of sheer hatred, and despite his height advantage over her, he seemed to hold his body awkwardly. Ephea suddenly felt fear for the

193

second time that day and she gripped the windowsill harder. In an attempt to sound braver than she felt, she stood upright and forced her head back, in order to look down her nose. How dare a cripple make her feel so afraid.

'What are you looking at? Get out of my way.'

Ephea shoved passed the man who stumbled slightly in his haste to move. Once again gaining the stairs, she hurried and didn't stop this time until she alighted on the ground floor.

Behind her, Fallon Kleinstock watched her fleeing skirts long after she had departed; the smouldering fire of disgust and hate burning within his soul.

Back in the main office, someone else had been interested by the usually proud and haughty woman, and the state in which she had left Nathan's office. Damien had been discussing a paper with one of his clerks as Ephea passed by. Both he and the clerk had looked up at the disturbance, then at each other in mild surprise and amusement. The clerk seemed to forget who was with him when he remarked. 'Well that was unexpected.'

Damien raised an eyebrow and the clerk flushed, stumbling an apology.

'I'm so sorry my Lord, I didn't mean any disrespect.'

Damien couldn't help but grin back.

'Nothing to apologise for, I am as intrigued as you are.'

He handed the clerk the papers he was holding and excused himself, then made this way back to his own office. Once inside, he stood facing his desk that sat under the high windows that would normally look out over the city; but today only a flat grey could be seen through the glass. To his left a door stood open as it usually did, he went over and popped his head through, seeing Daniel hard at work at his own desk. Before Damien could say

194

anything however, the fair head of the Chief of Imperial Justice looked up and grinned at his visitor.

'So, what's he done now to upset the old bat?'

'Did you hear what they were arguing about?'

Damien looked over to the other side of his office, to the closed door that mirrored the one into Daniel's room.

'No, I couldn't actually hear what was said, but that screech of hers can cut through to the bone. It didn't sound as if marital bliss abounded.'

'Well she was none too happy as she swept through the main office just now. Whatever was said, she is didn't like it.'

'Curious. I take it we are going to find out what happened.'

'Of course. Are you coming?'

Grinning, Daniel stood up and followed Damien to the closed door opposite that led to Nathan's office. They both placed their heads against the wood, like a couple of children checking if the coast was clear, before embarking on their next bit of mischief. Hearing nothing, Damien knocked and then turned the handle to enter.

Nathan was at one of the high windows that spanned the two walls of his large corner office. Polished wood panelling was predominantly hidden by the rows of bookcases that lined the walls. The carpet and soft furnishings were of deep reds and blues that would normally have made a room look gloomy, but with the expanse of glass that let so much light in, most visitors considered it comfortable and welcoming. Nothing, however, could hide the huge, solid, oak desk that sat beneath the still open windows behind it.

The man at the window had his hands planted either side of the frame, his arms were straight as if bracing himself, his head bowed in thought while he took in long deep breaths.

Nathan felt that it seemed to take him longer to calm down each time he encountered his wife. Dear Gods, he had to fight the urge to hit something every time he was forced to remember this fact. She was his wife; a simple, legal, but sickening truth. He knew he shouldn't have allowed her to get to him. He'd been around long enough to not let such things make him react, but his feeling of helplessness after reading the papers and her timing was perfect. He cringed inside as he thought of the way he let her needle him.

Suddenly something caught his attention, his senses heightened by the curious sensations he now felt, something out in the city had changed; a feeling of recognition, a warmth he'd felt only once before. Having been out of the city at his home in Devon for a number of days, he only returned early this morning. He found himself once more aware of the ever-encroaching rot that was spreading through Parva's streets. It had been pervading for weeks now, ever since the murders had started.

But this was something new. He tensed at the memory; it had suddenly dawned on him what the feeling was.

He heard the knock on his door and Damien and Daniel entered, making their way into the centre of the room. Turning to face his two friends, he had a new light in his deep blue eyes. The two men opposite didn't miss the slight tug of a smile at the corner of Nathan's mouth either. Glancing at each other they looked back at him enquiringly.

Nathan stood behind his desk chair, his hands resting lightly on its back and, with a positivity that he didn't think he'd feel again, he declared his good news.

'She's here.'

It barely took a heartbeat for his men to realise the significance of what he meant. The mysterious stranger was in the city. However, only Damien knew of the strange connection Nathan had with the unknown woman at Rassen.

Daniel, intrigued, asked. 'How do you know?'

The Emperor and Damien shared a brief glance, before Nathan enlightened Daniel as to his previous experience in the tavern at Rassen, what he had felt when he and the woman had briefly touched hands. Daniel straightened, the look on his face darkened, neither of the other two men were surprised at his reaction.

'So, when were you going to share this information?' He looked at Damien. 'I take it *you knew?*'

Damien nodded but it was Nathan who responded.

'I'm mentioning it now.'

Nathan stood grinning, with his hands in his pockets, feeling more positive than he had in a long while. Ephea and their recent altercation was banished to the back of his mind. However, Daniel wasn't impressed.

'Really? You have had a connection to this woman, and now you turn to flippancy to justify your silence.'

Nathan felt that Daniel was perhaps taking this a bit too much to heart.

'I told Damien.'

'And when exactly where you going to tell everyone else? Tell me?'

Daniel stepped towards the desk; anger flashed in his eyes.

'Always the secrets Nathan, would we even be in this mess if you weren't so bloody secretive?'

Damien tried to calm his friend, it was unusual for Daniel to be so angry; but again it was Nathan that answered. Moving around his desk he urged the two men to join him at the large sofas arranged around the fireplace, which was filled with flowers during the summer months. Though their scent was welcome during such miserable weather, they struggled against Ephea's overbearing perfume. As the three of them made themselves comfortable, Nathan sat forward.

'Hold on Daniel, this is not Damien's fault and I am not keeping secrets.'

I never have kept any bloody secrets.

Determined to keep calm, Nathan continued.

'I only mentioned it to Damien, because it was something I felt was curious at the time, but I couldn't be sure if it was real. We were all hungry and exhausted if you remember.'

Sitting back in the comfort of the sofa cushions, Nathan could almost feel every year of his long life.

'Only this time, I felt the same thing, but it was further away. I'm positive though, she is in the city.'

Daniel still kept a scowl on his face, it felt odd and he didn't like the feeling. He was a cheerful man by nature, even as his work led him to see the very worst of human depravity, he made a point of maintaining a positive outlook on life.

But dear gods. He thought. *It was getting difficult.*

He, like Damien, had been lumbered with one of the other two of Ephea's godawful sisters, and he felt that if there was any way their agony could be diminished, no matter how small, he should have been told.

Yollan was Ephea's youngest sibling, but unlike her sisters, she believed that Daniel actually had feelings for her; that their *marital arrangement* was something that he was happy with. He was beginning to think that the Earth expression 'a sandwich short of a full picnic' was an apt description for Yollan. Three times in the last week alone, she had come knocking on his office door when he had to work late into the night. It had finally taken half a dozen knights to manhandle her into a carriage to take her home.

Unfortunately, the letter he received earlier that morning, declaring that she forgave him and that she understood how busy he was, demonstrated that her enthusiasm hadn't diminished at all. He now considered only working while the office was full, and having the bloody woman banned from the Palace all together.

He leant forward with his forearms on his knees, a position Daniel took in court when he is about to make a particular point.

'Three times this week Nathan, three times.'

The look of anger and horror on his friend's face, made Nathan put aside his own annoyance of being accused of keeping secrets, he took on a more sympathetic countenance.

'I'm sorry Daniel, really, in your shoes the thought that Ephea…' The anger rose again. '…believing that there was anything else in our *contract*….'

He couldn't bring himself to say marriage, that would be a step too far. He shook his head and closed his eyes. A silent shudder passed through the three of them. Realising that

199

Daniel was still angry, but not so murderous, Damien tried to bring the conversation round to the reason they had joined Nathan in his office.

'So, what was the old witch up to this time? The look on her face when she left this office would curdle milk. Thunderous would be a good description.'

Nathan told them that, as they suspected, Johnson had disappeared and Ephea was panicking.

'She wants to blame me, because she can't possibly accept, that the nasty antipodean bitch may have left Kelan and gone back home, fed up with her mistress sending her on a hopeless pursuit.'

'But we don't believe it was hopeless though, do we?' Nathan and Damien looked at Daniel. 'There is always the other possibility.'

Nodding, they agreed, of course Johnson's cohorts could have seen their superior officer off themselves, but if that was the case where were they now? The only other viable option was that the female stranger, that Johnson was sent to look for, had dealt with all three of them herself. If she had, then she had also managed to dispose of the evidence at the same time, whilst it seemed, having gained the trust of those around her. However, it was highly unlikely that if she had made her way to Parva unnoticed by the authorities, it was not without some help. Mulling this information over Damien spoke up.

'Well if she, Johnson, is dead and your mysterious stranger is now somewhere in Parva, eventually Ephea is going to find out. That puts the woman in a lot of danger, do you still suggest we do nothing?'

Nathan considered this valid point and shook his head.

200

'No, though what we can do at the moment I have no idea. I still don't want to draw attention to her, but by the same token, I would like to see she is kept safe. What we need to do is identify her properly. We can't act on mere rumours, so keep your ears to the ground and speak to your own contacts, we may learn more within the next few days.'

Nathan, again leant forward, his elbows on his knees and his hands relaxed before him.

'In a few days it is the Midsummer Festival, Parva will be full of people wanting to celebrate, including those attending the ball here.'

Nathan stood and made his way to the fireplace, placing his hands on the mantelpiece and looking into the flower filled grate.

'Somewhere out there is a maniac apparently killing people at random, yet somehow, we need to keep the peace, without letting any more people die. If we're lucky, the festivities will pass without incident.'

He turned around and both men looked up at him, the scepticism clearly evident.

'Yes, I know, that is looking highly unlikely, but we can hope.'

Walking back to his desk, Nathan picked up one of the papers that headlined the previous night's attack.

'Find out what you can about this too, I have a nasty feeling about it. Have a word with the police and let me know what you find Daniel.'

Buoyed by the opportunity to do something positive for once, both men stood and made to leave. As they passed through the door leading to Damien's office, Nathan resumed his position at the open window.

By the time Damien had closed the door, Daniel was almost at his own office.

'Daniel.'

Turning, the man looked back, he looked tired. 'What is it Damien?'

'This isn't a conspiracy and Nathan really doesn't have any secrets. He isn't the reason for this mess.'

Daniel walked back into the room and seemed to consider something before responding.

'How do you know that Damien?'

Sighing he gently shook his head. 'I just do.'

The other man looked at him hard, then without speaking, turned and entered his own room, this time closing the door.

Damien returned to his own desk and stared at the papers that lay there. His eyes refused to focus and he placed his head in his hands. He thought he could cope with anything with Nathan and Daniel as strong as ever beside him.

But if that should fall apart?

He felt himself shudder at the possibility.

14

Murder

I t was the morning of the day following Morna's attack
and Ella had called on Jean at her lodgings. After Mrs
Moore had ushered her in, the PC found Jean at the
kitchen table, with a cup of tea in hand.

'Good morning, I'm surprised to see you up this early, I
thought you'd be sleeping off your night duty.'

Ella rolled her eyes. 'Luïsa, my girlfriend, decided that she
needed to clean the house this morning. Unfortunately, she likes
to sing while she works. Loudly.'

Jean laughed. 'Ah, I can imagine that she doesn't have a
voice that can send you to sleep?'

'You are joking, she has a voice that can raise the dead.'

Mrs Moore, who had followed Ella into the kitchen sniffed.

'Nothing like a good tune to get you in the mood for cleaning.'

Jean looked at her landlady incredulously.

'But Ella is in the police and she was working all last night. She has to sleep.'

Apparently, Mrs Moore felt that there was never any excuse for sleeping while the sun was up, so giving another sniff of disdain, left the two women alone in the kitchen. Both found it impossible not to laugh, but at least they had the sense to wait until the landlady was out of earshot.

Jean shook her head.

'I'm not even going try and convince her otherwise. In the world of Mrs Moore her word is law.'

Still chuckling to herself Jean got up and retrieved another cup.

'Come and sit down and have a cup of tea, it's freshly brewed.'

Ella sat down gratefully and took a welcoming sip of her tea. She had brought with her a small pile of newspapers and placed them on the table between them. Jean glanced at the headline on the top copy and frowned.

'What's this?'

Ella followed Jean's gaze; a look of concern crossed her face; she indicated that Jean have a look. Opening the papers out, Jean saw, emblazoned across the front of them all, the story of the attack and rape of a young girl in the night. No names were given fortunately, but it was still a surprise that the police would allow such information to be released so soon, she said as much to Ella.

'Oh, I can assure you that the police have nothing to do with this.'

She poked a finger of disdain in the direction of the tabloids.

'I dropped into the station before coming here, Inspector Graves was furious, and everyone was keeping well out of his way. I ducked out before he could see me there.'

'Would Morna's family have gone to the papers? Her father was understandably upset and angry last night.'

'Absolutely not.'

'How do you know that? He may have done.'

'I know, because I know how it works around here. There's no way Morna's family would release information that she had been so viciously attacked; it would put a black mark on the family.'

Ella went quiet for a moment and Jean watched as the anger crossed the young woman's face.

'If I'm honest, it wouldn't surprise me if the marriage to Aleix still went ahead. Probably sooner rather than later even.'

'What?'

'As far as both families are concerned, neither want the stigma of such an attack attached to them. I know it sounds awful, and archaic, and it is, but unless we have the full cooperation of the victim, we have nothing. It doesn't matter how much forensic evidence we have, be it DNA or otherwise, if she says nothing against him, there is nothing we can do.'

Jean was appalled and mirrored Ella's frustration, she struggled to keep her own emotions in check. Though the idea of going around to both families and giving them a piece of her mind, still felt like a good idea. However, it didn't solve the problem of who told the papers about the attack. Both Jean and

Ella tried to go over the details of the previous evening, discussing how both families were emotional, and the fight between both fathers. Then, as realisation hit them, they both groaned.

'How could I have missed it?' Ella put her head in her hands.

'It's not your fault, there was so much happening. Who looks twice when you're in a hospital, and a nurse or two helps to break up an emotional family outburst?'

Irritation crossed Ella's face.

'I need to speak to Graves. We have to find those two male nurses.'

To Jean's amazement Ella pulled out a mobile phone from her jacket pocket. She had to admit that she was becoming less and less surprised at the technology of Kelan society, but even this surpassed her expectations.

'Is that a mobile phone?'

Ella nodded. 'Of course.'

'I don't understand, surely they don't work here in the Empire. I had a torch that fell to bits after a few hours here.'

Jean bit her tongue as she realised her mistake. Ella looked at her with narrowed eyes.

'You're new to the Empire?'

Jean sighed, silently cursing herself.

'Yes, I'm originally from Earth, but before you ask, I have nothing to do with the Patrols, or anything else that Ephea is planning.'

'Then why are you here?'

Jean took a moment before she replied.

'I don't actually know for sure.'

The suspicious look on Ellas's face sharpened, Jean had to be careful here.

'I've spent a lot of time, travelling around a lot of worlds, and now I've somehow found myself here in Kelan. I know it sounds lame, but that's all I can tell you at the moment. I just ask that you trust me, and if I can help in anyway, I will.'

'And that's it? You just want me to trust you?'

Jean looked at her imploringly, but realised the young woman was right, she had no reason to trust her, and with the current social disarray, murders and vicious assaults, who could blame her? As a member of the police, her job was to keep the peace and ensure the law was adhered to. Now that the more assertive part of Jean was awakening, it was less likely that someone with passive tendencies would be affected by her empathy. She needed Ella's trust, so had to tread carefully.

At that moment the phone in Ella's hand rang, both women stared at it as if it was alive. Ella blinked before finally answering; it was Inspector Graves.

Jean, trying not to look as if she was listening in to a private conversation, started to flick through the nearest paper on the table. There was a story that caught her eye at the bottom of page five. The piece was only a small one, barely an obituary, let alone a story, but it was there, none the less.

Ella was now explaining to her superior, their suspicions regarding the male nurses at the hospital last night, when Jean tried to get her attention. Ella looked annoyed and turned her head to one side, indicating that she wasn't disrupting her call. But Jean was insistent, pushing the paper across the table, so the story was right under the PC's nose. She stabbed at the paper until she couldn't be ignored anymore.

'I am so sorry Sir, can you excuse me for one moment?'

Turning to Jean with a murderous look on her face, Ella hissed at her. 'What?'

'Look, read this.'

Ella looked down and read the brief article, slowly bringing her eyes up to meet Jean's, before returning back to her phone call.

'Sir, can I possibly call you back?'

Graves had obviously agreed, and the call was terminated.

'You think this is the same man from last night?'

Jean nodded. 'You obviously do too.'

Looking back down at the paper Ella reread the article. Early that morning, a naked male body had been pulled from the river. She looked up.

'It's interesting that a body has been found with its throat cut amidst a time when the city is under the fear of a killer; yet it is barely more than a by-line.'

Jean agreed. 'Exactly, someone didn't want this death to have too much attention. But made it look enough like the other murders should questions be asked. I think our unhappy Scouser was suitably silenced last night. The question is by whom?'

'And who sent them out to find us in the first place?'

Jean furrowed her brows.

'I have to admit, I've had a hard time trying to figure that one out. The Patrols are ultimately under Ephea's rule, though that is unofficial of course. But how would she have known about the attack and what would it have to do with her?'

'I can't imagine the Patrols would want it to be known that one of their own could have been a victim of our maniacal

208

killer either. But what if this Patrolman *is* another victim of the killer?'

Jean frowned. 'I didn't think the Patrols had been attacked before, I thought they were implicated in the murders.'

'That's just a theory that is travelling around the city. There's no evidence to suggest they are.'

'We seem to be gaining more questions than answers, and we're not going to find them sitting here.'

'No, I am not.'

The young PC stood up and thanked Jean for the tea.

'Ella, please don't shut me out of this, I can help.'

'I don't know. These are dangerous times, and trusting strangers is unwise.'

Shutting her eyes, Jean pushed the rising anger down. Opening them again, she looked straight at Ella. 'Why did you come here this morning?'

'What?'

Completely taken aback by the change of subject, Ella seemed confused. Jean stayed silent and waited.

'I don't know, I suppose I thought you should see the papers.'

Ella made a valiant effort to try and take back the advantage.

'It could have been you who alerted the papers. I had to make sure.'

'Really? That is your argument, that I'm the informant? You don't believe that now, and you never have done.'

The two women stared at each other, but eventually it was Ella who looked away first.

'Fine, I admit it didn't cross my mind that you would talk to the papers, and I don't believe now that you did. But the fact remains, you are a stranger here, a foreigner, how can I trust you?'

Biting back a retort to the foreigner comment, Jean tried to stay calm.

'Ella, there are people who have lived in this city all their lives, who are now conspiring against the Empire. Has it occurred to you, that maybe the only person you can trust *is* a stranger?'

She seemed to sag.

'Yes, alright, I do want to trust you and if I'm honest, I've no reason not to. But I love this city, it's my home, and despite whatever is happening to the Emperor, I believe in the Empire.'

'Then let me help you.'

Jean reached out and held onto the other woman's hand, Ella grasped it back after only a moment's hesitation, a small smile on her face as she nodded.

'Good. Well I suggest we find somewhere to eat some lunch, then we go over what we already know. Especially all you know about these murders; I'm convinced they are connected to the problems that have plagued the Empire for so long. But first of all, you can tell me how the hell you managed to get a mobile phone to work within the Ti'akai, without it falling to bits.'

Ella took out her phone to call back Graves. She let him know their latest bit of information before ringing off, then both women made their way to the door and out into the fog that still lingered. As they disappeared, a shadow passed across the kitchen window and Mrs Moore continued her ministrations in the garden.

Outside, the weather was as miserable as ever, and it didn't look like it was going to change anytime soon. The foghorn let out another eery blast, echoing the bleakness.

They made their way through the streets and Jean took the opportunity to ask Ella a question that had been niggling her.

'Why is there a police force here in Parva, yet places like Rassen have no-one to protect them from the Patrols? The Order at Fallport hasn't done anything to either.'

'Normally there is at least a local police presence within the towns and villages, depending on their size. But not long after the Patrols arrived and their numbers started to grow, there were a number of incidents, and during one episode a PC died. I don't know what was said by the powers that be, but soon after, the local police presence was withdrawn in all places other than the cities. It's been like that ever since.'

'What you're basically saying is, the Patrols are the only regulating presence outside of the cities?'

'That about sums it up, yes.'

Jean shook her head, things were looking worse the more she learnt about Patrols and their effect on the Empire. They were both quiet as they walked on, lost in their own thoughts until they came to a café that Ella suggested as a good place for food and somewhere to talk quietly. There were plenty of people out and about, completing their daily business, moving quickly with their heads down, eager to get inside as soon as they could. By the time the two women had reached their destination, their own moods were sombre and reflective. They ordered their food quickly from the harassed waitress, who soon disappeared into the kitchen.

'So, come on then, what's with the mobile phone thing?'

Ella, who had put off this discussion until they were sitting down and more comfortable, pulled out her phone and placed it on the table between them. It had been a very long time since Jean had seen one from Earth, but she knew that this one was still pretty basic compared to the ones she remembered.

'It's just for taking calls and texting messages. It can't do all the other things that *smartphones* can do, it's just a tool that we use.'

'Alright, I understand that, but how does it work? I haven't seen any phone masts around, and how come this hasn't broken down into bits?'

'There aren't any masts because this isn't Earth, the Ti'akai is the power source and conduit for all phones within the Empire.'

Picking the phone up Ella handed it to Jean.

'If you look at it and feel it, you will see there is no plastic at all, it's mainly made from brattine.'

Jean examined the phone and had to admit that there were differences to those she had seen before in her long distant past on Earth. Brattine, that metal again the Emperor and his little group of Knights held exclusive rights too. She didn't think Ella would be anymore likely to enlighten her as to why this was considered acceptable, any more than others had. For the sake of harmony, she didn't say anything.

'So how do you get one of these? And can you get them to do other things as well as make calls and text?'

Ella shook her head. 'Oh, you can't buy them. Only those on special business or duty get to use one, and that's mainly by the police or the Order. Apparently, you can get ones that have all the extras, but they wouldn't give one to a lowly PC like me.

The only reason why I have one now is because I am part of the investigation into last night's attack, and also the importance of the victim and her attacker.'

Jean frowned. 'So, no-one else can use these? They are not for sale?'

'Nope, there are strict guidelines on their use. Think of the experiences that Earth has had, we want to make sure that the Empire doesn't go the same way.'

Jean had to stop herself from audibly snorting her disgust.

'Sounds a bit like Big Brother if you ask me.'

Ella wasn't fazed. 'Hardly. Does the Empire seem Orwellian to you?'

'Well, no. But surely you should give people a choice?'

Ella laughed. 'The problem with giving people choices is they inevitably go for what they want and not what's good for them; in the end they blame someone else for their mistakes and expect others to clear up their mess.'

'That's a bit simplistic.'

'You started it.'

Jean was taken aback at this, resentment niggled at the fringes of her mind, and both women sat in silence for a while, indignation crackled in the space between them.

It was Jean who broke the silence first. 'Fine, well if you have such a Utopian life why is there so much unrest? And why is this Emperor of yours doing nothing about it? Perhaps he is not as good as his forefathers after all.'

Ella looked at her sharply.

'I've no idea why the Emperor has done nothing about all this.'

She waved her hands to indicate life in general.

'But what do you mean the Emperor's forefathers? His father never actually held the title of Emperor. Though history suggests he tried his damnedest to do so; and unsurprisingly a lot of people died for it.'

'But I thought the Empire has existed for the last ten thousand years?'

'It has, but with the same man as its head. Lord Nathan is our only ever Emperor.'

Jean took a moment to absorb this information.

'The Emperor is ten thousand years old?'

'Give or take a century or two.'

'He's been around for that long?'

Ella nodded and drank some of her tea.

'Yes, though how the hell they have managed it for that long I have no idea. You'll have to ask him and the other six Knights about that. The seven of them have been governing the Empire all this time, along with the councils of course, and until around five years ago no-one had reason to complain. Everyone was happy. Then Ephea and her sisters came along.'

She watched Ella's face and saw the look of someone confused and disappointed. She considered this new information, realising she had been working under a false assumption. This changed a lot of her own perspective and she needed to know more about the Emperor and his fellow Knights. An idea began to form.

Their food had finally arrived, and they eagerly tucked into their meal.

'Do you have a museum around here? One that gives a history of the Empire.'

Ella nodded as she tried to swallow her mouthful. Her eyes watered as a particularly large piece made its way down.

'Of course, over the bridge is a huge museum, it has everything you need to know about the Empire. There's even a special section on the Knights. I went there with my school once, it's very good.'

'Excellent, I will definitely look into that.'

A huge crash outside brought a hush to the café, then suddenly everyone stood up and rushed to look out of the big plate glass windows. Some of the waiting staff were nearly crushed in the race to get there first, while others caught trays of food and glasses as they went flying. There was a very angry head waiter stomping back into the kitchen, barking irate orders to his staff.

Across the road, a group of people were standing around, while two men fought on the street. A broken window of a milliner's shop now had the remains of a salesman's suitcase as part of its display. The case's contents of books were strewn across the hats that had been knocked off their perches and fallen onto the pavement.

A whistle blew, and several police officers appeared to break up the fight, dragging the men away. With the fun apparently over, everyone in the café eventually returned to their seats. Across the street, the owner of the hat shop was now gesticulating vigorously, as he imparted his anger to the policeman left behind to sort out the mess.

Ella stood up and told Jean *stay there*, and before any argument could be made, the PC was outside and walking through the mist to talk to her fellow policeman.

Jean tapped her fingers on the table in frustration.

Ella came back a short while later, one of the books in her hand, her face a mixture of anger and fear. Jean's frustration, momentarily forgotten, asked 'What's the matter, what happened?'

Ella shook her head and sat down at the table again.

'It appears that a member of the public took umbrage to books the salesman was selling.'

Jean said nothing but her face asked the question anyway. Ella obliged her with an answer.

'If this isn't bad enough, there's evidence that the man has even managed to sell some of this filth.' Ella laid the book on the table.

THE FALL OF AN OBSOLETE EMPIRE

Jean looked back at her companion's face, she saw the tears form despite her attempts to fight them.

'Jean, we can't let this happen. We have to do something.'

Jean felt the familiar force within her rise up a notch. In a voice that brook no argument she reassured her.

'Oh, PC Ella Croft, I will.'

Later that afternoon, Ella had been called in early for her nightshift to cover for the sudden upsurge in local unrest. Jean had heard from Mrs Moore that the Midsummer Festival was soon, and that many from across the Empire will be flocking to Parva for the celebrations. In particular the ball at the Palace.

Already the fog had begun to thicken again, it seemed that the foghorn had gained a few more decibels since that morning.

Jean mulled over the information that she had gleaned so far, there were far too many things that didn't make sense. In particular, why was the Emperor, who was such an experienced leader in running such a huge government, that had survived successfully for centuries, had now fallen silent when it all starts to go wrong? Ephea obviously had something to do with it, but what it was, no-one, whom Jean had spoken to, could answer. Whatever it was, she felt convinced it was something set in the past, and the best place to find out about that was the museum and library.

After enquiring, Mrs Moore told her that both buildings were across the river and within the grounds of the university. Assuring Jean that they had a *lovely section all about the Knights*. Jean decided to make a point of going there the following day after breakfast, that way she would have more chance to spend sufficient time researching and, should she get completely lost, have ample opportunity to ask for directions home.

While Jean spent the latter part of the afternoon settling down in front of Mrs Moore's kitchen stove, a message was brought to her from Ella. It was Lyal who delivered it, and he stood upright, keen and excited, but with a sad look on his young face as Jean read the short note quickly.

There has been another murder.

Come with Lyal.

Jean stood and told Lyal she just needed to grab her coat; she met him at the front door and called out to her landlady.

'Mrs M?'

Her landlady looked out into the hall from her parlour, apparently unperturbed by the shortened use of her name. Jean assumed that the idea that the police were asking her tenant for help was a useful source of gossip, so she was probably willing to put up with 'Mrs M' in the meantime.

'Yes dear?'

'I have to go out for a while, I have no idea when I'll be back.'

'That's alright dear, you just take care. I'll have the kettle on when you get back.'

'Erm, it might be very late.'

'Oh, don't you worry. I'll be here.'

Mrs Moore gave Jean her best smile and waved them both off.

'She's a crafty one. Any chance of getting the news first.'

Lyal gave a shy grin. 'Mrs Moore has quite the reputation for gossip.'

They both laughed quietly; considering their destination this evening, it seemed wrong to be seen sharing a joke. Walking in silence for about forty-five minutes, they eventually came across a scene with police in attendance. Ella, now back in uniform, saw them arriving and approached, thanking Lyal before sending him to help his fellow officers. When they were alone, Ella told Jean what had happened.

'A woman has been found in a side street with her throat cut, again with no evidence of theft or any other physical assault. Her purse is intact, and it doesn't look as if she had much time to put up a fight. She hasn't been formally identified, but we believe she is Shoman Torma, a mother that lives locally with her husband and two children. We have officers on their way now to speak to her family.'

Jean sighed and shut her eyes; another family torn apart by the needless death of a loved one. It never got any easier to accept.

'Can I see the body?'

'It isn't pleasant. Are you sure?'

'Death is never pleasant, but yes, I'm sure.'

Ella led her over towards the scene.

'Forensics are still on site, so try not to get in their way. I've cleared it with Inspector Graves that you can act as a consultant.'

She looked sharply at Ella.

'What exactly have you told him?'

'Nothing, only that I believe you may have knowledge that may help. The fact that you weren't in the city when the murders started helped a lot. At the moment everyone is under suspicion, so if we can be sure that you have a solid alibi, you may be the one to be able to stand back and see more than we do.'

'A fresh mind with fresh eyes.'

Understanding she followed Ella to the scene. The ground was swamped in blood, and both women donned boot protectors to help preserve the scene — as well as their footwear. Approaching the body, Jean noted it was that of a small woman; she looked as if she had been discarded haphazardly in the corner of a doorway. She spoke in quiet tones.

'What was she doing out? Do we know?'

Behind her, a familiar voice answered.

'Apparently she was shopping for the family dinner. She had forgotten a few things and told her husband she would be a few minutes. She never returned.'

Turning, they met Inspector Graves. Jean noted he averted his eyes from the body. Looking back at the scene, Jean seemed lost in thought.

'So where is her shopping?'

Ella shook her head.

'Maybe she was attacked before she made it to the shops?'

'Then where is her shopping bag?'

Ella looked back at the body and seemed unsure of what to say. Graves broke the silence.

'No, she had completed her shopping, some bread and vegetables from what I can gather.'

Ella caught the attention of one of the forensic team, and they exchanged a quick conversation. When she returned to Jean and Graves, she was frowning.

'Nothing, no shopping or bag has been recovered from here or anywhere close by.'

Jean felt an uncomfortable feeling begin to creep up her spine.

'The other murders, you say there was nothing taken. But what about food? Were they carrying any food?'

Graves and Ella looked at each other, then shook their heads.

The inspector said. 'I can't confirm that at the moment, but it will be something to consider. What is the point you are trying to make?'

She shook her head. 'To be honest I am not entirely sure myself, but I would really like to see the case files of the other victims and, if possible, the crime scenes.'

Graves nodded his ascent to Ella.

'Croft, make sure this young lady has all the information she needs.'

Ella inclined her head, then saying their farewells, led Jean away from the scene. They took off their protective clothing and made their way quickly towards the police station.

15

An Unquiet
Mob

J ean and Ella had been hours at the police station, pouring over the case files of the other murder victims; it hadn't been good reading. Whoever was responsible for such horrible crimes, it was becoming obvious they were efficient and quick killers. According to the autopsy reports none of the victims suffered, their deaths were swift and considered professional. A small but saving grace for the victims' families, Jean thought. Reading the transcripts from the families and work colleagues of those who died however, did suggest that the victims were either out shopping, or coming home from work carrying victuals.

Both women, were now sitting in a large dark office, the only light provided by orbs open on their desks. It was late and their eyes were tired. Jean stretched, arching her back to try and ease her muscles.

'Do you want any more tea or coffee?'

Ella was holding up her cup and heading for the kettle sitting on the small stove in the corner of the room.

'Dear gods no. I think I could sink a battleship with the amount I've drunk this evening. Where the hell do you keep it all?'

Ella grinned back. 'Part and parcel of being a policeman, you learn to drink copious amounts of tea and coffee. We can deal with anything you throw at us, as long as we don't run out of either.'

Jean laughed. 'I admire your constitution.'

When Ella returned with another steaming cup, she sat down and fiddled with the pages of the file open on her desk. 'Your theory seems to be holding water Jean.'

She looked up enquiringly. 'What theory is that then?'

Ella stabbed the file. 'The one about the victims carrying food but nothing being found on the bodies.'

'I can't imagine that a court would be convinced.' She looked sceptical. 'It could be argued, that any unscrupulous person may have come across a body, then stolen the food for themselves.'

Ella considered this for a moment.

'But why should they do that? If anyone is hungry, they just need to go along to any of the hostelries in the city, they always have a hot meal available. No-one starves in Parva.'

Jean was reminded of Niall's words all those months ago, how excess food went to feeding the less fortunate. She was now thinking aloud, and Ella listened carefully.

'So, you are saying, no-one should have a legitimate reason to steal food from someone else?' Pinching her bottom lip between her finger and thumb Jean frowned. 'If that was the case, wouldn't it suggest it's because they don't want to be seen out in the open? People tend to be a bit superstitious about stealing from the dead, and no-one in Parva should be that desperate for food, according to you. If that is the case, it does add more weight, albeit not much of one, that whoever killed these people, did it for their food. But nothing else was taken, their purses and clothing were intact. Why? A full purse would be perfect for someone wanting to buy more food.'

Ella shook her head. 'But the fact remains, no money was stolen from any of the bodies. As you say, why?'

Ideas began to form in Jean's mind; she didn't like them one bit.

'To use money would require being out in public, being seen. To just steal food means whoever is doing this can come out of hiding and then retreat quickly.'

Ella nodded. 'Sounds a good theory, but who would do that? The Patrols?'

Jean shook her head. 'Why would they need to hide? They are on the streets already, wearing a uniform that marks them out from the rest of the population. Discretion is hardly on their agenda. No, whoever is doing this doesn't want to be seen because they can be marked as different or recognised.'

Jean was quiet a moment while she considered this further. Ella watched in silence.

'What I would like to know is; is this one person killing to feed themselves or are they several people? Are they stealing their only food source, or are they topping up their menu?'

Ella shrugged. 'We can't know that.'

'No, but it is important we find out. If it is more than one or two people, then the food that has been stolen will not be enough to sustain them, which means someone else is providing food and shelter.

'If that's the case we then have to consider who? And why?'

Both women looked at each other for a while, contemplating Jean's theory. Ella closed the file in front of her in frustration, putting her elbows on the desk and rubbing her tired eyes with her hands.

'It's late, and I should start writing up a report on our thoughts and findings. You should go home Jean, try and get some sleep and I'll contact you in the morning.'

Jean also felt frustrated, but there was very little else she could do here, and Ella was right, she needed to sleep. Reluctantly agreeing she stood up.

'There is one thing you could do for me, however.'

Ella looked up. 'What's that?'

'You could find me a map of the city, otherwise I'm going to get completely lost getting back to Mrs M's.'

Ella chuckled. 'You really are going to have to find your way around soon.'

Rummaging in her desk drawers, she found a small map and marked where they were at the station, then where Jean's lodgings were. It wasn't far in the scheme of things, so taking the main roads Jean should be back in no time. Thanking Ella, she took the map and made her way out of the building. Behind her, the young PC was already writing at her desk.

Armed with her new map, it didn't take long for Jean to get home, and true to her word, Mrs Moore was still up, dozing at the kitchen table. As Jean entered, she woke with a small snore and blinked bleary eyes at her. Glancing at the clock, the landlady stood up and declared that she would put the kettle on and urged Jean to sit down. All Jean wanted to do was go upstairs to bed; the thought of more tea made her stomach lurch. However, as Mrs M had sat up waiting for her, the very least she could do was sit for a short while; but her tea was barely touched.

They talked for nearly half an hour, and Mrs Moore seemed satisfied with the small morsel of information Jean had dared to tell her. Bare details of the victim were given, but any theories she and Ella had discussed were kept to herself.

By the time Jean climbed into bed, she was asleep before her head hit the pillow. Despite the constant blast from the foghorn, which she barely even registered now, she managed to get some sleep. It was a fitful one, full of gory images and men stuffing their faces with bloodied food they had stolen; oblivious to the unrest and mayhem beginning to rise within the city.

John Corvier made his way out through the great double doors of the Imperial Palace. He stood at the top of the steps looking down over the parade square, past the high iron gates that separated the Palace from the main thoroughfare, and the avenue of trees disappearing into the foggy night. Looking at his watch he groaned, it was well after midnight, and the way things were going in the city, it didn't look as if he was going to get any sleep before morning. He breathed in the warm night air, the brine from the sea mixing with the scent of flowers planted around the buildings; softening the harshness of the white stone architecture.

Focusing on the group of angry protesters who now gathered at the gates, he sighed.

Might as well get on with it.

The square, predominantly used for parades and training, was bordered by the guest quarters to his right and the knights' barracks on his left. A single gate remained open at the corner of the barracks where the Order occupied the guard room; two knights stood at the door, apparently in discussion while watching the angry group at the gates.

John made his way down towards the guard room, skirting the edge of the square so as not to walk directly across it; old habits die hard for this old soldier. Aware that now both the guards and the protestors were watching his approach, he slowed his pace slightly, making sure they knew he was also watching them. By the time he had reached the guard room, loud whispering could be heard from the protesters; John smiled to himself, *good*, he needed all the help he could get.

The two guards had broken off their conversation and stood to attention as John approached; he stopped just before them, making sure the people at the gate were still in his view.

'Good evening, my Lord.'

'Evening Major Torvil, Captain Forrest. Please relax gentlemen, we have enough tension out there.'

Both men smiled and stood more at ease. It was always a point of amazement to the members of the Order, that the Lord Knights were always able to acknowledge them by name.

'So, what has been happening? Any trouble?'

It was Major Torvil that answered.

'At the moment, they are quite peaceful and calm. I admit they seem pretty angry, but they haven't done anything other than voice their bitterness.'

John nodded, he appreciated that these experienced and loyal knights, no doubt also had an affiliation to the concerns of those outside the gates, but they would never say so.

'Have there been any other disturbances? Reports are coming in that there's been a fair bit of tension in the city centre.'

'As yet we've not seen or heard anything my Lord, other than the latest murder from the city killer.'

Nodding his head, John said. 'Yes, a nasty business, I'll let you get along and I'll see if I can have a word with our visitors.'

'My Lord.'

Both men stood to attention again before returning to the guardroom and John turned, heading through the gate to meet with the angry group of protestors. By the time he had reached them, the mob had shown some organisation and nominated a spokesperson shoving him to the front of the group. He didn't look entirely pleased with the prospect, but he gathered himself up and put on a brave face; though John was sure he detected a slight gulp in apprehension. Holding his hands out in acquiescence, the Knight decided a softer approach would be a better way to broach this particular hornets' nest.

'Ladies and gentlemen, what brings you out here to the Palace on such a miserable evening?'

The delegated spokesman was prodded forward a bit further, so that he stared up into the face of the giant standing before him. John had become used to people being a bit cautious when near to him. At six foot seven, only his cousin Simon topped his height by a further inch; as hardened soldiers, they were particularly intimidating to those who met them for the first time. John would be happy if the mob's chosen spokesperson just remained on his feet and didn't let the whole situation overwhelm him. Fortunately, after a couple of awkward seconds, the man found his voice. It was bit garbled, but John managed to get his drift.

'My Lord, We…. we didn't expect one of your Lordships to actually come out to us personally.'

A voice from the back of the group, seemed to feel their spokesman was taking far too long to get to the point of their protest, and was far too polite. They also seemed to be bolstered by the anonymity of being in a crowd.

'It's about time you came out of the Palace, actually start doing something about what's going on here in the city, as well as the rest of the Empire.'

John looked up and over the heads of those before him, he saw a young lad with pimples and an unfortunate overbite. The look on the boy's face suggested he only now realised that he had been found out, and was trying his best to hide behind a large woman in front of him. She, however, was having none of it and shoved the boy into view. He watched the lad's bravado slowly fade from his eyes. Placing his hands in his pockets, John nodded.

'A valid point, and one I can't argue with if I'm truly honest with you.'

He paused and watched the look of confusion on the crowd's faces. They weren't expecting him to agree with them.

'I am here on behalf of the Emperor and my fellow Knights to speak with you, to discover the issues you have. I know how frustrated and angry you must be, feeling abandoned and your lives disregarded. I assure you this is far from the truth on all accounts.'

By now the crowd was looking at each other, confused with the reception they had received. The nominated spokesman again found his voice.

'That's all very well my Lord, but there are innocent people being murdered on the streets, no-one is safe. The Patrols are also running unchecked throughout the city, they are gaining popularity among the more disillusioned. Families are turning against each other, in either loyalty to the Emperor, or those who suggest his rule has reached its end.'

His voice petered off as he realised what he was saying, and to who; he gave an involuntary gulp and looked away, stepping back towards the perceived safety of the group behind him. Being urged to speak freely was one thing, to be brutally honest was probably foolhardy.

John felt a large stone seem to settle in his stomach, he was beginning to feel sick. He wished Nathan was here, he was much better at talking to people, but he was already engaged in sorting uprisings throughout the rest of Kelan, as were the rest of the Knights. John sighed and considered his next words carefully.

'Everything you have said here tonight is absolutely true, and yes, the situation that we all face is completely unacceptable. But it is a situation that exists nonetheless. The police are working constantly to try and bring this vicious killer to justice, and we are doing all we can to try and ease the tension that has risen in recent weeks. Ultimately, we are dealing with the issues that have brought us to this point.'

Inside, he desperately wanted to tell these people the true reason why they were the ones suffering, and who was responsible; but he knew that was impossible, at least for now. The spokesman seemed to be growing in confidence at the unexpected confession from one of the Lord Knights.

'But why? Why is this happening?'

All eyes were now firmly on John's face and he was acutely aware that behind him, a whole guard room of knights were also desperate to hear what he had to say. John just shook his head.

'That is information I can't tell you, and I wish I could. Believe me.'

The crowd looked at each other, unhappy mumblings passing between them.

'So, we're just expected to accept that and get on with it?'

Anger was beginning to boost the spokesman's resolve.

'People are being attacked in the streets, shop windows broken. Have you seen the filth they are peddling now?'

A small pamphlet-like book was shoved under his nose. He took it from the man, glancing at the title.

THE FALL OF AN OBSOLETE EMPIRE.

He felt the anger swell within him but forced it down. Having reached the point where these people needed to get home, he was determined to remain calm. Arguing with them wasn't going to help anyone.

'We will sort these issues, but standing here on such a miserable night is not going to help you, or us, resolve them. You should go home and stay safe.'

'While you return to your safe and warm home too, I suppose?'

The spokesperson suddenly stopped, realising he had gone too far. John said nothing but gave him a look that said the discussion was now ended. Turning to the guard room he gave instructions.

'Major Torvil, make sure these people have a safe passage home.'

He received an acknowledgment of his order, then turned back to crowd, who still looked unhappy and belligerent. In a voice that suggested he expected no argument, John said.

'Go home, we are doing all we can.'

With that he turned on his heel and made his way back to the guardroom, passing back through the single gate, forcing himself to maintain the same measured pace, when all he really wanted to do was get as far from there as quickly as possible. Desperately aware of the eyes that followed him, from both the gates and guardroom, he made his way towards the sweeping steps of the Palace. By the time he reached the large double doors, he finally dared to glance back. It was with relief that Major Torvil and his knights, were now escorting the unhappy group back towards the city and their homes.

Cursing under his breath he clenched his fists, feeling his fingernails sharp against the rough skin of his hands. Striding across the hall, he made his way up the staircase two steps at a time; one way or another they had to take action, and to hell with Ephea and her damned family.

16

Memories

The next morning, Jean woke up feeling more tired than when she first went to bed. Sitting up, she felt a tightness at the back of her head, threatening a headache later. She rubbed her neck, while making her way to the bathroom to stand under a hot deluge of water, trying to ease away the tension growing there. After her shower, she walked across the room and caught the image of herself in the mirror, the familiar, but tired, green eyes stared back. Raising her hand she ran a finger along the scar that ran from just above her right breast, down her cleavage and ended just above her left hip. Memories of pain, terror and hopelessness flashed across her brain and she looked away, rubbing her towel roughly across her skin to try and block out the memories that threatened to surface; she failed.

As clear as if it were happening now, she could smell the reek of blood and fear, feel the gore on her hands and feet as she tried to get away from the killing fields. Men and women dying in horrible pain, crying out for comfort, terrified of spending their last moments alone, buried beneath the butchered bodies of the dead. It didn't matter who they were, friend or foe, death welcomed them all equally. It had taken everything she had to wade through the dead and dying, desperately seeking out the comfort of safety; covered in cuts and bruises, blood and gore, she had almost made it.

When the attack came, she was completely taken by surprise. So much pain and confusion pervaded her senses, she couldn't feel the danger until it was too late. The blade had slashed across her body; a deadly wound that should have cost her life. Instinct had forced her hand to strike out and cut the throat of the assailant; a man whose eyes betrayed the madness of battle that had overwhelmed him. His blood bubbling in his open throat, was the last thing that Jean heard before pain and blood loss overwhelmed her and she passed out.

Her hand reached out for the wall; for a brief moment the room spun, and Jean shook her head to clear her mind of the memories.

Looking back into the mirror, she also saw the signs of change, a tightness around her mouth, her green eyes had a hardened glint. All indicating that the stronger, more assertive Jean was emerging. She looked away quickly. To most people they wouldn't notice, but to those who knew her, who had worked with her over the years, they would see them and understand. But work was needing to be done and a more proactive energy was required. She stretched and worked her muscles, ready for the day ahead; whatever it may bring she would be ready.

Forcing the memories down, she finished getting dressed before heading downstairs for breakfast and Mrs Moore.

She found her landlady bustling around the kitchen looking agitated, her usual immaculate image was now slightly spoilt by her hair sticking up as if she had run her hands through it once too often.

'Good morning Mrs M, how are you?'

The landlady threw herself against the wall, her eyes wide with fear. Jean thought she had missed her calling for the stage.

'Oh my goodness, what a fright you gave me.'

Holding her hands to her ample breasts, Mrs Moore demonstrated that whatever was bothering her hadn't affected her ability for the dramatic.

Jean rushed forward to steady her and help her to a kitchen chair. 'I'm sorry, I didn't mean to startle you. Is everything alright? You seem a little out of sorts this morning.'

Throwing her hands in the air, as if in resignation to some terrible fate that she had no control of, she flopped her arms down onto the kitchen table with as much dramatic flair as she could muster.

'Oh my dear, we are all heading for hell.'

'I'm sure you are destined for much more congenial surroundings Mrs M, and it will be a fair few years before you need to worry about that journey.'

'Well yes, you're perfectly correct in that regard, but I'm talking about out there.'

She waved her arms once more.

'The chaos, the bloodshed, the city is dying.'

Throwing her head into her arms Mrs Moore began to moan, which threatened to turn into a wail. It seemed a good night's sleep had recharged the more dramatic aspect of her landlady, and Jean began to regret talking to her last night. Seeing the imminent danger, Jean hurried to her side and placed a comforting, if awkward, arm around her landlady's shoulders. Fortunately, this seemed to help abate the threatened deluge of tears.

'I'll put the kettle on and you can tell me all about it. Nothing a cup tea can't fix.' *Though a glass or two of brandy would probably be more appropriate.*

Once the tea had been poured, and Mrs Moore was satisfied she had the full attention of her audience, she unburdened her woes regarding the fate of the city.

'It's been awful. I was out earlier this morning and I caught up with Mrs Thoms, from the corner shop, you know, the one whose son was at sea.'

Jean nodded encouragingly, she hadn't a clue who Mrs Thoms and her son were, but she didn't need Mrs M going off on a tangent now.

'Well, she was saying that the police and the Order have been out all night, people fighting in the streets, vandalism, and some very rude things written on walls. It seems the murder of poor Mrs Torma was the last straw; people have had enough.'

Folding her arms under her bosom protectively, she adopted a more self-satisfied look upon her face.

'Of course we wouldn't have heard anything around here; we're not that sort of area.'

Again Jean nodded in encouragement.

'So, these attacks have been confined to only a small part of the city? Do they know who's responsible? I didn't hear anything last night on my way back from the police station.'

'Oh no. They've been all over the place. Apparently, there has even been a rabble protesting outside the Palace gates.'

Jean fought hard to stop the laughter building inside. The irony that Mrs Moore considered that her home was not *one of those areas*, but the Palace was, had obviously not penetrated her conceitedness. There was a knock at the front door and Mrs Moore, obviously still feeling fragile after the shock of such awful goings on in her city, let Jean go and answer it. Jean wasn't surprised to see Ella standing there when she opened the door. She did note however, that the young woman was looking exhausted. Dark rings were beginning to form under her eyes and Jean was quite concerned.

'Come in Ella. Are you alright?'

Barely even attempting to stifle a huge yawn, Ella entered the house and followed Jean into the kitchen.

'It's been a busy night.'

'Mrs M here has been telling me, there have been a few fights and some vandalism, even the Palace has been targeted. She reckons it's down to our murder lighting the spark.'

This time it was Ella's turn to do the nodding dog impression. Mrs Moore was pleased to see her information confirmed, and eager to hear more from someone who had actually been involved, though her face fell when Ella suggested that Jean join her for breakfast elsewhere.

'I can make you something here if you want.'

Jean was quick to see the look of warning on the PC's face.

'No, that's alright Mrs M, we'll get out of your hair and leave you in peace.'

The landlady's face was quite mutinous as they both made their way back up the hallway and out of the front door, Jean could feel her stare boring into the back of her neck.

'Thank goodness for that. Good call about going out for breakfast, Mrs M was all set for a full rendition of the night's events.'

'She was there? Out at that time of night on her own?'

'Of course not, she was sitting up waiting for me with yet another cup of tea.'

Jean felt her stomach lurch again, she needed food.

'But she isn't going to let it stop her from regaling everything that apparently happened, no doubt with her own additional flourishes. Well, that's after those added by Mrs Thoms of course.'

'Ah yes, Mrs Thoms. I went to school with her son. He's at sea now.'

Jean looked sideways at her companion. 'Do you know everyone?'

'Not *everyone*, but I am a police constable, it's my business to know people, and Mrs Thoms does have some very useful gossip at times.'

Before she could reply, Ella was striding up the road in front of her.

'Come on, I'm starving.'

They made their way through the city streets, and Jean saw there was a marked increase in the presence of police and knights around. She also noted with relief, that the fog had started to thin into more of a mist, lifted by the breeze that had picked up from the direction of the sea. The foghorn was still blaring at intervals though, which suggested that visibility at sea was still bad, but the lightening of the air would be a boost to the gloom that had settled around.

Passing through the city, proof of the previous night's tension was more evident than Jean appreciated it would be. Broken shop windows were still being boarded up by their owners, whilst the presence of police was doing their best to discourage looting. Occasionally blackened stonework and stumps of wood told of possible arson, though the damage was limited, suggesting it was dealt with quickly before it got out of hand.

The most disturbing evidence of the troubles was still being played out however, a large crowd had gathered, and they had to force their way forward to see what was going on. At the entrance to one of the lanes leading to the harbour from one of the main squares, it seemed that residents had erected a barrier, stopping anyone from entering or leaving. More than a dozen police were making a valiant effort to persuade the angry mob to take down their makeshift wall, of what seemed to be anything they could get hold of at the time. Everything was game apparently in its construction; furniture, including tables, chairs, cupboards and one or two double beds were perched precariously on top. Watching with interest they observed the attempts to bring the standoff to a peaceful conclusion; there seemed to be people standing behind the angry residents, whispering and goading.

Jean felt Ella tense next to her.

'Patrols.'

True enough, those appearing to encourage the mayhem had all the hallmarks of the Patrols; their garb showing the makeshift uniform they preferred.

'What will the police do if they can't calm this lot down?'

Jean nodded to a group of knights, both mounted and on foot across the square, they remained detached from the scene while still watching intently.

Ella sighed. 'To be honest, for many, it will be too little, too late.'

Suddenly there was a shout, and something was thrown from behind the barrier. Whatever it was had hit its mark. Someone in the police line fell to the ground. For a terrifying moment Jean thought it was all going to end in a blood bath. The police line, angry at the attack on one of their own, made to rush forward. Behind the barricade, the residents seemed panicked, cries of *who did that?* rang out in the confusion.

But then, with a speed that Jean considered pretty impressive, the mounted knights were between the police and the barrier. They stood facing the police however, not the angry, confused mob.

The knights on foot didn't bother with the barricade. They had made their way through the buildings on either side and were now facing the mob, pinning them, and the startled Patrols, against the piled high furniture.

By then fight seemed to drain from the protesters when they realised the precarious position they were in and they soon surrendered. Arrangements were made swiftly to take them away, and the makeshift wall of furniture dismantled.

Impressed with the rapid and efficient way the Order had taken care of the incident, Jean asked. 'What will happen to them?'

Ella shrugged. 'Oh they'll have time to cool their heels in several cells around the city. The residents will probably be home, shamefaced and relieved by this evening. The Patrol members, however, may not be so lucky, the knights have been waiting for an opportunity like this for a long while now.'

'What do you mean?'

'The knights have effectively been confined to barracks, no idea why, but it means the Patrols have been fairly safe as long as they stay within the law. But while the police are the representation of the law in the cities, it is the knights who represent the Empire. You really don't want to piss them off.'

Jean nodded, already the barricade had almost disappeared. The police were now talking with the knights, it looked quite heated.

Probably letting them know their own views on the Order's interference.

Jean had to admit, for whatever reasons they had been curtailed from their duties previously, it was obvious the knights were still a highly trained and disciplined force. They must have been relieved to finally be free of their confinement; at least for a while.

Both women decided that they had seen enough excitement for the morning, and hunger pangs encouraged them to move on to more pressing matters concerning their stomachs. Finding seats in the café they were in the day before, they sat down and ordered from the waitress who still looked just as harassed as she did yesterday. Looking out of the window they saw that the milliner's shop window was now boarded up, closed for business. Jean turned to her companion.

'So what else has happened?'

'Obviously Mrs Moore's grapevine hasn't stretched quite far enough yet.'

She paused before continuing.

'Aleix Bales has been found dead. Stabbed.'

Jean looked at her, stunned.

'Dead? Where? Do they know who did it? Was it part of the disruption last night?'

'We don't think so. Actually, we've arrested Daven Hillside.'

'Who?'

'Morna's father.'

Ella looked at her as if Jean should have known this fact.

'I had no idea that was his name.'

'Aleix was found outside a tavern of, shall we say, less salubrious surroundings, down by the docks. He'd been stabbed through the heart.'

Jean was quiet for a while, when their breakfast arrived, she waited until the waitress had finally stomped away before shaking her head.

'There is no way Daven Hillside is responsible for this, or at least not the actual murder.'

Ella wasn't convinced. 'You can't know that for sure.'

'Oh I think I can.'

Ella's brows furrowed. She didn't look pleased that Jean dare suggest that the police could ever be wrong. Jean carried on, explaining her thoughts.

'First of all, Daven knows that Aleix has been accused of his daughter's rape, he even attacked him in the hospital and gave him a bloodied nose. There is no love lost between those two.'

'Exactly, Daven has already attacked once.'

'It was a lucky punch from an angry man. But in any other circumstances, Aleix, a strong young man, would never have allowed himself to be overpowered by an older man like Daven.'

'But what if he just got another *lucky* strike in?'

'Well that's another point; you say it was a stab wound directly to the heart. Was it from behind or the front?'

Ella sighed knowing where this was going.

'The front.'

'So a fit young man agrees to meet a man he that he can be pretty damned sure hates him, in a dodgy part of the city and lets him, not only get close enough with a knife, but also able to impart a single stab wound to the heart. Which, let's be clear, is not as easy as it sounds, you need to know what you are doing.'

Ella looked down at her breakfast and suddenly didn't feel quite so hungry.

'Alright, I concede Daven doesn't look such a good candidate now, but someone did deliberately kill Aleix. Who else had the motive to do this? I know the attack was all over the papers, but even the tabloids weren't stupid enough to print the names of those concerned.'

'I don't know Ella, but one very good possibility is that they knew Aleix, he trusted them enough to meet him in a dangerous place, while also letting them get close enough to kill him.'

Ella nodded. 'Alright, I'll get back to the station after this and have a word with Graves. It's just weird that Aleix's mother is adamant that it was Daven who sent a note to her son arranging a meeting.'

'Really? That is odd, and she didn't have any reservations about Daven's motive or that her son should go to such a meeting?'

'She has said nothing more than Daven arranged the meeting, and Aleix is now dead.'

The two women looked at each other, considering the possibilities forming in their thoughts. They ate the rest of their breakfast in silence, contemplating the events of the past twenty-four hours and it made for an uncomfortable meal. Eventually Jean broke the silence by discussing her intent on visiting the museum and library that morning.

'You might be unlucky today, one of the buildings attacked last night was the museum. I don't know how extensive the damage is, but it would be under the Order's jurisdiction. They may not let you in.'

Jean swore quietly and Ella raised an eyebrow.

'Sorry, but it's frustrating.' She shrugged. 'I'll just have to see when I get there I suppose.'

By the time the two women had left the café, a weak sun was trying to push through the gloom. Ella gave final instruction for directions to the bridge that would lead her up the main highway and then onto the university campus.

'The museum is part of the complex but is a separate building. It is signposted once you get inside; if you get inside.'

'Don't you ever look on the positive side?'

'Why?'

Jean shook her head and was at a loss to answer. Eventually the two bade farewell, Ella on her way back to the police station to report their awkward discussion to Graves; Jean towards the river Par and the North Bank. She crossed the bridge that spanned the river and mist swirled around the boats that anchored alongside both banks. Taking her time, she watched the stevedores at work, loading and unloading barges and tall sailing ships. Cargo moved from inland to sea and vice versa. This was a busy port and lock gates to the entrances of the many individual quays were open due to the high tide of the river, allowing craft to pass to and from the Par. It looked hectic and dangerous work, everyone was concentrating on their labours, quite oblivious to a single woman watching from the bridge.

Downstream, ships passed as they headed in and out to sea via the great harbour wall, still lost in the mist. Upstream, smaller boats carried their wares upriver to the towns that lined its banks inland. Jean saw, that while people had access to these gates or portals that Niall had referred to, they still preferred to transport freight this way. She was beginning to see this world called Kelan, and its association with the Empire, was a mixture of opposites that came together, but somehow, they formed a whole that seemed to work. Until recently that is, now things were slowly unravelling. Giving a last look out over the water, she turned her attention back to the North Bank and the university campus that resided there.

Nothing is going to get fixed with you daydreaming all day Jean.

Making her way up the main highway, she was impressed with the sheer size of the thoroughfare. It was wide enough that trees grew in the middle of the road as well as along the pavements, amongst well-tended flowerbeds. On either side of the street were large buildings that seemed to be offices alongside residential homes. Shops were also open, and Jean guessed that while this may be the municipal centre of the city, people still lived and worked here, so opportunity for retail was never going to be far behind. Finally, as she walked further up the treelined avenue, she eventually came to a corner that opened out onto a huge open expanse; it was set further back behind the buildings that lined the avenue.

Different buildings of varying styles and sizes were dotted within the grounds. A signpost beside a large statue of a man holding a number of books, indicated that these were the various colleges of the university.

She also saw, with both intrigue and dismay, that there were a hell of a lot of knights milling around. Whatever happened here last night, they were taking it very seriously. Checking the signpost for the museum, she made her way towards its general direction. She passed a number of knights on her journey, but none tried to stop her, despite the obvious looks of suspicion on their faces. This was the first time Jean had actually been up close to any of the Order since she had been in Kelan, until now they had been confined to their garrisons and barracks, only visible while guarding the city gate. She could easily imagine Niall as one of them in his black uniform and silver insignia. The Tree was present on all of their high collars, denoting their allegiance to the Empire and the Order; other regalia along sleeves and across shoulders, seemed to stand for their rank and regiment. She just assumed the shinier stuff, meant the higher up the ladder the wearer stood.

Eventually, after following the signs and passing though parks and copses of trees, she saw the building that was signposted as the museum.

It was huge.

Admitting to herself that she hadn't realised it would be quite as big as this, she worried she wouldn't have time to gather all the information she needed. There were a lot of knights around this area, and she saw that many of them carried a fair bit of silver on their shoulders and sleeves. She didn't think they were going to be so willing to let her walk in without some protest.

'Can I help you?'

Jean spun round, two knights, one man and one woman, approached her from her right. She attempted a disarming smile and answered.

'Erm, yes maybe you can. I was hoping to visit the museum today. I'm staying with my old aunt for the Midsummer Festival and she said this is an excellent place to visit while I am here.'

The knights shook their heads, the man, who wore the greater amount of silver, answered.

'I'm very sorry, but the museum will not be open today.'

'Oh really. Is everything alright?' Jean felt her acting skills were failing miserably by the lack of enthusiasm on the knight's faces. Her landlady could probably teach her a few dramatic techniques.

'It's nothing you need to concern yourself with.'

He smiled, but Jean was all too aware of the lack of warmth in his eyes. This apparently was her cue to leave.

'Maybe tomorrow then.'

He gave a barely perceptible nod of his head.

'Maybe.'

Neither knight moved, and she found that she had to retrace her steps, aware that now there were a number of eyes following her until she was out of sight. She groaned; she was going to have to do this the hard way. Making sure there was no-one around to see her, she skirted around the campus, making her way to the College of Science. It was apparently, in the general direction of the museum, but fortunately it hadn't been closed. Here she saw people in everyday garb, milling around, talking or making their way into the college.

Jean rolled her eyes. *Students, you can tell them anywhere.*

Taking a general stroll through the grounds, hoping she didn't stick out too much, and continued to make her way to the back of the building and out of sight. She could see the imperial museum across the park, and was relieved to see a number of mature trees planted around it. The work amongst the fields, since arriving in Kelan, had made her fitter and stronger than she had felt in a long time, and now, as she made her way through the grounds quickly to the trees, she was glad of it. Keeping her head low, she checked for the presence of anyone nearby by opening up her senses; finally she was in luck, there was no-one around, the majority of the Order appeared to be concentrated on the front of the building.

Soon she was close enough to the building to see that there was an open window on the first floor, all the lower windows were barred, which was probably understandable for a building that contained possible priceless artefacts. The open window was a bonus, if maybe a security error, but Jean wasn't complaining, having illicitly climbed into many a tight space over the years.

It didn't take long for her to cross the small expanse from the trees to the base of the wall, then checked again for anyone approaching nearby. When she considered it safe enough to continue, she checked her footing and began to climb, using the architecture and convenient downpipes that adorned the face of the wall. When she was finally at the open window, Jean alighted into a small room that was being used as an office, fortunately empty at present. She crossed towards the closed door and listened, sensing. For now, her luck stayed and the way was clear. Still being cautious, Jean opened the door gently, made a cursory check, then silently moved into the corridor.

17

Si Vis Pacem, Para Bellum

I t was early morning and Nathan stifled a yawn while he sat at the meeting table in his office, which, like the one at his home in Devon, was also a large circular, wooden structure. Surrounding it sat the other six Knights; they all had the slightly bleary-eyed look of men who had spent the night awake. With all of the troubles in Parva, the Knights had dared to step forward, trying to ease the chaos that was beginning to rise within the city. Unfortunately, Parva was not alone within the Empire dealing with the increase in public disorders, though not on the same scale. Once the Knights had intervened, peace was mostly achieved; albeit a tenuous one.

However, even though the Knights had finally dealt with the problems arising, for many it was seen as doing far too little, far too late.

The seven men around the table were feeling angry and useless, emotions were fuelled by exhaustion and shame of their impotence at their job. Nathan displayed his frustration by suddenly slamming his hands down on the table with a crash. He stood, leaning over the table with his hands spread upon the surface and looked about the table.

'What the fuck is going on?'

Brought out of their reverie by the sudden noise, the others looked up then at each other. They watched in silence as Nathan eventually moved to the window; no-one said anything, they didn't need to, they all shared his sentiments. Rubbing his hands over his tired face in an effort to wake himself up, Nathan turned and looked at his Knights sitting at the table. The pent-up fury was palpable, he had to do something to alleviate the situation, or he was going to have a mini mutiny to deal with here too.

Damien watched his cousin pace back and forth like a caged animal; he too was concerned about the possibility of uncontrolled anger exploding forth, not from the others, but from Nathan himself.

Nathan had a habit of keeping things to himself, not because he was secretive, but because more often than not, he felt that he alone carried the responsibility of dealing with such things. It frustrated Damien no end, as he knew how negative this could be. At times like this, Nathan needed everyone onboard, he couldn't be expected to deal with all this alone, not now. But some things really were easier said than done. Briefly glancing at his notes in front of him, Damien looked back into the concerned face of his cousin, best friend and Emperor.

'The reports from cities across the Empire have confirmed that any disturbances that arose overnight have been quelled. Unconfirmed evidence has been brought forward that much of the unrest has been provoked, and kindled, unsurprisingly by the Patrols themselves.'

Picking up a sheet of paper in front of him as if he needed a prompt, though Damien knew the words perfectly well, he continued.

'The general consensus is that, and I quote, "*The Emperor and those lazy bastards he calls Guardian Knights, should be getting off their arses and start protecting the people they swore to serve.*" Unquote.'

He placed the paper back onto the table and looked up at the faces around him, all, he noticed thankfully, had the decency to blush.

'Pretty eloquently put I thought.'

Nathan returned to his seat and sat down heavily.

'What happened to the protestors at the gates this morning? Please tell me they weren't dragged away and left seething in a cold cell somewhere.'

From the opposite side of the table John shook his head.

'Thankfully no; after a short discussion with the protesters themselves, they were escorted, peacefully, back to their homes. I can't guarantee that they will be so acquiescent next time though.'

'You think there will be a next time?'

Paul, sitting next to John asked.

'Don't you?'

John also placed the thin book, that had been thrust in his hand the previous evening, into the centre of the table.

'This apparently, is a reason for a lot of the fighting that has been taking place.'

He held Nathan's gaze.

'People are beginning to taking sides.'

Nathan picked up the book and briefly flicked through the pages. Angry, incendiary words stood out, but nothing that would stand up to a professional argument. But it was enough to cause a rift within communities that felt misused and forgotten. Dangerous propaganda.

Damien watched him put the book down amongst his own papers, aware that when this meeting ended, Nathan was likely to be scrutinising every page.

Nathan then looked up and faced him.

'Have you ensured that all the Order now know to help the authorities where they can?'

Soon after the first reports of the troubles the previous night, Nathan had made the decision to use the Order to help with keeping the peace. Aware that this action in itself could be seen as an act of aggression, they were ordered to only help when needed. Fortunately, reports so far suggested that, whilst the troubles had still carried on through the night, most uprisings were dealt with early and unable to grow into complete disasters.

But for how long can they keep this up? Damien thought.

Daniel, who sat on the other side of Nathan, caught his attention. Noting that his friend still had the look of mutiny in his eye, Damien hoped he would keep it in check for all their sakes.

Cautiously he asked. 'Have there been any reports from the police to suggest that things are now easing in the city?'

Daniel nodded; exhaustion etched in his face. He'd spent most of the past twelve hours moving around the Empire putting out fires both metaphorical and physical.

'For the moment everything has become quiet. People seem to have calmed down, at least for now.'

Next to Damien, Paul found it difficult to remain quiet.

'But isn't that the point? We've managed to keep things under control for now, but how long before things escalate again? And this time the police can't just rely on the Order for backup.'

Damien understood Paul's concern, he had very personal reasons to want the troubles to be kept in check in the city; then again so did he.

Simon spoke up. 'Surely one thing we can do, is enforce a curfew.'

Damien was dismayed to see several nods of agreement met with this suggestion, but it was Nathan who answered.

'To go down that route now, at this time would be disastrous. There are already people coming into the city due to the Midsummer Festival. Also, to be fair, the opportunity for people wanting to celebrate may be enough to keep their thoughts on less mutinous activities.'

The sceptical looks on the other faces mirrored his own, but he carried on anyway.

'Besides, people do have a right to protest, and to be honest, I feel like joining them myself right now.'

Simon wasn't willing to give in that easily.

'But these people are not just protesting, there is incitement here from other parties, parties who have no interest in the troubles of those that live within the cities.'

Nathan sighed and bit back his impatience.

'I know, but at the end of the day, the message we send out now will set the tone for the coming days, possibly weeks. If we go in heavy handed, we will become the ones who let the Patrols get away with their actions, while the innocent are punished for fighting back. We have to be careful. I'm not saying a curfew is out of the question, but things would have to get a lot worse before we go down that route. At the moment we have protests and the outbreak of petty fighting, if we're not careful we will end up with full scale riots.'

John sat forward in his seat. 'What about the vandalism? And these murders? The police are still no nearer to figuring out who is systematically killing off innocent people.'

Daniel answered him. 'A few broken windows and daubs of paint on walls, already being dealt with by the guilds and police. Regarding the murders, there is a suggestion that there is some sort of breakthrough there, but I have no further details.'

Everyone suddenly turned to Daniel, but it was Paul who spoke what everyone else was thinking.

'They know who the killer is?'

Daniel shook his head. 'No, not yet, but they have a start of a possible lead.'

Nathan agreed. 'To be honest, if there is any way forward on that one, I'll take it.'

Everyone else nodded, it was a relief to hear something positive.

'And the museum?'

Simon was sitting back in his chair, pulling at an annoying rag on one of his fingernails. Nathan looked up; confusion crossed his face.

'What about it? What can anyone possibly want to do there?'

Simon looked up. 'There have been reports that a particular area was targeted, though due to certain safety features, the prowlers were unable to gain entrance to do any further damage.'

Nathan put his head in his hands. 'Ah, *that* exhibit.'

Simon nodded. '*That* exhibit.'

'Someone is definitely trying to get a message across, I'll give them that.'

Stephen had spoken up for the first time.

'Do you think Ephea, her sisters and their father are responsible for all of this?'

Nathan shook his head.

'To be honest, no.'

Stephen was surprised by this.

'Really? Surely, they would love to see us running around, trying to put out fires and keep all of this chaos under control.'

Nathan laughed sardonically.

'No, they like the highlife far too much. They were happy enough to go along with all the threats and intimidation when it suited them, but this is a level that they haven't anticipated. Their cash cow could easily come to an end if this whole episode carries on.'

Simon nodded. 'So, whoever has been pulling Ephea and her family's strings, because let's face it we know they didn't start this, is now stepping forward?'

There was a general nod in agreement. Stephen cleared his throat and they all turned.

'There is of course another ideal candidate for this sudden rise in unrest.'

Daniel looked at him enquiringly. 'Who?'

Stephen spread his hands.

'Our new female stranger of course, things have been happening more so since she has been brought to our attention.'

John, Paul and Simon nodded in agreement, but Damien and Daniel just looked at each other.

Damien willed Daniel to keep quiet and not mention their recent conversation, he didn't need him to start airing his own frustration. Instead he put forward his own argument against Stephen's suggestion.

'While I see where you are coming from there, it doesn't explain why Ephea would send Captain Johnson out looking for her if she knew who she was.'

It was Paul that answered.

'Well, it fits the scenario that Ephea and her family don't know the whole story, and that whoever is responsible for all this mess is happy to keep them out of the way for now.'

More nodding ensued. Nathan sat forward; Damien felt himself brace for the coming storm.

'She isn't responsible for all this, I still believe that she is here to help us, not make it worse.'

'You can't possibly know that for sure.'

The look of consternation on Paul's face couldn't hide the fact that he was gearing up for a fight. Damien found himself groaning inside, they really didn't need to open old wounds, not now. But then Nathan seemed equally hellbent on self-destruction.

'I know, because we have a shared connection, I have sensed her in the city.'

Damien had to force himself not to bury his head in his hands, the dark looks on Daniel's face didn't give him much hope for any help in that direction. Nathan continued.

'When we were in Rassen, there seemed to be something that passed between this woman and I. At the time I dismissed it as tiredness and fanciful thought, but a few days ago I felt the same thing again, though this time it was somewhere out in the city. She is here.'

Paul wasn't to be put off so easily.

'All that shows us, is that she was in the city when the *shit really hit the fan* as they say. If anything, it strengthens the argument.'

Nathan furrowed his brows and Damien succumbed to burying his head in his hands.

Nathan carried on. 'I'm telling you she is not malicious.'

Paul was getting into his stride.

'That can be nothing more than just a fictitious notion, we don't even know who she is.'

'Yes, we do.'

Damien brought his head up quickly, all eyes were suddenly on Daniel. Nathan stared confused for a moment.

'We do?'

Damien began to notice a slight glint in Daniel's eye, he was sure Nathan hadn't missed it either.

Be careful Daniel

The fair-haired man who had spent most of the meeting in silence, just listening and watching, opened a file that sat in front of him.

'First of all, further to the headline in the papers concerning the recent appalling rape in the city, I now have all the details of the case.'

He lifted the file slightly off the table as if to confirm this.

'There is a lot of information that has now come to light, and I have to admit it is pretty disturbing.' He looked up as he spoke and caught Nathan's eye; he had his full attention.

'Names of the victim and her alleged attacker have been released. Morna Hillside and her fiancé, Aleix Bales.'

They all sat up at this.

'General Bales' son?'

Daniel nodded to Damien.

'The one and the same.'

'Shit.'

'And that isn't the end of it. Apparently both parties were accusing the other of leaking the story to the papers; of course they both denied it emphatically. However, information has come to light that it was in fact members of the Patrols, assuming the identities of two male nurses, that were responsible.'

'That's impossible.' Stephen was incredulous. 'My staff would never allow an imposter to enter the wards.'

'Well, it appears in this instance, they did.'

Stephen made to argue further but Nathan stepped in.

'I'm sure you will have plenty of opportunity to investigate later, but for now Daniel please carry on.'

It was now Stephen's turn to look murderous, but he said nothing.

Daniel continued. 'There has been additional news this morning that Aleix Bales was found dead in the dockland area, stabbed through the heart. The girl's father has been arrested and is now being questioned by the police.'

'Dear gods.' Damien shook his head in dismay.

'This doesn't tell us who the stranger is though does it?'

'Patience Paul, I'm getting there.'

Paul frowned; Damien could see annoyance cross his face as he felt the possibility for a good argument ebb away.

Daniel continued. 'There are also details of a witness who saw the rape itself, or at least the attacker, as he left the scene immediately after the incident. It was her statement, along with forensic evidence, that has enabled the police to consider bringing charges.'

Damien leaned forward. 'So, who is she? And how do you know this is the same woman as our stranger in Rassen?'

'I will get around to telling you if you would stop interrupting.'

Pausing as if to prove a point, Daniel then carried on.

'Her name is Jean Carter. She entered the city a number of days ago, and is currently staying at lodgings not far from the South Bank docklands. She has been helping the police since she arrived, in particular a PC Ella Croft, who has demonstrated an aptitude for her work and shown a great deal of potential for the future.'

Nathan nodded. 'That would be Major Croft's daughter. There is no love lost between General Bales and that family. But you're sure this Jean Carter is the same woman?'

'I've had some people asking around and it seems she arrived on a barge a few days ago. She was part of a group of labourers that have been working their way west on the farms between Rassen and Parva. The same description each time. Tall, fair, green eyes and not local to the area.'

As Daniel finished, Nathan stood up again and made his way to the window, this time calmer. When he turned back to the table, he seemed more resolute.

'We know from our own experience that when we are sent anywhere on one of these damned missions, it is usually when hell has already been let loose. More often than not, it can get worse before it gets better.'

The others sat in silence. Experience had taught them that Nathan had now made a decision, the time for arguments was over.

'Keep finding out what you can about this Jean Carter, but still keep a distance.'

He paused and looked out over the city; the fog was already thinning to a mist.

'Keep the Order's presence within the city up, but still only as an aid to the police. There will be no curfew, but there will be a more continuous, obvious presence of the Order. That should keep the peace around the city for at least a while.'

Damien nodded. 'But what about Ephea and her bloody family?'

Nathan shook his head.

261

'To be honest, I think they may have become superfluous to whatever plans have been made by our unknown puppeteer. If they have started to up the hostilities, we have to respond likewise.'

'But what about Ephea…?'

'I know, but that's something we have to deal with, if and when it arises. Pray to the Gods it won't come to that. But as a precaution just keep the Order as a continuing peacekeeping presence, not as a military force.'

He sat back down again and looked around at the faces of the Knights.

'There is a saying on Earth which I consider very apt at this time, '*Si vis pacem, para bellum*. If you want peace, prepare for war.'

18

The Museum

J ean stood in the corridor and listened. She couldn't hear anyone nearby, but her senses told her that there were people somewhere around. She had to be careful, and quiet. Satisfied she was safe for now, Jean took a few moments to take pleasure in her surroundings; she loved museums. As a child, she would spend hours walking around places like this, avidly peering through the glass panels of exhibits, reading their descriptions and imagining what they would have been like when they were brand new; part of someone's real life.

She was always a strange child, more likely to have her nose in some book rather than interested in boys and fashion as the other girls did. Of course, she paid the price for it, bullies found children like her perfect targets; pushing her desire to escape, hiding within other worlds and having adventures with imaginary characters.

Now she breathed in the cool, familiar air associated with such huge buildings. Looking around the lofty halls and vaulted ceilings, conscious of her footsteps making a noise in such open spaces. Before her, was a long stone balcony, skirting the first-floor corridors like the passages that surrounded a cloister. Looking tentatively over the balustrade, she was careful to stay out of sight of anyone wondering around. She peered down onto a large inner hall that housed, what seemed to be, an exhibition on polar exploration. Jean was itching to go and have a quick look, to find out more, but that would have to be for another day, when she had time for a leisurely peruse. Turning back to look along the corridor she was already in, she searched for any signs that might tell her where to find details of the Knights themselves. Ella had talked of a specific exhibit that would have all the information she needed, but apparently, for now its whereabouts would remain elusive. Choosing a direction, she made her way further into the building, looking for signs that may help in her search.

Moving throughout the museum she passed other corridors that tempted her to have quick look. History, both ancient and modern; Science, Zoology and Geology; every subject enticing her in, but she resisted. One exhibit very nearly succeeded in pulling her in, simply entitled

EARTH

Ducking her head around the door, a huge model of a steam engine stood, marking the entrance to the rest of the exhibit behind. She sighed longingly and dragged herself away; this would be the first point of call when she had the time.

Eventually, after passing through numerous halls and floors, she saw the signs she had been looking for;

IMPERIAL KNIGHTS
Guardians

As Jean neared the area, she began to hear voices somewhere close by. She stopped short at a corner that led into a main hall, and peering round slowly, she swore to herself. There were a group of people, whom she assumed were a forensic team, working at the entrance to the area that she was interested in.

The exhibit doors were open.

One man stood up and held his hand to the small of his back, while another looked on and chuckled.

'You're getting old, perhaps you should consider a desk job.'

Rapidly taking his hands from his back and making a particular effort to stand straight, the older man grumbled.

'There is nothing wrong with me, I'll still be here a few years yet.'

The first younger man, looked to his fellow workers for assistance in the possibility of some fun, but he found them averting their eyes. He would find no sport amongst this lot, he dropped his head and carried on with his work, scowling. The older man seeing the tension tried to change the subject.

'It's a good job this is area is protected by extra security at night, the god's alone know what damage could have been caused if they'd got in.'

A middle-aged woman looked up and nodded.

'Don't you think it's strange that this is the only part of the museum that has been damaged at all? No other exhibits have been touched as far as we can see.'

'Maybe that's the point, whoever did this was trying to make a statement. It's not just blatant vandalism, it's targeted to a very specific group of people.'

'Well, whoever did this must be mad; I wouldn't want to piss them off.'

There was a general murmur of assent around the group, and the younger man put his head up again.

'They've not exactly done themselves any favours recently, have they? I'm surprised it hasn't happened sooner.'

The look of shock and disgust from his fellow workers made him shake his head. Putting his head down, the look on his face was mutinous.

Jean watched the team at work and listened to their exchange, feeling the tension grow between them. Above them, paint had been daubed across the walls and doors to the exhibit.

EMPIRE BE DEAD

Not exactly poetic, Jean thought. Probably just a delinquent doing a job they'd been hired to do, imagination was unlikely to be a requirement. There was nothing she could do for now though, but sit and wait, so settling down out of sight, Jean bided her time.

Eventually, after what seemed an eternity, the team started to pack up and make their way out of the hall. Jean assessed it was probably lunch time by the grumbling of her own stomach. She heard the last remnants of their passing as they headed out of the building and sensed she was alone at last. Standing up she made her way to the large open, double doors that marked the entrance to the Knight's exhibit and went inside.

She found herself in a large, circular room, a domed glass roof was set into the centre of the ceiling, spreading daylight throughout the space. Raised above the floor, and all around the walls, were full length portraits of eight men and one woman, all wearing the uniforms of the Order. Beneath each portrait was a small biography, detailing who the person was and their rank. Set further into the centre of the room, in front of each painting, was a stand-alone glass cabinet that could be viewed from all sides; all but one contained a sword, balanced on its blade, pointing downwards. Within the centre of the room, display cases showed smaller items, with their descriptions alongside.

But Jean wasn't looking at the display cases, she was looking at the portrait of a man that hung directly in front of the double doors. He wore the distinctive uniform of a member of the Order, with the Imperial trees upon his high-necked collar. His rank was not only depicted by the additional amount of shiny insignia across his coat, but also, unlike any of the other portraits of the Knights hanging within this room, his was in gold. However, what drew her to this particular portrait, looking down from its lofty position, was the face which held two bright blue eyes. She had to admit, it was a face that could be considered quite handsome set under a mop of dark hair, but she had seen this face before; when she first arrived in Kelan, confused, exhausted and hungry. Two piercing blue eyes staring out as she made to steal a desperate meal; the shock of familiarity as he grabbed her hand. A feeling, she realised, that had tugged at her subconsciousness since she had arrived in Parva.

She winced, not content with stealing just anybody's food, she had to pilfer the cheese and pickle sandwich of the Emperor Nathan himself!

Though she grinned when she had to admit that it was a very nice cheese and pickle sandwich.

Getting over this initial shock, she gave each of the other portraits a quick inspection. From her position near the centre of the room, the portrait to the left of the Emperor was another man she recognised. He was the one who gave her the map and whispered in her ear. Now she had time to look closer she saw the resemblance to the Emperor. At a quick glance they could even be mistaken for each other, but for the fact that this man had eyes that seemed almost black. His biography stated that he was Lord Damien and he was, in fact, the cousin of the Emperor, not his brother as she first assumed. The silver insignia on his uniform mirrored that of the others in the room which set them apart from Nathan.

The men depicted in the portraits on the other side of the Emperor were also familiar from that night in Rassen. The first was a man with fair hair and grey eyes, Jean considered the artist had done well to capture the look of amusement on his face. He, like Damien and Nathan, had a familial look about him, but it was not as marked as the other two. His biography stated that his name was Lord Daniel.

The second was a blonde-haired man with blue eyes, Lord Stephen. While he had strikingly handsome features, he shared none of the countenance that picked him out as a family member of Nathan, Damien and Daniel.

However, the man next to him did share similar genealogical characteristics to Stephen. He was apparently Lord Simon, and Jean noted that while all the portraits presented everyone at the same height, this man had a bearing that implied he was a much larger and stronger man than the others. His hair was a light brown, and, despite his apparent height, his green eyes suggested a pleasing warmth.

She turned her attention to the portraits hanging on the other side of Lord Damien. Here was the face of a man that looked as if he was angry; his features seemed unnecessarily hard; his green eyes looking at her with disapproval. His biography stated his name was Lord Paul, and Jean felt it was a shame that he seemed so unhappy, as like the others in the room he had a face that could be considered handsome, if his features didn't look so bitter.

Next to him, in contrast, was a man known as Lord John. He had a bearing similar to Simon, which suggested, he too was a big man, and between the two there was an implication of a family connection. Jean was drawing nearer to the painting, when she realised that beneath the light brown hair, the irises of his brown eyes appeared to be ringed with gold. It was odd to see at first, but didn't look out of place within his face as a whole.

Turning around and facing the entrance, she saw two further portraits hung on either side of the doors; their position slightly separate from the other portraits. One of a man and the other of a woman; they were both wearing similar uniforms. She took a few moments to look up at the woman's portrait and smiled, but chose to investigate the man first. He too had a biography, but his also displayed the date of his death.

Lord James it seemed, was no longer with us.

Something familiar struck her and she looked back across the room, yes it was there, the same grey eyes and fair hair; even the look of amusement was apparent. But she also noted that he had a slight hardness around the mouth; unlike Lord Daniel, his smile didn't quite reach his eyes.

Now finally, Jean made her way back to the portrait of the only woman in the room. She too had the bearing of someone who was tall, her raven black hair hanging loose around her shoulders, framing her strong face in a dark halo. Her eyes were a vivid violet, and while the artist seemed to have painted someone hard and cold, Jean could see a dull light of sadness and pain in her eyes. Her biography simply stated she was the Lady Katherine, twin sister to Lord Nathan. Last positive sighting 7000 years ago; her current whereabouts unknown.

Katherine alone, didn't have a sword exhibited in a display case in front of her picture, though her portrait did show her hand resting on a sheathed sword. Instead, within the glass case that stood before her likeness, was a beautiful sapphire blue stone, sat on a pure white velvet cushion.

As far as gemstones go it was huge, at least the size of a large man's fist. Intrigued, Jean read the inscription that accompanied it.

The Blue Star

Several years ago, the Blue Star was brought to Kelan by a monk who had travelled across the universe to bring the stone home.

Legend has it that 7000 years ago a woman came to the monk's monastery; tired, hungry and exhausted. She spoke of the pain and anguish the stone had caused her and the people she loved. She had been the Blue

Star's guardian, but eventually, after years of abusing its power it finally rejected her. Now she had come to the monastery in the hope that she could leave it in their care, until the true heir to its energy came to claim it.
Eventually the woman left, and the monks waited, guarding their charge until someone claimed their precious inheritance.

Unfortunately, after thousands of years, the monastery began to fall into disrepair and eventually, after several raids from pirates, to plunder the wealth that had been accumulated there, the monks were forced to send the Blue Star away. Now, one of their most trusted brethren was tasked to find the Blue Star's true home on Kelan.

After years of searching, and by the grace of the gods, the brave monk found his way to the Empire, finally able to entrust the Stone to its rightful place of rest.

This is a replica of the original Blue Star; the original stone is kept at a secret location due to the enormity of the power it holds.
To this day it still waits for its rightful heir.

Jean stood and read the inscription a few times and then looked back to the portrait of the striking woman who had caused and felt such pain and anguish. She felt as if a lump was settling in her stomach and looked away.

Finally, she stepped into the centre of the room, inspecting the swords displayed in their own cases. These too apparently were replicas of the originals, but that due to the Knights themselves keeping them by their sides. She noted the inscriptions on each blade; three words that were pertinent to each of its owners. She was contemplating the Emperor's engraving,

PEACE, HONOUR, LOVE

when a loud, deep voice, shattered the silence of the room.
'WHO THE HELL ARE YOU?'

19

Sisters and Sons

As the vase hit the snowy white stone wall, lethal shards of glass where flung around the room. The two women sitting on a sofa nearby screamed hysterically, covering their heads, trying to protect their faces from the sharp projectiles.

'Oh for heaven's sake, don't be so ridiculous, it's only a bit of glass.'

Ephea was furious and wasn't in the mood for her sisters' over dramatic episodes.

'Are you mad? Look at the state of me? There are sharp bits everywhere. It could have sliced my face open.'

Ephea's youngest sister, Yollan, gingerly touched her cheek and then her neck, checking that indeed she hadn't been cut by the glass; abject horror written all over her face. Ephea rolled her eyes, whilst continuing to stomp around the room, her bright red wig seeming to have gained a slight tilt to the right. It looked dangerously like decanting from her head altogether.

'Ephea, will you please sit down, you're making me feel sick with all this pacing.'

Gradine, the middle sister, was also getting agitated, wafting her face with a napkin in a vain attempt to gain some respite from the ferocious heat of the brazier glowing in the corner of the room. Her eldest sister still refused to open the windows, and the herbs she continually threw onto the hot coals, was giving the air within the room a cloying stench that made it difficult to breathe. Gradine winced, Ephea was screeching again.

'Sit down? How can I possibly sit down? Have you read this?'

Storming over to a spindly table she grabbed the letter, that had previously been slammed down in her anger, and thrust it under her sister's nose. Gradine was going cross-eyed as she was forced to look at the offending object so close to her face. She looked away in disgust.

'I am fully aware of *its* contents thank you, but stomping around is not going to change anything.'

As it became obvious that no one was going to take the, now crumpled, paper from her, Ephea used it to vent her anger further. Screwing it up as hard as she could, then opening it out

274

again in order to efficiently rip it up into tiny pieces, before finally throwing the offending confetti onto the brazier.

Her sisters groaned, all they needed was more fuel to create extra heat.

'Maybe father really does have the whole situation in hand and doesn't want us to worry. That is his way after all.'

Ephea and Gradine looked at their youngest sibling in disgust. Gradine shook her head as she gave her scathing response.

'Yollan, we know you have never been exceptional in the brain department, but surely even you have to realise that father has practically thrown us to the wolves.'

Yollan's blue eyes opened wide in shock, making her moonlike face even more reminiscent of an oversized baby.

'How can you say that? Father would never desert us.'

Rolling her eyes again, Ephea walked away while Gradine carried on.

'Father couldn't care less what happens to us, as long as nothing interferes with him and his barely legal new wife, we can go to hell for all he cares. He has what he wants, which means we are now surplus to requirements.'

Bitterness forced Gradine to bite her lip as she saw the hurt in Yollan's face.

'He doesn't care anymore. He mollycoddled you as a child because, quite frankly, you were too stupid to do anything to annoy him.'

Yollan shrieked as she flew to her feet, her hands out, clawing at her sister's face, who recoiled back from the potential assault; pushing Yollan away hard before retreating to safety behind the sofa. Yollan shrieked in protest, falling back against the spindly table that had previously held the letter. Soon there was a pile of broken wood, along with voluminous skirts and exposed flesh sprawled across the floor.

'Stop it, stop it, stop it.'

Ephea's temper threatened to explode again and she stamped her feet in furious frustration.

'She started it. She said daddy doesn't care and that I'm stupid.'

Ephea rounded on the figure struggling to rise from the floor. Grabbing Yollan roughly by the arm, Ephea dragged her up to her feet, thrusting the flushed and teary woman back into her seat. Her own spite and anger fuelling her retort as she thrust out her numerous chins.

'To be fair, Gradine has a point.'

Yollan gave another shriek, but it was cut short by the vicious slap she received from her eldest sister. Tears run down her face, while humiliation and confusion contorted her features as she held a plump hand to her reddening cheek.

Finally satisfied with the ensuing silence, Ephea restarted her angry pacing. Gradine retreated to a seat in the corner and brooded; scowling through sulky eyes and only speaking when she felt it safe to do so.

'If father doesn't know what is going on, why can't he get Nathan to do something about it? He managed to control him with Belby, why can't he do that again?'

Ephea sighed, it seemed she was the only one of the three sisters blessed with brains.

'Because Nathan has nothing to do with all the unrest going on. He's struggling to keep the peace as it is, he's even brought the Order out to help the police on the streets.'

'Father told him not to let the knights out on the streets.'

'I know, but if he doesn't then we will have anarchy out there.'

Yollan sniffed indignantly from the sofa.

'If it's not the Emperor, and father doesn't know what is going on, who is doing all the bad things out there?'

Ephea buried her head in her hands and leaned against the wall.

'I don't know. I really don't know.'

A cough broke the silence in the hot cloying atmosphere. The three sisters' heads shot up and they looked around them in confusion. A man stepped forward from a far corner in the room. They had forgotten he was there. Looking at each other, they tried to act as if they were more in control, and that the previous argument hadn't happened. Ephea walked towards him, attempting her usual superior look, but her wig was still askew, and she just looked slightly drunk.

'Captain Mason, what do you want?'

The man sneered at her and she recoiled as he moved further into the room. Mason had become Captain Johnson's replacement, though for the life of her, Ephea couldn't recall when exactly he had been appointed such a position. In fact, she was hard put to remember him within the ranks of the Patrols previously either. He just appeared one day, taking up the vacant post, hardly leaving her side since. When he did, it was only briefly to issue commands to his subordinates. Commands that she found had less to do with her authority, and more to do with his own agenda; he increasingly left her completely out of any edicts he chose to give.

Mason frightened her.

Unlike many of those within the Patrols, taken from the ranks of the underworld of Earth, this man had no accent that she recognised, his grasp of the Kelan language had been quick and exceptional. His bearing was of a battle-hardened soldier, and he was huge, carrying many scars and tattoos across his face, demonstrating previous campaigns he'd been in according to the few conversations Ephea had managed to have with him. But it was his eyes that put the fear of the gods in her, to Ephea they seemed dead, carrying no life at all. If the eyes were the windows to the soul, as she'd heard said before, then this man either didn't have one, or it was as black as hell.

Mason now stood in the centre of the room, armed to the teeth, as was his custom, addressing the women before him. His voice was low and rough, as if it was used rarely and he was out of practice.

'The stranger that Johnson failed to find.'

His reluctance to use the title of Captain, when referring to someone who Ephea felt deserved far more respect than this man gave, annoyed her. But for now, she was wise enough to keep her own council.

He continued. 'There is word that a woman carrying the same description has entered the city, she is currently helping the police with their enquiries.'

Ephea was reluctantly intrigued by this news.

'Do we know who this woman is?'

Mason paused before answering, then shook his head slowly.

'No information has been available as yet.'

Ephea got the distinct impression he was lying through his teeth, but again she didn't push it. Instead she grasped the significance of his suggestion and questioned him further.

278

'Do you think this is the person responsible for the recent unrest in the city? The murders?'

Mason just shrugged. 'No idea.'

Gradine didn't have Ephea's wise council of keeping quiet, she challenged him on his lack of efficiency.

'Surely it is your job to find out who she is and what her involvement is in all this?'

His head barely moved as his gaze fell on the other woman, still hunched sulkily in the corner.

'I am fully aware of what my job is, Madam. And I can assure you I am carrying out all of my work perfectly well. You on the other hand are slowly becoming surplus to requirements.'

He left the obvious threat hanging, all three women were shocked into silence, their fear now palpable within the heat of the room. Satisfied he had made his point; Mason turned and left the room without any further comment. There was barely a click as the door closed behind him.

It was some time before the sisters felt able to speak, but now their voices where more subdued. The contents of the burnt letter forgotten; their differences settled.

Reality had slowly dawned; they were on their own.

Nathan took a sip of his tea, watching the man sitting in the large leather sofa opposite. Irritation gripped him just by the way the man held his cup; balancing the china object between his fingertips of both hands. His unwanted guest was a man of medium stature, though he looked small and insignificant in his chair; both knees together and shoulders hunched. His sharp features highlighted the hawklike eyes that moved constantly, seemingly looking for unknown threats in every shadow.

He reminded Nathan of a weasel.

How the hell did you ever become a General in the Order?

There was no way Bales would have passed scrutiny for such a lofty promotion and rank had Nathan had any say in it, which normally he would. But this time unfortunately, he didn't. In fact, Bales barely made the grade as a Captain; a mediocre leader at the best of times. Perhaps with perseverance, and a lot of mentoring, Major could eventually have been a possibility. But to jump over several ranks even higher to achieve General was, or should have been, inconceivable.

Yet here he was, a man that Nathan should rely on to lead armies; to advise him and inspire those under his command; who instead barely drank tea without inspiring Nathan to wrench the cup from him and commit serious assault on his person.

Aware that Bales had also had a recent bereavement within his family, Nathan forced himself not to reach across the coffee table, take him by his shoulders and force him to sit up straight. It was killing his own back just looking at him. Bales' recent bereavement, however, didn't exclude him from his duties as a senior knight of the Order. Having already dispensed with condolences, Nathan got to the point so this farce of a meeting could end, preferably sooner rather than later.

'General Bales, you requested this meeting to discuss a matter you considered urgent. I am sure you're as busy as the rest of the Order, with the troubles within the city. With time being something we have precious little of, perhaps we can get straight to the point.'

Bales took another sip from the cup between his fingertips, before barely moving the cup away from his lips, allowing him to speak. Nathan, again, forced down the urge to not snatch the damned cup from his hands.

'There appears my Lord, that there has been a miscarriage of the duties expected amongst the police force.'

Nathan looked questioningly back.

'Oh? How so?'

'Daven Hillside, the murderer of my son, has been freed without charge.'

Nathan nodded. 'I'm aware that Mr Hillside is back at home with his family. But I'm also aware that there is absolutely no evidence to suggest he was responsible for your son's unfortunate demise.'

A furrowed brow and a darkening of his features were the only indication of the change of any emotion in the General's demeanour.

'No evidence?' There was a distinct pause before Bales continued. '*My Lord!*' He shifted forward slightly as his anger rose. 'My own wife gave witness to the man; he lured my son to his death.'

Nathan growled inwardly. The use of the epithet 'My Lord' was something he barely noted in conversation with others. It was used so often that he would be hard pushed to recognise whether it was spoken or not at all. Personally, he didn't see the point, everyone knew who he was, and he knew his duties as their ultimate leader, he didn't need reminding of the fact. But it seemed to make everyone happier to call him something; and he refused point blank to be called Your Majesty. And with regards to the custom of bowing, he had put a stop to that before he even became Emperor. As far as Nathan was concerned, he preferred to look those around him in the eyes when dealing with them.

Bales, however, wanted to make a point. Nathan ground his teeth and, in his mind, ran the horrible man sitting before him, through with his sword. Outwardly he was the epitome of calm and respectability.

'There is only your wife's word that such an invitation was given, no evidence has been produced to back up this statement. Further investigations have also indicated that persons, other than Mr Hillside, are more likely to be responsible for your son's death.'

Bales was furious. He threw himself forward in his seat and slammed his teacup down, sending the cold liquid contents all over the highly polished table.

'My Lord, are you accusing my wife of lying?'

Nathan held the other man's eye, pausing before speaking slowly and left no doubt as to the level of his anger.

'You forget yourself General, I suggest you calm down. I will not tolerate that tone.'

Bales seeming to suddenly realise the danger, sat back in his seat, his eyes refusing to look at his Emperor. His Adam's apple bobbed in his throat as he gulped.

'My apologies My Lord.'

Nathan continued. 'I make no accusations; I simply state that there is no evidence to back up your wife's version of events. Mr Hillside is no longer considered a suspect in the murder of your son.'

Bales just sat and seethed.

'There is of course the question of your son's involvement in the sexual assault of Morna Hillside.'

Bales suddenly sat up, alert, he appeared to have gained several inches in height.

'My Lord, my son is dead, he can't stand trial. His respectability can't be brought into question now.'

Nathan stared at the man a few moments, before giving his final blow to the arrogant upstart.

'Surely… *General*.' Two could play at this game. 'You are more than aware of Imperial Law? A man of your rank should be versed entirely in the nuances of its workings?'

Bales looked on blankly, aware that he was now in a position where admission of ignorance could have dire consequences to his own rank and standing within society. He sat in silence, unsure of how to answer. His ultimate superior was satisfied with the involuntary gulp in the man's throat again.

'Perhaps, due to the emotional times we are dealing with, I will remind you.'

Nathan took up the file that he had lying on the sofa beside him, he opened it as if needing to be reminded of the details. Bales wasn't fooled.

'While the evidence of a single witness is not enough to convict a man of such a heinous crime, the forensic evidence has finally come through, showing that your son did indeed have sexual intercourse with Miss Hillside.'

Glancing at Bales, he was satisfied to see the colour drain from his face.

'Also, her injuries are consistent with a vicious sexual attack. Witness statements and forensics, in my view, are pretty conclusive, especially considering Aleix Bales denied even being in the vicinity at the time.'

Looking back at the report, Nathan made a point of checking a fact before continuing.

'An alibi was given by your wife, stating that he was at home when the attack occurred. It seems, General, that your wife does seem determined to be a bit circumspect with the truth when it comes to her son.'

Nathan put his head to one side and watched Bales slowly realise what he was saying. He continued.

'Of course your son wouldn't be tried in a court of law. Dead men can't be brought to trial. But that doesn't mean he won't be judged for his actions.'

'My Lord.' Bales barely whispered his response.

Nathan sat up and ensured he now had the man's full attention before adding the final blow.

'I alone can judge a man for his crimes; I alone can pass a verdict and deal punishments accordingly out with the court of law.'

Nathan sat back in his seat, relaxed, watching the arrogance drain from the man opposite him.

'I admit, it is something I very rarely have to do, but I feel a final verdict is needed now, to allow those affected to move on with their lives, and for justice to be served. In this case, Aleix Bales has been found guilty of rape and as such, his character will reflect this. Do we understand each other… *General?*'

Bales sat stunned, only replying when Nathan repeated his question.

'Yes My Lord. I understand.'

'Good. Now I suggest we move on. We can discuss this matter further at a later date, but for now there are other urgent issues I must address.'

Nathan stood up and Bales, realising he had been dismissed, scrambled to his own feet. His stature was such that his head only just came to the height of the Emperor's chin, even when he stood to attention, which he did more out of habit than respect for his superior.

As Bales left the Imperial office and closed the door behind him, Nathan felt uneasy. He reflected that this man was a problem that was going to have to be dealt with at some point, preferably, sooner rather than later.

20

Love, Hope and Trust

J ean turned slowly on the spot. Engrossed in the portraits
and the information within the exhibit, she had been
totally unaware that anyone else had entered the
building, let alone finding her illicitly wandering around
a crime scene. When she saw the man standing by the large
open doors, however, she was momentarily taken aback, so
striking was his appearance. She had spent a long time living in
her part of the universe, having grown used to the eclectic mix

of people who lived there, she had taken their differing colours, shapes and sizes in her stride. It was their emotive energy that concerned her most, not what they looked like.

However, since her arrival in Kelan, she had grown used to the fact that its inhabitants pretty much fitted the description of anyone you could find on Earth.

But not this man. He was different.

For a start he looked really pissed off, an emotion that was emphasised by his eyes; they were icy blue, and like the portrait of Lord John, they had a halo around the irises. But this man's were a silvery white which made them seem to almost shine. His hair was also striking, it appeared to be an inky blue rather than black, shot through with silver, cut short, but thick enough to stand on end, making him look even taller than the great height he already was. He must have been at least six and a half feet tall. Wearing the uniform of the Order, its silver insignia on the black cloth only helped exaggerate the effect.

Jean was feeling a bit nonplussed; she couldn't say she enjoyed the feeling.

Having dealt with even bigger and more numerous enemies in her time, she knew she was more than capable of giving this man a run for his money. But instead she just stood, quite speechless, caught in the fact that he was probably, one of the most beautiful men she had ever seen.

'I asked you a question. Who are you, and while you are at it, what are you doing here? This is a crime scene.'

Jean blinked and forced herself to answer.

Dear gods, get a grip woman.

In a vain attempt to bluff it out, she answered.

'I'm sorry, a friend of mine suggested I saw this exhibit while I was visiting the city.'

Indicating the displays around her and laughed.

'Bit of a fan.'

What are you talking about woman?

Cringing to herself at how bloody daft she must have sounded, she noted that he didn't look impressed either.

'There are knights all around the campus, they have made sure all visitors are told the museum is closed for the day.'

Jean tried for an innocent look, she thought she must have looked ridiculous.

'Oh, I must have missed them.'

The man's eyebrows shot up, surely she didn't think he would fall for that pile of rubbish? She certainly wouldn't. Apologising again, she held her hands up in appeasement.

'I'm sorry, really I am, but I had to get in and see this exhibit, it has information I really needed to see.'

'What sort of information?'

He glanced around the room as if to assess whether anything had been moved or taken.

'Just things about the Emperor, his Knights and his sister.'

He instinctively turned around to the portrait of the Lady Katherine, which hung just slightly behind him, to his right. Until now, his left hand had rested lightly on the pommel of his sheathed sword. Now, she noticed, he seemed more agitated, especially as his eyes passed from Katherine's portrait to the stone displayed in front of her. His gaze finally returned to Jean and he seemed to come to a decision. Stepping forward, his long legs made short work of the distance between them.

'You are coming with me.'

Jean started to protest; this was the last thing she needed right now.

'What? Why? I'm sorry, I know I shouldn't have been in here but surely, we don't need to take this too far. A slap on the wrist and I promise to be a good girl before we go our separate ways.'

She gave him her biggest attempt at a disarming smile she could. He still wasn't impressed. Taking her arm, he started to lead her to the door. Instinct began to kick in and Jean pulled away roughly, catching him by surprise at the strength she seemed to have. She continued to protest.

'No, I really don't think we need to do this. I have too much that I have to do.'

He had obviously decided he'd heard enough. With a speed that took her aback, Jean was in a set of handcuffs and being frogmarched out of the doors and through the museum halls. Several attempts at trying to talk to him failed. Apparently, he wasn't up for discussing the matter further. Desperately trying to save the disastrous situation, she began to calm her thoughts and sense the motives of the man beside her. To her relief she sensed honesty, determination and integrity and was fortunately without deceit — he was a good man. Though at the moment Jean considered him a colossal pain in the arse.

As they passed through the main doors and out into the misty campus, other knights, who were still working around the museum, looked up. Including, she noted, the two who had spoken to her earlier; they looked rather angry. Jean decided to just brazen it out and gave them a big smile.

'Afternoon again.'

The two knights looked at each other as if she was completely mad, she felt their eyes on her back as she was led out of the campus towards the tree lined avenue. However, instead of heading towards the river though, her captor turned her right, northwards, in the direction of the Palace.

The man at her side still said nothing as he strode with her along the pavement, while people they passed stopped and stared, many whispering to each other. They were soon hurrying off, probably eager to tell friends of the latest bit of gossip. When they neared the Palace, Jean realised it was actually more of a complex of buildings surrounding a main square, rather than a grand royal house as the name suggested. However, she was unable to appreciate it for long, as her companion was now hauling her past the main gates and towards the right of the complex. They entered what was appeared to be the stables; rows of stalls, some with curious long faces staring out over their doors. People were busy with the care of the horses, the comforting smell of horse sweat, and leather tack caught at her nostrils. But once more, she was whisked away from the scene, this time to the left and what she realised was the back door of a guard room. She was hauled along a corridor with several rooms leading off, heading towards a door with a view of the parade square beyond it. They stopped at a high desk that ran at right angles to the door, another knight was behind it listening to *Mr Frosty*. She smiled to herself for that one; beautiful he may be, but he was no bundle of laughs.

The knight on duty was now nodding his head and writing something in a large book in front of him, he then turned it around while *Frosty* signed the page. Producing a set of keys from behind his desk the duty knight came around to join Jean and her nemesis. Then the pair of them proceeded down another corridor, which led further into the building; Jean unceremoniously dragged along behind. Making one final attempt at saving the situation, she opened her mouth to speak, but suddenly she was staring at a blank wall with a window set high above a hard bench, her handcuffs removed, and the door slammed shut behind her.

'What the fuck?' This had gone too far. 'Oi. Come on. A joke's a joke, and I like a laugh as much as the next person, but this is ridiculous.'

She banged on the door in frustration.

Turning around in disbelief, she assessed her best course of action.

Over the years there were a few rules that Jean had figured out, regarding who she was and the work she did. One of the first, and most important rules she discovered, was not to translocate to get herself out of trouble while on one of her missions. It appeared that while it may resolve an immediate problem, it invariably created a much bigger one further down the line. There were countless times Jean had been tempted, but she couldn't do it; the possible disastrous consequences would never be worth it.

Standing here in her cell however, she did wonder if it would be worth just translocating to PC Croft, then return back to her cell while Ella came to sort this mess out with Frosty. The more she thought about it, the more she convinced herself that it wouldn't be entirely cheating; she would still be under lock and key, but she would have help on its way. Resolved that she needed to do something, she set her mind to sense the signature of where her friend would be, and using the energy within her, prepared herself to translocate.

Nothing happened.

She stood for a few moments, completely confused. Trying again there was still nothing. Something was stopping her from translocating, and she could feel the panic begin to rise within her. Trying to think of anything that was different since arriving at Kelan it dawned on her, the Ti'akai, was it preventing her from travelling? Anywhere? But that couldn't be the case because she had managed to translocate to the hospital at Aria with George and Niall, so what was happening now?

She began to pace, trying to calm the rising panic and think rationally. Whatever the issue was, she wasn't going to find out within her cell. So, she was back at her original problem; how to get out.

'This is ridiculous.' She repeated, then shouted louder. 'I need to speak to someone. Where's *Frosty*? I have to tell him something.'

She listened. Nothing.

'Oh come on.'

She began to pace again, aware that getting angry was not a good idea right now, but the urge to beat the crap out of something was becoming very desirable. Taking deep breaths, she forced the negative thoughts out, instead focusing on the information she had gleaned today. The people known as the Guardian Knights, the swords and the Blue Star. But most of all, the Lady Katherine.

And why the fuck can't I translocate anymore?

She had to get out.

Leaning her head against the stone wall, Jean allowed its coolness to help calm the anger that threatened to rise. How long she had stood there for she didn't know, but when the cell door finally opened, she realised the light from the high window had shifted the shadows on the floor. Not moving from her place against the wall, she felt rather than heard someone enter, then the door close once more.

There was no danger, she knew who it was. When he spoke, she turned to face him.

'Frosty?'

It was an unexpected question and try as she might, she couldn't stop herself giving him a wry smile. For the first time, she saw him smile too, it transformed the coldness of his features. Damn, she couldn't help but like the man. He had dragged her through the city streets, then chucked her, rather unceremoniously in her opinion, into a cell. While she wasn't happy about the situation, Jean found it was like being annoyed with a big brother; although admittedly, a very large, big brother.

He seemed to realise that though her cell was small to start with, now his presence made the space look tiny. He looked around and indicating the bench, he suggested they sit down. Once seated they both studied each other. Out of a sense of urgency, it was Jean who spoke first.

'Look, I know I shouldn't have broken into the museum; although technically, I climbed through an already open window, I didn't break anything. I promise that I will answer to any charges you want to bring, but please, I cannot stay here. I have things to do and they can't wait.'

He seemed to contemplate her words for a while before answering.

'I think before we discuss whether you remain our guest for the evening, we should deal with the formalities. You still haven't

293

told me who you are and why you were in the museum, when it was clearly out of bounds.'

She pushed down her frustration, this was his game and she would have to play by his rules, at least for the moment.

'Jean, Jean Carter. And you are?'

He smiled and acknowledged it was a fair question.

'I am Captain Ty Coniston, and I would still like to know why you were in that particular exhibit.'

Sighing, she closed her eyes.

'If I told you will you let me go?'

Again, he contemplated her question. Apparently, he was not one to speak unnecessarily.

'That all depends. You see, that area of the museum was targeted specifically, last night. Whoever it was, tried to get through the doors, but they are protected by forces that make it impossible, at least that is, until the staff arrive the following morning.'

He spread his hands. 'So, when I find a stranger wandering around that particular room, when it is supposed to be a cordoned off crime scene, I have a tendency to be a bit suspicious.'

Jean sighed, she couldn't fault his logic and if she was honest, in his position she would have thought exactly the same. Somehow, she didn't think benign excuses and attempts to conceal the truth, was going to cut the mustard. Contemplating her previous analysis of this man's countenance and the situation she was in; she made a decision. Praying to the gods it was the right one, she knew there was no going back once she started.

'Captain. I need you to trust me. While I have only just met you, I have to take you into my confidence, and I believe you are a man of integrity, someone who I can rely on for discretion and understanding.'

Coniston looked at her, puzzled. He had listened to what she had had to say, but the look of surprise on his face when he saw what she did next, was priceless in Jean's opinion. Instead of giving a verbal explanation, she had stood up and made her way to the door. Turning to face him, Ty saw a woman who was completely unarmed, but when she reached over to her left side with her right hand, she drew a sword that hadn't been there a second ago. He stood up and drew his own sword, though, in such a confined space, it was doubtful either of them was in a position to harm anyone. Jean held out her hand in supplication.

'No, wait. Please this isn't a threat. Just look.'

Taking her sword, she moved past him and placed it down on the bench, then moved back towards the door. Completely stunned, he looked at the blade and then back to Jean.

Silently he re-sheathed his own sword and, making the most of the light available from the high window, he crouched down and scrutinised the wonder that lay before him. Because he realised that this is what it was, a wonder. Holding his hand out towards the inscription that ran the length of the blade, Ty didn't quite touch the metal, instead his fingers just hovered above the ornate wording.

LOVE HOPE TRUST

Behind him, Jean stood, silent and unmoving. Both of them knew she was in no danger now.

Finally tearing himself away from the sword, Ty slowly turned to Jean, he was still crouching down and he had to look up to see into her face.

'This is part of you, joined to you when you made your vow to be a Guardian.'

Jean realised this was not a question, he was stating a fact he already knew. She inclined her head but said nothing.

'Only you can summon your own sword, your own weapons. Do you have any other weapons?'

She eyed him cautiously, then reached behind her and withdrew two daggers, the same inscription on their blades as on her sword. He raised an eyebrow.

'Two daggers?'

'I have a bow too if you are taking an inventory.'

He looked impressed.

'Who are you?'

Confusion flitted across his face. She went to him and knelt down, picking up her sword she placed it against the wall, before indicating that they both resume their seats.

'Captain Coniston. Actually, do you mind if I call you Ty? I don't really feel this is a conversation that requires formality.'

He just inclined his head, hardly daring to move. He couldn't speak, his eyes never left her's.

She smiled and took his hand in hers, it was warm and calloused, a soldier's hand. She could sense the frisson of excitement running through him.

'I was born in London, England, and I lived a full and perfectly normal life. I worked, married and had a family, then eventually, at the ripe old age of ninety-two, I died.

'I can't say that I have any knowledge of what to expect in the afterlife though, because I never really had the opportunity to find out. If I'm honest, it is a part of my past that is quite confused. I have memories of being aware of people who played a part in making me who I am today, but when I try to capture their images they fly away and escape me.'

Jean didn't feel it was necessary to tell Ty everything that happened then, she wasn't even sure herself.

'Anyway, after a while I found myself in, what I now know as the Seventh Sector, and I have been there for a very, very long time. My work has primarily been keeping the peace and making sure some seriously bad guys don't get away with even more seriously bad stuff. Many of those occasions have meant that I end up in some strange new worlds. Basically, dumped in the middle of someone else's nightmare trying to clear up a hell of a mess.'

She paused and he looked at her questioningly.

'Why have you stopped?' His strong baritone now barely a whisper.

'Do you have any idea how dangerous this information is?'

He understood but he urged her on.

'Please, tell me.'

She sighed and continued.

'A few months ago, I arrived in Kelan, at a town called Rassen. I met four men there, briefly, and I had no idea at the time who they were. Today however, I saw their portraits in that exhibition, where I also saw the replica swords that they all carry, swords like this one.'

She put her hand out and brushed the hilt of the blade beside her.

'Until now I believed I was alone in my work.' She looked away. 'I couldn't be more wrong, could I?'

I'm not alone anymore.

Ty squeezed her hand and she looked back up.

'They need your help.'

She inclined her head.

'I know. I need to speak the Emperor; I must speak to Nathan. I have to find out what has caused all of this chaos; and why the hell they have done nothing about it.'

Ty sat up straight, his eyes bright with a passion that wasn't there before.

'That is something I can help you with. I know all about the events that have happened, but I won't be able to get you an audience with the Emperor. However, I know someone who can, or at least they can find a way.'

Jean felt relief that her instincts hadn't let her down, this man was the one to help her, maybe she could finally sort this particular mess out. Ty stood up.

'First of all, we need to get you out of here, then we can go somewhere safe where we can talk privately.'

He went to the door and banged it hard. A small hole opened, allowing a pair of eyes to peer through. Seeing Ty's face, they closed the hole and the door swung open, Ty turned and beckoned Jean to follow him.

As she rose, he noted her sword and daggers were no longer anywhere to be seen.

Part Three

North

Bank

21

Morecross

Captain Coniston led Jean out of the cell, with the knight holding the keys looking on curiously as they made their way back through the guardroom. They paused briefly while Ty signed the book on the high desk again, then he led the way out; this time towards the guardroom main door, and not the back entrance.

Stepping out into the misty late afternoon, Ty nearly collided with a fellow knight who had come storming down the pathway that ran from the Palace towards the gates. His head was down, causing people to keep out of his path. Everyone, except Ty that is.

The man, who had not been looking where he was going, was much smaller than Ty. He bounced back dramatically, falling against the rail that separated the guardroom from the parade square. His furious face was almost purple with rage and wiping spittle from his face he roared his anger.

'WHAT THE HELL ARE YOU DOING? GET OUT OF MY WAY.'

Ty, realising who he had sent flying, looked mortified. He immediately stood to attention.

'Sir, General Sir. I apologise, this was my fault entirely. I didn't see you coming.'

Jean frowned from behind Ty and thought. *It was his bloody fault, not yours.*

'No, of course you didn't, because you're a big stupid lump of a buffoon.'

Brushing himself down, General Bales made to continue storming through the gates. However, he seemed to change his mind and turned with a malicious look on his face, throwing in a final vicious jibe over his shoulder.

'I wouldn't be too comfortable with your rank Captain; you would have made more use as a Sergeant, I think. It will be something I will have to look into.'

Jean glanced at Ty, his face was one of anger and shock. Bales seemed satisfied with his reaction when he saw Ty's confusion and discomfort. But then his gaze fell on Jean standing behind him, he couldn't fail to see the look of utter contempt on her face. Anger crossed his features again, and he jabbed a finger in her direction.

'WHAT THE HELL IS THAT WOMAN DOING HERE?'

By now, several more knights had come to see what all the noise was about. When they saw the General, they looked wary but didn't leave. Ty looked thankful for the extra numbers around him, even if it was only from curiosity. Not moving from his position of attention, his voice carried his feeling of loathing for his superior.

'This Sir, is Jean Carter.'

'I know who she is, I want to know what she is doing here.'

Ty tried to hide his confusion and replied.

'She has been helping us with our enquiries into the break-in at the Museum. Sir.'

Bales considered this a moment.

'She is the one who attacked the exhibit? Why isn't she in a cell? Have the prison guards at Balen been informed?'

His eyes gleamed at the thought.

'Miss Carter is not a suspect, Sir. We are still investigating and looking at all of the evidence.'

Bales didn't bother to hide his disappointment. Instead he stepped closer to Jean, who was taller than him, she wrinkled her nose at the smell of his sweat and stale breath; making sure Bales saw her.

'Helping with enquiries again *Carter*? You seem to have a knack for finding trouble.'

Jean felt that having remained quiet throughout the whole farcical episode, she now had to say something. The high state of fear and loathing, that emanated from the knights that witnessed this awful man's actions, struck a chord; and she didn't like bullies. Something, she recalled, Captain Johnson found out eventually to her detriment.

'Funnily enough, *Bales*, the trouble I find myself in, has eventually involved you or your family one way or another. I can see where that vicious bastard son of yours got his wit and charm from now.'

Feeling the unease rise from the knights, Jean moved forward and closed the gap between her and Bales further.

'And it's *Miss* Carter to you.'

All around there was an air of panic forming, while the knights watched their General's face turn a horrible puce colour. Behind her, a man came out from the guardroom at speed and brought himself to attention.

'General Sir. My apologies, Miss Carter is a visitor from the country and has yet to appreciate our manners.'

Jean turned around to face the new arrival, but before she could give him what she considered her thoughts on manners, Bales was once more in full flow.

'Major Torvil, I have seen nothing but an appalling display of incompetency from you and your men. I will be writing a full report on my findings so I hope you don't mind the cold; I hear the frozen north of Lorimar can be biting in winter.'

His threat was obvious and the Major winced. Jean turned back, once more face to face with the General. When Bales spoke, his voice was barely a whisper.

'And you have not heard the last of this.'

She wasn't threatened and she made sure Bales was more than aware of it.

'Oh I guarantee, this conversation has only just begun. *Bales.*'

Backing away, unused to threats, the General checked himself. He looked at the faces of the knights around him and was satisfied that at least they were suitably chastised, he turned on his heel and made for the gate that led out to the avenue, throwing a final remark over his shoulder.

'Get your mess sorted Major. While you still can.'

Those by the guardroom stood in silence, watching Bales stomp down the avenue. Jean sensed the knives of hatred emanating from those around her, and she threw her own into the mix for good measure. *One day.* She thought. *They were going to be very real.*

Ty turned to Major Torvil.

'Sir, can he do that? Reduce our rank on a whim I mean.'

The panic in his voice was obvious.

Torvil shrugged. 'Technically I suppose, he is a General after all. I doubt if we could do anything about it, but with any luck he will calm down and will have forgotten about it by morning. In all reality, the man barely has a backbone, and with all the troubles we are dealing with at the moment, I can't see the Lord Knights worrying about his little tantrums.'

Despite his previous remarks concerning her apparent lack of manners, Jean appreciated his words. He was a soldier that had probably seen more of life in the Order than Bales could ever hope to achieve. The knights around him seemed to rally, the feelings of anger being replaced with cautious relief. But Jean could feel her restlessness rising, she was getting agitated with her lack of progress; the urge to fight was growing stronger, and it was going to intensify further before this whole sequence of events was over. She stared into the lined face of Major Torvil, he looked exhausted.

'I can assure you all, he will not be in a position to interfere with anyone's rank. Your careers are all safe.'

Torvil studied her and frowned.

'You into fortune telling now Miss Carter? Because I sure as hell have no idea what is going on, what makes you think you can figure it out?'

Ty shook his head. 'Actually Sir, I think she can.'

Torvil didn't look convinced and shook his head.

'Well Captain, I hope you know what you are doing.'

Ty looked at Jean, the determination etched on her face, echoed his own thoughts.

'Yes Sir. I believe I do.'

Torvil turned to Jean. 'And you Miss Carter, can you possibly stay out of trouble? At least for now.'

Jean gave the Major a rueful smile.

'Erm, unlikely, but it's a nice thought.'

He shook his head and ushered the rest of the knights back to work. Looking back, he replied.

'Then may the gods look down on you generously.'

That would be a first. She thought.

Feeling Ty take her elbow, she allowed herself to be led towards the avenue and south towards the river, while Torvil was left to watch their departure with curiosity.

What could possibly make a man like the Captain so sure?

Feeling tension and anger still coursing through her companion, Jean asked him about the buildings that they passed, hoping it would take his mind off of the uncomfortable conversation he had had with Bales. Fortunately, Ty was happy to oblige. He then started a little lesson in the administrative aspects of the North Bank of the City of Parva.

Once they were through the Palace gates, he indicated the first building on the left-hand side of the avenue. It was a solid, stone structure, with no evidence of windows or doors, other

303

than the front doors which were accessed by a set of broad stone steps. At the top were two members of the Order standing guard. This was the Imperial Bank, the main responsibility of Damien, Lord Chancellor. Ty paused briefly and Jean sensed a moment of sadness, she looked enquiringly at him, but he didn't elaborate. Instead he indicated that they should cross the road towards the building directly opposite.

They traversed the highway to its centre, with the rows of trees that would provide travellers with shade from the sun and some shelter from the rain. Then continuing to cross, they came to another large building. This was a sharp contrast to its twin across the road; the steps that rose up from the pavement led to large double doors, which were also guarded by two knights. But this was the only similarity. Here, there were plenty of windows that let in copious amounts of light. People were milling around the entrance, some in gowns denoting a uniform, and others dressed in ill-fitting, smart clothes that made them look uncomfortable.

'Let me guess, this is the Imperial Law Courts?'

Ty grinned. 'That obvious eh?'

'Just a bit. I'm assuming that those in the gowns are legal staff, but it's those wearing clothes they normally reserve for weddings and funerals, trying, unsuccessfully, not to look guilty that clinched it for me.'

She was glad to see Ty laugh; it brightened his face and added a warmth to the coolness of his features.

'Yes, this is the domain of Daniel, he is the Lord High Judge within the Empire. Only the Emperor has a higher legal authority.'

Jean studied the Court for a moment, then glanced across to the Bank and the University campus behind it, finally turning back to the buildings known as the Palace. The main factors of power; Government, Law and Economy, surrounded by Education. Whoever planned this city knew what they were doing. She pointed back to the Palace complex.

'I know that is known as *the Palace*, but is it actually a place of residence? Does the Emperor really live there?'

Ty shook his head.

'No. Apparently a very long time ago, before the creation of the Order, they used to live on the top floor. But now the whole complex is made over to administration and formal entertaining. But even the buildings here are relatively new. They are only a few hundred years old or so.'

He pointed to a large rectangular structure on the other side of the gates that sat between the harbour wall and the Square.

'That is a guest hall that accommodates many visiting dignitaries, it is one of the older buildings and used to be the main administrative building. It's been pretty quiet of late, but it is filling up now with those attending the Midsummer Ball at the Palace.'

She looked at him sharply.

'There are more people entering the city? Even with all the unrest and murders?'

Ty sighed and nodded.

'I know, it's going to be a logistical nightmare. But at least the Order can enter the city again and not just be an armed guard at the gates.'

Jean shook her head and started chewing at a thumb nail.

'I don't like it Ty, not with all this trouble, not when people will be more interested in celebrating than their own safety.' She looked back at the Palace. 'It's not a coincidence all this is happening now.'

As if to prove a point, a large group of people made their way out on to one of the balconies of the guest hall. They were laughing and had obviously been drinking. Looking at each other, Jean and Ty shook their heads and groaned.

Ty said. 'Come on, let's get moving, I'm starving. I hope you don't mind basic cooking.'

Jean laughed. 'If someone else is cooking, I'll not be complaining.'

He grinned again and led her down the avenue, passing the court buildings and coming onto an area that was more residential. Shops and taverns were more prevalent here, providing services to those who worked at the Palace, Bank, Law Courts and university. Also, of course, the members of the Order who chose to not live in the barracks, along with the never-ending supply of students.

It was a colourful residential mix, that included people from all over the Empire and their differing bank balances. There were buildings that seemed to teem with students as they wandered to and from the university. Occasionally, Ty acknowledged several people wearing the uniform of the Order heading towards or from their duties.

There was one house they passed, that sat back from the road, surrounded by large gardens full of trees and flowers. Unlike other buildings around it, that had windows and doors flung wide open now the fog had finally dissipated, this one was closed up tight; though Jean could see people moving around inside, flitting past windows as they worked. She looked enquiringly at Ty and noted that his face had darkened. Realising her interest, he nodded towards the residence.

'That, is the home of Ephea, the wife of our Emperor.'

'Ah, I take it he doesn't live there too?'

Ty Laughed. 'Dear gods no. He does his damnedest to stay as far away, from that harridan as possible.'

Giving a final glance at the house, Jean followed Ty further along the road, eventually arriving at a square that had a terrace of town houses on either side of a small grassy area. The farthest side, away from the road, was taken up by a high eight-foot wall, and Ty led her to a house that abutted against it. Climbing the steps up to a gleaming black front door, Jean was able to see over the wall and saw the harbour below. This part of the harbour was more of a marina, with vessels more likely used for leisure rather than for carrying cargo. Ty followed her gaze, explaining that many of the rich in Parva liked to spend a lot of their spare time on their boats. He also added that many of them hardly ever saw the open sea.

Nodding, Jean understood, she thought it a shame though, as the joy of sailing on the open water was a rare but treasured pursuit of hers. Standing here by the expanse of the ocean, the briny air filling her lungs, was a small glimpse of heaven as far as she was concerned.

Ty broke her revery. 'Come on, we can't stand here all day, I'm starving.'

Reluctantly, Jean followed her host inside the house, throwing one final envious glance to the vessels below before closing the front door.

Adjusting her eyes to the change in light, Jean saw that this house had actually been divided into separate apartments. Ty brought his finger to his lips in a request for quiet, then pointing at the door opposite, he mouthed a silent explanation.

'Landlady.'

Nodding at the ominous suggested threat that inhabited beyond the closed door, she followed him up the stairs and stopped at the first floor. She assumed his landlady had particularly sensitive ears as he kept his voice to a whisper, pointing to the only door at this level, he said this was his apartment, indicating upwards he continued.

'That's Kate Bridger's, she's just made Captain. She couldn't wait to get out of barracks.' He grinned. 'Don't blame her to be honest.'

When he opened the door to his own apartment, she was surprised at how homely it was. She half expected Ty to have a sparse bachelor pad, but instead it was tastefully decorated and welcoming. Jean thought that maybe this was due to the disturbingly anonymous landlady, yet there were many personal touches here too that Ty had added. Pictures of himself and other people she assumed were friends and family, along with awards adorning the shelves; Jean kept her manners and didn't look too closely for a good nose, but it was difficult.

Ty suggested she sit and make herself comfortable, while he changed out of his uniform and made some tea. Jean welcomed the comfortable embrace of the big squishy sofa; she was all too easily able to stretch out and make herself at home. It didn't take long for Ty to come back in with steaming mugs of tea in hand, he looked much less rigid and militant in his cotton slacks and shirt. He also had a big smile on his face as he sat back and reclined in the sofa opposite hers.

She looked at him enquiringly.

'What are you looking so cheerful for?'

He shrugged. 'Things are looking up. That's something to smile about surely? '

She laughed. 'That's a lot of faith considering the mess things are in at the moment.'

Ty inclined his head.

'True, and you don't even know the half of it yet. But you're here, that must be a good sign at least.'

'I hope for everyone's sake that isn't misplaced faith.'

He spread his hands. 'Alright, let's call it quiet optimism.'

Drinking her tea, Jean took the time to study Ty. Thankful that he had decided to trust her, but unsure what it was that convinced him that she was the answer to the Empire's prayers. Yes, as a soldier he was more likely to be connected to her more assertive state, but the level of trust he showed, especially as it wasn't so long ago he had frogmarched her up to the Guard Room in handcuffs, was quite a turnaround. Hopefully she would learn more as she got to know him. She put her mug down on the coffee table and made herself more comfortable on the sofa. As she now had his attention, she asked her questions first.

'So, now seems as good a time as any for you to finally tell me what exactly has been going on here. Because I have to admit, I'm at a loss as to how such a strong, and apparently stable, government system, can just start to fall apart. And, I don't believe, for one moment, it is just down to an annoying little woman who was fortunate enough to get herself married to a powerful man.'

Ty also put his cup down and settled down in his seat. For a while he seemed to be examining his hands in silence, thinking. She said nothing and let him tell his story his way. When he finally spoke, her patience was infinitely rewarded.

'First of all, I think I should mention who Ephea and her family actually are. No doubt you have heard various stories of a woman that has managed to marry a man, that many have considered the most elusive bachelor in the Empire, if not the universe. There were even stories throughout history that he was a misogynist, but I can assure you that couldn't be further from the truth.

'Are you aware of the system of rank that we have within the Empire, and the associated responsibility that goes with each level?'

Jean nodded, remembering Niall explaining this on their journey from Rassen to his farm.

'Well, Royce Morecross, Ephea's father, inherited his rank, along with substantial lands and property. He was an only child, and I believe there was no-one else to take over when his father died. Unfortunately, Royce was weak and a terrible landlord. He apparently bullied his staff and treated his tenants as nothing more than a means to fill his own coffers.

'He had been warned, on several occasions, by the Imperial Council to change his ways and, from what I can gather, he curbed them just enough to keep below the Council's gaze.

'That was, until his delightful daughters grew up. Their mother had disappeared many years before, I'm not entirely sure what happened to her. She could have died, or just left,

310

exasperated by her family's actions. However, by the time Ephea, Gradine and Yollan had grown into spoilt and vicious female versions of their father, their mother had been long gone.'

Ty stood up and began to pace the room slowly. Jean kept him in her gaze as he continued his story.

'Eventually the Emperor had had enough. He ordered a report into the conduct of Royce and his daughters and, in conclusion, he made the decision to strip the Morecross family of their responsibilities and, as such, their rank and entitlements. Their lands and properties came under the Guardianship of the Empire until such time someone could be found to replace Royce.'

'What happened to him? Royce and his daughters I mean?'

'Ah well that is it, he became a tenant of a neighbouring landowner.'

'Ouch, that must have hurt.'

'Oh, it did.'

'But that doesn't explain why his daughters hold such lofty positions now.'

'No, but I will come back to them later. For now we move forward in time by about a year or so. In fact, it will be just over five years ago it all started.

'One day a monk arrived in Parva, details of the man himself are scarce to be honest. I had only just arrived in the city myself and I was more concerned with other things. Anyway, this monk entered the city, and took himself to the main Crossroads within the South Bank. From there, he spent days proclaiming that he had come from across the other side of the universe, the Seventh Sector. For a while people completely ignored him as a crazy man, until one day he produced a large blue crystal stone. Its copy sits in the museum.'

Jean nodded, remembering the large blue sapphire like stone, residing in its case before the portrait of the Lady Katherine.

'People began to take more of an interest; then the press got hold of the story, suddenly our lowly monk had become a sensation. He told a tale of being brought to Kelan by the Gods, and that it was his task to bring justice for a terrible wrong. He spoke of a woman who came to his monastery seven thousand years ago calling herself Katherine, saying that she had been banished from her home by her brother Nathan, apparently because of something terrible she had done. It seems she never spoke of the crime she had committed that her own twin brother turned his back on her. Anyway, she carried with her the stone he called 'The Blue Star', and she entrusted it to the monks, saying that one day someone will claim it as rightfully theirs. Only the stone itself will know who that person will be, but until then, it needed to be kept safe. Katherine then left the monks to their 'sacred task' and disappeared into history.'

Ty shook his head in disgust and continued.

'The crowds had gathered around this lonely monk, listening to his fantastic story and wondering of the fate of Katherine. Their curiosity got the better of then and they eventually turned to the Emperor for answers.'

'What did he say?'

Ty shrugged. 'Nothing. He refused to comment, stating that the details, as he knew them, were private and not for public scrutiny. So of course, everyone obviously believed the monk. It seems that whatever Katherine had actually done to get herself exiled was ignored, so Nathan became the villain; deserting his sister and leaving her to wander the universe alone.'

Jean sat in silence for a while. Ty went to make more tea and she was thankful for the respite, already there were many questions spinning around her head that she herself needed answering. As another welcoming mug of tea was placed in front of her, she watched as Ty sat down.

'So what happened to the monk and the stone?'

'Good question, and to be honest, I don't really know. The monk disappeared soon after his proclamation, and the stone fell into the hands of others.'

'The Emperor?'

'No, Nathan never actually met the monk, or saw the stone, as far as I can tell. It probably would have saved a lot of pain and heartache if he had, but hindsight is a wonderful thing.'

Jean considered this information and urged Ty to continue, she had a nasty feeling that things got a lot worse from now on.

'So what happened next?'

'Ah, well now we return to our tale of Royce Morecross and his daughters. Within a matter of weeks of the Blue Star arriving in Kelan, he was once more the prosperous landlord, his bullying worse than ever.'

'How do you know that his change in circumstances was due to the Blue Star?'

'Because it was Nathan who gave him back his lands and properties, eventually agreeing to Ephea and her sisters marrying him, Damien and Daniel.'

Studying Ty, she sensed a sadness overcome the man, there was more to this than just a telling of an unfortunate story. He stood up again and this time his pacing was more agitated.

'The Order was practically brought under house arrest. Their influence was to be no more than guard duty of the city gates, along with the portals that each garrison was responsible for. It's been a bloody nightmare, made even worse when people like Bales, are promoted to positions they are clearly not capable of doing.'

Ty stopped pacing and stood behind the sofa he had been sitting on. He rested his hands on its back, breathing deeply, trying to control the anger that threatened to spill out. Jean sat in silence as he gathered himself, until eventually, he straightened and continued his pacing.

'I come from a world within the Empire called Juno, there is…. was, a large town called Belby. Five years ago, Royce Morecross contacted Nathan and the other Knights, telling them he now had the Blue Star. At first he wasn't believed of course, but when Royce was found to be responsible for some pretty nasty attacks on local people, particularly by incomers from Earth, Nathan had to listen.

'They arrived on a hill outside Belby, where they met and confronted Morecross. Apparently, he didn't say much except produce the stone. It seemed that he had managed to capture the power of the Blue Star and, for want of a better way of putting it, basically flattened the town. In fact, he completely crushed it…Everything… Right there, in front of the Emperor and the Knights; he had destroyed an entire town and every living thing within it.'

Jean was confused. 'How did he do it? What did Nathan do?'

'Royce used the stone of course.'

She made to say something but thought better of it.

Ty then said. 'What could Nathan do? Morecross threatened to do the same to another town, or even a city, if he didn't do as he was told.'

Now she understood.

Ty sighed. 'So all Nathan could do, was sit back and watch as Morecross and his daughters systematically took control away from him. Just as Nathan had previously done to Morecross.'

Jean shook her head. 'Royce didn't do this himself. This is the work of someone far more interested in things that have nothing to do with petty revenge and blackmail.'

Ty nodded in agreement.

'The question is who, why and how?'

Jean took a moment before speaking again.

'Of course, one question I have, is how do you know all of this? Everyone whom I have spoken to knows nothing of the fate of Belby, let alone the threat held over the Emperor. But you seem to have information that a Captain of the Order wouldn't normally be privy to.'

Ty sighed and nodded. 'That is very true… and very personal.'

A moment of sadness flitted across his face before he replaced it with a big grin. Jean wasn't fooled for a minute. Ty then completely changed the subject, rubbing his hands together he made a declaration.

'It is also a story better told on a full stomach; how's about some dinner?'

Jean smiled back. 'Sounds like an excellent suggestion.'

With that, Ty left to go into the kitchen and a short while later, Jean joined him and together they were soon chatting idly while they made dinner.

22

General's Fury

Bales made his way home after leaving the Palace grounds, in a foul mood; scowling at everyone he went past. Fellow knights seemed to find more interesting things to do, ducking down alleyways and buildings as they saw him approaching. He barely seemed aware of them; he was too caught up in his fury.

Having left his home that morning, glad to get out of the awful atmosphere of his grieving family, Bales had been determined to salvage the situation his son had created; his wife had been in full wail and he was relieved to close the front door behind him. He couldn't understand all the fuss himself; the idiot boy shouldn't have allowed himself to get caught.

Dear gods, he was due to get married to the silly girl, what he did behind closed doors then was his business. But no, Aleix couldn't wait, couldn't even find someone else to satisfy his urges, it had to be Morna. The girl with the big 'come and get it' eyes.

Bales snorted. The little tart was no angel, she'd waved those hips and ample breasts in his own direction more than once. If he didn't have his position to protect, he'd have made sure no-one else knew when he took her. However, Aleix obviously took his brains from his stupid mother, letting him get away with far too much; not enough back hands to keep him in check.

Too bloody soft. Well it's about time she learnt a thing or two about discipline.

He clenched his teeth in frustration. She had obviously forgotten the lessons her father had taught her.

Now there was a man who knew how to keep people in line.

Everyone in his household knew their place and what was required of them, and woe betide anyone who thought the authorities should poke their noses in. Bales sighed, damned authorities every bloody time; if it wasn't the police, it was the bastards in the Order.

And no-one is a bigger bastard than the one who sits on the top of the stinking heap.

His mind brought up an image of the man who had stood over him, trying to make him feel small, *Nathan L'guire.*

'Fuck.'

317

His sudden outburst startled a mother carrying a child in her arms, while walking up the avenue. She moved back in shock, causing the child to whimper at the sudden movement.

Bales snarled. 'Get out of my way. Don't you know who I am?'

The woman shook her head, but she understood the insignia on his uniform as a high-ranking knight. She hurried past, shaking her head at his rudeness, while trying to resettle the whimpering child. Her ignorance to who he was, only succeeded in fuelling Bales' anger and contempt of others. Again, he was reminded of Nathan, it was the Emperor's fault that people had no respect for him, a General of the Order no less. Nathan had allowed the lower masses to get away with such little respect for their betters.

Anger rose within him again when he thought of Nathan's damning verdict, declaring Aleix as a rapist. How the hell could his family come back from this one?

'Stupid, stupid boy.'

Then the image of Jean came to mind, he closed his eyes and felt his stomach plummet.

Who the hell is this woman?

It was her fault Aleix was caught, her fault he was now lying dead in the mortuary. And, she was found near the vandalism in the Museum.

How the hell was she still free?

Bales scoffed to himself, if Aleix wasn't already dead, they would probably try and pin that one on him too. But no, she had that oaf, Coniston mooning around her.

Probably thinks his luck is in if he works at it.

He turned into the road where his large family home stood, making his way up the winding path to the large red front door. Letting himself in, he concluded that something had to be done about the *bloody* Carter woman; he would make an effort to speak to the Lady Ephea the following day, before the Midsummer Ball. She would have just the right people to ensure *that* little problem didn't crop up again.

As the front door clicked shut, he was confronted with the wailing howls of his wife. He groaned and shut his eyes.

Where the hell does she get her energy from?

She ran into the hall and practically fell into her husband's arms; his anger was still running high and he didn't have time for her dramatics. He pushed her away, causing her to fall against the stair banisters. Rubbing at her shoulder that had taken the most of her fall, tears welled in her eyes.

'Victor, please. That hurt.'

He snarled in disgust. 'Then sort yourself out and gain some composure. Wash your face and make sure the rest of the house is in a respectable order too while you are at it.'

She flushed at his anger, flinching as he threatened to follow his remarks with a meaningful blow. Turning her face away, she acquiesced.

'Yes Victor, I'm sorry.'

Bales, satisfied his dominance was once more unquestioned, moved towards the stairs.

'I'll have my dinner in the study, make sure it is hot this time.'

Acknowledging his unveiled threat with a wince, she asked how his day had been with the Emperor? Had the matter been sorted?

319

Bales had gained the first step of the stairs and paused before turning to face her, relishing the look on her face as he sent home the fateful blow. Jabbing his finger in towards her face, punctuating every damning point.

'Oh, it's been sorted, alright. The Emperor, himself, has passed judgement... Your Son, is a rapist... A disgrace to your family... You, should be ashamed of yourself... I wipe my hands of you all.'

He then stalked upstairs leaving his wife shocked, silent tears rolling down her already puffy face.

A door slammed above as Bales entered his study. His wife walked into the kitchen to give instructions to feed her husband, her life already draining from her body.

23

Mason

After their dinner, Jean and Ty were back on the sofas, facing one another with mugs of tea on the coffee table cooling, happily replete. Once they were settled Jean waited for Ty to begin.

Ty considered his thoughts for a short while before he started. If he was honest, he wasn't sure how to explain anything without going back to the start, all the way back to what seemed someone else's life now. Staring at his hands resting in his lap, he was aware of the woman across the table, watching. Taking a long low breath, he started.

'When I arrived in Parva five years ago, a newly made up Captain, I was ready to take on the Empire. I had worked hard since leaving Pernia, serving in several posts, including Earth.

Looking back now I was young, innocent and a complete arsehole.'

Jean raised an eyebrow and laughed.

Ty joined in. 'I can't lie, I must have been insufferable, but such is the way of the young.'

'It was only five years ago.'

'Five years? It might as well be a lifetime, to be honest. But I digress. Part of my duties here eventually brought me into contact with the Knights themselves. I have to admit, it's a bit nerve wracking when you finally meet one of the men you've spent your life emulating and honouring. I was so nervous standing outside the office of Damien, that by the time I was called in to see him and make my report, I was a gibbering wreck. I'm surprised I wasn't demoted and sent to Aria for a mental health evaluation right there and then.'

He laughed at the memory, and Jean recognised, once more, the light that had been hidden since he had started.

'However, instead of sending me away, Damien left his office and asked his secretary to bring in some tea. Apparently, he was convinced I was going to fall down if I didn't sit down, he'd also just had his carpet cleaned.'

Ty laughed again, but this time quietly, his mind momentarily in a different time and place.

He continued. 'The next thing I know, we are sitting in his office, just as we are talking now, about anything and everything. By the time I had left his office, I had made my report and, to my complete surprise, left my heart there as well.

'I told myself so many times over the next few weeks, that I was a complete fool and to get over it. I had a crush, and that was all it was. I'm not entirely sure who I thought I was fooling at the time, but it was a mantra I insisted on repeating silently, often several times a day.

'It didn't work.

'No matter how much I tried, I could not hide from my feelings. At first, I found myself dodging duties that would mean I was anywhere near Damien, even volunteering for the duties no-one else wanted to do. But in the end I wasn't strong enough, I would make a point of being the one who had to be there, anywhere he was, but always in the shadows; just in case he realised how much of an idiot I was.'

Ty leant forward on the sofa, his arms resting on his knees, hands clasped lightly in front of him.

'Needless to say, Damien is no fool, and one day he called me back into his office. I felt sick, I was sure he was going to have me transferred as far away from Parva as possible. I entered his office, desperately wanting to see him again and dreading it would be for the last time.'

Ty looked down into his hands, a smile slowly grew on his face and he returned his gaze back to Jean.

'He didn't send me away though, in fact, he wanted to know why, every time he arranged for me to be around, I would avoid him? He was concerned that he misunderstood our first meeting and was worried he had upset me.' Ty shook his head. 'Once we realised we had both been complete idiots he asked me to join him for coffee in the city when I finished my duty. The Emperor and the other Knights often went into the city before Royce Morecross happened, until the events at Belby that is, so it wasn't unusual for them to frequent the coffee houses there. Damien and I had our coffee, several in fact, and I

323

would love to say the rest is history — but then everything went wrong.

'Morecross and his daughters were becoming a real menace and anyone close to the Knights were considered a threat. Damien was terrified that if they found out about our relationship, especially as Gradine was demanding to be his wife, that something would happen to me. Neither of us were happy about it, but Damien was so adamant, what could I do?

'So for the past five years we have met secretly, though rarely, hoping that one day this nightmare would be over and we can be open about our relationship.'

Ty rubbed his face with his hands.

'Every time we have to say goodbye now, it's getting harder to leave. I can't lose him Jean, but I don't know how much more either of us can take of all this.'

Ty put his head in his hands, he was exhausted from such little sleep and the effort of his emotional outpouring. Jean stood and quietly moved to his side, holding him.

'We will sort this Ty, I promise.'

She took his face in her own hands and looked into his sad, beautiful blue eyes.

'And I promise, you will once more enjoy a coffee within the city with Damien.'

Later that evening, the mist was now just a few tendrils around the river quays, even the stars were managing to come out, though no moon was visible. The night was dark except for the orbs from the city street lighting, casting their gentle glow through the gloom. It was an hour before midnight and Ty and Jean were making their way back to her lodgings. Ty had

324

insisted on accompanying her, stating it gave him a chance to see how the streets were after last night's occurrences. Jean didn't argue, in fact she felt relieved. She had enjoyed his company, and despite the unfortunate start, considered theirs as the beginning of a good friendship, someone she could trust. Between her keen senses and many years of experience, Jean had come to learn quickly who she could and couldn't trust, there were even a very few she would consider as friends.

Earlier, once Ty had gathered himself, the two of them had sat talking quietly about Ty and his relationship with Damien, and what he knew of the other Knights. Jean gathered, that while his relationship was to remain secret from the rest of the Empire, Damien had confided in those closest to him; to the point where they often helped in ensuring that clandestine meetings went undetected by the Morecross family and their Patrols.

Ty then asked Jean about her own life and how she came to be here in Kelan. While reluctant at first she told him of her previous life as a wife and mother, and the joy of eventually becoming a grandmother. He was full of questions and she was quite impressed with his interrogation techniques. Eventually she resorted to telling a few tales of her other escapades, featuring the often weird and wonderful people she came across, spending the rest of the evening laughing at the antics she, and those who accompanied her, often found themselves in.

By the time the pair were walking towards the bridge, crossing over to the South Bank, they had forged the beginnings of a happy friendship. As they travelled, they both remained alert to those around them, Ty noting that there were a lot more people in the city now, determined to enjoy the festival period despite the recent murders and scuffles in the streets.

There was now a marked increase in security however, not only were the police making a more visible presence, but a notable number of the Order were out too. Evidently the threat of more protests had been taken seriously, and a more concerted effort was made to deter anyone from stirring up trouble that may have been planned for that evening. But it was still unnerving to see so many people about when trouble wasn't that far away.

Eventually they reached the street of Mrs Moore's lodging house where, unlike the previous fog filled evenings, the view down the road was clear. Suddenly, Jean grabbed hold of Ty's arm and, with some considerable effort, she dragged him into an alleyway. Possibly the one she and Ella had hidden in previously, Jean thought ironically.

'What the hell...'

'Shhhhh.'

When Ty looked down enquiringly at her, she pointed towards a house situated about a hundred yards further down the street. Two men were coming out of the front door of Mrs Moore's house. One of them had all the markings of the Patrols; he looked as if he would cut your throat just for looking at him. But it was the man who followed him out of the house, that was cause for concern to Jean. He was large, very large, and he carried himself like a soldier, not a street thug. He was cautious as he moved, constantly scanning the road and the houses around him.

Tucking back into the alley, Jean looked up into the puzzled face of her companion, she whispered her concerns.

'That was *my* lodgings that they have just come out of. Poor Mrs Moore, I have to make sure she's alright.'

Jean made to enter into the street again, but Ty held her back.

'Wait.'

She tried to free her arm. 'I need to find out where they are going.'

Ty let her go but barred her way out of the alley.

'Why? They are just another couple of Patrolmen out to cause trouble. We only need to make sure your landlady is alright.'

Jean shook her head. '*You* have to check on Mrs M, *I* need to follow those men.'

She stepped quietly into the street, but was dismayed to note that both men had already disappeared.

'Shit.'

By now Ty had joined her. He shrugged his shoulders.

'They'll be surrounded by the crowds enjoying the festival now, I doubt if you'll find them amidst all that lot.'

Jean shook her head again. 'No, they won't be among the revellers. They were here because of me, and they will return to whatever nest of vipers they have set up in the city. They won't be interested in having fun.'

'You seem pretty sure of that.'

Jean looked up at him. He was shocked to see the look of fear etched into her face.

Concerned he asked. 'Who are they?'

Jean leant against the wall and rubbed her face; this added a whole different light on the situation. She needed to think and, now more than ever, she needed to speak to Nathan.

327

'It's only one of those men I have any concern about, though his companion must be a vicious piece of work to be allowed to accompany him. The big guy, his name is Mason, and I know him.'

'How?'

'We've met before, it was a couple of years ago, but time wouldn't matter to his kind.' Jean shuddered. 'Ty, he's from the Seventh Sector and I don't mean Earth. He comes from a long way away, and he will be here for only one reason. I have to find out what that reason is. I hate to think what poor Mrs M has been through.'

Ty considered this for a moment.

'Very well, but you stay here, and I'll check on your landlady. The chances are they will have someone keeping an eye on the house.'

He pulled a set of keys out of his pocket.

'You should go back to my apartment and stay there tonight.'

Then, without allowing her to argue, he stepped out into the road and down the street towards her lodgings. He returned a short while later carrying a small bundle.

'Mrs Moore is pretty shaken up but she's made of stern stuff. They didn't harm her, they just wanted to see you. When they discovered you weren't there, they searched your room; I'm afraid they ripped open furniture and some of your clothing for some reason. I did manage to gather a few things I found still intact though, I'm sorry, but this is all I have.'

He held out the small bundle and Jean took it from him gratefully. She had to admit that there wasn't really anything of value left in her room, but she appreciated his thoughtfulness.

She did, however, find herself checking the pocket of the jacket she was wearing, feeling the comforting data pack that resided there. Her thoughts were interrupted by Ty asking questions.

'Are you sure you have recognised the right man? I talked with Mrs Moore as I made her a cup of tea. She said that the big man deliberately made sure the smaller one didn't harm her. That hardly seems the sort of person you have described.'

'As I said, he is here for a reason. He won't care about other people's issues here, only completing his task. The only ones who need to worry, are those who get in his way, and if he knows that I am here, I will be one of them. You said they destroyed my clothing, was there a dark blue suit?'

'Yes, I believe there was.'

She nodded. 'Figures, that suit was armoured, and believe me the last thing he wants, is me protected in anyway.'

She took Ty's arm and they left the alley, making their way back up the street.

'If you're sure Mrs M is alright, then I am the last person who should be anywhere near her now. When this is finished, I'll make her the biggest pot of tea and take a whole pile of cakes, feeding her as much gossip as she can deal with. Until then we have work to do.

'Ty, you have to find a way to get me in to see the Emperor.'

Nodding that he understood her urgency, he left her at the entrance to the road of his own home. Then hurrying, he made his way back to the Palace and the Guardroom, ready to take up his duties for the evening; a plan already forming to speak to the one person whom he trusted to help Jean now.

By the time the sun had come up and he was making his weary way back home, Captain Ty Coniston had at last received good news for Jean.

24

Careen

Bang. Bang. Bang

The crashing in his head was getting louder, irritating the hell out of the headache threatening to explode in his skull. His throat was so dry, his tongue felt stuck to the roof of his mouth, he needed water, and soon.

Bang. Bang. Bang.

His eyes shot open, the blazing sunshine streaming through the window, burning into the back of his already painful brain.

Bang. Bang. Bang.

'General Bales, please open up or we will be forced to break down the door.'

Hiding his head under the blanket, he tried to steady his already churning stomach. His voice sounded muffled from beneath his covers.

'Dear gods no, go away.'

'Open the door Sir, this is the Police.'

Bales forced the covers down and blinked painfully.

Police? What the hell were they doing here? Shit, what has she done now?

'Stay where you are officer, I'll be with you in a moment.'

He attempted to shade his eyes from the agony of the sunlight and tried to sit up. The world spun, and his stomach did multiple summersaults. It took all his effort not to throw up. On the table there stood an empty bottle of whisky, a souvenir from his trip to Edinburgh last year. Bales groaned, what was he thinking? Even he knew he wasn't a drinker, he rarely touched the stuff; but last night he was so angry, he just wanted to obliterate his misery. Now, he still had his misery, but it was spectacularly accompanied by a raging hangover that he wasn't sure he would ever see the end of.

Bang. Bang.

'Sir?'

'Alright, I'm coming.'

Getting up from the sofa he had used as a makeshift bed, he worked his way along the wall until he was at the door. Summoning all his efforts into making, what he hoped was, a look of superiority and displeasure, he flung open the door. Before him stood a senior policeman in full uniform; Bales was sure he had been there when Aleix was accused in the hospital.

What was his name again?

'Good morning Sir, I'm Inspector Graves. We had a problem rousing you, we were concerned something had happened.'

Graves, that's it.

Bales felt decidedly sick now.

'What the hell are you talking about? What are you doing in my house at this ungodly hour? Get out and make an appointment to see me when I am more disposed to accept your company.'

Making some effort to close the door on his unwelcome visitor, Bales was dismayed to see the Inspector block the door with his foot. The Inspector smiled, but it didn't reach his eyes.

'I'm afraid that will not be possible Sir…. There has been an unfortunate incident.'

He studied Bales and looked him up and down.

'Perhaps it would be better if you dressed yourself before following us downstairs.'

'Are you trying to be funny Inspector, how I dress in my own house is my business.'

It was then he caught the face of the young maid standing just behind Graves, realising she was staring in horror at something, he looked down. To his mortification, he found he was only wearing his shirt; apparently, he had stripped off everything else before collapsing on to the sofa. His morning erection stood proud for all to see. Rapidly trying to cover his embarrassment, he shouted that the maid should get him some painkillers. He regretted the increase in decibels instantly. Facing Graves, who seemed to be doing his damnedest not to laugh, he snarled.

'I will be with you shortly Inspector.'

Slamming the door in their faces, Bales made his way to the small bathroom he had installed as part of his study, before making himself more presentable to be seen in public. Staring into the mirror at the bloodshot eyes and the shadow of his beard, he decided that shaving was one task too much at the moment. Turning to the toilet he started to relieve himself.

Dear gods, could this day get any worse?

By the time he reopened his study door, the Inspector had been joined by another PC. He thought he recognised her too, but his brain hurt too much to try and remember. A footman stood behind, holding up a tray with two pills and a large glass of water. Bales leant forward and grabbed the tray, dismissing the man as inconsequential. He missed the glance that passed between the two police officers.

Graves stepped forward and introduced his fellow officer.

'Sir, you of course remember Sergeant Croft here?'

Croft, of course.

'Sergeant?'

'Yes, a recent promotion, and one well deserved.'

Bales studied Graves, was that a dig at him?

'Well, I'm sure you think so Inspector. Now what is this all about?'

Again, Graves and Croft glanced at each other and this time Bales saw it.

'Is there a problem?'

'If you will follow us Sir.'

Curiosity now getting the better of him, he joined Graves and they made their way down the staircase, with the newly promoted Ella following behind. To Bales' surprise, however, when they reached the bottom of the stairs, instead of making

334

their way to the drawing room where he would normally receive visitors, he was led towards the garden, where many more police officers were working.

From somewhere behind him, a woman flung herself around his neck and began to sob. His anger flaring again he grabbed her arms, forcing his only daughter away, demanding that she pull herself together and find her mother. This seemed to make the girl worse and she fell onto the churned-up grass and sobbed even harder and louder.

Unfortunately, the painkillers still hadn't begun to take effect, and the person in his head with a very big hammer, had yet to relent their task. But Bales had had enough.

'Will someone please, tell me what the hell is going on? Where is my wife?'

Graves stood in front of the General, his face sombre.

'Your wife is dead Sir. One of your servants found her hanging in the garden from the beech tree this morning. They tried to rouse you, but there was no answer. They didn't know what else to do, so they called for us.'

Bales was stunned, what was the man talking about?

'Dead? But I was just talking to her last night. You must have the wrong woman.'

'I am afraid your wife has been formally identified by your son and daughter. I'm very sorry Sir.'

Bales was incredulous.

'How? Who did this?'

He could only think of one person, that bitch Carter. Graves was speaking again, and he looked up.

'The coroner has yet to make a formal report, but his initial findings suggest this was suicide. A letter has been found that would support this theory.'

'Suicide? Never. She wouldn't do that to me. She wouldn't dare.'

The Inspector looked shocked. 'I beg your pardon Sir?'

'Where is this letter? I want to see it now.'

Graves looked back at Ella, she nodded and left the two men standing there in an awkward silence. When she returned, it was with a letter inside a protective evidence bag. Handing it to Bales, she stood back as he read the contents.

> *I'm sorry,*
>
> *I cannot cope with the responsibility of my shame any longer.*
>
> *To my father, I was the failure destined to ruin everything I touched. It seems that he was right after all.*
>
> *To my children, who must now suffer the loss of the reputation that my beautiful son, Aleix, and I have brought upon them.*
>
> *To my husband, I cannot rest knowing that he has been right, that I am too weak, that even though I had tried to make things right, it would never be enough.*
>
> *The Emperor has made his judgement and my family will pay the price. Even the sacrifice of Aleix was not enough to save us.*
>
> *May the gods save us all,*
>
> *Careen Bales*

Bales went over and over the familiar handwriting, his anger growing. Almost forcing the letter back into the hands of the sergeant, he turned and made his way to the patio table, slumping into a seat. He held his head in his hands and sobbed.

To those around him, it was a scene of a grieving husband trying to make sense of a terrible tragedy. The truth was, Bales grieved only for the loss of the man he had fought so hard to become.

Within the matter of a few days he had lost everything; position, rank and power, all those years wasted. Someone had to pay, and he knew who to start with.

'Carter'.

25

Belby

By the time Ty had walked through his front door, Jean was making breakfast. The cooking smells emanating from his kitchen, perked up his tired brain at the prospect of a decent meal. He'd been awake for nearly thirty-six hours and he was bone weary. She looked up as he entered the kitchen.

'You look done in.'

He tried a tired grin.

'Thanks. And good morning to you too.'

She laughed. 'Good morning.'

She put her hand on his arm.

'You do need to sleep though. Here, eat this and then get yourself off to bed, you're no use to anyone if you are dead on your feet.'

Placing a large plate of scrambled eggs on toast in front of him, Ty just grinned and nodded before devouring the welcome breakfast. Halfway through the contents of his plate he finally came up for air.

'I'm sorry, this is really good. I barely managed a sandwich last night.'

Jean sat opposite him at the table with her own breakfast.

'Was there any more trouble in the city?'

Ty shook his head.

'No, well nothing out of the norm for a Midsummer Festival, but people were still determined to let us know how they feel about the Emperor, the Order, and how they have handled the whole Patrol problem.'

'To be fair, they have a point.'

Ty sighed. 'I know. That doesn't make it any easier to deal with though. They seem to forget that when we're not working, we have to deal with the Patrols too. We know how bloody annoying it's been.'

He resumed his eating, though this time at a slightly less gut busting pace, then seemed to remember something.

'I have good news however, I've managed to secure a meeting with someone who can at least get you into the Palace while Nathan is there. Tonight is the Midsummer Ball and all the Knights will be there too. However, before she does anything, she wants to see you.'

'Needs some proof eh?'

Ty at least blushed at this.

339

'She, like me has a lot to lose. In fact, she has a lot more to lose.'

'It's fine Ty, I understand. So, when do I get to meet this mysterious woman?'

'This afternoon, 2 o'clock.'

Jean looked at her watch and nodded.

'Excellent. That gives me plenty of time to look into a few things. How about I meet you back here an hour beforehand? There is something I need you to do for me first though.'

'Now?'

He looked more exhausted than ever, and after a hearty breakfast all he wanted to do was collapse in his bed.

'Don't worry, you don't have to actually do anything, just give me your hand and concentrate on this Belby place.'

'That's it?'

'That's it.'

Reaching across the table they clasped each other's hands and Ty set his mind on the town he had visited as a boy; its buildings, its people and the beautiful countryside of his home world of Juno. Jean gave his hand a squeeze before she released it.

'I can't help the people of Belby, but I'll make sure what happened there won't happen anywhere else.'

Ty gave her an exhausted smile. Then taking his plate away he placed it in the sink before Jean turned and ushered him out of the kitchen.

'Now go, you need to sleep. I'll be back here around lunch time.'

Picking up her jacket, Jean headed for the front door, throwing back a final instruction as she left.

340

'Sweet dreams.'

The door closed behind her, while Ty let himself into his bedroom. He barely had the energy to remove his uniform before collapsing into dreamless oblivion.

The previous evening, Jean had lain in her bed, mulling over the information that she had learnt that day, in particular the tale told by Ty. Someone had actually destroyed, or believed they had destroyed, a whole town by using a mystical stone. In doing so, they had held an entire Empire to ransom, slowly bringing it to its knees.

Jean came to the decision that before she did anything else, she wanted to see Belby and its fate. During their dinner, Ty had explained that it was impossible for anyone to translocate from Parva directly, except through the portals that were located at the city gates. Nathan had created a barrier over the city, which meant that anyone entering had to pass through a guarded portal or gate first. There was also, apparently, a portal situated beside the guest quarters at the Palace, but that was always locked and guarded. Only to be used in special circumstances.

She breathed a sigh of relief, at least now she knew why she was unable to translocate while she was in her cell by the guard room. She decided to not share that bit of information with Ty.

With the early morning sun now clearing away the shadows, Jean headed out towards the river and crossed the bridge to the South Bank. Following the road that led east, and the gate that she had passed by only a few days ago. This time she was on foot, so she had to pass through the gate itself. Its structure was a tower, built into the rock of the caldera walls surrounding the city, extending upwards to the full height of the cliff face. It joined a manmade, fortified wall that ringed its ridge line, with similar towers set equidistant apart around the caldera walls, each with their own defendable steps linking each tower to the city below.

The gate itself, was high enough to allow a mounted rider through, and wide enough to allow two carts to pass each other. On either side of the entrance, was an open door where a knight stood sentry; both keenly watching those who moved in and out of the city. Small windows in the tower walls indicated that there were more knights within; this was an important access to the walls and towers above and despite any issues elsewhere, the security of the city depended on a strong force at its weakest points.

Passing out into the countryside beyond, she breathed in the fresh air. As far as she was concerned it didn't matter where you were, cities were always smelly and full of far too many people. Looking around, she made her way further along the caldera walls, away from the busy traffic of the road and river. There was evidence that until recently there had been some attempt at habitation here, but no doubt they had been moved on. With all the unrest going on within the city, the threat of allowing people this close to the walls unchecked, was probably unacceptable.

Making her way to an area that was away from the view of the main gate, she set her mind to the information she had gleaned from Ty that morning regarding Belby. Not even a heartbeat passed, and she had left Parva behind.

Looking around, Jean took in her surroundings; she was on top of a small hill, topped with a copse of trees. The air felt fetid and the ground wet and mouldy. The trees around her carried leaves, but they were wilted and covered in black spots; she shuddered, this was not a healthy place. Instinctively she drew her daggers.

Making her way to the edge of the tree line, she tried to sense the life that should have surrounded her, but instead, there was nothing but a cold eerie silence.

When she had left Parva on the world of Kelan, the sun had just newly risen. Here at the place where the town of Belby once stood, on the world of Juno, it appeared to be around midday. However, a thin, low layer of cloud hung over the area that left the atmosphere cold, dreary and damp. Moving around the edge of the copse, she saw below the hill on which she stood, were whole areas of devastation spread out in all directions. Evidence of trees and buildings having been ripped from the ground was all around. Where grass and crops once grew, there was now a sickly brown dust bowl, littered with tree stumps and battered foundations.

But it was the scene that met her as she continued around the hilltop that caused her to moan in shock.

On a large promontory were the remains of the town of Belby. Its once solid stone walls now lay broken, the ramparts razed by, what seemed to be, the debris from the surrounding area having smashed through them. Within, the buildings that once stood there were now demolished, the debris piled high; combined with trees and barns that had crashed into the town. Again, Jean tried to sense life of some kind, but still, there was nothing. Everything was dead. Even the trees behind her were dying. Jean could only liken the scene to a war zone, she had had to witness far too many of them, recognising the signs and ultimately what caused them.

This time, instead of feeling for life she opened her senses to release the power that usually remained quietly within her. She frowned as she felt a barrier somewhere in the distance, surrounding the dead town. Slowly making her way down the hill, she walked towards the invisible wall. As she approached, her skin began to prickle from an unknown source of heat, growing stronger as she drew nearer.

Finally, Jean was at the base of the hill that Belby had sat upon, she could feel the intensity and heat of the invisible barrier. It was so strong she had to fight to stay this close. But by now she understood the heat she felt; one she knew that, for a short while at least, she would be immune too.

Radiation.

It accounted for all the lifelessness that surrounded her, but it was within the town that the source existed. Jean was considering the possibilities that would cause such devastation, but she couldn't see how it was feasible, not within the Empire, or anywhere else outside of the Seventh Sector for that matter. What she did know, was that no trumped-up landowner, with an ego to match his grievance, was capable of this, no matter how pissed off he was.

Jean turned and made her way back up the hill, considering all the facts she had gleaned so far. She didn't like her conclusions, which accounted for everything she had heard about the horrendous fall of Belby, and the consequences to the Knights and the Empire. To deal with it however, she would need help, so once more she returned to her need to see the Emperor Nathan.

Returning to the copse at the top of the hill and the dying trees, she took another look around her. She felt troubled, and it

344

wasn't just because of the fate of Belby and its citizens, but because she could feel herself breaking her one personal rule. She was beginning to care.

Not that she didn't care about the people she worked with and helped over the years, that was normal. But she was beginning to feel concern about the future of the world of Kelan, the Empire and the people in it. It seemed important to her that whatever happened over the next few days, to not succeed and see the people she had met suffer, would hurt her deeply. Normally, she would finish the work she had to do and leave, those left behind were once more on their own. She had done what was required, they needed to deal with the consequences.

It hadn't always been like that of course, there was a time she would stay and help if she could; even to the point of revisiting and making sure everything was well. But that all ended one fateful day. She found herself placing her hand across the scar under her shirt, the memories washing over her.

It had been a fairly straightforward mission; everything had worked to plan, and she had helped those affected in the aftermath. But while she dealt with the oddities of the universe; the wrinkles in the fabric of the cosmos that distorted the natural course of time and space, life had to be responsible for its own fate.

Everything had happened so fast; she had been drawn into their politics, their petty squabbles, and suddenly, battle lines were drawn; war was the devastating but inevitable outcome. She had unwittingly found herself in the middle of a manmade horror and she couldn't get out. The ensuing bloodbath still haunted her dreams, often waking, screaming into the lonely darkness, soaked in sweat and reliving the fear and horror.

She should have died that day, but she didn't. Once she had fallen unconscious at the hands of the man driven to madness within the hell of that battle, she had been unaware of the many hands that had lifted and taken her away. It was apparently over a week later, before she woke to the administrations of the Chevil; a race of healers that lived out with the confines of the universe's time and space. They had been watching over her for centuries, aware of the danger she had fallen into, so when the time came, they were ready to not only heal her body, but also help heal her mind; but even for the Chevil, her soul was out of the reach.

Once she had recovered and her saviours had done all they could for her, she returned back to the universe she knew, however this time she had vowed never to be that close to the people she worked with on a mission again.

Resolute in her decision she had found it worked, she did what she needed to do before moving on, refusing to look back.

That is until now.

With everything that she had gleaned about the Empire and the people within it, Jean could not throw off the desire to stay, but the thought still terrified her. She wasn't sure what frightened her more, the consequences of staying, or what it would do to her soul if she didn't?

Taking a deep breath, shook her head to clear her mind. That was something she would have to deal with at some point, but now she needed to deal with the present. Setting her mind back to the city of Parva, until once again she was standing outside its city walls, her mind on the task in hand.

Making her way back to Ty's apartment, Jean was still unable to shake the melancholy feeling as she walked. Wandering through a market that had been set up in one of the squares, she bought a couple of pies for their lunch, but barely noticed the bunting and gaily coloured market stalls that surrounded her.

By the time she reached the apartment, Ty was already up and dressed. He looked much better than he did earlier that morning, and he happily devoured the proffered pie; finishing Jean's too. She couldn't summon an appetite after the scenes she had witnessed that morning.

Dwelling on the images that flitted across her brain, she felt the anger rise again, but this time she focused it and her senses once more hardened. Even Ty could feel the change in the atmosphere and looked at her enquiringly; the quiet, smiling woman he knew yesterday seemed slightly harder around the edges.

Once they had finished their quick lunch, Ty and Jean made their way back into the city to meet up with the person Ty was convinced could help Jean finally meet with the Emperor. They were making their way back across the river to the South Bank, Ty steering Jean towards the edge of the city and its caldera. By now, the Midsummer celebrations were getting into full swing; many people were out in their holiday finery, determined to enjoy themselves despite the hostilities and unsolved murders. Extra stalls had even been set up in the market squares; there was always money to be made when people were having fun.

Jean was alert, on edge, she looked around and noted the general merrymaking and laughter of those around her; but she couldn't be happy for them. By now she fully sensed the rot that underlined the city, the festering wound that had been five years in the making. She felt sickened by the fake gaudiness of it all; and in amongst the foulness, sat Mason. Her stomach lurched at the thought, and she vented her anger and fear.

'Why can't people understand how wrong all this is? How much danger they are in?'

Ty looked at her surprised, he'd just been landed a big kiss from a passing group of young women, who had obviously been enjoying the revelry in one or two inns since earlier in the day.

'It's only a kiss. They are just having a bit of fun. What's wrong with that?'

She shook her head. 'I don't have a problem with people having fun Ty, the gods know I would be the first to enjoy the festivities usually. But not now. The danger is all around, just waiting for the right moment, these people shouldn't be getting drunk in the city; they should be running for the hills. Looking for safety.'

'You are kidding right?'

'You think I would joke about this?'

She stopped and looked up at him, he gave her a resigned smile.

'No. I don't think you would joke about this, but we have to be realistic. This is a huge city, with many more people coming in, you can't evacuate them just like that.' He snapped his fingers to prove his point. 'The Emperor isn't going to even consider it, not without a hell of a lot more proof that there really is a threat.'

'You still don't believe me about Mason?'

'He's one man? We have a huge garrison of experienced knights. You think we can't cope?'

Ty drew his eyebrows together, his pride rising to the fore. Jean closed her eyes and tried to control her frustration.

'No Ty, I have no doubt about the ability of the Order, but this is not about whether you are good enough. But, I know Mason, and I know what he is capable of. I also know he won't be here alone. They have an agenda and a lot of people will die, including members of the Order, in the misplaced belief that they are just normal soldiers. If I'm honest, I believe they have already killed, and are   the ones responsible for the recent murders that have hit Parva.'

Ty suddenly looked much more serious.

'I don't understand, what do you mean? What can they possibly do that we can't cope with? And what makes you so sure they are the killers?'

Jean looked at her watch. 'Do we have time before we have to be at this meeting?'

Ty nodded. 'We have a short while. Why?'

'Let's find somewhere for a coffee.'

He looked around, then took her arm and led her down an alleyway. They entered a small shop that had the most delicious aroma of coffee as they walked through the door. Ty ordered at the counter and they sat down. Aware that time was short, Jean leant forward and began.

'Ty, I've been doing this game for a very, very long time. I have met people and creatures from all over the Seventh Sector and, some way or another, I've dealt with them all. There are some amongst those, however, that even I have thought twice about. Not because of their size, or their ability to fight, but because of what makes them tick; and Mason is definitely under that category.'

She paused and thought for a moment.

'Have you ever come across anything like an android? A robot? That sort of thing.'

Ty shook his head. 'No I haven't, but I'm an engineer by trade, I understand the mechanics involved.'

'Good, so you know that a machine can be built with strength and that they can be programmed to do pretty much anything. But at the end of the day, they are only as good as their software.'

'Are you saying Mason is a machine?'

'No, I am saying if he was, I wouldn't be so worried. Besides I doubt if there is an android that could be built that could survive the Ti'akai.'

Their coffee arrived and Jean noted the extra smile the waitress gave Ty as she put down his beverage. She raised an eyebrow and he grinned back at her.

'I can't help it, it's not like I can put a sign up that says 'sorry, wrong gender'.'

Despite herself Jean had to laugh, and for a moment the tension was eased. They both took a sip of their hot coffee before Jean continued.

'The first time I met anyone like Mason was about ten years ago. They are known as the Kaimiren, though they are generally known as just Ren for short. They're not machines, but are a race genetically bred as soldiers. They are engineered to have reinforced skeletons and have abilities to withstand huge extremes that would normally kill your average human. But it isn't that which scares me.

'As I have said, I've met them before. Kaimiren, are beings bred with no conscience; they are given a task and no matter what, they will do whatever they have to, to complete it. Unlike the limited parameters of a machine, they can adapt and overcome, whatever comes their way, but they won't be side-tracked by inconsequential events. Mrs M was safe last night because she didn't get in Mason's way, and he ensured his *friend* didn't do anything that may cause people to investigate further.'

She took another sip of her coffee.

'These men are mercenaries that are available for hire, but at stupid prices. Funnily enough though, not for their own profit, it's someone else who owns them, reaping the financial reward. But they are rare and very expensive to create, it takes many failed, and often fatal, attempts to make a final product that could be called a Kaimiren. As such, to lose even one in the field would be a disaster, so costs must be covered. Whoever has hired Mason will no doubt have hired at least a couple more. They will have an agenda, and whatever it is, it will be catastrophic. These men don't do subtle. This is why it worries me about the Order, they will see ordinary men and will try to stop them. But it can only end one way, and that is with many knights who will have died needlessly.'

'You really think they are that much of a threat?'

'I know they are.'

'But you think they have been responsible for the murders?'

Jean nodded and explained the theory that she and Ella had considered regarding the stolen food. 'The Kaimiren need a lot of calories, so if they get hungry, they will go on the hunt for it, even coming out of hiding and into the city.'

'Then how are we going to deal with them?'

351

'You're not, but when I have spoken to Nathan, I will have a better idea.'

'Damien will be in a lot of danger, won't he?'

Looking down into his almost empty cup, Ty couldn't hide his concern.

'I can't lie to you Ty, there won't be an easy end to all of this.'

He nodded his head, he understood. Looking at his watch he stood up and beckoned her to follow. Jean was both relieved, and saddened, so see a more resolute mood in his demeanour.

'We need to get moving, Anna will be waiting.'

Assuming Anna was their point of contact Jean followed, continuing their journey in silence, both concerned with the consequences of the Kaimiren and their hidden agenda.

26

Anna Priestly

Making their way through the festival crowds was becoming more difficult, several times they had to elbow their way past overzealous revellers. By the time they reached their destination both of them were hot, bruised and thoroughly fed up. They had arrived outside the base of a stone tower of fortified steps leading up to the caldera ridge line way above. Entering the building, they made their way to a knight who sat behind a desk, he looked up and acknowledged Ty as someone he recognised, even though he wasn't in his uniform.

'Afternoon Captain Coniston, just wait here and I'll let her know you've arrived.'

He glanced briefly at Jean before knocking on a door behind him and entering. A moment later he returned and held the door open.

'She'll see you now.'

Nodding his thanks, Ty walked into the room with Jean following, no sooner had they entered, the door was firmly closed behind them. They were in an office and Jean instinctively knew that whoever it belonged to, wasn't someone who dealt with fools gladly. She reckoned the woman sitting at her desk was about fifty years old, a touch of grey was streaked within her thick auburn hair, which had been pulled back into a neat bun at the nape of her neck. Wearing the uniform of a knight she had the bearing of a seasoned soldier; she expected respect and no doubt, had earned it. Her eyes missed nothing, and Jean felt herself scrutinised as much as she scrutinised her. While her face showed the lines of someone who had experienced the hardships of life, Jean sensed that she wasn't embittered by it.

Standing up, she was probably just an inch shorter than Jean, she moved around the desk and approached them, offering Ty her hand; he shook it, and a broad smile split her weather worn face. She was more striking than beautiful, but Jean considered she looked better for it.

'Hello Ty, lovely to see you again.'

'Afternoon Anna, yes, it's been too long.'

He indicated Jean, who stepped forward.

'This is Jean Carter, the person I spoke about in my note. Jean, this is Colonel Anna Priestly.'

Both women shook hands and Anna indicated for everyone to sit down. Just then the door opened, and the knight who had shown them in, carried a tea tray which he left on Anna's desk. The Colonel thanked him, and he left. Pouring out three cups of tea, the Colonel passed them around. Jean liked her instantly, no standing on ceremony with this one, she would be just as happy making guests feel welcome, as commanding an attack on a battlefield. Jean briefly thought of the idiot Bales, and the irony that he had such authority and so little respect.

After Ty and Anna had exchanged their pleasantries, the Colonel sat back with her elbows on her chair-arms with her hand resting lightly in front of her; fingertips gently touching. She studied Jean before glancing at Ty to indicate that he should continue. He inclined his head in acknowledgement, then surprised Jean by turning to her and saying.

'Jean, show Anna your sword.'

Jean gave him a sharp look, her eyebrows raised.

'And why exactly would I do that?'

'Anna needs to know she can trust you.'

'Well I've got news for you Ty, that's a two-way street.'

Ty looked a bit confused for a moment. It obviously wasn't a response he had expected, and he shot a glance at Anna who seemed quite at ease with the situation.

'Jean, please, Anna is a Colonel within the Order.'

'And Bales is a General, and I wouldn't piss on him if he was on fire.'

Ty winced. Anna leant forward and held up her hands, an amused smile on her face.

'Stop panicking Ty, Jean is perfectly right. I would have no reason to trust me if I had Bales as an example of a Senior officer either.'

Placing her forearms on her desk Anna turned to Jean.

'Let me tell you something about myself, then, hopefully, you will be able to judge for yourself how much you are willing to share with me.' She relaxed back in her seat. 'Yes, I am a Colonel, and I have been a knight of the Order for nigh on thirty years now. I have been to many worlds throughout the universe, and have seen and done things both wonderful, and terrible.'

Spreading her hands Anna continued.

'Would I do it again? In a heartbeat. But that is not the point of this meeting.'

Absentmindedly, she lightly brushed the wooden arms of her chair as she continued.

'Personally, I have three children, two of which are also serving within the Order, the other is an artist, currently living in a tent, somewhere on Juno.

'Fifteen years ago, I lost my first husband to cancer; it was an awful time in my life and I still miss him. But that is in my past. Now, for the past ten years, I have been with a man, who can sometimes be difficult, often grumpy and on occasion unapproachable. But we fell in love, and I couldn't imagine being happier with any other man.'

Anna paused as if reflecting, a smile lit up her face and her eyes seemed to sparkle with emotion.

'Just over five years ago, shortly before all of this shit happened, we were married. It was a very quiet affair, with just a few close family members and friends. It was one of the happiest days of my life… However, since that bitch Ephea and her sisters arrived on the scene, I can count on two hands the amount of times my husband and I have been able to meet each other.'

Jean sat in silence, intrigued, waiting for her story to continue.

'My second husband is Lord Paul, he's one of the Knights and, like Damien with Ty, he felt it would be safer for me if we distanced ourselves. I admit I didn't handle it well at first, and I probably hurt him badly with the things I said.'

Anna hesitated, unsure why she felt able to tell this complete stranger so much of her personal life. Ty seemed to understand what she was thinking.

'It's alright Anna, carry on.'

Anna gave him a thankful smile, then returned her gaze back to Jean. It was a few more moments before she seemed to come to a decision and carried on speaking.

'Our relationship wasn't a secret, everyone in the Empire knew, it never had a bearing on either of us or our work. But Damien of course has to be careful, because of Gradine and the possible threat to Ty. I couldn't see what they could do to me though.'

Jean felt rather than saw Ty tense at the emotion that rose within him, it was a raw subject that had never had time to heal.

'Unfortunately, it became all too clear that my involvement with Paul was unwelcome to Ephea and her sisters; a reminder of their past, and that was something Ephea and her father couldn't have. After a few veiled threats to me and my children, I stepped back. Since then, the meetings between Paul and myself have been few and illicit. Ty believes you may be the key to helping us sort out this mess; to be honest with you, I'm at a point where I will try anything. I miss my husband, and I'm not a young, sprightly woman anymore. I want to enjoy the rest of my life with him in peace. If you help us achieve that, then you

357

will have my full support. But I need to know my family and my husband will be safe.'

Jean contemplated her words and considered her reply carefully.

'Anna, yes, I believe I have answers that may resolve this mess, but I can't, with all honesty, say it will be a clean way. There is every likelihood that Paul and the rest of the Knights will face a danger that could have dire consequences.'

Anna nodded and gave a sad sigh. 'I understand, and so will he, but I would rather it wasn't so.'

Jean looked at Ty and then back at the face of the woman across the desk and stood up. Like before, she made to draw a sword that wasn't there, she laid the blade on the astonished colonel's desk; the inscription as clear on the blade as the day Jean first took possession of it. Anna's voice was barely a whisper.

'Is it real?'

Ty couldn't stop himself from chuckling.

'Try lifting it.'

Anna looked at him and then at Jean, who nodded her agreement.

Running her hand gently along the flat of the blade, feeling the inscription under her fingertips, Anna reached for the hilt. Then, with the action of a practiced swordsman herself, she tried to lift it.

It didn't budge.

Taking a stronger grip, she tried again, she couldn't even make it move across the table. Anna was dumbstruck.

'Leameum.'

Jean nodded. 'That's it, *steel of the gods* apparently. Only someone chosen as a Guardian is able to lift a weapon made from it.'

Anna looked at Jean closely, not sure what to say.

'It's incredible. How is it possible that there is another Guardian?'

Jean spread her hands.

'To be honest with you, until yesterday, I thought I was the only one with a sword like this. It didn't occur to me that someone else would have one, let alone another seven people, eight if you include James.'

Suddenly something flashed across her memory, it was there for a moment as clear as day, but just as quickly it was gone. No matter how she tried, Jean couldn't retain it. She swore under her breath.

Anna and Ty looked at one another, then Ty touched her arm.

'Are you alright Jean?'

She looked at him, slightly embarrassed.

'Yes, of course. Don't worry, it's nothing.'

He didn't seem convinced, but he let it go anyway.

In an attempt to change the conversation, Jean brought her attention back to Anna.

'Ty said you can help us … I need to speak to Nathan as a matter of urgency, and it won't wait any longer… Can you get me into the Palace to speak with him?'

Anna shook her head slightly.

'I can't actually gain you an audience with him, Ephea's supporters are everywhere, and the last thing you need is to be associated with me. But I can give you authorisation that will get you into the Palace tonight. You will need Ty's help too, but I can give you a pass that means you will have a valid reason to be there. Nathan and the others will be attending the Ball, so how you manage to secure a meeting will be up to you. But you will have a limited time, and if you're found out, you're on your own.'

Jean nodded. 'Fair enough, if I can just get in and know he is there, I can deal with the rest.'

Anna understood and handed Jean an envelope, it contained all the relevant documents she would need that evening. Standing up, Anna came around from behind her desk and extended her hand. As Jean took it in hers, the two women locked eyes in a wordless comprehension. Then Anna shook Ty's hand before opening her office door. Her guests made to leave when she said.

'Good luck, and may the gods be with you.'

Both Ty and Jean echoed Anna's sentiments before crossing the outer office, heading to the front door and acknowledging the knight sitting there. They were careful as they left the tower, both acutely aware of the merriment around them, and how easily all the festivities occurring could soon become a catastrophe.

Making their way towards one of the bridges that would take them over the river, Jean suddenly seized Ty's arm and dragged him behind a stall selling sweetmeats. The smell of sugar made Jean want to gag, but instead she tried to concentrate on the man she had just seen leaning against a wall further up the lane.

'What's wrong? Who have you seen?'

Without taking her eyes from the man, she hissed back the name Ty didn't want to hear.

'Mason.'

'Shit. Where?'

Jean nodded in the direction of her gaze, and heard her companion emit a low growl, she appreciated how he felt.

Jean whispered. 'We can't lose him again. This may be our only opportunity.'

At that moment, Mason moved away from the wall, where he was joined by the man who had been with him the previous night. He had come out of a shop, and together they both moved up the road. Careful not to be noticed, Ty and Jean followed. It seemed Mason and his friend were following a prepared route, where the friend entered into various premises, then after a short while, returned to Mason before carrying on to the next stop.

'A protection racket do you reckon?'

Jean shrugged. 'If it is I have no idea why? It certainly isn't the norm for Kaimiren.'

'Do you think they are branching out?'

'Unlikely, as I said, they're not self-employed. They are owned and are created to not care about making their own wealth.'

Jean would have loved to check out one of the premises the two men were interested in, but she daren't lose Mason. Eventually, after following them for another hour, Mason and his companion stopped visiting various properties around the city, and the two started to head in the general direction of the harbour. The crowds were thinner here, and following without being seen was far more difficult. Reluctantly, Jean and Ty had to hang back, only just keeping their quarry in view.

At one point, there was a moment of panic when Jean thought they had lost them. Having dodged into an alley, Mason suddenly disappeared. They pursued him into the semidarkness of the lane but were unsure where to go next. Fortunately, the friend wasn't as switched on as Mason, and his head came briefly into view just before turning right, disappearing down a flight of steps leading to an underground cavern. Relieved, they followed, keeping close, making sure they themselves weren't the subject of someone else's curiosity.

The cavern led into a tunnel and they appeared to have entered into a different world altogether. The darkness was lit only with occasional small orbs and the air was damp and musky. They could hear the sound of rats scurrying ahead, but neither of them were bothered. There was evidence around that the tunnels were used as storage for the buildings above; they passed several steps that led up to trapdoors and caged areas with unused stock bolted onto the stone walls. They also saw that some of the locks had been broken before being repaired; someone had been helping themselves to the produce stored there. Moving on, intent to not lose their quarry, it appeared the further they travelled through the tunnels, they were moving back towards the centre of the city. Both Jean and Ty were now becoming increasingly concerned about the time.

However, eventually the tunnels finally opened out into another, larger cavern, the glow of more orbs cut through the gloom, but they failed to brighten the shadows. It stank of sweat and stale food, and there was a suggestion of sewage nearby, probably from a makeshift latrine. What met their eyes however, made both of them pale in horror. Hiding behind a stack of provisions, they looked out onto a makeshift lair full of men, some were lounging against the walls, while others were engaged in combat training drill; both hand to hand and with weapons. Most of those lounging, had the appearance and uniform of normal members of the Patrols, but it was those primarily concerned with their exercise that concerned Ty and Jean, these were without doubt Kaimiren. They were big and strong, and carrying many scars, all sharing similar distinctive tattoos over their bodies and faces, so it wasn't difficult to distinguish them from the other men. They had large heads, that looked even bigger, when wearing the heavy looking helmets donned by some of those training. It was the first time Ty had seen one up close, and as he watched them train, he began to understand Jean's concerns.

The Kaimiren didn't actually do each other harm, as no doubt they are aware of the price such damage could cost them. There were, however, several Patrol members donning bloodied bandages, and even missing bits of their anatomies, they either sat, or lay, in a corner that appeared to be a makeshift hospital. All of them were averting their gaze from the Kaimiren.

The brutality in the eyes of the Kaimiren as they sparred was frightening, there was none of the camaraderie normally associated with soldiers as they trained; no encouragement or laughing. Not even the usual grunts as a blow landed wide, or through the sheer effort required. The whole scene was like watching one of the films shown on Earth with the volume turned down, Ty found it both fascinating and creepy.

Jean felt she had seen enough and indicated they move back. So in near silence, they each contemplated the scene they had just witnessed as they made their way back up the tunnels.

'I thought you said there may be another couple or so as well as Mason?'

Jean shook her head. 'It's unheard of, there must be nigh on seventy of them there, probably half of the total that exists within the whole Seventh Sector. No wonder they have been off scavenging food, it must be quite a feat trying to keep that lot fed.'

'But what are they all doing here?'

Ty tried to keep the panic out of his voice. Jean had a nasty felling she knew why, but didn't think it would be wise to share her thoughts with Ty just yet, instead she just shook her head and pleaded ignorance.

Suddenly there was a movement behind them and they just managed to back into the shadows just in time. They watched with interest as Mason's new friend strode past, all arrogance and swagger. Without a word they followed behind as he made his way back up the tunnels. But instead of heading back through the way they had come, he stopped at the bottom of one of the steps that led to one of the trapdoors. He gave a final look around him before starting to climb the steps, then at the top he disappeared through the door. Ty followed and made his way up, lifting the door slightly and peering through the crack, assessing the danger. Jean watched as he finally opened the door fully, beckoning her to follow. Quickly, they made their way through a cellar and, after making sure the way was clear, they entered the back of a haberdashery shop.

Fortunately, there were enough people around due to the holiday festivities, that they were able to mingle without being noticed. It was Ty, who due to his greater height, was able to point out the figure of Mason's friend as he passed the shop window. Attempting to make their way through the crowds they eventually caught sight of the friend again, pursuing him to a smaller, quieter street; eventually coming into a dark and dank yard surrounded with high walls on all three sides. He was about to place his hand onto the latch of a wooden gate set into one of the walls, when a large hand grabbed his shoulder and pulled him back off of his feet.

Taken by surprise, the friend took a moment to react, but when he did, it was to twist his body and produce a long, vicious dagger, lashing out at Ty as he tried to overpower him. Using the training and flexibility his size belied, Ty swerved, and the dagger caught fresh air. Fuelled by his anger at the audacity of the Patrolman, Ty slammed the smaller man against the wall. There was a crack as Friend's head hit the stonework; a bloody stain was left as his body slid down the wall.

Ty grabbed him by the scruff of the neck and pulled him up to his feet again, forcing him back against the stone; the man shook his head and blinked as he appeared to desperately clear his mind.

Then, with a vicious kick out at Ty's legs, he made another attempt with the blade he still held in his hand. Dodging another potentially deadly blow, Ty gave a nose crunching punch to the man's face, followed by several hits to his chest and torso. The smaller man went down, gasping, holding his hands to his face as blood poured through his fingers. His dagger hit the floor, forgotten in his agony.

'Who the fuck are you? You don't know who you've pissed off you bastard.'

His cockney accent was audible but muffled, even though the blood and broken nose. Ty, already buoyed by the fight, pushed his own face into that of the blood-soaked man.

'Oh trust me, we know.'

Spitting blood everywhere, the Patrolman wasn't giving up.

'Yeah, right. They'll rip your fucking head off.'

Having stood back from the brawl while Ty took his anger out on Mason's lackey, Jean finally stepped forward and hunkered down. Taking a scruff of the Patrolman's bloodied hair, she pulled his head up. It was difficult to see properly in the gloom along with all the blood that had splattered around, but she could still discern the tell-tale scars and deadened eyes of the drug addict.

'Fuck off.'

The blow to his ribs caught him off guard and he sprawled to the floor holding his chest. Ty standing over him, ready to deliver another if needed.

'Fuck sake, call your gorilla off.'

'I suggest you start talking, he's not in the best of humours right now, and I think you're just the tonic to put him in a better mood.'

The Patrolman began to cough as blood caught in his throat.

'He'll fucking kill me.'

Jean studied the sprawled body on the floor. This time she picked him up by the scruff of the neck and hauled him back against the wall. Her face within inches of his, she could smell his stinking breath and sour body odour, but she didn't care.

'You're already a dead man.'

She put her head to one side, his eyes opened wide in horror.

'The question is, how quick and painless the process will be.'

The man, now panicked as well as in pain, looked to Ty standing behind her. The light went out of his eyes as he realised he had no hope of salvation there, he slumped heavily against the wall. Slowly he began a sardonic, cynical laugh as he looked Jean in the eyes.

'It doesn't matter anyway. You'll not survive when they are finally set free in this stinking shit hole.'

'Who is their target?'

'Who the fuck do you think? Those trumped up bastards in their big Palace; they won't see much past dawn tomorrow. Then all hell will break loose. See how those fucking knights will strut around when their Emperor's head is paraded around the city on a fucking spike.'

He made to let out another burst of laughter, but Ty had had enough. He seized the Patrolman's head, and twisted it, breaking his neck so hard, it was virtually looking the other way by the time he had finished.

Stepping back, Jean and Ty looked down at the broken body on the cobbled ground. They glanced at each other, no words were needed, they both understood. Ty looked around and saw a manhole cover and made to lift it.

Jean put her head to one side and grinned. 'What are you doing?'

Pointing at the dead man, Ty suggested they hide the evidence. Jean shook her head.

'Leave this one to me.'

A quick look around the alleyway confirmed their presence had been unobserved, she held out her hand, once more produced the blue flame that engulfed the dead Patrolman's body. Her companion gave her a look that suggested he had given up being surprised. Within minutes the Patrolman's remains were nothing but dust, and taking Ty's arm, Jean guided him back up the lane. Raising her hand, a cloud of dust rose in the air behind them; then, which a click of her fingers, it disappeared into the dank air of the alleyway.

Needing to prepare for her meeting with Nathan, they emerged out into the late afternoon sun. When Ty spoke, his voice was quiet and determined.

'Did you see which shop we came out of when we followed him?'

He jerked his thumb back up the lane.

'No.'

'It was one of those Mason and his friend visited earlier.'

They stopped and looked at each other, realising the significance of this information.

'You think it wasn't extortion they were dealing with, but access to the city from underground?'

Ty nodded.

'Shit.'

'Exactly. After we get you into the Palace, I'm going to have a word with the watch in the city. That's one nasty surprise we can do without.'

Jean agreed, biting her lip as she contemplated this latest piece of information, reinforcing her determination to get into the Palace that evening. 'Come on Ty, let's get moving. I have a party to get ready for.'

They moved through the city quickly, and soon, as the sun began to dip behind the caldera walls, they made their preparations for the evening ahead.

Part Four

Retreat

27

The

Midsummer

Ball

B y the time they had returned to Ty's apartment, it was already dark, and the avenue was busy with people heading for the Palace and the Midsummer Ball. Fortunately, Kate Bridger, the newly promoted Captain from the flat above Ty's, hadn't left for her own watch yet, and she was intrigued as to why Jean would need a knight's uniform. However, when Ty pulled out all the charm he could muster, Kate relented and dropped it in on her way out without asking any more questions.

Ty had a rummage through some old boxes stored away in a cupboard, where he found a set of insignia for the rank of sergeant. They thought it better if Jean didn't have any higher rank, the last thing they needed was for her to have to take charge of some issue that arose, whilst also trying to contact Nathan in the limited time she already had. Fortunately, the overall fit of Kate's uniform was pretty good, except that she was somewhat taller than the Captain. Hopefully, when wearing her boots nobody would notice that the hem of her trousers sat several inches above her ankles. The jacket sleeves however were noticeably short, there was nothing they could do about that in the time available, but Jean kept subconsciously trying to pull them down so often, that in the end Ty had to pull rank and tell her to stop fidgeting.

They grabbed a bite to eat while finalising their plans, sparse though they were. Jean didn't want to be detected before she managed to find Nathan, and once she did, she still had to find a way to get him alone. They were both painfully aware that Jean was going into a situation completely blind, despite Ty's rudimentary plan of the Palace, it still didn't give any ideas where Jean should start looking.

Ty wanted to send knights out into the city and check out the buildings that Mason, and his now deceased friend, visited earlier. Also, Jean didn't want to spend time drawing attention to herself; so, they gave themselves an hour before they were to meet up again. It was pushing it in Jean's eyes, she hoped it was going to give her enough time.

Walking up to the Palace they began to feel the tension rise, time wasn't on their side and there was still so much uncertainty. Apart from the obvious threat to Nathan and the Knights themselves, Jean was worried sick about the possibility of a blood bath if Ty wasn't able to persuade his fellow Order members, as well as the police, not to engage the Kaimiren if they encountered them. She didn't even want to contemplate the nightmare of trying to keep an entire city of drunken revellers safe, while the Patrols were still hell bent on causing mayhem. By the time they arrived at the guardroom her head was spinning.

They were pleased to see that Anna had been true to her word, ensuring the Watch this evening was completely different from the previous day's. They didn't want people recognising Jean wearing the uniform of the Order and asking awkward questions. Ty nodded to the knights standing by the gate, telling them he would return shortly once he had taken Jean, their newly arrived sergeant, to the Palace and given her instructions. The knights nodded and they both continued on, following the path alongside the parade square, leading up to the main buildings.

That night, the Palace had been decorated to mark the Midsummer celebrations. Torches of fire lit up the walkways, and the building itself was decorated with flowers and greenery in abundance. Every window was alight and the whole display was spectacular. Around them, people dressed in their finery wandered through the elaborate decor, laughing as they slowly made their way up to the main entrance.

During the day, the buildings themselves were not notable for their architecture, the whitewashed structures were more than merely utilitarian, but they didn't display frivolous, unnecessary adornments. The Palace was a work of stone and glass, with an enormous set of double doors which opened above the broad, stone steps. Unusually they were not set in the centre of the Palace frontage but were situated to the right-hand side of the building. The reason for this became apparent as they neared the building and Jean could see inside. A huge hall was situated on the other side of the entrance doors, splitting the building in two as it rose the full height of the structure. With the front doors offset it ensured that one side of the Palace could be used without having to keep crossing the hall.

Ty led her away from the main entrance, towards the barracks that abutted the Palace on the righthand side, coming to a door that was mainly unnoticed by visitors walking around. Passing through unchallenged, they stepped into a long corridor, where to their right it curved off away from the barracks and Palace, towards the back of the building. But Ty led her off to the left, towards the sound of music and merriment from the main hall. He left her on the edge of the celebrations, where they checked their watches (Jean had borrowed an old one from Ty) and agreed to meet here in an hour. They wished each other good luck before she found herself once more alone.

As Jean had suspected from her view outside, the hall itself was actually a huge atrium. It rose from a beautiful stone floor, to the glazed ceiling three storeys above. It was difficult to see the floor clearly due to the amount of people milling around, but from what she could see, it was made up of different shades of pink stone set out in an intricate pattern. The pink stone

374

theme continued up the walls and to the balconies that identified the separate floors. The ceiling was of panes of glass set within a metal framework; during the day she assumed the light must be amazing in this space. The hall ran the full length of the building from front to back, where there were more glazed windows leading out into another area, though she couldn't make out what it was from this angle. Across the hall and leading up to the opposite storeys, was a curving staircase opening onto separate balconies for each level. Remembering Ty's description, each balcony had corridors which led further into the Palace complex beyond.

On the side of the hall where Jean stood, a single flight of stairs led up to the first floor, with the wall on this side covered in paintings of landscapes and portraits. A prominent painting was one of Nathan and the other Knights, including she noted, Katherine and James. However, it was the portrait that hung on the wall opposite the corridor where she stood, that caught Jean's eye. It was situated near to a set of doors that appeared to lead to the main festivities, judging by the sound of music and laughter that emanated from there. The picture itself was of a woman, sat in a swirl of silks and lace. Her dark hair was set in intricate braids around her head and her eyes were the most vibrant violet; her face seemed almost sad, but also with a definite note of pride. After her visit to the museum previously, she assumed that this woman was likely to be related to Nathan and his twin sister Katherine; very possibly their mother.

Arrangements of coats of arms and weaponry were also set around the walls in elaborate designs, a nod to past campaigns no doubt, with flags of regimental colours draped proudly alongside. Unfortunately, there was no time for appreciating her surroundings further, as she had to get on with finding Nathan. This however was going to prove difficult, as just behind her, a loud and rather annoyed voice close to her ear, cut through her thoughts. Jean jumped and very nearly reached for her sword, managing to stop herself just in time.

'Hello Sergeant. Anybody there?'

Spinning round, Jean came face to face with a woman wearing the uniform of the Order; her insignia marked her out as a Lieutenant. She was staring at Jean with a particularly unimpressed expression on her face, and it took a brief second for Jean to remember that she was now in the uniform of the Order herself, and that she was being addressed by a senior officer.

'Er, yes ma'am, sorry.'

The Lieutenant softened and gave a small sigh.

'First time in the Palace eh?'

Jean nodded. 'Yes ma'am.'

'Oh for heaven's sake drop the whole ma'am bit. This is Parva, you'll be *Siring* and *Ma'aming* all over the place, driving everyone nuts if you don't loosen up. You'll get nothing done but manage to piss everyone off. I'm Vicki and that's Clay.'

She pointed to a Sergeant sitting on the staircase that led up to the first floor, he was propping up the head of a short plump woman who sprawled comatose, on the lower steps. Clay grinned and gave Jean a nod.

'Right, grab a leg.'

Confused, Jean spun back to the Lieutenant.

'I beg your pardon?'

Vicki pointed to one of a pair of large stockinged calves, protruding from a garish yellow silk dress. Aware of the time,

Jean tried to explain that she had an errand to run, but Vicki wasn't having any of it.

'Whatever it is, it can wait. We've got to get this lump out of the way first.'

'Who is she?'

'This, is our *Lady* Yollan. Wife of Lord Daniel.'

Jean raised her eyebrows.

'Does she normally get into this state?'

Both knights nodded, the look of disgust on their faces evident.

'Often, unfortunately. Tonight, we drew the short straw, and it looks like it's going to be your night too, so grab a leg.'

With little choice, Jean took hold of the leg, while Vicki held the other. Clay heaved at her shoulders, and together, they dragged a very drunk Yollan up the stairs. Jean thought the woman, with the overly made up face and the stink of too much perfume, was liable to be black and blue the next morning by the way she seemed to hit every step on the way up. She also noted, that no-one within the hall took a blind bit of notice of the proceedings, or the subsequent fate of Yollan.

After much heaving and swearing at Yollan's awkward bulk, they eventually reached the top step of the stairs. Then grabbing an arm each, Clay and Jean dragged her down another corridor; her head hanging backwards, drool running from her open mouth towards her hairline, creating a sickly sheen across the woman's features. Vicki stopped and opened a door some way down the hallway, and between the three of them they managed to manhandle her into, what could only be described as a store room. Shelves to one side held piles of linen, whilst opposite, was a pile of old sheets, presumably ready to be sent to the laundry. A small window was set high in the wall. Yollan seemed unconcerned with her lowly surroundings however, snuffling into the dirty linen and starting to snore quite loudly.

Jean said. 'Should we leave the window open?'

Vicki seemed to consider this for a moment, and Clay added, with what Jean thought was his concerns.

'The daft woman may wake up and try and climb out and fall to her death.'

Vicki frowned. 'Good idea.'

Jean watched in silent amusement as the Lieutenant opened the window fully, before ushering the others out. Then closing the door carefully, she locked it. The three then turned and made their way back to the main hall.

'Do you usually do that to her?'

Vicki looked at Jean wryly.

'To be honest, she usually gets dumped into a spare bedroom; but to hell with it, the bloody woman is a menace. Last time she woke up, she started wandering half naked around the great dining room while the Emperor was giving a banquet.' Vicki winced. 'It wasn't pretty, poor Lord Daniel ended up having to help get her out of there pretty sharpish. He really wasn't a happy man.'

Jean couldn't help it; she was laughing with them both. When they had descended the staircase, Vicki thanked her, and they left her to continue her task (whatever it was) and she was once more surrounded by people in various states of drunkenness. She couldn't really see a thing from where she was standing, and had no idea where to start looking, so retracing a few of the steps of the staircase, she tried to gain a better view of the atrium and the people within it.

Then she saw him.

Nathan had just entered the hall through the doors that led back into the party beyond. He seemed intent on something or someone and Jean followed his gaze gaining her first glimpse of Yollan's older sister, Ephea. The Emperor's wife was currently hanging onto the arm of a Captain of the Order, giggling and waving a wine glass around, seeming to be thoroughly enjoying herself. The couple were making their way to the other end of the atrium, where the large glazed doors stood open. Moving down the hall, Nathan followed at a distance, his face impassive and gave nothing of his thoughts away. In his right hand he held a large brandy glass still half full of a thick amber liquid, which he sipped at occasionally as he watched the antics of Ephea and her friend. Then he too disappeared through the glazed doors.

Afraid of losing sight of her quarry, she hurried to catch up, forcing her way through the throng of carousing guests, almost falling over the legs of a couple fumbling on the floor, across the threshold of the glazed doors.

Finally, she was at the top of a flight of stone steps, leading down to a smaller glazed room, more like a large orangery, Jean thought. Scattered around the area were comfortable chairs and low tables, where a few people sat talking amongst themselves, acknowledging Nathan with a nod when they saw him, before carrying on with their own business as he passed.

Nathan crossed to another set of doors that led out onto a terraced garden; an area lit by orbs that gave off a gentle light amongst the flowers, trees and bushes. Jean breathed in the intoxicating scent as she followed, closing her eyes briefly, she relished the peace as she left the sound of the party behind.

Seeing the back of Nathan disappearing along a path, Jean hurried to keep up, just keeping his back in view as the path twisted through ornate flowerbeds and hidden niches amongst the undergrowth. They passed several couples in various states of undress while producing much giggling; Nathan ignored them all. Jean eventually caught up with him as he stood beside a low, ornate wall that overlooked a lower terrace. He was looking out into a darkened patch of undergrowth, where a lot of squealing and giggling was taking place amongst several shuddering and trembling bushes. But Nathan hadn't gone any further, instead he stood looking over the wall, his face and manner still impassive.

For a moment she wasn't sure what to do or say. Here was a man who had just watched his wife leave with another man, who had led her into some bushes, and where it was unlikely, they were discussing the finer points of topiary. If she didn't know the truth of their relationship, Jean would think Nathan was a man contemplating revenge.

Approaching Nathan cautiously, she stopped at the wall next to him, finding herself slightly embarrassed considering the circumstances. Voyeurism wasn't something she was really into. At her arrival, Nathan turned. She saw emotion cross his face for the first time, surprise and then recognition. Her spine tingled, the same sensation she had felt back in Rassen when they had first encountered one another.

Damn, what is it about those eyes?

Even in the semi darkness of the garden, with only the gentle glow of the orbs for light, his eyes were a deep blue and Jean was drawn in.

For heaven's sake Jean, get a grip and snap out of it.

Trying to concentrate on something else, she nodded towards the quivering bushes.

'Bit of late-night gardening?'

Nathan didn't take his gaze away from Jean, instead he laughed.

'Good luck to him, I wouldn't like to think what might be dug up in there.'

Jean tried not to think about that prospect. Nathan now gave Jean his full attention, the giggling bushes forgotten.

'Am I correct in assuming, you are the elusive Jean Carter?'

Jean was surprised. 'You know of me?'

He laughed again, an easy deep chuckle.

'Miss Carter, you are quite the celebrity. I've been hoping to meet you again for some time now.'

She felt a bit taken aback at this; it didn't occur to her that Nathan may actually know that she was around. How much did he know of who she really was?

More wary now, she realised that he was studying her, his eyes travelling across the uniform she wore. The silver trees and sergeant's rank were in sharp contrast to the gold braid and insignia of the Emperor on his own dress uniform.

'You've had a sudden inclination for the Order I see.'

She looked down and instinctively started tugging at her sleeves again.

'Do you have any idea how difficult it is to get into this place and try and see you? We had to do something, and time was short.'

She gave another self-conscious tug.

'We?'

'Yes, Captain Coniston and Colonel Priestly.'

He looked at her sharply. 'You know Ty and Anna?'

'Yes, and time is running out. Ty will be waiting for me by the east door soon, so I don't have long.'

There was a sound of people on the path behind them. Jean turned her head sharply, peering cautiously into the gloom. While she couldn't see anyone there, she was aware of several people nearby. She stepped closer to Nathan, trying to instil the sense of urgency of why she had come to see him.

'You have to listen to me Nathan, this is important.'

If he was surprised at her use of his name, he didn't show it. Instead he looked up and she saw that they had been joined by the rest of the Knights.

'So, Nathan, how are they getting on?'

It was the man Jean recognised as Damien. Even though it was the second time she had encountered both men, it was only now that she appreciated just how much like his cousin he really was. Nathan grinned and returned his gaze to the trembling bushes.

'Still at it from what I can tell.'

All of a sudden, Jean found herself pinned against the low wall, as the Knights rushed forward; the bushes well and truly convulsing now. She had to cling on to the edge to stop herself from falling onto the lower terrace. There was a general murmuring of, *impressive* and *hilarious*, when, as one, they all started to laugh at the spectacle.

'This may be very funny to you, but some of us would like to be able to breathe.'

The laughing stopped, and she was able to take in air as they all stepped back in surprise, only now seeming to see her properly.

Damien looked confused. 'We are sorry Sergeant.'

They all looked at Nathan questioningly.

Daniel looked back at Jean 'Is something wrong? Can we help you with anything?'.

Nathan shook his head. 'This, gentlemen, is the elusive Jean Carter; the uniform is just a disguise apparently.'

All eyes were once more on Jean. She felt even more self-conscious now; at this rate she was going to pull her sleeves off completely.

Nathan introduced the rest of the Knights and she made a huge effort to get her head back in order. She was feeling her darker side begin to grow within her, not in anger, it was more in recognition. These men seem to be awakening a part of her that Jean would rather stay sleeping. She wasn't sure how she felt about it and conflicting thoughts scattered about her mind. Standing up straight and mentally shaking herself down, she tried to gain control of her senses once more. The beast within seemed to growl as it submitted, reminding her that it was still there, before returning to the farthest aspects of her mind; but only sleeping.

Turning back to Nathan, she continued to implore the urgency of their situation.

'Look, I don't have time for social niceties, or watching what other people get up to in the shrubbery; and neither, for that matter, do you.'

They all looked at one another and then back at Jean. It was as if a switch had been turned on, they settled around her, listening intently. This brought on another bout of tugging and she heard Ty in her head, ordering her to stop fidgeting. Despite herself she smiled.

'Nathan, you have to put a stop to the festivities. Get people indoors, or preferably, out of the city.'

Of all the things he expected her to say, it obviously wasn't this. He opened his eyes wide in surprise.

'Are you mad? Tell an entire city in the middle of a giant party, to just stop and go home?'

She sighed and closed her eyes in frustration.

'If you don't, a lot of people are going to get killed.'

Nathan put his glass down onto the wall beside them and looked hard into Jean's eyes.

Shit, keep it together girl.

'Miss Carter, the days when I could authorise that kind of action within the city disappeared years ago.'

He glanced at the still rustling bushes and grimaced. Jean forced herself to return his gaze.

'The Blue Star.' It wasn't a question.

He nodded. 'No Doubt Ty and Anna have informed you of the details concerning the bloody thing. I can't afford to allow such a disaster as Belby to happen again.'

Beside them, Jean felt Damien and Paul tense on hearing the names of people they cared so much for. But such sentimentality would have to wait and she closed her heart to it.

Stepping nearer to Nathan, she tried, but failed to ignore his eyes boring even deeper into her own.

'I can absolutely guarantee, that neither Ephea, or any other member of her family, was responsible for what happened at Belby five years ago. And I can also assure you, that no chunk of rock brought here by some poor delusional cleric is guilty either.'

Nathan furrowed his eyebrows and Jean caught a flash of anger cross his features.

'You can't possibly know that, and to suggest it is dangerous.'

She took a deep breath and shook her head slowly, then returning his own intense gaze she told him the true nature of who she was.

'I know, because seven thousand years ago, your sister Katherine, gave me what they are now calling the Blue Star. No one else could possibly have used it, because technically it no longer exists. I am everything it ever held; it is now part of my me and my soul.'

All around there was a stunned silence. Nathan turned to the others and they all looked back Jean, shocked.

'You?'

'Yes Nathan, me. Now will you please listen?'

He sat down on the wall, and Jean felt his scrutiny of her escalate. She sat along side him, aware now that everything she said now would be crucial to what happened in the hours ahead.

'There are men within the city who are hell bent on achieving only one goal. You. They want you dead, and they will destroy anyone, and anything, that gets in the way of that goal. You have to make sure the Order keeps the Patrols at bay, and the police must ensure the people of the city are kept safe, out of harm's way.'

At this Damien came to stand next to Nathan, confronting Jean.

'And you think we are just going to hand Nathan over?'

She gave him a withering look. 'No, of course not. It's just we are the only ones in a position to do anything about it.'

Suddenly, a huge rush of adrenalin hit her senses, as a jolt of anger flared from those around her. She flinched at the unexpected force, but it was the response from the others that surprised her more; they had felt it too. For some reason, where Jean was normally able to draw on the emotions around her to enhance her own, the Knight's had reacted to her as well, as if their own natural responses had been heightened too. This was something new and it took a moment for her to realise what had happened. Immediately, she shut down her senses, willing herself to keep calm; maintaining the peace around her. If her reaction increased the Knight's emotional level, it would have an immediate effect on her too. The result could be an enormous rush of adrenaline, that continually rose between them, building up into dangerous, and possibly, explosive levels. Looking around her, She realised the effect hadn't gone unnoticed by the Knight's either. Acutely aware that she was now being highly scrutinised, she checked her watch for something else to focus on.

Shit. She was late.

'I have to go; Ty is waiting for me.'

Damien shot her a look. 'Ty is here?' He couldn't hide his concern in his voice.

She nodded. 'And he needs to know he has your authority to stop the Patrols, you can't let anyone else tackle the Kaimiren when they surface.'

'Who?'

Jean groaned, this was all taking far too long to explain. 'I don't have time to go through everything now, but they are the ones after Nathan.'

Beside her Nathan stood up and she followed suit. The others recognised the signs and knew he had made a decision; once more, time for discussion was over.

'Damien, go with Jean, speak with Ty, then go with him to make sure every knight in the city helps the police enforce a curfew, effective as of now.'

He looked at the others, they were listening intently.

'The party is over, close down the Palace, making sure everyone leaves through the Portal above the guest quarters. It doesn't matter where to; they can make arrangements on the other side. Then help Damien to enforce the curfew in the city.'

He turned back to Jean.

'What time am I expected to meet my fate?'

'Dawn, apparently.'

He nodded. 'It gives us a few hours to prepare, but if they want me, they will have to come here for me. This will be a no-go zone to everyone by dawn.'

Jean felt relief that her concerns had finally been taken seriously.

'I'll be here by then, no matter what.'

Nathan gave a brief nod, his mind already working on the information Jean had provided.

'Until dawn tomorrow.'

Satisfied she had done all she could for now, Jean made to leave with Damien. Suddenly, a high-pitched screech ripped through the air.

'What is going on? Who are you?'

Gradine had stormed down the garden path and shoved past the rest of the Knights, making straight for the woman standing with her husband. The smell of too much perfume and alcohol reminded Jean of Yollan, and mixed with the nasty whiff of bad body odour, it made her feel quite queasy.

Jean turned to Damien. 'Is she with you?'

Armed with Jean's recent declaration regarding the truth of the Blue Star, Damien growled angrily.

'The bitch can rot in hell for all I care.'

Jean shrugged. 'Fair enough.'

At that they both made to continue on their way, ignoring the enraged woman standing with her mouth open in shock. But Gradine soon collected herself and reached out, grabbing hold of Jean's arm and hauling her back, forcing her round to face her. Unfortunately for Gradine, instead of pulling her arm away, Jean seized her restraining arm and grasped the bare flesh tight, pulling Gradine so close, that the smaller woman had to stand on her platformed toes just to stop her arm being wrenched out of its socket. She winced at the pain.

Jean's anger was barely a whisper. 'Never, touch me, again.'

Then just as quickly, Gradine was forced away. She fell to the muddy ground in a billow of silks and unpleasant smells as Jean let go. Without any further concern for the prone woman, Jean turned back and nodded to those around her.

'Gentlemen.'

Then she and Damien left.

Gradine, however, wasn't finished. Furious, she screeched her demands to the men around her, undisguised contempt upon their faces.

'Somebody help me up.'

Nobody moved. Struggling, she finally made it onto her feet again, but now her skirts were muddied, and her hair had taken on a wild look — she was furious. Staring around, she waved her arms in anger.

'She pushed me, and you did nothing.'

Daniel scoffed. 'Pushed you? It looked like you stumbled.'

His sister-in-law looked incredulous.

'That knight deliberately attacked me.'

Nathan looked innocently at the rest of his men.

'What knight? I don't think I saw any other knights here, did you?'

Gradine's face seemed to take on a darker shade of fury, when there was another air wrenching screech, this time from below, her elder sister, Ephea, was now scrambling furiously from out of the bushes.

'YOU FILTHY BASTARD.'

Stumbling, Nathan's wife fully emerged from the shrubbery with exposed breasts, and skirts caught up around her waist, showing glimpses of her bare arse. Following behind, the Captain was tucking himself back into his trousers and roaring with laughter, while Ephea's wig balanced precariously on his own head. Letting out another ear-splitting screech, she reached up and snatched the hairpiece back. Staggering in her desperate attempt to escape back to the Palace, while she simultaneously tried to rearrange her dress.

Gradine, horrified at the spectacle her sister was making of herself, ran to help her up the steps, trying to tuck one of Ephea's wayward breasts back in as they went. From below, the Captain called up to Nathan.

'That's a bottle of brandy you owe me My Lord.'

Nathan retrieved his glass from the wall and raised it to the man below.

'Indeed it is, and well-earned too. Now get your filthy arse up here, you have work to do.'

Still laughing, the Captain joined the other Knights and listened to his orders intently, while Ephea's wails could still be heard as she was helped back to the Palace by her furious sister.

By the time Jean and Damien had reached the east door, Ty was pacing and constantly checking his watch. When he saw Jean he stood forward, about to admonish her for her tardiness, when he noticed her companion. For a moment he forgot about the danger to his city and his Emperor.

'Damien.'

Damien smiled. 'Hello Ty.'

Jean stood back, becoming intent on a picture of a bowl of fruit that hung further down the corridor. For a moment, both men allowed their fingers to entwine, their heads touched in a brief show of intimacy, before reluctantly pulling apart. Work had to be done. She looked around as Damien suggested they get going, and the three of them then made their way down the path to the main gates. When they arrived, Jean asked Damien where she might find Anna at this hour. When he had given her the details she required, she turned to Ty and touched his arm.

'Stay safe my friend, if the gods are with us, we will meet again tomorrow.' She looked at him wryly. 'And please try to stay in one piece.'

He gave a sad grin back. 'The same goes to you too.'

Then, she did something that was totally unexpected that surprised all of them. She squeezed Ty's hand, and reaching up she kissed him on his cheek. 'Thank you.' He squeezed her hand back, his face full of emotion.

Reluctantly she turned away before inclining her head to Damien.

'Until tomorrow morning.'

He mirrored her gesture. 'Until tomorrow.'

Then both men watched her stride down the tree lined avenue, her head bowed in concentration on the work she had to do. In the distance, evidence of soon to be disrupted parties could be heard.

Damien turned to Ty. 'Do you know who she is?'

'I know she carries the same sword as you and the other Guardian Knights.'

Damien looked surprised. 'You've seen it?'

'Yep, you could say it was her get out of gaol pass.'

Damien looked back at Ty raising an eyebrow.

'It's a long story.'

'I look forward to hearing it then.'

They both enjoyed a shared moment of laughter, then they returned to the guard room, issuing orders that would be performed throughout the rest of the city.

Already from within the Palace, there were the sounds of revellers discontent that their party was being abruptly broken up.

Nathan was now standing on the Palace steps; he too watched Jean leave, and considered all that they had learnt this evening. From within, he could feel the anger that had been suppressed for so long, begin to stir. He felt the shackles that had tied his hands falling away, and he breathed in the night air.

Whatever happened with the bringing of a new day, he would face it head on; the gods only knew he was ready for a fight. Tomorrow, these Kaimiren that Jean spoke of, would feel the strength of his fury; forced to be kept buried for five, agonising, long years. He was under no illusions regarding what lay ahead at dawn, experience had shown him not to underestimate any enemy. But it had been a while since he and his fellow Knights had drawn swords in anger, and the prospect of meeting an enemy in battle was not unwelcome. Turning and making his way back into the atrium hall, he ignored the howls and complaints from the unhappy party goers, setting his mind on more deadlier matters.

28

NICI

Taking the directions that Damien had given her, Jean made her way down the avenue back to Ty's lodgings where she could change back into her own clothes. It was on the way to Anna's house and she was relieved to not have to fight with her sleeves anymore.

With orders now being sent out to mobilise all available knights to help within the city, she wasn't even sure if Anna would be home at this time. Fortunately, she lived, like Ty, on the North Bank and soon she was walking down a leafy lane with large houses set back from the road. When she had reached her destination, Jean could see a large half timbered, two storey house. It was accessible by a long driveway that led around to the back of the property, where she assumed there must be a stable. Making her way up to the house, she knocked on the shiny black painted door, the brassware gleaming in the moon light.

Anna herself answered, and when she saw Jean, she welcomed her inside, leading her into a sitting room that overlooked the darkened garden. Aware of time slipping away, Jean came straight to the point.

'I'm sorry to call on you so late Anna, though you'll probably be getting another call soon, the Emperor has ordered an immediate curfew.'

A look of surprise flitted across Anna's face before she asked Jean to sit down. By the time they were both comfortable, Anna had regained her composure.

'So, you managed see Nathan then?'

Anna paused and tugged at a thread on the old, but comfortable looking armchair she was perched on.

'Did you see anyone else while you were there?'

Smiling, Jean was happy to say she had, albeit briefly.

'Yes, I have seen all of them, including Paul. He's obviously very worried about you.'

Anna seemed to relax slightly.

'Jean, I won't lie to you, I miss him terribly.'

Clasping the other woman's hand, for a moment, the force that had been steadily rising within Jean subsided, slightly.

'And with any luck, you will be together again, hopefully by this time tomorrow.'

Anna looked up, a small tear had escaped down her cheek and she brushed it away in irritation.

'Things are moving that fast?'

Jean sighed. 'There have been a few things that have happened since we saw you earlier today, and yes, I believe that whoever is controlling these events, has chosen the cover of this evening's revelry to make their decisive move. By dawn tomorrow, the city is supposed to be sleeping off a very big hangover, and with the Order supposedly confined to guard duties, an attack on the Palace would be pretty straightforward.'

Anna considered this for a moment.

'You think the Patrols are organised and strong enough to defeat the Order at the Palace?'

Jean laughed. 'Hell no. The knights would slaughter them. No, the Patrols are merely a diversion to keep the police and citizens busy, while the real threat makes their move.'

Jean told Anna about Mason, his friend, whom she and Ty had followed earlier that day, and what they had discovered. When she heard about the fate of Mason's Patrol friend, Anna smiled in satisfaction.

'I could have told you it would be wise not to mess with Ty when he's angry.'

Jean gave a small chuckle. 'I'm glad he's on our side.'

As the two women laughed, Anna offered some tea and went to the kitchen. When she returned, she was wearing her uniform, ready for when the call came. She poured the tea and when they were both sitting comfortably Anna looked up, her face once more serious.

'Assuming this isn't a late-night social call, even if it is to convey my husband's wellbeing, what can I do for you now Jean?'

Taking another sip from her cup, Jean set it down onto the coffee table between them.

'I have a very large favour to ask of you. To be honest I don't even know if you can do anything to help, but if there is a possibility….' She trailed off, unsure how to continue.

'Why not just start at the beginning?'

Jean looked at Anna gratefully and nodded. It was difficult at first, there were things she said that she hadn't told anyone else, and things she wasn't entirely sure about herself. But by the time she left Anna's house sometime later, both women were prepared for the day ahead, whatever it may bring.

When Anna opened the door to let Jean out, they saw two knights making their way up the drive to their Colonel. Jean and Anna looked at each other; at last her call had come.

Walking along the avenue towards the bridge that would take her to the South Bank, Jean considered what would be her best move now. Nathan and the Knights were, at last, taking charge of the City. Also, no doubt issuing instructions to the Order throughout the Empire, that they were no longer confined to barracks and Guard duty only. She had a feeling the Patrols were about to get a very nasty shock over the next few hours.

Ty, along with Damien, had hopefully ensured that any sightings of the Kaimiren were only noted but not to be engaged. It still made Jean sick to think of the possible blood bath that could ensue, should any foolhardy knight consider themselves up to the challenge. It was a simple fact that outside of the Seventh Sector, the Kaimiren were an unknown quantity, and if Jean's advice wasn't adhered to, then lessons were going to be learnt the hard way. Jean brushed these thoughts aside, worrying now wasn't going to achieve anything, she had to trust

Ty and Damien to do their job — she needed to concentrate on hers.

So far, she had gleaned a fair amount of information from Belby, but not all of it was concrete fact. She had made a lot of surmising, now she needed to find the evidence to back it up. Crossing the bridge to the South Bank, she then turned left and made her way back along the road, adjacent to the river, to the main gate out of the City. In the distance she could hear the first indications that the people of Parva were not going to take the enforced curfew quietly. She thought of Ella and Lyle trying to persuade party goers it was time to go home, she didn't fancy that job at all.

Fortunately, the main gate was still open. With orders to either remain inside or leave the City, some people were making their way out into the countryside. A brief discussion with the guards told Jean that everyone had until an hour before dawn to leave if they wished, after that they were to remain inside their homes until the Emperor said they could leave. Judging by the few travellers she saw, most had chosen to stay, she had a feeling a few parties may still be going on behind closed doors. As long as the revellers didn't try and make their way home the next morning, she had to accept that there was very little that could be done about it. Passing through the gate and making her way around the base of the wall, Jean made sure she was out of sight, then with a single thought of the all too familiar bridge on her spaceship, she translocated away from the City of Parva and the world of Kelan.

As soon as she arrived on the main deck, NiCI sensed her presence, lights and life support, that had been left to tick over during her absence, were brought up to full power. Blinking in the artificial light after the darkness outside the city of Parva, she gave the command for NiCI to reduce the brightness. Breathing in the air artificially produced in the spacecraft's engines, she felt slightly sick, it was a testament to how used to the clearer air of Kelan she had become.

Making her way to the controls, and satisfied that NiCI was in full working order, she considered where to go to next. While it was relatively easy to translocate NiCI to anywhere in space, the problem was actually flying anywhere afterwards. NiCI, like any other ship, required fixed locations in order to navigate from. Within space, there are specific three dimensional points that enable a ship to know where it is at all times. When it moves from that point, it can plan and track its trajectory through space. But, if Jean physically moved NiCI from a known point to an unknown area of space, there was no way of plotting where she was or where she was going. She would effectively be flying blind, and when travelling at huge speeds that required meticulous route planning, this was impossible; it only took one planet to be in the way and it was game over.

Jean had devised a way around this, by having set points within known galaxies that were pre-programmed into NiCI's navigational systems. So that if she translocated her ship to one of these points, the computer was able to adjust accordingly. It had been a lot of work, but worth it in the end.

Over the years, she had discovered the requirement of having a spacecraft, despite the ability to translocate, when many of those she dealt with took to space rather than remain on a planet's surface. It was nigh on impossible to translocate to another ship while it was moving at speed; so, she had to level the field as they say. It had taken many years, but over time she had adapted NiCI to her own wishes, and now she was unique in her design and build. Technically speaking, she was a ship capable of taking a full crew, but Jean and NiCI's programming was enough to get by and it suited her needs.

Now she intended to take NiCI, not to a known navigational point, but to a familiar location, nonetheless. Earth's solar system. Having spent time within the Empire, Jean was, at last, now able to locate Earth and its position within the Seventh Sector. With her ship's sensors powerful enough to easily reach the length of the whole system, she decided to take her to the farthest side of Saturn's rings; just in case anyone on Earth now had the means to sense that far into space. Once in place, Jean located Earth and NiCI was set to work scanning the computer systems that functioned there.

Given specific parameters, it didn't take long for NiCI to produce the information required. Satisfied she now had all the pieces to the puzzle she needed; she decided to keep the spacecraft out of sight within Earth's solar system.

Before she made to return to Kelan however, Jean scanned the information before her once more; her gaze pausing over the date. She felt her heart in her mouth as the numbers seemed to dance before her. Closing her eyes, she forced herself to keep her mind on the task in hand, everything else would have to wait for another day.

Making her way to the centre of the bridge she concentrated her thoughts, and with one final look around the ship, she returned to the base of the walls surrounding the City of Parva, NiCI already powering down all necessary systems.

29

Retribution

Ephea made her way home, escorted by one of the guards on duty who had been coerced into the task by a furious Gradine. Once Gradine had finally contrived to get her into a state of dress suitable to be seen in public, she was then frogmarched her down to the Palace gates. With the sudden orders to abandon the Midsummer party, along with all the guests to be escorted from the city by portal, Gradine was now concerned about Yollan. She hadn't been seen for some time and she could be out cold, sleeping off yet another hangover anywhere within the complex. Satisfied that someone else was now responsible for her elder sister's safety, Gradine made her way back up towards the Palace.

The presence of the Order once more out on the streets of Parva, hadn't gone unnoticed by its residents. With emotions running high from the midsummer festivities, they considered it a good sign that life was at last getting back to normal. Parties were springing up all over the place, including the staff of Ephea's home. They had taken up the gauntlet and their party was in full swing by the time their mistress arrived home. Ephea had been unceremoniously dumped outside her own house by her guard. No sooner had she stepped onto the path to her front door, her escort had turned about and quickly made their way back to the Palace, eager for new orders that would hopefully get them some decent action in the city.

Ephea was tired, humiliated and angry at the way Nathan had treated her in front of so many people, only to be left alone by Gradine and passed into the hands of some lowly knight. She was heading for an almighty self-pity sulk and needed someone to take it out on. Aware that most of her household should now be asleep in their beds, she considered all the tasks she could wake them up for and force them to complete. That would teach them all not to laugh at her.

However, on opening the door, the house she expected to be quiet and sleeping, was in fact hosting a drunken party that was in full swing. Ephea blinked in the bright light, slowly recognising her own staff dancing and singing, whilst… Oh dear gods, no…they were wearing her clothes…HER WIGS

Ephea ran around, trying to grab at her hair pieces that were deliberately being held out of reach. Servants laughed in her face as she clawed at her dresses, some paraded around by men in a parody of their mistress.

Her stomach churned and her head pounded as she screamed at them to stop and go to bed; but she was blatantly ignored.

Why didn't they listen to her and do as she told them?

The rage boiled within her, these were her servants, her subordinates, they had no place treating her home and possessions in this way. Who did they think they were? In her confusion the house began to spin. Everyone was laughing and jeering, she felt sick, and needed to calm down, find somewhere to rest.

Making her way to the stairs, Ephea was tripped and pushed, her own wig was once more lost, and her stays threatened to loosen their hold on her ample bosom again. Finally, reaching the bottom step, she started to half crawl, half stagger up the staircase. As she ascended, her face came into close proximity with a dress she recognised as her own, but this one was covering an arse that was in the process of seeing to one of her parlour maids, who also wore one of her favourite dresses.

Transfixed in horror, she watched as the two revelled in their fornication surrounded by her own silks and tulle. It was as they reached their climax it all became too much, grabbing her own skirts she ran up the rest of the staircase to her rooms, slammed the door behind her and promptly threw up.

After emptying her stomach, she wiped her face on the back of her hand and stood up, shaking as she made her way towards the bathroom. She reached out at the furniture to steady her legs, oblivious to her surroundings; until she tripped and fell over something on the floor. Crying in pain and frustration, she sat up to see what had caused her fall, it was then she became aware of the devastation around her. Furniture had been thrown across the floor, along with clothes, underwear and scarves strewn everywhere. Half staggering, half crawling she finally made it into her own private space that had also been ransacked. Jewellery boxes lay empty on the floor, mirrors had been smashed and her precious make up, to hide her scars, smeared everywhere. It took a while for Ephea to comprehend what had happened to her lovely world. Sitting amongst the wreckage, she sobbed until she had no more tears to shed, her body exhausted from the effort. She had to get away from here, away from the city, away from Nathan.

The bastard, this was his fault.

She'd go to father; he would know what to do.

Satisfied she now had some sort of plan, she removed her already torn and filthy dress and hunted at the back of her wardrobe for her old clothes. They had been kept, but hidden, as a reminder of how far she had risen in life since her father's first disgrace. Finding an old felt hat, she covered her head and made her way out of her rooms.

The hall was now empty, the party broken up. Smashed glass and bottles were strewn amongst her abandoned dresses and wigs; though she noted that none of her jewellery was left behind. Without a further look back, she descended the stairs and crossed the hall, closing the front door behind her as she made her way towards the South Bank. Once she reached the East gate, she would take the portal to her father. She would be safe there.

The city itself was now mainly quiet. It had been some time since Ephea had left the Palace with her escort, and there was a faint lightening of the sky in the east. The streets were empty except for companies of the Order and bands of police, determined to keep the curfew enforced. Ephea had no intention of coming into contact with either, so keeping to the shadows, chose the smaller, darker streets as she made her way towards the edge of the city.

Alone in the darkness, Ephea thought of Johnson and she wished she was here with her now. She would have kept her safe, made sure the servants paid for their desecration. Instead she had that bastard Mason, and he had abandoned her when she needed him most. So intent was she on herself pity, that Ephea had failed to notice the figure following her until he stepped out into her path.

They were alone in an alleyway, dark with only the orbs from the street ahead to shed any light. Just the two of them, Ephea and the silent stranger. Fear caught in her throat and she stepped back, but the figure followed and made to stop her leaving. As he turned, Ephea saw his face, lit up in the dim light of the distant street orbs. Scars ran down the left-hand side of his face, and he seemed to hold himself awkwardly, his left arm held close against his body as if he favoured it. She thought she recognised him, but for the life of her she couldn't remember where from.

'Hello Ephea. Remember me?'

Fear gripped her spine, but after all the humiliation of the previous evening, she was determined to brazen it out. Standing up straight, she assumed her natural pose of looking along her nose.

'I have no idea who you are, now get out of my way.'

But Fallon Klienstock didn't move, instead he held her gaze, and she found it impossible to look away.

404

'Oh you are not going anywhere but to hell Ephea.'

Trying to step back out of his way again, she finally recognised who he was, but it was too late. He pushed her back, pinning her against the hard, damp stone of the wall; her heart thumped frantically against her ribcage. Gulping air in her panic, her voice was thin and barely a whisper when she answered.

'I thought you'd left the city, gone back home to your father in disgrace.'

There was no mirth in his laugh, his voice still quiet and calm. 'Oh poor Ephea, I didn't go anywhere. I've been here all this time, waiting.'

She gulped; he was so close now she felt his breath on her skin.

'What are you going to do?'

'What do you think I'm going to do Ephea?'

She shook her head, eyes wide. Suddenly his hand jerked and then she saw it, a sharp wicked blade held close to her face. He let the cold metal touch her cheek, pressing a little harder so that a rivulet of blood began to flow. Her eyes were now wide with terror.

'You're mad, you'll never get away with it.'

'You're probably right, on both counts, but of course Ephea, you assume I care.'

She cried out briefly, but her voice was quickly silenced. The blade was drawn across her throat before Fallon plunged it deep into her heart. He may have been a disappointment to his father as a man, but as a boy Fallon had learnt the skills of using a blade as any son of a knight off the Order would.

Letting her limp, lifeless body fall to the ground, he cleaned his dagger on her shirt before re-sheathing it. Then, without a second glance, he turned and limped back towards the street, and the safety of his aunt's house.

As he passed a darkened doorway, Fallon failed to notice the form of a tall woman standing there, someone who had witnessed the whole proceedings. She waited until he had disappeared from view, before she stepped out and walked down to the crumpled body of Ephea. Nudging the body with the toe of her boot, she avoided the blood that flowed along the cobbles. Satisfied she was dead, Jean Carter retraced her steps back up the alleyway, continuing in her quest to help the Order and police. Ephea wasn't going anywhere and this time there would be no hue and cry, Justice had already been served.

30

Kaimiren

J ean knew the storm would be coming soon, and while the Patrols had certainly made their way into the city through various access points from the caverns and tunnels below, the Kaimiren were still out of sight.

The police had taken charge of making sure the curfew was observed by the general public, though they had had quite a night of it, trying to convince not just one, but many drunken parties that they had to end their revelry early. There were even occasions when it was necessary to call in the help of the Order to encourage the carousers to politely, but firmly, go home. However, all the inns were emptied (much to the disgust of the landlords) and the stalls, that had opened to catch extra business during the festivities, were shut down. The streets were empty, and apart from the odd sound from a few determined private parties, the night was quiet.

The Order was out in force to watch the streets for the emergence of the Patrols. They had been warned to steer clear of anyone answering the description of the Kaimiren — very big and well-armed. As yet though, only the Patrols in their familiar uniforms were observed and followed, then rounded up and taken to cells within the various Guard Rooms throughout the city; which by now, were becoming alarmingly full. Some groups of Patrols, however, had managed to evade the Order, but even they were only minor factions, confused and lacking direction as their leaders were rounded up. Eventually, a few found themselves trapped within small sectors; unable to escape, their panic beginning to take over until the Order intervened and the last remnants removed.

Eventually, the inevitable storm came; rising from below, armed and ready to kill.

In a closed café bar, several streets from the South Bank of the river Par, a group of people sat around tables, listening to a man as he voiced a list of their own complaints. Once again, the Emperor had failed to act in the people's interest, if it wasn't a lack of security and the blatant blindness to the appalling acts of the *foreigners*, it was the determined effort to halt any laughter and enjoyment that the populace managed to achieve.

'Last night, we stood at the gates of the Palace, we were assured by Lord John himself, that all was being done to rectify the appalling treatment of the loyal citizens of Parva. We have had to endure so much due to the lack of action by the Emperor and his Knight's for so long; and now they choose to punish us. All because they can't control those who are truly

408

responsible for the evil taking place upon our streets. It's not good enough. We gave them an opportunity to stand up and make a difference; instead they want to keep us quiet, afraid of what might happen if others start to listen. Well, people are listening already, and we will be heard again. I suggest we make our way back to the Palace, but this time we don't let them send us away, silenced and ignored.'

All around the room people cheered, they would see action at last. Buoyed by the enthusiasm of his audience, the man made his way to the door, and opening it wide, he called to the others to follow.

'WE WILL BE HEARD.'

Again, a resounding cheer and the crowd stood as one, following their new leader out into the pre-dawn light.

Out to the east, the sun was beginning to rise, the first rays yet to reach the high walls of the city.

The ruckus the group of protesters were making as they made their way down the street towards the river, could be heard streets away. Passing the doors of shops tightly shut up, windows above still darkened as their occupants slept; their previous partying at last catching up with them. Out of the gloom a figure ran towards the angry crowd, holding out his hands to make the mob stop. The baleful looks he received told the young policeman he wasn't welcome, but Lyal stood his ground anyway. The young PC's face was stern as he tried to make the protestors stay quiet and go home.

'You have to get off the streets, the Emperor has instilled a curfew. If you don't comply you run the risk of arrest. Please find somewhere to go now and stay inside until you are told it is safe to come back out.'

The mob jeered; their leader bolstered by his first opportunity to voice their anger to a member of the establishment.

'You have no right to tell us to go anywhere in our city. We are not the problem, it should be the Patrols you are dealing with, threatening to throw them into cells, rather than the good citizens of Parva.'

There was much nodding and sounds of encouragement from the crowd, though Lyal noted that it had become short lived, their jeering petering out into a stunned silence. Seeing the faces of the people before him, he watched their gaze rest on a point behind his shoulder. The fight seemed to suddenly drain from them.

Then he heard it, the subtle sound of breathing, its warmth caressing his neck. Turning slowly, Lyal wasn't sure what he expected to see; perhaps a company of the Order, ready to arrest the unhappy protestors, or even a group of Patrol members, hell bent on causing trouble. But the reality struck the fear of the gods deep into his heart.

Before him stood ten or eleven huge men; tattoos marked their faces. They didn't speak, they didn't need to, their eyes told Lyal his fate. Before he even had a chance to say anything, barely even open his mouth, the nearest Kaimiren had run his sword through the young PC's heart — the shock of fear and pain etched onto his face, before his lifeless body fell to the floor.

The Kaimiren kicked Lyal's body from his blade, before returning his gaze to the terrified mob before him, then, as one, he and the Kaimiren behind him, bore down on the hapless crowd. Some of those towards the back of the protesting group had managed to find their voices before they were also caught

410

and cut down, their screams brief and futile. Curtains from surrounding windows twitched, but the people behind were too terrified to come out, to offer any help against the horror below. Within no time at all the street was silent, nothing moved but the body of Kaimiren making their way back towards the river, meeting with their fellow killers, ready to seek out their quarry. Behind them the hacked and broken bodies of sixteen people lay scattered about the street, blood flowed along gutters and into drains. Among them a young policeman, his lifeless face framed by a mop of blonde hair, ruffled by an early morning breeze.

Dawn was slowly breaking over the city, and as the Kaimiren left the bloody scene, a few brave souls emerged from the surrounding buildings, calling for help, desperate to know they hadn't been abandoned to the hell they had just witnessed. From around a corner a policewoman came running. At first, she tried to calm the people, telling them to get back inside until told otherwise. But then her anger turned to horror as she saw the awful scene before her. There was an anguished cry as the newly promoted Sergeant Croft ran to the dead, feeling her stomach lurch as she saw the slaughtered body of her work partner, her friend, Lyal.

Grief rushed over her and anger surged through her soul. They couldn't ignore this, they couldn't just run and hide, no matter what the Order and the Emperor said. By now other police officers had arrived, also realising that one of their own had fallen with these hapless victims; raising angry voices, demanding revenge for his murder. Sergeant Croft and the band of police hurried to catch those responsible for their butchery. Running towards the river, they were caught by a

411

company of the Order led by Captain Ty Coniston, cutting them off in their charge.

'What the hell do you think you are doing? Get back inside, this is not a time to be out on the streets.'

Ella spun on the Captain. He towered over her, but she stood back so as to make sure he understood that she wasn't going to be stopped in her quest.

'Those bastards have just killed a fellow policeman, along with over a dozen members of the public. We can't just let them get away with it. We have to do something.'

Tears of anger and frustration filled her eyes, she battered them away angrily with her hand.

Ty looked horrified. 'They've killed people already?'

Ella nodded, eager to get away.

'They must have been out on the streets when those bastards came out. They didn't stand a chance.'

Ty took her shoulders and felt the frustration and anger of the police behind her.

'And do you really believe you stand any better chance than they did? You need to stay focused sergeant, the people of this city depend on you to keep them safe, not run off in a fit of vengeance.'

His voice softened as he saw the anger flash in her eyes again.

'I can only imagine the grief you feel now, but you have to wait before you can deal with it. Right now, you must stay safe.'

Ella seemed to suddenly come to her senses, his words cutting through her pain. Pulling herself away from the knight, she stood up straight.

'Yes, it pains me to say it but you are right.'

Behind her there was an angry cry, several policemen had broken away and decided they were not so willing to give up on their quest for vengeance.

'Shit.'

Ty stared after them, but before he could do anything, three of his own knights had taken off after the renegade police, calling them back. Ty turned to the remainder of his company and ordered them to stay with Ella and her fellow police officers. He made sure they understood to stay away form the invaders and to keep safe.

Following after his men, not entirely sure what the hell he was supposed to do when he caught up with them, Ty prayed silently that it was before any of the Kaimiren were encountered. He sprinted down the hill towards the river, swearing bitterly at the scene that met him as he turned the final corner. It was carnage. The enraged police and pursuing knights hadn't stood a chance, the horde that now ranged around one of the squares that backed onto the river had cut them to pieces, their bodies strewn across the cobbles. While he stood horrified, a hand caught at his shoulder and he spun round, ready to fend off the attack, but instead came face to face with Jean. Relief rushed over him until he saw the look of horror and anguish on the woman's face.

'Ty, what the fuck has happened?'

Briefly, he explained the small amount of information he knew about the disaster. Movement in the square caught their eyes, it seemed that now was the time the Kaimiren were considering their advance across the river, to the North Bank and the Palace.

'Shit Ty, we can't deal with that now, I've got to do something about these numbers, there must be seventy Kaimiren out there.' Jean reached out and held Ty's arms, concern etched across her face. 'Once I start however, this lot are going to be seriously pissed off. You need to be out of here and fast.'

Ty didn't move, how could he let her face the Kaimiren on her own? But Jean wasn't having any of it, she recognised that look. The sound of urgency in her voice was unmistakable as she urged him again.

'Ty go, now.'

By now the Kaimiren were heading down the hill, towards the road that would lead to the bridge. Time was up, she had to go. Using her left hand, instead of drawing her sword, Jean took a device that opened out into a bow. Ty watched and would have sworn it wasn't there a moment ago, but now she stood beside him with a fully strung bow. It had markings along its curving limbs that were the same as those on her sword and daggers. Pulling back on the string, an arrow appeared, and picking out a Kaimiren towards the front of the large platoon, she let it fly. The look of surprise as the arrow caught him between the eyes was almost comical. No ordinary arrow could have pierced that bone; but of course, these were not ordinary arrows. For a moment the advancing horde faltered and several more men fell to Jean's onslaught. Their leader, she recognised instantly as Mason, looked around for the person responsible, when he found his quarry he shouted out, his men following his call as one. If she wanted to gain their attention, she had certainly got it now. Deciding that it would probably be as good a time as any to make a swift retreat, Jean dashed down the hill

414

towards the bridge and up the avenue towards the Palace. A final call over her shoulder as she ran.

'Ty, get the fuck out of here.'

She looked around, and with relief saw that he had gone.

But unbeknownst to Jean, Ty had not run for cover. He knew this city like the back of his hand, and while Jean had been letting fly with her arrows, he was already on his way to the river. He saw, sitting unmanned at an alleyway that backed onto the quayside, a wagon full of tree trunks that had been brought in by barge from the country. Its position was above the river itself, perched on a slope that led down to the bridge.

Without any further consideration, Ty leapt upon the wagon and released the brake. Wheels turned as gravity lent a helping hand, and soon he was hurtling down towards the bridge, noting with relief that Jean was just able to make the bridge before the wagon. He grinned ruefully as he saw the look of surprise on her face as she turned at the noise. Behind her the company of Kaimiren, who hadn't fallen to her arrows, were charging with Mason in the lead. Ty acted instinctively. Taking his own sword, he sliced through the ropes that held the huge trunks in place, and as the wagon crashed into the bridge railings, huge heavy logs spilled out onto the Kaimiren. Even their reinforced bone structure couldn't withstand that much of a pounding.

Across the bridge, Jean could only look on in horror as she saw Ty disappear below the wagon's load, and into the chaos of crushed Kaimiren and timber. An uncontrollable cry of grief escaped her lips, as Mason and his henchmen cut their way through the wreckage of the wagon, giving no thought to the plight of their fallen comrades. Firing a few arrows to gain the

Kaimiren's attention, Jean then took her chance and turned on her heel, continuing full pelt up the, now empty, tree lined avenue to the Palace. She knew the Kaimiren wouldn't be diverted for long.

Jean pounded up the avenue, unable to stop the flow of tears that poured down her face. Nothing could have prepared her for the loss of Ty, he was a friend she had grown fond of; in her work such friends were few and far between and her heart ached at his loss. Roughly she rubbed her cheeks, she couldn't afford to be emotional now, there would be time for grief later. Letting out a roar of fury she forced her emotions down, let the bastards come, she'll make them all pay.

Her heart was pounding by the time she finally passed through the Palace gates and saw, with dismay, that the guard room was still manned. Not even bothering to speak, she made her way to the back door and reached in, startling the watch as she closed and barred the door on them. Then making her way back to the front of the building she was confronted by an angry Major Torvil.

'Go back inside Major, this is not your fight.'

Before he had a chance to argue further, she pushed him back into the guardroom with a strength that belied her, locking and barring the door. Angry voices from within were followed by loud banging in frustration. Despite their orders, Jean couldn't trust that being so close to what was about to take place, the Order would stay put without being under lock and key.

Ignoring their protests, Jean hurried up the Palace steps, behind her the Kaimiren were almost at the locked gates.

She knew they wouldn't hold them for long.

31

The

Guardians

athan and the other Knights had already gathered in the main atrium. Having spent the night organising the evacuation of the city and subsequent curfew, they were agitated and not in the mood for general chit chat; prowling around the space in silence, waiting for the arrival of Jean as expected. One of the great doors to the hall stood open, and the early morning sun was beginning to filter through the glass ceiling above.

Daniel had found himself looking at an exhibit of weaponry for something to keep his mind occupied. He'd seen it thousands of times before, but anything was better than the unknown impending threat they were expected to face. He studied the work's intricate patterns; swords and daggers arranged around a large embossed shield. The shield's surface was covered in thick black leather, with the Imperial tree depicted in large, pointed studs emblazoned on its front. He tensed. From somewhere within the city to the south, faint sounds of people shouting could be heard. Curious, he made his way to the open door, but he stopped and cocked his head to one side as if listening. Something had caught his attention from within the Palace itself, a loud banging noise was coming from somewhere on the floors above. Knowing the Palace should have been evacuated hours ago, he turned to his companions and asked.

'Can you hear a banging noise?'

The others stopped and listened too, nodding their heads when they could hear a faint rapping coming from above. Daniel made his way towards the sound, taking the stairs that lead to the first floor two at a time, before disappearing around the corner at the first landing. It was a short while before those in the hall heard a loud screech, as Yollan vented her fury through a very bad hangover.

'YOU FUCKING BASTARD. YOU DID THIS. HOW DARE YOU LOCK ME IN A FUCKING CUPBOARD.'

Downstairs, the Knights all looked at each other and smiled broadly. Simon folded his arms, and with a big grin, commented as if he was imparting some great words of wisdom.

'I do believe, that our Daniel is no longer flavour of the month with his doting wife. You never know, he might get some peace now.'

John grinned back. 'Not if the racket she is making has anything to do with it. Has she come up for air yet?'

It was true, if Daniel had any say on the matter, he was finding it hard to get a word in edgeways. The high pitched shrill of a fuming Yollan, came ever closer as she approached the staircase. It was at this point that Gradine came into the atrium, wanting to know what all of the noise was about. The Knight's turned in surprise to see her, they thought that she had left with the rest of the guests the previous evening. From the corner of his eye, Nathan saw Jean enter quietly through the open front doors.

Suddenly there was an almighty scream, everyone turned to see Yollan clattering down the stairs, head over heels, yellow silk skirts ballooning around her. There was a sickening crack, and by the time she reached the bottom step she was a heap of soiled yellow silks and smudged makeup.

Everyone stood in stunned silence, before looking towards the top of the stairs where Daniel stared down upon the lifeless form below.

An ear-piercing scream rented the air, and Gradine stood pointing at the man at the top of the stairs.

'MURDERER.'

Gradine ran to her sister's body and was still screaming up at Daniel.

'YOU EVIL BASTARD. YOU THREW HER DOWN THE STAIRS. WE ALL SAW YOU.'

419

She looked around at the Knights, who stood with emotionless faces; no one moved or said anything. From above, Daniel began to descend the stairs, shaking his head. He looked shocked.

'You don't believe that I actually pushed her?'

'Of course I do. You hated being married to her. What a convenient way to get rid of someone you considered such a burden.'

By the time he had reached the lower steps, Daniel had to manoeuvre himself over Yollan's broken body. The angle at which she had landed, meant she was sprawled out over several steps, making the climb around her awkward.

'He didn't push her. She fell. She was flailing so much she wasn't watching where she was going and she missed her footing, so she fell.'

Everyone looked up, spinning round to see Jean standing in the doorway. Gradine became incensed. 'LIAR!'

Jean remained impassive, her own anger and grief had forced her to push her emotions behind even greater walls. She felt numb and cold.

'I can assure you I am not in the habit of lying. I had an excellent view of the top of the stairs when I entered the hall, and she fell; she wasn't pushed.'

Gradine, exhausted, angry and full of grief for her sister, ran at Jean, her talons out ready to scratch at the woman's face. It was a fatal mistake. Jean had had enough. These stupid women had instigated a string of events that had resulted in the death of good men and women, of Ty.

She would receive no quarter from Jean today.

Before Gradine could make any contact herself, Jean had grabbed her by her dress and hurled her away; lifting her off her feet, sending her backwards towards the wall and the arrangements of weaponry. There was another sickening crack, then a thud, as her body smacked into the tree embossed shield that had so interested Daniel earlier.

For a moment, Gradine just hung there, her body impaled upon the spike like studs, a look of complete surprise fixed upon her face. Then, slowly, she started to slide to the ground. By the time she lay crumpled on the floor, a thick smear of blood was running down the wall, with bone, brain and body tissue clinging to the spikes. There was a silence as Stephen made his way to the body to check for life signs having just finished checking Yollan. He shook his head and stood up.

'Well, that's two divorces no longer required.'

'Three actually. Ephea sort of ran into an old friend. It didn't end well.'

Nathan frowned but didn't have the opportunity to comment further, as the sound of the main gates giving way under the force of the Kaimiren caught their attention. Ignoring the lifeless bodies of Yollan, Gradine, and the question regarding Ephea's demise, Jean and the Knights quickly made their way out to the top of the broad steps that led down to the parade square. Instinctively they all drew their swords, and Jean again felt that tug of the familiar, a curious warmth.

Before them were the remains of the Kaimiren that had survived Jean's onslaught of arrows, along with the barrage of timber that Ty had sacrificed himself for. Now she guessed that barely thirty to thirty-five remained. Considerably better odds, but tough all the same. She could also see that approaching the

Palace, Anna was leading, what seemed to be a small army of knights and police up the avenue.

She groaned. 'Do your people ever do as they are told?'

Paul looked up and laughed sardonically.

'I think you'll find that has more to do with Anna if anything.'

However, Jean need not have worried as the company stopped short of the Palace gates; their faces grim and determined, but they would go no further. From the guard room the shouting and banging had stopped, instead concerned faces peered through the barred windows. All eyes were on the Kaimiren.

Though their ranks had been reduced considerably, they still looked a very formidable sight. Standing now, waiting, their faces were impassive, eyes dead to the rest of the world around them. They had at last found their quarry. In front of them all, stood Mason, his tattoos and scars etched deeply into his face and neck. Nathan looked at Jean standing beside him.

'Who, or what, are they?'

Her own hardened green eyes looked back into the azure blue of his.

'Genetically and physically engineered men. Their skeletons are reinforced, and their vital organs enhanced; bred purely to complete the tasks their owners have been paid vast amounts of money for. When they are given a task, they will do all that is necessary to achieve it. They don't recognise pain, and they consider death as part of their contract. No honour, no conscience. Just big, deadly, professional, killing machines.'

'Shit.'

'Shit indeed.'

The Knights looked at one another. Jean sensed their concern and underlying fear.

'There is a way I can even the odds, but I have no idea of the consequences to you, or me. Do you remember what happened last night? In the garden there was a moment of emotional connection.'

Nathan nodded as if understanding.

'But you believe it will be enough?'

She took a deep breath.

'It has to be. Are, *you* prepared though, to take that risk I mean?'

Nathan's face was a grim mask.

'Whatever it takes, let's just get this nightmare over and done with.'

Jean said nothing, but once more, brought up the previously hidden bow in her left hand and drew back the string.

'Once this starts, they will charge; you should get ready.' She gave a sideways grin. 'Oh and be prepared for the biggest adrenaline rush of your lives.'

Opening her senses, she tore down the walls that kept the emotional world at bay, aware that now, she was also letting in the huge adrenaline hit of the men around her. She had to stop herself from reeling as the force hit, shaking her head slightly, bringing back her focus.

Then, with the familiar feeling of the rest of the world disappearing into the distance, with her mind trained only on the impending battle settling upon her, she pulled back on the bow string. Taking aim, an arrow appeared, drawn and ready to fly to its chosen mark.

Several Kaimiren fell to her volley, but their fellow soldiers were not to be stopped by this additional attack, they charged.

By now there were less than thirty of them — it was all or nothing.

Abandoning her bow, Jean drew her own sword and released the adrenalin rush she had gathered from the Knights, sending it back towards them with force. If they were shocked by the hit, they didn't show it, used to countless battles themselves they would not be surprised by the sudden sensation.

Hearts began to beat faster, breathing slowed and minds sharpened, concentrating on nothing but the battle itself.

As the adrenalin of the Guardians rose, Jean was able to sense the escalation, she sent it back to the Knights who responded again, so that within seconds a rhythm was formed, and the energy pulsed between them. Pain and fear gone, only experience, power and determination moved them forward.

They met the charging Kaimiren head on.

Those who witnessed what happened that day never forgot. Many were themselves veterans of campaigns for the Empire; called by their Emperor to act at a time of need. Sometimes to fight, at other times to help build up the fallen. Always the Knights were there to lead, direct and help. But it was rare for anyone within the Empire, to actually see them fight a battle; to overcome adversity and deal with the very lowest life within the universe. That was always something the Knights did alone, this was when they were Guardians. All symbols of power and privilege meant nothing, only the will to survive and ensure those intent on destruction failed.

To the citizens of the Empire, the Emperor and his Knights were symbols of power, an authority that made sure the people they were sworn to protect were safe. Of course, it was their code, and their example, that was taught to every knight who passed through Pernia. Their history, the stories of their battles and accomplishments, both good and bad, were the stuff of legends.

It had been difficult to correlate the myths with those of the real-life men they knew.

Yet here they were, facing a formidable enemy that in all probability should be impossible to defeat. But their very presence gave hope, a belief that even the impossible was possible.

The blood bath that ensued belied the truth; while the Kaimiren were efficient killing machines, they lacked the drive and purpose of the Knights. As the energy surged between the eight Guardians, they felt no pain, fighting the battle as a single unit, a subconscious drive to destroy, before being destroyed.

Spread out along the line, Jean and the Knights found themselves averaging about four Kaimiren each. As expected, the vast majority aimed for Nathan, but Simon and John soon put paid to that.

At close quarters it is difficult to wield a sword efficiently, and while the Kaimiren reckoned on overcoming Nathan quickly with numbers, they suddenly found themselves corralled together.

Damien stood by his cousin, and even Jean was impressed with his sword skills, making short work of the attackers.

The advantage was turning against the assault on Nathan, the four Knights, now able to fulfil a better swing, with far more

425

power behind their blades. The extra adrenaline, strength and durability of the Guardians' swords brought several more Kaimiren down.

Mason had detached himself from the bloodied group, heading for Nathan himself; it was his biggest mistake. Without the protection of the other Kaimiren, he fell almost immediately against the defending sword of Damien. Even before Mason drew his last breath, he was forgotten, left to die as the battle raged around him.

With the main body of the force focused on Nathan, the rest of the Knights and Jean soon picked off the outliers. The Leameum swords were able to cut through the reinforced bone of the attackers with a single blow. If there was enough force behind it, a mighty swing could cleave the unfortunate in two, before injuring any adjacent adversary in the way of the deadly blade.

They were also painfully aware of the threat if the Kaimiren could make their way behind and attack their flanks. The Guardians kept each other's backs, ensuring they were not drawn out, leaving themselves vulnerable. As such it was difficult for the Kaimiren to get through.

In the end it was the underlying rule of the Kaimiren, that they achieve their goal no matter what, that caused their final defeat. Every time they pushed forward to get to Nathan, the Guardians cut them down, with a skill and strength the Kaimiren were not expecting, and hadn't planned for.

The final dozen or so eventually made a stand, but it was to no avail. The last Kaimiren went down dead or dying as the sun finally rose above the city's caldera wall.

The parade square was awash with blood as the Guardians stood alone, surrounded by the dead and dying. Covered from head to foot in blood, brains, bone and gore, exhausted with exertion, they staggered against the large open gates that separated the Palace complex from the main road of the North Bank.

The roar of battle still ringing in their ears, the desire to continue the slaughter raging within them. Once she realised the battle had ended, Jean forced herself to fight the urge to destroy, shutting down the pulsing, destructive energy. Walls were raised in her mind, allowing the men around her to begin to recover as the adrenalin slowly declined.

Within their minds, the roar was suddenly replaced by an overwhelming silence. The world around them seemed disconnected, a series of silent pictures viewed through a glass wall. Shaking their heads to try and recover, it took a few moments to be aware of people rushing forward.

For Jean, her problem now was the huge volume of energy surging within her, it was too much for her to release and it had nowhere to go. Her heart continued to race, her chest constricted, her breathing becoming short. She felt sick, with an overwhelming feeling of panic taking over.

Collapsing on to the blood-soaked ground, someone was holding on to her, a voice in the distance was shouting.

Pain surged through her body with every muscle taught, the nerves under her skin seemed to be trying to burst out, she felt as if she was ripping apart.

Still someone was shouting her name, but she couldn't see who. All around the world had begun to grow dark.

32

Aftermath

athan caught Jean just in time, before she fell to the ground. Laying her down gently he held her in his arms; she was barely conscious as she shook uncontrollably. While he had been aware of Jean shutting down the link between them, reducing the surge of adrenalin to a level that they could manage, Nathan still struggled to ease his own desire to lash out at anything that dare to cross his path. The beast that he fought hard to conceal had momentarily been set free, and he had to constrain himself to remain calm. Focusing on Jean he forced his mind to try to figure out what was happening to her. She seemed to be dying and he didn't know what to do. He could feel panic form in the pit of his stomach, he had to do something fast.

A voice sounded somewhere in the distance, he thought it could be Anna shouting, but everything around him was still muffled and he couldn't be sure.

Then suddenly the world seemed to burst with sound. Once the shock of the battle was over, the noise around them rushed in, everyone was shouting to be heard.

Aware that Stephen was now at his side, Nathan felt relief that help was at hand. Stephen would know what to do, and as he had seen so many times before, Stephen used his own energy to examine Jean, holding her hands, sensing for vital signs of life and anomalies. It didn't take long and Nathan was dismayed to hear his findings, it wasn't what he hoped for. Stephen looked grave.

'Whatever is happening to her, it is not due to medical reasons. Basically, she is having a massive heart attack.'

Nathan was shocked, trying to push the panic down further.

'Surely you can ease the symptoms?'

Stephen observed the look of concern on Nathan's face and felt his frustration. Jean had only just appeared in their lives, and now it was very possible she could die before they even got to know her.

'This is more your department Nathan; all I can say is you had better do it quickly.'

Before he could say any more, Anna had pushed her way past the other Knights, even giving an unceremonious shove to her husband as she went. Rushing to Nathan's side, she was breathless and gulping air as she tried to explain what she had been told the night before by Jean.

'Jean is empathic, she can sense the emotions of other people and animals. She said that last night something

429

happened that made her think that all of you could pick up what she senses too. If that was so, then you could all use it to beat the Kaimiren.'

Nathan was agreeing with her but was unsure what point she was trying to make; he wished she would hurry up.

'I know that, but right now I'm more concerned with just keeping her alive.'

Anna found it hard to keep her annoyance in check.

'I'm trying to explain.'

'Anna.'

Behind her, Paul put his hands on her shoulders but she shrugged them off.

'If it worked, Jean knew that she would be able to shut down the energy that she passed to you. But it concerned her that it may get to the point where she wouldn't be able to control the build-up of energy within herself. She has never had to deal with that much before, she was worried what the possible consequences would be if it consumed her.'

She reached out and caught at his arm.

'When I told her what had happened to James when he died, she became even more panicked.'

Now Nathan understood, the sudden release of energy would be catastrophic.

'She's getting worse Nathan; you've got to do something.'

Stephen had hold of Jean's hand, the look of helplessness etched into his face as he watched her dying in front of him. Around them, the rest of the Knights looked on in helpless horror.

430

Jean was vaguely aware of voices around her, pictures flitted teasingly across her mind. Memories of people who had been so familiar, who had helped her become who she was today. There were feelings of happiness, and of betrayal; feeling her heart break as she was forced to leave those she loved so much behind.

Someone was calling her name, she tried to run back, they wanted her after all, but the images were becoming less clear. She felt herself panic as she tried to refocus, she had to get back to them.

'Jean.'

In her mind she tried to call back, but her voice wouldn't come.

'Jean can you hear me?'

The images faded; no matter how much she tried, she couldn't keep them, and they were gone; her heart aching at their loss.

'Jean, I need to you listen.'

It was a man's voice and it was close. She tried to force her eyes open, there were people around her, staring.

Do I know them?

Then there was pain. She gasped as the tightening in her chest seemed to force the air out of her lungs.

'Jean let it go. Let the energy go.'

The voice belonged to the man beside her. A strong face with blue eyes, framed with a mop of dark hair. He seemed familiar but she couldn't place where from. He was covered in blood, the familiar scent of iron filled her nostrils, her head was now spinning with the pain. She wanted to throw up.

431

It took all her energy, but she managed to find her voice, it was barely a whisper.

'I can't, I know what it will do to you. You have to leave me and get as far away as you can.'

'It won't do anything to me. You have to trust me Jean, I know what I am doing. Just let the energy inside go, please.'

The man tried to keep the panic out of his voice, but she felt it all the same. She was in so much pain, so exhausted, it was a relief for someone else to take control. She had no idea what would happen, but in the end, she didn't think she had much choice. With both reluctance and relief, she let the energy pounding within her go.

Nathan felt the force of her energy as she finally released it, he was shocked at how much had been concentrated within her. But he knew it was never going to be a problem, he didn't even have to tell the others. Bracing themselves, they felt the energy's impact as Nathan dispelled the force amongst the seven of them, and in doing so, the threat to Jean was easily consumed, then dispersed.

Nathan felt Jean relax in his arms, and Stephen immediately re-examined her, satisfied that she was now fit and well, and out of danger; he wished all of his patients recovered so quickly. The smile on his face told Nathan all he needed to know. The relief that flooded over him helped to push the beast within down, smothering it until it submitted and returned to its slumber.

Jean tried to sit up, but with so many people around her it was difficult to move. She felt like pushing them all away, she needed air. Fortunately, Stephen had taken over his patient's care and was ordering everyone to give her space. Grateful and relieved, Jean finally managed to stand up with Nathan's help, Stephen hovering like a concerned mother hen.

Looking around her, she and the Knight's were still covered, head to toe, in drying and congealing blood. They looked as exhausted as she did. Beside her was Anna looking on anxiously; Jean was pleased to see a man, she took as being Anna's husband, Paul, standing beside her. His face was full of pride for his wife as he held her hand.

From across the parade square, they could hear the disgruntled watch finally being released from the guardroom, and members of the Garrison were now gathering around the square, standing beside where the gate once remained closed. Further down the avenue a substantial crowd had formed and by the sound it, more people were joining it, making their way across the bridges from the South Bank, hurrying to find out what had happened up at the Palace.

The parade square itself was awash with blood, broken bodies littering the ground; Simon and John had already searched among the dead and dying, sending the rest off to the afterlife they no doubt deserved. It was pointless in trying to save any lives amongst them, no one could survive that slaughter for long. Damien stepped forward and Jean's heart sank as she remembered the loss of Ty.

'We should clear up this mess I suppose.' Indicating the square.

Nathan agreed, and everyone stood back while he held out his hand, he looked surprised when Jean joined him in raising her own. They looked at each other enquiringly and Nathan cocked an eyebrow and grinned. Jean hoped the blood covering her own face was sufficient to hide her cheeks as she felt herself go red.

'A joint effort then?'

She nodded and together, they again, raised hands, letting out their energy that formed the consuming blue fire. Flames passed over the bodies, engulfing the dead, finally reducing them to ash. However, something else unexpected began to happen, as the two sources of flame mingled, they grew into a bright blue inferno, spreading from the bodies to Jean and the Knights themselves. While they knew that the flames were safe to the living, the flames had never spread like this before, even Jean had a moment of concern on her face. Then, as the cool heat enveloped their bodies, Jean and the Knights realised that the gore that had coated them was now being cleansed away. By the time the last flicker had disappeared, the ground around them was thick with ash, and not a speck of blood was seen anywhere on the ground, or on themselves. Those who stood by, and had witnessed the scene, were awestruck. Once again, they had heard legends of the blue flame and the phenomenon of destroying the dead, but rarely had anyone seen it. Especially in such spectacular fashion.

Nathan looked down at Jean and gave her a wry grin.

'Well Miss Carter, I have a feeling life is going to get a bit more interesting from now on.'

This time she had nothing to hide the redness in her cheeks.

Once Nathan had dispelled the excess energy within her, the anger and desire to fight had gone too. She gratefully felt the calm and peace within her body again, but she couldn't shake the exhaustion that still wrapped around her. Jean knew it would take time, but she didn't like the fact that she was probably now more vulnerable than ever. She couldn't help but hold on to his suggestion that there was a possibility of working with the Knights in the future. Was there really a chance that she didn't have to do this god forsaken job on her own anymore? She tried to push down the hope that such a dream was possible.

Aware that the Knights were looking at her curiously, she busied herself to hide her awkwardness. Holding up her hand to dispel the ash lying around them, Nathan took her cue and they both snapped their fingers, ash rose in a haze before being blown into the wind. A moment's blur, then the air was clear.

Nathan and Jean both glanced at each other and grinned, when a familiar voice was heard behind them.

'Typical, I missed all the fun again.'

Damien turned with a beaming smile and made to greet Captain Ty Coniston as he joined their small group. However, he was almost knocked off his feet as Jean ran past and threw herself at the man she thought was dead, crushed beneath the weight of timber and the killing blows of the Kaimiren. A moan of pain from Ty caused Jean to pull back, he was holding his right arm gingerly against his ribs.

'Oh Ty I'm so sorry, what happened to you? I thought you were dead.'

An exclamation from Damien cut through Ty's answer.

'What do you mean you thought he was dead? When exactly did you intend to tell me this?'

Jean's stomach churned as she remembered the guilt she had felt when she saw Damien, believing Ty dead. She turned to him; her eyes full of regret.

'I'm sorry, how could I say anything, knowing what we were about to face?'

Damien, however seemed to be taking it very personally.

'You should have said something, you had no right to hold that from me.'

From behind Jean, Nathan stepped forward.

'That's a bit harsh, if you'd thought Ty was dead, it could have proved fatal during the battle, you needed to keep you head clear. Jean was right to not say anything until afterwards.'

Damien turned on his cousin, the other Knights around them were shocked to see the look of fury on someone who was usually so calm and level-headed. He had moved so close to Nathan; they could barely hear what was said. In his anger, Damien's voice was barely a whisper.

'It's hardly a surprise that you would defend the keeping of secrets from those who matter.'

Nathan's anger flashed and for a brief moment it looked like he was going to reach out and grab at Damien. But he forced himself not to react, instead he let the atmosphere that hung between them show his cousin how he felt.

Sensing the tension rising dangerously, Jean stepped forward and stood between the two men.

'Please, this was my decision, no one else's. Damien, I don't know you and I was so intent on the Kaimiren, I couldn't even contemplate talking about what I'd seen. I thought I had just seen Ty fall and die; I could barely believe it myself at the time.'

Ty ran the finger of his good hand under his collar, he seemed uncomfortable by the interest he was now receiving from the Knights. Looking around him he saw that while the crowd was far enough away to not hear what was being said,

436

they were still aware that something interesting was happening. He looked to Damien for help and was relieved when his face softened and he joined him. Taking Ty's uninjured hand, Damien spoke.

'What happened? Why would Jean think that you had died?'

Ty had the grace to look abashed as he glanced at Jean. He explained about the killings in the city and how he had met Jean at the market square just over the bridge on the South Bank. Around him there were murmurs of anguish when he told of the people who had died, civilians, police and knights, all dead.

Jean then asked. 'But what happened when I left and tried to make the Kaimiren follow me? I told you to stay away.'

She looked at Damien.

'I thought he was safe, I had no idea he had decided to play the big, brave hero.'

Damien looked sharply at Ty, who looked down at his feet; the colour rising in his cheeks. Everyone was now silent, and expectant. Looking up he cleared his throat and continued, though he avoided Damien's eye.

'Well, there was a large dray sitting on a rise above the bridge that Jean was heading for. Those bastards were right behind her, I had to do something to slow them down. So, I loosened the brake and climbed onboard. As it smashed into the bridge, I slashed the ropes holding the wood, managing to crush a fair few of the Kaimiren along the way. Unfortunately, because I had to stand on the logs to cut them, it meant I landed on my backside as they fell.'

Jean nodded. 'That's what I saw, I thought you had been crushed by the logs and then caught in the backlash.'

Ty started to laugh, Jean thought this was rich considering the pain and anguish he had just put her through. Seeing her expression, he held up his injured arm and winced at the effort.

'I have to admit I thought I was pretty much done for too. But instead, as I landed several hands grabbed me and pulled me to safety, I distinctly remember seeing your Mrs Moore wading into the injured Kaimiren with a huge meat cleaver; there were members of the public hacking at anything that moved. Fortunately, they saw fit to get me out of the way first. I have a renewed respect for our city folk, they are damned scary when they are angry.'

Damien shook his head.

'But not all of these Kaimiren were caught under the dray, surely they didn't just walk away.'

Ty agreed. 'No, apparently Jean started firing arrows at them again, so they focused on following her. I hate to think what would have happened if she hadn't distracted them.'

Damien looked at Jean and gave a single nod of his head. He may not have appreciated her silence, but he understood she had played a vital part in saving the life of Ty and his rescuers.

Satisfied that Ty had finished his tale, Stephen checked him over as he had done Jean. It seemed he had badly bruised his arm and cracked a few ribs, otherwise he was in fine health. Informing Ty that he was to get himself to the hospital as soon as possible, the Captain protested vigorously. But Stephen was having none of it and was in the process of placing Ty firmly in the hands of Major Torvill when Nathan intervened.

'Actually Stephen, I think Ty should stay here for the moment.' He turned to Damien. 'Keep an eye on him.'

Stephen tried to protest but again Nathan stopped him.

'Just for a while, he should be here beside Damien, as long as he's not in too much pain.'

Ty nodded vigorously. 'I'm fine.'

Nathan accepted this and after a brief glance to Damien he set his attention to the crowd now forming along the avenue as people still streamed in from them South Bank. It seemed that news of their victory had spread quickly, and there was much anticipation as to what the Emperor and the Knights were going to do now.

Nathan looked back at the knights of the Order spread around the parade square. Aware that their Emperor was now focusing on them, they realised that they looked more like a bunch of spectators rather than an elite fighting force. Almost as one they snapped to attention. A single look from their Emperor and they knew that they had been given a reprieve, but they wouldn't get away with that again. Satisfied he had their attention, Nathan issued orders for the bodies of Yollan and Gradine to be removed from the Palace, then taken to the morgue. After a brief conversation with Jean, he also sent for Ephea's body to be retrieved from the alley.

He would deal with the demise of the three sisters later, right now he had more pressing matters to deal with. The crowd had swelled considerably, even after such a short time; the people of Parva wanted to know what was going on and it was about time he at least spoke to them. He issued orders for something to be brought from the guardroom that could raise him higher in order to see above the crowd, and they could see him.

Not long after, a large desk was being dragged across the parade ground and placed in front of the open gate of the complex. Major Torvill following behind, scowling, every time the wood of the desk was scuffed he winced, giving a growl at whoever the culprit was at the time. Once Nathan was satisfied the desk was placed into position, he jumped up and looked around at the crowd stretching far back down towards the river. Major Torvill looked as if he was going to cry as his Emperor's boots scuffed his precious desk's surface.

Behind Nathan, the Knights stood in a line, Ty and Anna also standing next to Damien and Paul respectively. Jean tried to stand out of the way, but Daniel caught her arm and pulled her to stand between him and Damien. She attempted to protest but Daniel just gave her a look that suggested it was pointless to argue. She relented and stood in silence behind Nathan, as he addressed the people of Parva. As Nathan began, Daniel leaned into Jean and whispered into her ear.

'Thank you.'

She turned her head and looked up into his face, she said nothing, there wasn't any need. Instead she just inclined her head before they both turned back to face the crowd.

Nathan's voice carried out down the avenue to the people who had gathered. Jean was notably impressed with his ability to project his voice so far, but also with the hushed silence despite so many people; Nathan might have been speaking to an empty room for the quietness of his audience.

'Citizens of Parva, I bid you good morning. It is inspiring to see so many gathered here on a day in which we can claim glory over the tyranny that has held us in its grip these last five years. I know you are angry and disillusioned. You feel let down by the very establishment you believed could keep you and your loved ones safe.'

He paused; the crowd listened in continued silence.

'I cannot blame any one of you for your anger and bitterness, for too long strangers have been allowed to cast fear throughout the Empire. However, I can assure you that at no point did we ever turn our backs on the people we have sworn to serve, never have we ceased in our endeavours to serve the Empire, nor have we abandoned you in our hearts. We too have been angry and frustrated; we have also seen how our peace and way of life has slowly crumbled under the tyranny of the Patrols.

'But not anymore, today truth became our banner and we followed it into battle. Today the lies and deceit that has plagued our security and peace, were crushed under the weight of truth and honour. Yes, it is with a heavy heart I must convey the sad news that people lie dead at the hands of these invaders. Our friends and family have died trying to keep the people of this city safe, their numbers including those from the police, the Order and civilians alike. These souls have paid the ultimate price and will not be forgotten. But also, we will not forget those citizens who came forward and fought beside the Order and the police, risking their own lives for the peace and justice they believe in.'

He paused again, this time his eyes ranged over the enrapt crowd.

'Now I say to you, the people of Parva, I urge you to take up the torch that lights the way to a better, stronger future, where the Empire will prevail over its enemies. Go tell of the bravery of those who died today, of their sacrifice so that you can once more be secure in the knowledge that your future is safe.

'Yesterday our festival was marred by suppression, today go forward and celebrate our freedom and our peace within the Empire.

'To the people of Parva, I, Nathan, your Emperor, uphold my oath to protect you. I ask you to join me in sending this message to all. The people of the Empire are its virtue, its backbone and its might. I stand before you humbled by your strength and determination to overcome our past, your courage swells my heart with pride.

'As we move forward into our future together, people of Parva, of Kelan and the Empire, I salute you.'

With his final words he lifted his sword high, and the rest of the Knights around Jean followed suit. The crowd went crazy.

Jean could only watch in awe.

Satisfied he had gained the confidence and eagerness of the crowd behind him, for now at least; Nathan came down from the makeshift dais. Major Torvill nearly ran to his desk and personally supervised its careful journey back to the guardroom. As Nathan made this way back to the Knight's and Jean, she managed to catch his attention.

'So basically, you've just congratulated the general populace on fighting a battle that they had nothing to do with.'

Nathan didn't break his stride as he answered.

'That wasn't about saying who did and who didn't do anything; it was about making everyone realise we are all in this together. I don't care if they didn't do anything then, I'm more concerned with what they are going to do from now on.'

He stopped and shared a solemn glance with Damien and Daniel.

'Unfortunately though, it's going to take a lot more than a few words to change the views of the disillusioned, and in all honesty, I don't blame them. It is going to be a bumpy ride from now on.'

He gave Jean a serious look.

'You may have picked a tough time to join us.'

Jean made to reply but realised that she had nothing more to say. Torn between the possibility of once more being caught up in the politics of a world she barely knew, and the possibility that she was being welcomed by the only people she knew who could understand her own life. Nathan briefly touched her arm, then began giving instructions to those around him. She felt someone watching her and she looked up, Daniel gave her a brief smile, then turned to give his Emperor his full attention.

Ty was dispatched, under Stephen's strict orders, to have his injuries seen to, while Anna went to join her own ranks and command. Nathan had decided that while they still had to deal with the fake Blue Star and Belby, there were also pressing issues concerning the government of the Empire. He gave instructions for John, Simon and Paul to take charge of the Imperial Council, ensuring the chaos left by the Patrols around the Empire was dealt with as smoothly as possible. He had every faith in his Council, they had after all taken control of the Empire while he and the Knights were left with their hands tied behind their backs. But to add the authority of the Knights behind their actions would ensure there was little argument from any dissenters who might see an opportunity for mischief.

Stephen was to make his way to Aria and supervise any medical help that may be needed. That left himself, Damien, Daniel and of course Jean, to make a visit to the one person who instigated this whole sorry business in the first place; Royce Morecross, the father of Ephea and her sisters.

When everyone knew what they were doing and before they left to go to their respective duties, Daniel groaned and clutched his side.

'Surely I'm not the only one who feels as if they have been trampled by a herd of bulls?'

A unanimous low groan from the others confirmed he wasn't alone in his discomfort. Paul was looking a bit green and Stephen went to check him over. The effects of the adrenalin that had surged through their bodies and made them oblivious to the pain and injuries they sustained, was now unfortunately wearing off.

'You're not looking so good my friend. What happened?'

Paul spoke through clenched teeth as pain wracked his body.

'To be honest I'm not sure, I was rushed by two of them bastards, and the next thing I know I was forced against the wall. The whole of my righthand side is not feeling good.'

Stephen held Paul's hand as he had done Jean and Ty, he looked at Paul concerned.

'You've managed to crack that hip. You should come with me to Aria.'

Paul shook his head vigorously.

'I have too much to see to here, I'll deal with this when we have time.'

'Hang on.'

Everyone turned to Jean as she approached a rather mutinous Paul.

'It may not take away the pain completely, but this might help a bit.'

Holding her own hand against Paul's chest, she closed her eyes. His brows furrowed as he felt the pain subside to at least manageable levels; he thanked her but still sounded cautious.

Stephen looked at her suspiciously.

'What did you just do?'

Jean shrugged. 'I haven't done that much; I've just helped share the pain.'

Stephen looked aghast. 'You mean you now hurt as much as him?'

'No, he hurts less, and I've helped to ease it. It's pointless in arguing, it's done now, so shall we get going?'

Stephen and Paul were left speechless as Jean moved away, none of them failed to see her wince as she moved.

33

Royce

Morecross

Finally, the small group split up and went to their various duties, agreeing to meet up soon at the site of the devastated town of Belby. Members of the Order were sent to encourage the crowd to disperse, who were reluctant to leave at first but when they realised there was nothing more to see, they slowly made their way back towards the South Bank. *No doubt*, Jean thought. *'To the many hostelries that will happily open their doors to those wanting to celebrate their Victory.'*

Nathan led the way for Damien, Daniel and Jean to leave the city via the portal above the guest quarters. Jean recalled Ty saying this gate was usually locked and barred, mainly because of its proximity to the Palace and the possibility of invaders using it to get into the city. The irony of recent events wasn't lost on Jean, she doubted if it was lost on the Knights either. Falling into step with Daniel as the other two men walked ahead, Jean broached a question that had been on her mind.

'What happens to the Patrols now?'

Daniel smiled.

'They are being taken to various garrisons throughout the Empire to be questioned. Our first priority is to find out who has been responsible for recruiting them from Earth, someone has a lot of questions to answer.'

'And then?'

'And then they will each be dealt with accordingly.'

'What do you mean *dealt with*?'

Daniel considered her for a moment.

'We're not monsters. What do you think we are going to do? String them up on the roadside as a warning to others who would rise against the Empire?'

The awkward silence from Jean made Daniel chuckle.

'Most of the Patrols are nothing more than men and women who thought they were being offered a way out of the life they were living. Prison will no doubt be an option for most of them, but not necessarily all.'

'Will they be able to go back to Earth?'

'Probably, one day.'

Jean stopped and looked hard at him.

447

'You'll just let them go? You're not worried that they will tell anyone about the Empire?'

He laughed again. 'You'll be surprised how many people choose not to tell anyone about us. To be honest, the Empire is probably the biggest open secret that no-one talks about on Earth.'

Jean looked at him, shocked. Grinning, Daniel held out his hand and encouraged her to continue walking. She had to admit, of all the answers she could have been given, that wasn't the one she expected.

They made their way up several flights of steps that ran around the exterior of the guest quarters. By the time they had reached the roof, Jean had a spectacular view of the city and harbour area. They were under a covered space that had a solid stone balustrade on two sides, the entrance to the steps on another and set into a wall on the final side, was a large, solid double door. It was made of wood and was bound in a metal that looked like iron, but knowing what she did of the Empire now, it was very likely to be brattine, the metal the Knights held sole rights to. That was another issue she would dearly like to discuss soon.

She looked out over the walls and across to the city below. Restricted by the walls of the caldera that surrounded it, the buildings and open public areas jostled for space. With so many people within such a relatively small area, it made for a lively place to live and work. Jean began to see the nightmare the police and Order must have had trying to ensure Parva's citizens kept to their enforced curfew.

'Miss Carter?'

Jean turned and Nathan was standing behind her.

'If you are ready, we should be leaving.'

Jean realised she must have looked as if she had been daydreaming, she was embarrassed to admit she probably was.

'Yes, of course, after you.'

Nathan watched her a moment longer, then indicated to the guards standing either side of the great doors that they should unlock them. The gate was opened and the Knights passed through, with Jean close behind.

Once clear of the portal, they found themselves on a long, sweeping driveway that led up to a large house sitting within expansive gardens and manicured lawns. The clouds overhead looked ominous and full of rain, threatening to pour down any moment.

It was the first time, since the battle with the Kaimiren, that the four of them were finally alone. Jean could feel the tension from the Knights around her ease as they left the city of Parva behind them. They started up the driveway and the atmosphere was much more relaxed, Jean was keen to ask a question that had intrigued her since talking with Ty.

'Nathan?'

He seemed surprised on hearing his name and turned.

'Yes?'

'How are you able to stop anyone from entering and leaving Parva by translocation?'

Nathan gave a slight shrug to his shoulders.

'It's easy enough; I just manipulate the energy around the city to form a natural barrier.'

'You can manage that much energy and still keep it stable?'

He nodded, as if this was an everyday occurrence and perfectly normal. It was Damien who answered though.

'To be honest, the city is nothing. How do you think the Seven Worlds of the Empire remain connected? How they remain hidden?'

Jean was shocked.

'You did that? On your own?'

Nathan nodded his head, still acting as if they were discussing the weather.

'As far as I am aware no-on else is around to do it. But anything bigger or requiring a larger amount of instant energy, then I have these guys around to help.'

Jean considered the implications of this for a moment.

'Then if the plan to kill you had been successful?' She left the question hanging.

It was Damien who answered again.

'The Empire would have been completely exposed. In particular, Earth would have been at risk with its link to the other six worlds and their relative sectors. Keeping Earth hidden means that we can control who passes through between the Seventh Sector and the other Sectors.'

'What makes you think that would be a bad thing?'

The Knights looked at each other. Daniel answered this time.

'We're not suggesting it's a bad thing, only that until we fully know the risks, we would rather not take any chances. Besides, we have enough problems at the moment, dealing with people from the Empire wanting to completely cut all links with Earth. It's a delicate process that needs handling carefully.'

Nathan nodded in agreement then continued.

'It wouldn't be the end of the universe of course, if I was to die. If the truth be known, people would find a way to cope, but….' He spread his hands. 'The whole point of us being here is to keep a balance within the universe. You know yourself, we're not around to sort out other people's problems….'

Jean understood.

'No, we generally end up in a whole pile of hell that some other sod has created, causing discourse within the universe.'

All around her was a general muttering of agreement, and Jean found herself in deep thought as they neared the house. Suddenly, she realised what it was that had been niggling at the back of her mind.

'That is why I could never find Earth. All this time I have never been able to find my way home, no matter how hard I searched. It was because you've been keeping it hidden.'

Nathan looked contrite. 'I'm sorry.' He gave her a wry smile. 'I suppose it proves it works.'

'Is that the reason why Earth doesn't have many visitors from space?'

Nathan thought about this for a moment.

'Well apart from anyone who happens to run into it on the way past, no. Except us of course.'

They finally arrived at the house, and making their way towards the front doors, that stood surprisingly open, the weather finally broke; it poured down.

Making their way inside, rushing to avoid the sudden deluge, it took a moment for them to realise that there was an old man standing on a chair, trying to hold up another old man that had apparently tried to hang himself. A noose was suspended from one of the banister railings of the broad sweeping staircase that dominated the hallway. The old man looked relieved and begged them to help him cut the other man down. Hurrying to

451

help him, they soon had the half dead man, that Jean now realised was Royce Morecross, down and laid on the floor. The old man introduced himself as Garth, Royce's man servant, and he gathered his master in his arms, tears rolling down his face.

Nathan questioned Garth to try and find out what had been going on. Royce's manservant looked up through bloodshot watery eyes, but he spoke with venom and disgust in his voice.

'The servants have all abandoned us. Once word arrived that you were no longer confined to the Palace, Royce knew he was lost. He's been ill for so long now; he just didn't have the strength to fight anymore. I found him as he was lowering himself over the banister.'

Nathan looked around the hall.

'I thought Royce was newly married, where's his wife?'

Garth's face grew even angrier.

'That bitch left long ago, taking everything that wasn't nailed down.'

Looking at the man on the floor, they could see he was in a very bad way. Jean recognised the symptoms of someone who had been exposed to a large dose of radiation, Royce Morecross was dying. Hanging himself had only brought forward something that was soon to be inevitable anyway. Garth sobbed louder and hugged Royce closer to him.

Wanting to question the dying man further, Nathan moved closer, but Jean pushed past him, kneeling by the two men on the floor. She held onto the old man's frail hands while Nathan scowled at her rudeness. But Jean ignored him.

'Who told you the Blue Star had power Royce?'

He looked at her through dimmed eyes, but belligerence still sat there. He refused to answer and looked away, snatching his hands out from hers.

Jean persisted. 'I know you were given a date and time to be at Belby with the Blue Star. I don't doubt that you believe it has power, and that you are the chosen one to wield it, but it has all been a lie, none of it was true.'

Royce was struggling to breathe now. From the men behind her, Jean could feel anger rising. She continued to ignore them and persisted in her questions.

'Royce, you are dying, your daughters are all dead, and yes, at the end of the day you can stay quiet, that is your choice. Just another failed footnote in history. But you are dying because of a lie. Someone told you about the Blue Star and you believed them.'

His voice was so brittle in his anger, how dare she doubt him. 'It *is* the Blue Star.'

'No Royce, I've had the Blue Star all along. It's a part of me, as I'm part of it. All you have is a worthless chunk of rock.'

His eyes widened, refusing to accept what she said.

'No.'

She held his hand again. This time he didn't pull away and she could feel the pain of realisation wash over him, tears running down his face. Barely audible, Royce spoke.

'A man, I never knew his name, came to see me. He wasn't anything remarkable, but his friend, him I will never forget. His eyes were like pure evil, they shone with insanity. He frightened Ephea so much she refused to be in a room with him. Fortunately, they only visited the once.'

453

The effort to speak was beginning to take its toll, so Jean asked one last question.

'Where is the stone he gave you now?'

Royce looked at Garth, emotion welling between the two old friends, and Garth nodded his understanding. The old man finally gave a rattling sigh and as he died in his retainer's arms he was finally at peace.

Wanting to be rid of these unwanted visitors, and needing to be alone to grieve, Garth laid his master down and led them through the house. He took them down dark corridors and staircases, until they eventually arrived at a door that opened into a small windowless room. Garth then turned without another word and left them alone.

No furniture adorned the space, except for a large box on a single plinth standing in its centre. Nathan briefly looked inside the box and nodded, confirming that the stone was indeed there. Closing the lid, Damien and Daniel carried the box between them. Then the four of them walked back the way they had come, passing through the house again eventually arriving back at the hallway. Garth and Royce were nowhere to be seen, and Jean and the Knights made no effort to look for them.

Before they entered the rain-soaked gardens again, Nathan touched Jean's arm.

'The men who Royce described were not men at all. Do you know who they are?'

She nodded solemnly. 'Oh yes, Gellan and Duran. Two of the gods I'd rather not have to deal with again. It doesn't surprise me at all to learn that they are responsible for all of this.

But it doesn't bode well when they realise their carefully laid plans have completely gone to pot.'

Nathan had to agree. 'Do you know what happened, how they managed to cause all of this?'

Jean inclined her head.

'I believe so, especially when you consider what else I have discovered.'

'Which is?'

'Let's go to Belby and I'll explain.'

With that, they closed the front doors behind them and silently, Nathan took them all to the devastated town of Belby.

When they arrived, the other Knights were already waiting, so now the eight of them stood within the same wooded rise that Jean had visited previously. It was the first time the Knights had been back since the day Belby was destroyed, the look of shock and sadness was obvious on all of their faces. Jean sensed their pain and stood back, leaving them as they dealt with their grief at the desolation that had triggered so much misery. Nathan, Damien and Daniel spent a short while discussing the efforts the others had made; Nathan seemed satisfied with their progress.

After a short while, he sought Jean out. The other Knights resting against the grey and sick looking trees, while he asked her to explain what she believed had happened here.

Jean sat down on a fallen tree and began to describe her thoughts while they listened.

'I began to have an idea of what happened after talking with Ty. I came here yesterday to look around and see for myself what had occurred, and everything I've seen points to proving my theory.' She sighed sadly. 'I've seen this kind of devastation

455

before, and once I approached the ruined town, I could feel the familiar heat of radiation emanating from its centre.

'Knowing we have a certain amount of immunity to the effects of radiation, I thought it would be interesting to see who else had been here when the town was destroyed. The fact is, Royce and Ephea, were the only other people around, and only they developed the signs of radiation poisoning. Unlike Gradine and Yollan, who were never here.

'When I talked to Anna last night, she confirmed the exact date and time of the event, she then helped to translate that into Earth's time. So earlier this morning, before the sun came up, I returned to NiCI….'

'Who?' Nathan mirrored the look of confusion on everyone else faces.

Jean held up her hands. 'I'm sorry, of course you have no idea who, or what, I'm talking about. NiCI is the computer program on my ship; I admit I do tend to anthropomorphise her.'

Nathan raised a sceptical eyebrow, but Simon suddenly stood up and came to sit next to Jean, he had a weird glint in his eye.

'When you say ship, what exactly do you mean?'

She smiled. 'My spaceship.'

Behind them, John groaned. 'Oh no, here we go.'

Simon ignored him. 'You have a spaceship? You travel through space?'

'Er, yes.'

Jean was sure she heard slight, gurgling sounds, from the man next to her.

'Are you alright?'

456

John laughed. 'Trust me, he's definitely alright. Just expect to be bombarded with constant questions and requests to visit your spaceship.'

Jean looked blank and John continued.

'Simon is an engineer. He spends most of his time pulling things apart and trying to make them work better. Unfortunately for him though, most of the kind of things that fascinate him only work in the Seventh Sector. Earth is about the nearest we get to him being able to carry out his experiments. Now you've given him a whole new area to play in, he's going to be a nightmare.'

Simon scowled and Jean laughed.

'To be honest, if you know how to fix a warp engine without having to disconnect the kettle, that's a bloody good job to me.'

Simon gave her the biggest grin he had, while John and the others looked at each other and shook their heads. Nathan, however, wanted to know more of Jean's story.

'So, what happened when you went back to your ship?'

Beside her Simon continued to grin broadly while she continued.

'First of all I translocated NiCI to Earth's solar system, behind Saturn's rings to be precise, trying to avoid detection from any sensors. Though I admit, I'm not sure Earth has the sort of sensors that could have seen NiCI, but better to be careful.

'Anyway, I managed to connect to the computer systems that exist on Earth. NiCI then found that on the date and time Anna gave to me, the Chinese had been doing some underground nuclear testing. However, for reasons unknown to them, much of the data they had hoped to collect, was corrupted. They had

457

also assumed, that there was a geological reason for the unexpected way the damage had effected the area.'

She paused briefly.

'The next bit is all theory, but it fits the facts, and with the knowledge that Gellan and Duran are involved, gives it weight. What I believe happened, would require someone with an enormous amount of power and precision timing.' She looked at Nathan. 'To be honest, if it wasn't you, the only other possibility is that it was performed at a deity level. Only the gods could truly have achieved what they did, especially without you knowing.'

She stood up and looked out over to Belby.

'A barrier had to have been placed around the town. Then, once the nuclear bomb was set off on Earth, they were able to capture the return blast.'

She turned back and saw they were watching her intently.

Simon was nodding his head in understanding.

'A nuclear blast produces a large amount of energy that rushes away from the blast centre so fast that it produces huge winds. A vacuum is formed, and the air is forced back to the centre.'

Jean smiled back and agreed.

'And I believe that the return blast was responsible for destroying Belby, which had suddenly become the centre of a huge vacuum, dragging everything around it into its centre. The force was so great that even the barrier was sucked into a tight ball around the town. Since then, radiation that had become part of the barrier, has been leaking out and affecting the land around it.'

Jean went back and sat down on the fallen tree again.

'I believe, that only a disaster of such epic proportions, would be enough to stop Nathan from dismissing the stone as a fake. The effort and organisation of such a plan; from the first visit of the monk to Parva, to the hiring of the Kaimiren, would almost certainly make doing a repeat undertaking quickly, virtually impossible. They had to make it big enough for you to believe it the first time.' Jean played with her bottom lip as she considered something else. 'Why has no-one questioned what happened here? Surely the families of those living here are missing them.'

John sat down next to Simon and sighed. 'We put it out that there was a natural disaster here, an earthquake that destroyed the entire town and no-one survived. There were still many questions but there was only so much we could cover up. Nathan put a barrier over the area so no-one would enter, and a memorial put up in the city of Gemin. Eventually people just stopped asking, but I doubt if they have given up on wanting to know what happened.'

'At least you can give them the truth now. It will be a small comfort, but a comfort they can cling to.'

Nathan agreed, and he realised that after Jean's revelation he now had many things to consider. The most significant of which was what to do with Belby now. They couldn't leave it the way it was. Despite the biohazard consequences, along with dangers with leaking radiation, this was a town that was a home to many, who also had families elsewhere in the Empire. This was one big toxic grave, with huge social and environmental issues attached. Daniel suggested that they use the blue flame to at least clear away the dead inside and give their families peace of mind. Then maybe erect a memorial to those who have died

459

here, they would at least have something to mark what had happened to them.

Nathan shook his head.

'That is not an option. To do that would require taking down the barrier, and that would release the radiation that is still inside.'

'There is a way.'

They turned back to Jean.

'If you are happy that all you want to do is clear the site and disperse the dead, then we can translocate the entire site into space.'

Damien looked uncomfortable. 'I can't say I like the idea of dead bodies floating around. Hardly seems fitting somehow.'

'No, I mean sending them into the Seventh Sector space. There, NiCI can destroy everything down to an atomic level. Everything will be dispersed, there won't be anything recognisable left.'

They all thought about this for a minute, unsure. There were several sideways glances before everyone rested their gaze on Nathan and Jean.

'I can pinpoint the best place to move everything, but I don't know if I can move that much myself.'

Nathan gave a small smile. 'I think we can help you with that. You show me where, and we'll move it.'

He beckoned her to stand with him, then, taking Jean's hand, they stood opposite each other while the other Knights drew their swords, forming a circle around them, facing inwards. Nathan looked over at the broken town of Belby and then back at Jean.

'When you're ready.'

Then he closed his eyes in concentration.

Jean was confused as to what was to happen next, but she followed suit. Seeing in her mind NiCI and where their ideal target to place Belby would be. Then, a surge of energy passed between all eight of them. It seemed to create a connection she had never felt before, and if asked to explain, Jean could only have said that it was as if for that moment everything was right with the universe. She immediately dismissed it as fanciful thought and told herself to get a grip.

She felt the power reach out to the site of the stricken town and the force required to move it. Her heart seemed to swell as her mind opened to the expanse of their combined energy, merging with the ever-present Ti'akai.

Once Belby was relocated, along with the box that contained the fake Blue Star, Jean felt an overwhelming reluctance to let go of Nathan's hands, to separate from a bond that had momentarily formed between the eight Guardians. When she opened her eyes, Nathan was looking at her with a similar expression of confusion and regret; only the movement from the other Knights reminded them that they were not alone, and they pulled apart.

They all looked around in silence.

Belby was gone.

Simon was the first to speak, his tone was quiet and solemn.

'What about destroying the remains of the town?'

Jean answered. 'That has already been sorted.'

Nathan frowned. 'What do you mean, sorted?'

'Well, while I was with NiCI earlier, I set a program that as soon as Belby came within her range, she would destroy it. I didn't really want to turn it into a three ringed circus, it would

461

have been very quick. There is now nothing left of Belby and its residents, except as atoms in space.'

The Knights stood in stunned silence until Nathan spoke in barely suppressed anger.

'That should have been a decision that all of us made.'

Jean felt her hackles rise.

'Well seeing as you were not around at the time, it was a decision I had to make for myself.'

'It wasn't as if I was in a position to help at the time, being stuck in the bloody Palace or at home on Earth.'

'Exactly. So, I took the initiative.'

While Nathan and Jean began to get into the stride of their argument, the other Knights exchanged glances; this was getting interesting.

Nathan was furious.

'So, arrogance can be classed as one of the less agreeable aspects of your character.'

He jutted his finger to the site where Belby once stood.

'Those people, were part of the Empire, they deserved more than being abandoned in space, obliterated without any witnesses present.'

Jean wasn't having any of it.

'Why don't you admit it? This has nothing to do Belby, this is all about you not being in control. A decision had to be made, so I made it. Just as I always have done. On my own.'

Nathan raised his hands.

'What the hell does that mean?'

Jean stepped closer, they both glared at each other.

'Some of us haven't had the luxury of knowing there are six other people around when you need help. When you've spent as long as I have, being alone, making my own decisions is a necessity.'

Nathan stepped even closer, they were now inches apart.

'But you're not on your own anymore, are you?'

Jean blinked. '*That* remains to be seen.'

Seeing trouble escalating to a level that someone was going to regret, Daniel stepped forward and tried to calm the situation down.

'As interesting as this discussion is to watch, it's not really getting us anywhere is it? Nathan, it may not have been ideal, or how we would have liked to have seen the situation sorted, but what is done is done. Jean, we can't possibly imagine what it has been like to be alone, but please understand, we need to talk to each other from now on.'

Daniel gave Nathan a hard stare.

Damien also came forward, aware this argument had the potential to grow if Daniel decided to air his grievances too.

'I agree with Daniel, arguing doesn't help. It's been a very long day and there is still a lot to do. We need to organise people to come and clean up this mess for a start.'

Simon and John agreed and said they would get people onto it. Jean and Nathan were still seething but said nothing, Daniel tried to change the subject.

'Nathan, what are the chances of us finally going home? Back to the Retreat.'

Nathan's expression softened and he sighed before nodding.

Jean was confused. 'Where or what is the Retreat?'

Daniel smiled sadly. 'Home. We're finally going home.'

Then, without looking back, Nathan took down the barriers that he had raised around the Retreat five years ago, and the Knights were once more back home.

34

The Retreat

J ean had to blink several times to make sure her eyesight
hadn't gone completely. She was reminded of when she
first arrived at Rassen, in that old barn all those months
ago.

It was very dark, and being hemmed in by the Knights
didn't help. They stood so close together, Jean was beginning to
feel a bit claustrophobic. Someone beside her, she thought it
might be Daniel, started to laugh.

'I think we may need to employ an entire brigade of
gardeners to sort this lot out.'

There was a general hum of agreement and laughter all
round. Fortunately for Jean, before she ran out of air
completely, the Knights started to move away allowing her to

breathe properly again. Finding herself with more space and light, she could see her surroundings more clearly. It looked as if they had arrived under a large gazebo, its wooden frame supporting a solid wooden roof.

Apparently, the darkness was due to the overgrown bushes and trees that had been allowed to grow wild around the structure. The air smelt of damp earth and mould, the ground directly under the gazebo felt like stone, but she couldn't see it for all of the low trailing plant life that had spread over its surface.

'Are you coming?'

Jean looked up and saw Daniel was smiling at her; holding out his hand, he encouraged her to follow. They walked out onto what seemed to be a garden path, but it was so overgrown it was hard to tell. It was still dark, even when out of the cover of the gazebo, the rays of the afternoon sunshine struggling to penetrate the overgrown trees and bushes.

Somewhere, further up the track, they could hear someone trying to hack their way through some particularly tough greenery. Fortunately, by the time Daniel and Jean had arrived, the path was fairly clear and trodden down. Ahead, John suddenly called out in pain, evidently, he had lost a fight with a particularly nasty prickly bush. Jean found she was quite impressed with his vast, colourful array of expletives. Once the other Knights joined John in his battle to beat the offending bush into submission though, the path was soon cleared, and their way forward was much easier. Jean had managed to pick up a few scratches herself from low lying branches, and she was beginning to wonder if Nathan had lost the plot and had just landed them in the middle of nowhere. Fed up and exasperated, she stopped and held onto Daniel to gain his attention.

'Where the hell are we?'

Daniel had a big grin on his face.

'We are home of course.'

'You live in a jungle?'

He laughed and those in front had also stopped. It was clear, that despite the effort of having to fight their way through the greenery, they all seemed to be happy and annoyingly cheerful. This didn't help her mood, as she was still smarting from her altercation with Nathan earlier. Daniel raised his hands and looked around at the tangle of woodland that surrounded them.

'No, we don't live in a jungle, though it certainly has turned into one over the years. This, is the Retreat, our home, or at least this is the garden to our home.'

He pointed past Jean, and although the sun was partially obscured by the trees she managed to ascertain he was pointing south.

'In that direction is a rise that separates the city of Parva and these gardens. You can only access the Retreat through the Palace, or via the area under the gazebo.'

He pointed back the way they came.

'But only we are able to use that portal, or on occasion a very small few others.'

A look of sadness passed over his face briefly, but then the smile was back.

'We haven't been here for over five years, but normally this would be a beautiful garden, full of colour and life at this time year.'

Jean put her hands on her hips, she still didn't understand.

467

'But why haven't you been here for so long, and why did we have to translocate so bloody far from the house?'

Everyone turned to Nathan; he looked as if he was still rankled from earlier as well, and at first it appeared that he wasn't going to say anything at all. But then sighing, he changed his mind and walked back to stand in the middle of the small group.

By now the trees had thinned to provide sufficient sunlight through their branches, the damp smell replaced by the sweet scent of flowers, that had spread freely through the undergrowth. In the warmth of the sun Nathan studied Jean for a moment, then spreading his hands, he began to explain.

'As Daniel has said, these are the gardens to the Retreat, our home. It is a place we have always been able to come back to, where we can leave any troubles outside and be ourselves. Here we have very little in the way of staff usually, and those that we do have, only come in a few days a week, generally to clean, tidy up and fill the fridge.'

Simon interrupted as if he suddenly remembered something very important.

'The fridge. It'll be empty.'

The look of horror on his face told how much he considered this a priority. It was only when everyone else also had the same look, that Jean had to laugh. Clearly, the idea of an empty fridge in a house full of men was considered as a form of hell. John put his hand on Simon's shoulder, his face was grave.

'We'll get onto to it as soon as we arrive at the house my friend.'

Simon and the others sighed, evidently, the possible disaster had been diverted and Nathan felt he was now able to continue. Jean inwardly rolled her eyes.

'The most important thing to us, next to a full fridge of course, is our privacy. As a general rule, we are pretty self-sufficient in most things. We have been around for so long now, that an army of servants milling around is the last thing we need.'

He paused for a moment before carrying on.

'Five years ago, when Royce and his daughters arrived on the scene, our privacy became a rare option. Now we all have homes on Earth — it's convenient for the work we are doing there. Fortunately, Ephea and her sisters hated anything to do with Earth, which is ironic when you consider that is where she recruited most of her Patrol members. Anyway, we have spent most of our time living and working on Earth, returning only when we have to see or speak to the Imperial Council, or carry out official duties.

'Our problem was, the Retreat was becoming of interest to Ephea, and we had no idea what she and her father were capable of with the Blue Star. It became extremely important and personal to us, to protect the one thing within the Empire that no-one else could touch. So, I put a protective barrier around the whole house and gardens, making sure it was as strong as possible. In doing so, none of us could return until I removed it. What state the house and gardens would be in we didn't know however. The gardens are obviously overgrown, but whether the house is untouched, or in a state of disrepair, remains to be seen.'

469

He looked up the path in the direction they had been travelling.

'We will soon find out.'

He inclined his head back towards the overgrown gazebo.

'The reason we have arrived so far from the house, is because when we first built the Retreat, there was some concern that if anything unwanted did come through, then they would need to make their way through the garden first. By that time, I would have known we had visitors.'

Jean nodded, it made a lot more sense now and once she had heard Nathan's story, she had an overwhelming desire to see this house they called the Retreat for herself. Looking around at the men watching her, Jean was grinning back. It was like being amongst a group of schoolboys who had just been let out for the summer holidays.

'Well, we had better get moving then, and see what state this house is in.' She said. 'Oh, and Simon, make sure there is tea on that shopping list of yours.'

He gave her a brief salute and assured her that it would be on the top of his list. The tension between Jean and Nathan hadn't dissipated entirely, but the feelings of hostility had at least, it seemed, subsided. The rest of the group was now more concerned with seeing their home, than worrying about arguments. Continuing their way back up the path towards the house, Jean caught Damien and Daniel glance at one another. Was that relief she saw?

The rest of the journey was made in a pleasant silence; each Knight and Jean, contemplating what they would see when the Retreat finally came into view. Jean had found that she was so enjoying the peace in the sun, that she walked straight into the back of Paul when he had stopped without warning, he had hung back a bit from the group, as his hip had begun to hurt more again.

Bloody hell, the guy is solid

Steadying herself to stop landing on her backside, she saw what the Knights were all looking at. Across a large overgrown lawn, bordered by trees and flowers, was a beautiful two storey, half-timber, half stone house, with additional extensions to the rear. Jean just stood and took in the whole scene. The ground floor was predominantly glazed with French windows, opening onto a large patio that led into the garden. Looking closer she saw that a structure had been built to one side of the patio.

Is that a barbecue?

The first floor also had large windows, which allowed daylight to flood the rooms behind them. Jean had no trouble understanding why someone would want to protect such a lovely place.

'It looks as if everything is still in one piece.'

Stephen, like everyone else seemed quite emotional.

'Only one way to find out for sure.'

Daniel moved to the front of the group and led the way up towards the side of the house. Jean was about to follow when she saw that Nathan hadn't moved. Despite their clash earlier, she touched his elbow.

'Are you alright?'

For a moment he didn't speak or move, then turning he looked at her. His face was serious, and she felt as if he could see right through her.

'Jean, whatever happened and was said earlier at Belby......I meant what I said about you not being alone anymore. You are

471

one of us and this is as much your Retreat as it is ours. If you want to, this can be your home too.'

Jean was completely speechless, and despite all her efforts, she couldn't stop tears falling onto her cheeks. They were both standing there in an awkward silence, unsure what else to say, when the other Knights returned. Apparently, they had heard most of what Nathan had said and Damien slapped him on the shoulder, while Daniel came over and gave Jean a big kiss on the cheek. Then he declared.

'Welcome home to the mad house.'

Still choked and full of emotion, including a certain amount of embarrassment at the attention, Jean could only smile and laugh back. Nathan looked around them as Jean wiped her face on the sleeve of her jacket.

'I thought you were all off to see if the house was still in one piece.'

Damien rolled his eyes.

'You've locked the house up as well; we can't get in. Beside we wanted to know what you two were talking about.'

Nathan sighed and gave a resigned look at Jean.

'Bunch of nosey bastards. If you thought you had any secrets, they will soon wheedle them out of you.'

They all grinned back, and Jean gave them an awkward smile. Ushering everyone to the side of the house, Nathan stopped at a solid looking, half glazed, wooden door. He turned the handle and unlocked all the barriers that had kept it safe from unwanted visitors. Soon they were walking through into, what appeared to Jean, a large boot room. To the left of this lobby was an enormous kitchen, where a wooden table dominated one end of the room, while the business end, with a

472

range cooker, sink, fridge, and lots of cupboards, was at the other. Simon made his way straight to the big fridge, and on opening the door, he quickly closed it again, sporting a green tinge, not unlike the one Paul had earlier.

'Yep, definitely need to restock the fridge. It may need a good clean out too.'

A limping Paul followed John over to an island of cupboards and took out paper and pens from a drawer. Simon then proceeded to open and close cupboards, inspecting their current food situation. Paul, perched on a high stool, started to write, what Jean must have thought was, a shopping list. She considered how organised and domesticated the scene appeared, and it was hard to believe that not so long ago, the eight of them had joined in a battle with some of the most formidable soldiers in the universe.

'That will keep them quiet for a while.' Said Stephen, who then rushed off through another door.

Damien looked at Daniel.

'Where's he off to in such a hurry?'

Daniel rolled his eyes.

'He probably wants to check no-one has swiped one of his precious scalpels while he was away.'

Jean looked confused.

'But the house has been shut up, no-one can get in.'

Daniel laughed sardonically.

'Stephen won't let a little fact like that get in the way. He'll check everything he owns before he's satisfied that it is all intact.'

He put his hand under Jean's elbow and urged her forward.

'Come on, let's show you the rest of the house.'

Leading her through the same door that Stephen had just exited, Damien and Nathan followed. They entered into a huge hall that opened all the way up to the oak beams of the eaves, with a balcony running all the way round the first floor. Doors could be seen that led off, to what Jean assumed were bedrooms, and which were accessed by a huge, sweeping, oak staircase. The floor of the hall was of solid oak, that despite having been neglected for five years, still gleamed with the sunlight that flooded in from open doors that led off the hall. The balcony was supported by solid oak pillars, and the walls had been painted a very light cream colour. But what really caught Jean's attention, was that all the walls and tables were covered in pictures. Not formal portraits like elsewhere in the Palace; instead these were photographs of the Knights and, Jean assumed, close family and friends in happier times.

There were a few paintings, but these were more likely to be personal pictures, chosen artwork to be hung in their own home. More evidence of personal touches became apparent, when Daniel led her into a room with double oak doors to their left. They had entered a large comfortable looking sitting room, where sofas had been arranged around an empty fireplace. More photos and artwork hung on the walls or were displayed on tables, along with objects no doubt collected over the centuries. To one side a grand piano stood in pride of place.

Along one wall, French windows led out to the patio area and the overgrown lawn. Jean imagined, that once the garden was restored to its former glory, this would be a lovely place to enjoy the view at any time of the year. She eyed up the sofas and considered how wonderful it would be to curl up and sleep on one right now, instead Daniel directed her into another room. This was obviously a library, the walls lined from floor to ceiling with shelves of books, the floor space taken up by tables and chairs, ready for someone should they wish to work in the quiet atmosphere. However, they didn't stop to survey the vast array of books that were displayed there. The next room was the most masculine space she had seen so far, a billiard table stood centre stage; with smaller tables, sofas and armchairs laid out around the walls. Jean doubted whether a fluffy cushion had ever darkened these rooms, and if it did, it probably ended up swiftly in one of the fireplaces.

Before she had a chance to explore the room any further though, Daniel had ushered her back into the hall. There they met Simon and John coming back into the house from a door opposite the kitchen. They had been delivering their shopping list apparently, whilst managing to pilfer a few victuals from the duty watch that stood guard between the Palace and the Retreat. Simon saw Jean's face and he assured her that tea was on top of the list. They mentioned that Paul and his hip were now being seen to by Stephen, which made Jean feel a twinge of guilt. She should check that she could help with his pain. However, Daniel it seemed had other ideas.

Leaving John and Simon to make their way back to the kitchen, Jean realised that Nathan and Damien had disappeared somewhere too. Daniel then showed Jean into another room situated opposite the sitting room. This appeared to be a meeting room, a large boardroom table and chairs being the only furniture. Floor to ceiling windows looked out onto this side of the house, and ignoring the rest of the room, Jean went to the windows, it was the view that took her breath away. Daniel opened the glazed doors and they walked out onto a decked area, where they stood by a balustrade that ran the length of the house. There they looked out over a sandy inlet, made private by the high cliffs that surrounded it. The spectacular, unbroken view, out over the ocean was stunning, and Jean closed her eyes and breathed in the sea air as the wind whipped at her face.

'You like the sea?' Daniel was studying her.

She opened her eyes and smiled back.

'I love the sea.'

Daniel joined her in silence for a short while before encouraging her to follow him. To their right, they walked along the decking until they came to one of the building extensions Jean had seen from the garden. She gasped when she realised what they were. Entering back into the house they passed through a very well-equipped gym and a full-length swimming pool.

'You have a swimming pool?'

Daniel looked at her as if surely everyone had a swimming pool, didn't they?

'Of course, you need to be fit in this job.'

He seemed to consider something for a moment.

'We may need to get this one checked out after five years of neglect mind you.'

Jean was quite overwhelmed. When Nathan had said it was their home he really meant, *their home*. The Retreat may be a large house, but everything about it said welcome and make yourself comfortable.

However, despite Nathan's assurances, Jean was still too afraid to hope that this really could be home to her as well. She was struggling to not fall in love with the place as it was.

There was a noise behind them, and John came in, carrying three mugs of something hot to drink.

As he passed them over, he said. 'We promised tea and so tea is what you get.'

Jean took the mug gladly, hoping that the duty watches still had some left for themselves, and that their entire stock hadn't been pilfered.

From back inside the house, they heard Damien call out for everyone to join him and Nathan. Following Daniel and John back through into the hall, they met everyone else gathered in the sitting room. Making themselves comfortable on the sofas, Nathan addressed all present with a look of concern on his face.

'Alright then, so we are back at home and everything seems to be in one piece. I've had a message from the Council, after their meeting with John and Simon, to say that no immediate disasters have come to light since this morning's events. They have everything in order concerning the Patrols, and they are clearing up the city; so that is one less thing to worry about for now.

'We will, of course, deal with any issues as they arise, but right now we really should be considering what we have learnt over the past twenty-four hours, in particular with regards to Gellan and Duran.'

Everyone agreed and waited to hear what else Nathan had to say. Jean sipped at her tea, welcoming the hot liquid as it slid down her throat, finding herself desperately trying to stay awake. She was so comfortable, she considered that she may have to stand up and start pacing to keep her eyes open, though she tried talking first to keep her mind focused.

477

'I don't know what your own experience of these two are, but mine has been pretty limited. I've only met them once, but to be honest that was enough. I do try to steer clear of insane gods, as they have tendency to be a lot of trouble.'

Nathan grimaced.

'Unfortunately, we've had considerably more experience of the both of them. For some reason, Gellan has a problem with Earth, with the Empire and with us. Though I have to admit, it's been a while since we've had an issue with them on this scale.'

Damien sat forward in his chair and spread his hands.

'The fact is though, we are no nearer to doing anything about this whole matter than we were before we knew they were involved.'

Jean sat up.

'Actually, I think we are.'

Seven pairs of eyes turned in her direction; Jean wished they wouldn't keep doing that, it was very unnerving. Taking another sip of tea, she put her mug down onto the coffee table and reached into one of her pockets. She pulled out a small object, not quite the size of her palm.

'Bearing in mind the whole mobile phone thing, I don't suppose you have a computer around here too?'

It was Simon who answered.

'Yes, we do as a matter of fact.'

He stood up and opened a cupboard that sat in a corner of the room. Inside was a computer screen and keyboard, he reached over and switched everything on.

Jean grinned. 'Excellent.'

Standing up and making her way to the screen, she looked back at Nathan.

'How does this work? Surely you don't have Wi-Fi here?'

He shook his head.

'No, apparently the connection between Earth and the rest of the Empire may have made it impossible for you to find Earth; but it does allow information to flow. If I'm honest, I'm not entirely sure how, but it seems the energy of the Ti'akai acts as a kind of conduit.'

'Fair enough.'

Jean held up the small object in her hand.

'This is basically NiCI, the computer system on my ship; once I put this into your computer she will take over. But be warned, she will automatically break into any programs and files she finds.'

Jean held up her hands as the voices of consternation rang out.

'It's alright, she will lock them again unless I give the code to open them. I can assure you I have no intention of interfering in any business you have. But this will connect me to NiCI's computer on my ship. Though the information we need will only be valid up until late last night. Once I brought NiCI into Earth's solar system, the ship would have been too far away from any viable information source within the rest of the Seventh Sector.'

Jean stood and did nothing until Nathan agreed, then she plugged the device into their computer.

The effect was instant. Programs flitted across the screen, until after a few moments the words, *Good Afternoon Jean,* appeared. She then began to type something onto the keyboard, when Simon asked a question.

'The device that you have just used. How has it managed to survive the Ti'akai?'

She smiled back.

'Ah, that is because it's actually made from an organic material, it's a bit like a mini brain. It was made for me about two hundred years ago, by a very nice man on Primus Five.'

As if this was a perfectly acceptable explanation, Jean returned to the computer. Simon turned to the others and shrugged his shoulders. He obviously still had a lot to learn. Having finished typing in her commands, Jean made sure that the speakers were switched on, then they all heard a female voice emanate from the computer.

'Good Afternoon Jean.'

Jean answered, pleased that so far things had worked.

'Good afternoon NiCI. Good to hear you.'

Behind her the Knights sat in stunned silence. Jean continued.

'NiCI, I need you to run a search for me on all those known to have Kaimiren on their books for hire. Specifically, those who have a large number on offer.'

The screen flashed various pictures, that scrolled too quickly for anyone to see. Then they stopped.

Several faces now appeared, and the Knights gathered around the computer to see the results. However, John disappeared when there was a knock at the front door. NiCI read off the names and the current known locations of those people who had Kaimiren on their books.

Then, NiCI surprised Jean by adding. 'This information is only valid up until twenty-four hours ago. All current information has been revoked.'

Jean furrowed her eyebrows. 'By whom?'

'Galactic Police.'

Jean considered this. 'How long before you can retrieve this information when we are within communication range?'

'Once encryption has been identified, three minutes.'

Jean noticed John walk past, heading towards the kitchen with a large box, and an idea began to form in her mind. Smiling to herself, she retrieved her device from the computer and turned back to face the Knights. They were looking at her expectantly. Giving them a mischievous grin, she held up the device and thought of all the delicious food that had just been bought into the house.

'So, who's up for a trip in a spaceship?'

Printed in Great Britain
by Amazon